THE PRIVATE SECTOR

JOSEPH HONE

THE PRIVATE SECTOR

E. P. DUTTON & CO., INC. / New York / 1972

First published in the U.S.A. 1972 by E. P. Dutton & Co., Inc.
Copyright © 1971 by Joseph Hone
All rights reserved. Printed in the U.S.A.
First Edition

Published simultaneously in Canada
by Clarke, Irwin & Company Limited, Toronto and Vancouver

Library of Congress Catalog Card Number: 70-179843
SBN 0-525-18469-4

FOR JACKY

Contents

BOOK ONE

LONDON, MAY 1967

1

I DON'T know. Certainly I'm not going on Williams's calculations. It may have been a week before—or a day. Anyway, sometime before he disappeared, for no good reason I could think of, Henry had given me an Egyptian ten-piastre note: the remains, among other pieces of grubby paper—hotel bills, ticket stubs and so on—from one of his trips abroad. He'd thrown the mess down on my office table, just after he'd come back from Egypt—from one of his 'missions', as he described his visits to that part of the world which interested him most. When he went further afield—east or west—he talked simply of having been on a holiday, as if the only real work he did took place in the Middle East. And that was probably true though I didn't know much about his work. We were friends in other ways.

Perhaps he had meant to encourage me with this collage of foreign bric-à-brac—encourage me to travel or to sympathize with my not having travelled (I did very little of that); or perhaps the rubbish which he emptied on my desk that afternoon was his way of saying the journey hadn't really been necessary. Again, though I knew Henry well, I'm not sure what effect he intended—which was fair enough, I suppose, for a man whose job it was to conceal things. Later it struck me that this clearing out of his pockets might have had something to do with his disappearance—but it's not the sort of thing one thinks of questioning one's friends about when it happens. It was one of the few details which Williams didn't manage to worm out of me so perhaps it had a significance.

I'd been with Henry in Egypt years previously—we'd both been teachers there before I'd joined Intelligence—so later that day in the tiny afternoon drinking club round the corner from our building in Holborn, I'd listened willingly to his account of the trip; days spent in empty, panelled bars we'd both known in Cairo, places the English had once patronized, like the Regent at the top of Kasr el Nil with its flaking discoloured mirrors advertising long-vanished tonic waters. And other days when he'd gone across to the Gezira Club on the island, drinking with the last of the old-style Egyptian playboys. Henry had been looking for someone, looking for leads—another of our men had disappeared, I gathered. It was happening all the time then. But he didn't go into that. It could wait until he saw McCoy. McCoy was his immediate control. In fact on that trip I remember him saying he'd not spent much time in the smarter, previously European parts of Cairo—the centre, around Soliman Pasha Street, Opera Square, the corniche by the Nile and the smart Embassy apartments in Garden City beyond the new Shepheard's Hotel. He'd been in the back streets behind Abdin Palace, in old Cairo beneath the Citadel, in and around the dusty flarelit alleys which clustered about the Mousky bazaar.

Somewhere on these slopes of the old city he'd been staying with Robin Usher, our Cairo Resident, a man he'd first met years earlier when he lectured at Fuad University just after the war.

'I was with Robin most of the time. You should have got to know him better. An incredible house, rather like a male harem with cushions and boys littered all over the place. But genuinely Mameluke. One of the very few left. A jolly old party, especially when he's had a few. Though I must say the boys were inclined to get under one's feet. "A thing of beauty is a boy forever"—that was rather his style. That and the *Daily Telegraph*—it's all the English have left in Egypt. Can't blame them really.'

Henry, without being aware of it for he was a displaced colonial, used a slangy Edwardian shorthand when talking about the truly English. It was his way of admiring them without admitting it.

He had been talking about Cairo ten years after Suez and it was this new situation in the country which attracted him. 'The fun of going back somewhere and finding it quite gone to seed,' as he put it.

He'd talked as little as possible in my office in Information and Library.

'What a terrible place to meet again,' he'd said as he shuffled through his pockets, staring sadly at the haggard walnut furniture, the files of Arab newspapers, the half-carpet, and the hat stand I never used. And then, looking out at the mass of hideous concrete that had cropped up all around us: 'You used to be able to see St. Paul's.'

I liked the way he used the phrase 'meet again' as if we'd met that afternoon quite by chance and he and I didn't work for the same organization. Not that I'd ever thought he worked for 'somebody else' as Williams used to describe whoever the 'other side' happened to be at the time. I thought then that Henry was simply being his own man.

We went on that evening to a wine bar further down the Strand, a place we'd gone to for years and where Henry ordered champagne—as he did whenever we met after he'd got back from a trip. I don't think he really liked the drink; he bought it, I always thought, because it was expensive and because he could run his finger down the side—tracing a line through the condensation like a child playing on a clouded window pane—to see if it was cold enough. He enjoyed touching things carelessly, as though wondering whether to steal them—looking warmly at strangers as if he'd suddenly seen an old friend. He had that trick of immediate intimacy, a headlong approach to any experience, and he drank too much.

Because I liked Henry's humanity—envied it obviously—and envied his sense of invention and ease of manner, I thought them to be the qualities that had made him good at his job. One never likes to think of one's colleagues in a dull occupation as being less tied to it than oneself so it never properly struck me until after he'd disappeared that this naïveté and freshness were quite at odds with the sort of work he had to do—the depressing daily grind of extracting information from people or things—of spying on them. Though that word evokes a drama which our work never had.

I had done very little work in the field, not since I'd been a teacher in Egypt after Suez and even then there had really been a minimum of danger or personal confrontation in the job. I had prepared elaborate memoranda on the situation there when I came back on leave to England and now I did the same thing in London, from Arab newspapers, without going anywhere. Sometimes I 'evaluated' reports from people in the field, which went on to the Minister, but McCoy liked to do most of that now, hogging the few excitements of our department for himself. I thought Henry by comparison was happy with his position, which at least took him all over the place, and I was surprised that evening when he said he wanted to get out.

'It's a hack job. We shouldn't fool ourselves. If we hadn't

been together in Cairo then we'd never have been involved. If we hadn't had some Arabic, had connections there . . .'

'If we hadn't *wanted* it . . .'

'What?'

'The excitement. That Embassy party. We thought—didn't we?—that our bits and pieces of information were important. We were stupid enough. If we hadn't been—things would have been different. We might have still been there. Teaching. I suppose we thought it more exciting than that.'

I spoke of the past indefinitely, as if I'd forgotten it. I knew we both had thought it was more interesting then—that summer after Suez. There had been those madmen, Usher and Crowther, at the Embassy then—whose veiled suggestions and eccentricities in that empty Egyptian summer had been a happy reminder of secret and important purposes elsewhere—when we had chatted vaguely about some distant political mischief on the Queen's Birthday and the *suffragis* had chased to and fro beneath the flame trees on the huge lawn, stumbling under the weight of ice buckets and martini trays.

There is an innocence about the beginning of things, a blindness I suppose most would call it—even in work as sordid as ours—which keeps one at the job for years in the hope that we may be able to recapture the freshness of the original impetus which drew us to it, some of the morality which we gave to it all then. And I thought this was what must be worrying Henry: the disappointment of a wrong turning long ago, of expectations lying in the gutter. Once, it had worried me too. But I'd soon come to see that sort of loss as being part of the deal.

Henry looked at a woman across at another table in the quiet back room. The commuters, the Principal Officers from Orpington and Sevenoaks, had had their dry sherries and left. The candle flames on the barrels were dead still in the air. She must have been a secretary from one of the Government offices nearby, getting on a little, with an older man who didn't look like her husband or her boss. There was an intense awkwardness between them—as if they'd just started on something, or had just ended it.

'I wish I could wake up one morning only knowing Irish. And just the name of a village near Galway. I'd like it all to stop. And start again.'

'The Olive Grove Syndrome. The song of a man at forty,' I
said. 'You can't stop it. And you'd be no good at anything else
if you did. They've seen to that. You've got a job after all, a
trade: how would you describe it?—to pretend, to cheat, only
to go for the man when he's down and so on. The dark side, like
insects under a stone. The real world would kill you, if you ever
got into it again. With its haphazard, petty deceits, its vague
decencies—you'd be quite out of your depth. There'd be
something wrong in it for you, things you wouldn't follow at
all. You'd feel like an innocent man in prison. When you
accepted your language allowance for colloquial Arabic you
accepted all the rest.'

I was facetious since I didn't really believe Henry was being
serious. But he was, I suppose. He smiled at the girl, hopelessly.

'It's all a toytown. A lot of sour old men who can't forget
their youth and their good sense over Munich—who think they
can live it all over again by casting Nasser as another Hitler.
They're as stupid now as Chamberlain's mob were then. One
could resign.' And then he added, as if he'd already made the
decision—but this may be only hindsight—'You should leave
too.'

Afterwards we dropped the subject and talked again about
Egypt ten years before—about everything we'd done then,
except the woman I'd married towards the end of my time
there and who at that moment seemed as remote as it.

When we left Henry didn't have enough money to pay and
he'd somehow mislaid his cheque-book—probably among the
debris he'd thrown down on my desk—so I gave the barman, a
friend of ours, the ten-piastre note as a sort of deposit. 'Don't
worry, he'll be back,' I said.

Anyway, when McCoy said Henry had gone I'd assumed he
meant on another trip, and I said, 'So soon—where to?'

'No, I meant "disappeared" not "gone".' He underlined the
difference like a schoolmaster, looking at me as if I'd been
responsible for the inaccuracy.

'He was to have reported on his whole Mid-East operation
last Thursday. At the area committee. He never turned up.'

I said nothing. I'd known Henry to be away for days on a
drinking bout without too many ill effects; he'd always turned
up again and I was sure that McCoy knew this too. He'd

probably been the first to report him as a security risk for his drinking years before. But people didn't listen to McCoy—not the sort of people who ran our section. He wasn't one of them.

McCoy was from Belfast, a Navy man and a Nonconformist who'd been a shipping movements officer in Port Said for part of his war. An abrupt, short-sighted fellow, he'd been taken off active duty—there had been one or two near collisions in the harbour or something—and had joined Middle East Intelligence. He was good at picking up languages—perhaps the missionary spirit of his creed hadn't quite died in him—and he'd made his way up through the ranks in London after the war. It was one of his jobs to co-ordinate reports from the field for 'processing' at 'committee level'—his words for the endless, pointless, claustrophobic chatterings which went on all over our building—and he treated his informants, and their information, like a breach of Queen's Regulations. He wasn't at ease in matters of deceit. He didn't like his position as a filter between the sordid and respectable and he looked at me now like a shopkeeper I'd not paid in full.

'You mean he's left—for good,' I said flatly, playing as limp a hand as possible since I'd no intention of making things worse for Henry by being helpful. None the less McCoy perked up a little as if I'd presented him with a vital clue to the mystery.

'Yes, that's one way of putting it. Nothing good about it though.'

'Anyway, why should I know about his leaving? I'm just a friend of his. I'm not his operator.'

'You were the last person to see him apparently. He came to your office the day before—well, sometime before he left. Perhaps he told you something and perhaps—' he paused like a ham actor settling into a role—'perhaps you might tell me. There'll be an enquiry. It might help if you spoke to me about it first. It looks as if this may be something on the Blake scale all over again. You may want to sort your ideas out beforehand. I shall want a full report from you anyhow.'

McCoy paused after each sentence, like counsel bullying a witness with inessentials before slipping in the loaded question—looking at me each time for a response I didn't give.

What with the disappearances, deaths and defections over the

years—and the odd person who had genuinely retired—the ranks
in our Middle East section had thinned dramatically by the
spring of 1967. We were a few survivors, still snooping around
by hand as it were—planning cunning sorties along dark
alleyways in Cairo and through hotel bedrooms in Beirut only
to find when we got there that the lights had gone on again all
over the Middle East; that whatever bird it was we'd had in
mind was flown or dead, the blood already congealed by the
time we turned the body over. Other powers ruled the area
where once we had been the sword of punishment and
mercy—and did so with a thorough modern brutality which we
couldn't hope to emulate, much as our superiors would have
wished it. We could only work off our energy by keeping up
appearances at home, for the sake of the press or a new
Minister—or the Americans. And of course everyone sprang to
attention and looked like Kitchener whenever someone
defected from our section—when one 'disappeared' as McCoy
put it, as if one had been the victim of some fiendish conjuring
trick and we only had to put the squeeze on the magician to get
him back. For even after so many such tricks McCoy still
couldn't face the fact that one of his men had gone for good.
When this had happened before, like the headmaster of some
wretched prep school trying to placate a parent, McCoy had
always implied in his approach to the enquiry that the laggard
would be back in time for chapel.

Still, even if Henry had done something careless it didn't
seem important. He'd always struck me as being too sensible a
person ever to want to defect; he was too sure of himself, his
pleasures and his friends and the way they all fitted into his
London to want to throw it all over, I thought. In our section
there wasn't much left to betray anyway. Blake had pretty well
cleared the shop. But perhaps Henry had been involved in some
drunken accident, some schoolboy nonsense—as when he'd
broken his ankle lunging out at a taxi at a zebra crossing.

'Has he been in some brawl? Have you checked the hospitals?
He lived alone you know. And are you sure I was the last to see
him? Have you been in touch with any of his other friends?'

McCoy sat there quietly. It was my turn to ask the staccato
questions; the chance that Henry had been hurt seemed to me
something to worry about. Like a parlour game McCoy let me

run through a variety of suggestions. None of them got a response. In the end he smiled.

I knew then that Henry really had disappeared, that there hadn't been any stupid accident and that in so far as McCoy could manage it there would be a fuss. It was McCoy's fashion to smile when something really serious occurred—that's to say when something big enough happened to ensure him a substantial role in the matter.

'Where do you think he is then?' Williams said, in his usual violet shirt and polka-dot bow tie. He asked the question with a monumental lack of interest as if Henry himself had simply been late for the meeting. I knew Williams liked these preparatory enquiries with his subordinates even less than McCoy did. He would be at home in the matter only while making his confidential report to the Minister. McCoy sat next to him, feeding him papers every now and then—mechanically, invisibly, like a dumb waiter—and there were several other people from Whitehall in the basement room which had just been repainted so that my eyes were smarting.

'I don't know. You've read my report. I don't think he's defected. He could be anywhere—just gone off on a holiday or something. He was like that.'

Williams's face winced painfully as if he'd been stuck with a pin. His eyes closed and he drew his face back into a hideous grimace—nostrils dilated, his mouth twisted up above his teeth in a colossal sneer. Then he sneezed twice, his whole body surging to and fro across the table uncontrollably.

'Gone on holiday did you say? McCoy—has Edwards simply taken leave?'

'Well—gone somewhere . . .' I interrupted. I wasn't really interested. Edwards would turn up and being in the room was torture.

'Exactly. "Gone somewhere", as you say. And that's why we're here. To find out. Where.'

McCoy handed him another piece of paper and he was off again, this time in his scolding tone, like a girl let down on a date, and I had the easy feeling of just being a cog in the wheel again.

'As some of you know,' Williams looked at the dry men from

Whitehall, 'Edwards was our provisional replacement in the Middle East for Everley, who was head of our operation there, and it was his job to re-activate the network: the "Cairo-Albert circle" as we know it. Edwards had the go on all our new contacts, codes and so on—right through the area . . . Losing Blake was bad enough.' He paused and I thought for a moment that he might be going to echo Wilde's remark about the carelessness of losing two parents. But the same thought may have occurred to him (Williams had been brought up in all the right places, indeed he had been born somewhere near Goring-on-Thames) and he veered away from what looked like being a catalogue of all the embarrassments which Henry's sudden departure had caused. We knew of them already in our section—the Whitehall drivers chatting with the receptionists downstairs, Williams arriving an hour earlier in the mornings instead of an hour late; and many of us knew too of Henry's fresh responsibilities, since we weren't supposed to know. It's difficult to keep a secret among men who are already a secret in a building which isn't supposed to exist; the strain is too much and people start giving away odd things the moment they get inside the doors.

'Well, I don't have to go into every detail—except to impress upon you all the seriousness of the matter.'

Williams was marking time, I thought, before moving into his final peroration. Nothing would be decided but we'd be out of the frightful room in a minute. McCoy passed him another piece of paper.

I knew then that I'd been wrong in my calculations about the outcome of the meeting, indeed that I'd probably misunderstood its whole purpose—for pinned to the top of the sheet was the ten-piastre note I'd given the barman. Someone, McCoy no doubt, had been hard at work at quite a different angle.

I suppose by my saying nothing of importance about Henry's disappearance—by inventing nothing—they had detected a certain evasiveness in my attitude towards the whole thing and had decided to check more carefully. I didn't mind being a temporary scapegoat, that was to be expected, I'd been the last person in the section to see Henry apparently. But it was obvious that Williams was looking for more than that. If Henry really had defected and there was a public scandal when the fact came to light, then Williams wanted a permanent scapegoat, a victim. As had happened so often before when someone had left us—he was followed by his friends. Williams had at last decided to bolt the stable door. I'd been unlucky enough to be caught inside when the music stopped.

'What was Edwards talking to you about when you last saw him?' Williams continued in a livelier tone.

'About Egypt. We were talking about Egypt,' I answered at once in as tired a way as possible, hoping that my words might slip by unnoticed in the stream of previous banalties. 'We taught there together. I was recruited in Cairo, as you know. Just chatter, that's all. Old gossip.'

But already the others round the table had perked up, noticing the personal level the meeting had dropped to and sensing it might go deeper.

'And this note. Why did you pay your bill in the pub with this Egyptian ten-piastre note?' Williams was fidgeting with the grubby piece of paper, twisting it about with his fingers as if it were counterfeit. 'Where did it come from?'

'Henry hadn't any money with him. So I paid with that instead—a sort of deposit until we came back and settled up. A joke, I suppose. We knew the barman. Henry had given me the note earlier that day, I don't know why.'

The others round the table were fully roused now, as if my last words clearly hinted at a confession of some terrible truth. And certainly, if they thought, as they seemed to, that a man could be bribed or paid off with the equivalent of a shilling, the business over the note looked incriminating. No one said anything. I felt they were trying to decide which of us had been buying whom: had Edwards been anxious for my silence—or I for the barman's? Or was the note part of some elaborate code—a signal passed from hand to hand heralding some devious Arab plot?

The tired piece of paper could only arouse their wildest suspicions for they were incapable of seeing in its movements through that day the casual attributes of friendship.

I said, 'The whole thing, the money and so on—it was a bit childish really. But I don't see that it's got anything to do with his disappearance.'

'I hope you're right.'

Williams was happier now, as if, in the matter of the note, he'd elicited another vital piece of information and was considering all its implications. Yet suspiciously, I thought, he didn't go on about it. He said nothing more to pin me down, though with these shocking intimacies I'd surely given him every opportunity. Perhaps he was working on a next incisive, embarrassing question, so I said the first thing that came into my head to stall him, thinking of the note again—the ten piastres which had done as a tip for so many good things in Egypt in the past.

'Perhaps he's gone back to Egypt. He had a lot of friends there. He liked the country.'

But McCoy had already eased another piece of paper in front of Williams and I didn't think he heard me. I could see it, the yellow office memo paper we used. It was the frugal report I'd written.

'Why do you think Edwards told you he wanted to leave the section that last evening you saw him?' Williams said, looking at the piece of paper very carefully.

'He didn't say that. That's not in my report—'

But I'd been too eager. For the first time I'd flatly contradicted Williams while the sudden urgency in my voice was enough to discredit everything else I'd said as unimportant and suggest that my last response had been a lie. I'd made the oldest mistake—of suggesting murder in an enquiry about a natural death. But no one noticed. Williams simply looked puzzled.

'I'm sorry. Didn't McCoy show you his letter? His letter of resignation—it was posted some days after he'd seen you. I thought you knew about it. He says you can explain about why he left, that he told you all about it that evening.'

Williams shoved the paper across the table. The letter had been typed and it looked like Edwards' scrawled signature at the end; a short note on office paper pinned in front of my report. Of course, it could have been forged.

'I'm sorry to have gone off the subject—about *why* he left. That's not so important. What interested me was your saying he'd gone to Egypt. You mean he told you this?—it's not in his letter.

'On the other hand if he actually *told* you beforehand he was going back to Egypt that puts it all in a much more certain light. We may gather that he *was* going back—just to work for them.'

Williams broached this last phrase as if such an exercise in free will were a far more serious matter than being bundled up in a trunk.

'So you see our problem. Either way we shall have to find out what's happened to him. We can't wait till he crops up on their side—in Moscow or Cairo or wherever—and makes a fool of us. Like the others.'

There were always the others for Williams—the others who'd left us and lived to tell the tale. Like a tune reminding him of an unsatisfactory affair Williams couldn't stand a change of heart.

'I'm afraid he'll have to be stopped.'

McCoy shifted in his chair and the others raised their eyebrows, like a jury in a bad courtroom drama. For what Williams meant in his discreet, Thames Valley manner was that if Edwards had gone back just to work for the Egyptians—or if even he'd simply been kidnapped by them—we'd have to get him. To kill him. When Williams used the word 'stop' he always meant 'kill'. It was a euphemism which he'd introduced into our section long before, an ideogram for death quite in keeping with the polite, slightly academic reputation our section had.

'One way or another we shall have to be certain about him,' Williams continued, as if concerned about his welfare. 'And I'd like you to be responsible for the arrangements.' He detached the ten-piastre note from my report and pushed it across to me. 'You've not been in Egypt for years. They'll never connect you with Edwards.'

It was no use telling Williams that Edwards's being in Egypt had just been an idea of mine. Williams didn't believe in ideas—except his own or his superiors'.

I said, 'I'm not going to kill him.'

Williams had two offices, one in our building—sparsely furnished and looking out over the back courtyard and car park—and another, a much smarter one I'd heard, in Whitehall. We were in the grubby one where he managed his routine affairs.

'I didn't speak of killing him, Marlow. You do dramatize

things. You said he had friends in Egypt, that he liked the place. You were there with him—you should know. I'm going on that. It's only a possibility. For the moment it's all there is.'

'He has friends in London. He liked it pretty well here too.' I expected Williams to say 'We've looked'.

'He's not in London. We've looked. He's taken his passport.'

'Well, even if he is in Egypt and I happen to find him—when you said "stop him" you meant "kill him", didn't you? That's what you've meant before. I can't do that—even if it turned out there were very good grounds for doing so. And I can't see that there are.'

'I should have said "find"—that's what I meant.' Williams, like McCoy, was always having trouble with words—the trouble one has to take to make them suit every eventuality. 'You just find him, if he is to be found. That's all I'm asking.'

'Finding sounds the same as killing him.'

'Why do you harp on about killing him? I never mentioned the word. We simply want to know what's happened to him. Don't you? You were a friend of his. If people just disappear—if a member of this section simply vanishes—don't you think we should make every effort to find out what's happened to him? Really.' Williams looked at me with pained distaste, as if I'd kicked him in the crotch during a house match. 'We've no one reliable left in Egypt. I should think it quite fair to say that if Edwards is there, or in any trouble, you'd be as good a person as any to find out. They won't connect you with him—yet you know the place, you have the language and . . . connections.'

He must have meant my wife's family and friends. Her parents were dead now, I'd heard, but Bridget had been half Egyptian. Her mother was English, from Aldershot. It was a connection certainly—one that I didn't want to renew. 'Incompatibility' her mother had afterwards written to me, describing our failure. I suppose the vague legal expression had been a comfort to her—a way of avoiding the real reasons for the disaster, which were quite precise. Could that be a part of Williams's reason for sending me back there, I wondered? As a sort of subtle punishment for my having failed in a sexual arrangement so opposed to his own proclivities in that field? Anything was possible with Williams.

'Start in Cairo, I should,' Williams said. 'That's where the gossip is. If he's anywhere else in the Middle East, they'll know in Groppi's.

Williams shared with so many others in our section the habit of an awkward facetiousness when speaking of something he considered important—as if he didn't really believe in it but it was an entertaining thought anyway. Certainly I didn't believe him; the whole idea seemed preposterous, a wild goose chase. Yet for a charade, it was dangerously elaborate. Williams usually stopped his nonsense long before—this, after all, was going to make quite an additional rent in his travel allocation for the year. I didn't really know whether to believe him or not. One could never completely lend oneself to anything Williams said, or any of us for that matter, even if it were the truth. We had all of us, in the backwater of our section, moved so far away from reality in the hopes of establishing some purposeful, secretive, slightly eccentric personality which would justify the nonsense of our work. And in this attempt we didn't lie but clung desperately to imagined truths. Which is what we'd done all day. On the face of it Henry had certainly disappeared and we were supposed to be looking for him; yet all we'd done was jockey for position, establish a role for ourselves in the matter, complicate the issue.

'I might as well go and look for him then,' I said.

If Williams had some crazy reason for sending me to Egypt, I now had my own: Henry had been right about the toytown—the useless imbecility of our section; the layer upon layer of deceit and half truth which we had all so carefully involved ourselves in for so long. Our lives suddenly seemed like a prologue to an act that would never come and in agreeing to go and look for Henry the only real reason I had was of wanting to find him and tell him he'd been right.

2

HENRY had a small flat at the top of a decrepit terrace house near Kentish Town. Just down the street, on the opposite side from him, was an imposing red-brick Victorian council school.

From Henry's rooms you couldn't see the wire netting and the broken concrete playground—just the arched tops of its tall, church-like windows and the steeply slated roof with its long chimneys, so that on summer evenings, when the light turned the brickwork a pale yellow, it looked a little like a minor château. But the rest of the area lacked any suggestion of romance; it was decidedly shabby, resolutely lower-middle and working class.

Several of the houses in the street had disappeared, either in the blitz or through neglect, and a rotten wooden fence lurched over into the road, saving one from a fall into the razed basement areas and exposed cellars but preventing one from using the pavement. People obviously didn't come this way often and I suppose it was due for development. Certainly Henry could have done better for himself—but I'd imagined his living here to be all part of his scheme of things; not to bother with the daily mechanics of living, with having any permanent image, but to spend his money and energy on champagne in London and brothels in Addis Ababa.

I went with Mr. Waters from Home Security in our section who had an immense bunch of skeleton keys and a borrowed Foreign Office van—with that legend clearly stamped in gilt on either side. We parked it round the corner from Henry's house. 'Not to make it too obvious,' as Waters said. And then we were off, skirting suspiciously around the drunken fence, as if it were we who were being pursued and not Henry.

I thought Henry might have left something behind, I suppose; something I'd notice, by knowing him, which the others who'd been there before would have missed. 'A clue to his whereabouts'—a phrase which even Waters wouldn't have sunk to using—kept running through my mind. There was, of course, something quite unreal about going there with Waters—cold sober to a place I'd been at home in so many times. And there were far too many 'clues': the crease in one of his ties, lying on the floor in the bedroom; the sticky empty bottle of Cointreau and the Egyptian cigarettes on the mantelpiece; the Brassens record on the dusty turntable which worked through the expensive multiband German radio—did they mean something? Was this how he'd spent his last night—drinking Cointreau and listening to Brassens—or a night weeks before? Or had he been with a girl, looking at the portable TV set at the end of his bed?

That was more likely. A lot of girls liked Cointreau and Brassens and exotic cigarettes. I knew Henry didn't.

Waters said confidentially, 'The only thing missing is his passport.' He'd been in the flat before with the others and was showing me round the place now with the self-importance and hushed reserve of a churchwarden describing some historic mutilation in the crypt.

'How do you know? How do you know what was here in the first place?'

'Well, I mean—he didn't take any of his clothes or luggage. They're still in the bedroom. He must have left in a hurry.'

'Why? He never took much with him when he went away.'

'He'd been with someone recently.' Waters was holding up a minute navy blue suspender belt as I turned. 'A girl I should say,' he added in a deeply considered tone.

'Well, he wasn't queer you know.'

A girl. A schoolgirl to judge by the size of the thing. Perhaps from the school opposite. With Henry, there had been so many girls; it was pointless to try and trace anything about him that way. 'That's what they really want, you know. We fool ourselves about the rest,' Henry had once said to me. Girls were another of his insatiable traits—what did it matter if he thought that every woman shared his appetite? He'd always been lucky with them.

There was a bottle of horseradish sauce in the fridge, frozen solid, and a plastic bag of black olives. By the gas cooker there was a little whisky left in a half bottle and a sugary saucepan with some lemon peel in it. Waters said, 'He couldn't have been eating. He must have had a cold. Unusual for the time of year.'

'Perhaps he liked a grog before bed, even in warm weather and perfect health. He wasn't English either.'

The bare flat with its remnants of Henry's few essential pleasures seemed so much a staging point in his life that it was difficult not to think of him in the past tense—not because he'd died, just that he'd so obviously gone on to the next station. It was true, what Waters had said—he just upped and disappeared.

'I suppose that's the sort of life one has to expect—a man in his job. Here today, gone tomorrow. I'm not surprised. I couldn't stick it myself. You'll want to take a look at his papers. There's nothing there of course. He kept the rules and all that. Nothing to associate him with us, I mean.'

There were several drawers full of books and typescripts, carbon copies of articles he'd written, proofs of book reviews for a national daily, a travel feature on Egypt for one of the glossies. Henry had written quite often about the Middle East—vivid, colourful pieces, well informed and shrewd. It had been an easy cover for him.

'I wonder he didn't keep his books on shelves,' Waters said as I piled them up on top of the desk.

'Because there aren't any.

Leigh Fermor's *The Traveller's Tree*, *The Leisure of an Egyptian Official* by Edward Cecil, Greene's *The Quiet American*; they were the sort of books one keeps, that one can read a second time, and I was surprised he'd left without them.

Perhaps he had gone back to Egypt. Perhaps things had rather died for him in London. Grog, horseradish sauce, schoolgirls—even the strongest tastes must pall. I'd said to Williams that he had friends in London but I'd no idea where to start looking for them. And even if I found them—what could they say?

His friends, I realised, would be the last people to know what had happened to him since he had never involved them on a personal level. He didn't talk to them, as he hadn't to me, about his plans for next week or his failures last year. Instead he spoke of gazing down some small crater in East Africa, of watching the animals, and saying it felt like looking at something happening at the beginning of time and making you believe him. He shared his obsessions, not the pains he took to arrive at them. That was the basis of his friendships. It meant that in looking for him one had nothing to go on except the odd remembered vignettes from his conversation—the girl he'd once met in Singapore or the bus he'd taken from Nairobi to the coast. His friends would remember him well enough but they wouldn't know anything about him.

'Just as if he'd gone away. For the week-end,' Waters said, picking up the bills and newspapers which had come for Henry and which had piled up just inside the door. The *Times* and *Express* and last week's *Bookseller* rolled up in brown paper.

'Hadn't you better have them stopped?' I asked. 'Tell someone at the section?'

'He might be coming back.'

'I don't think so.'

His papers had gone on coming, turning up each morning like an abandoned dog looking for its owner. It was the only real 'clue'. In this alone could one feel that Henry had sacrificed something: last week's news whimpering at the door. These were his roots in London: his morning story of the world, a look at the autumn books—to have given them up he must have found something else more compelling. And perhaps too that was sufficient reason for leaving a country—having no one to stop the papers; that could be happiness for a man who had seen too much of the world—finding a place where one didn't need them.

'You'll be pretty much on your own of course. Except for Cherry and Usher. We haven't got an Ambassador in Cairo any more,' Williams had said the next day.

'Cherry? Is he at the Embassy now?'

Cherry was an Irish teacher I'd known in Cairo ten years before. It seemed unlikely that he'd graduated from the mission school in Heliopolis to the Residency by the Nile.

'No, he's not at the Embassy. Just a stringer. He's been told simply that you're taking over from Edwards, setting up the new circle there. That's all. Don't trust him with anything else except helping you make contacts. He's good at that, knows everyone, married to an elderly French woman, the widow of one of their Embassy people out there who took a fancy to his blarney.'

I'd gone with a tape recorder. Williams had suggested it as if Egypt were still in some sort of dangerous revolutionary turmoil and one couldn't go there quite openly as a tourist. It was a cover we sometimes used—those of us who could ask presentable questions anyway. I was doing a radio programme, an article, a book—it didn't matter. It was no good anticipating a long stint lurking around the back streets with dark glasses; even Williams had seen that.

'Keep us informed,' he said. 'You know the routine in Cairo, it's still the same—through the council library, next to the Embassy. They'll be expecting you. Got your passport, visa, money—your tickets?'

Williams had seen me off with all the careful zeal of an undertaker. He'd even offered me a warm gin and tonic from his private cabinet.

'Cheers,' he'd said, with the genuine release of a man thankfully at the end of a meeting with a wretched visitor, and I'd taken a taxi straight to the airport.

We'd crossed the Alps, the small green valleys at the bottom of the great shafts of rock and snow—glittering in the afternoon light like a pre-war travel poster, a promise of things never done: a winter holiday, learning to ski, hot chocolate in the sudden dark and the journey homeward from Basle in time for the New Year; something from an age when one didn't have to go beyond the Balkans with Ambler for adventure.

I'd fallen asleep without finishing the tiny bottle of burgundy which had come with my dinner. I dreamt I'd fallen through the ice on the lake at home as a child, looking for a fountain pen I'd lost there the previous summer holiday—something precious I'd been given for my birthday—and only finding the top of it in the dark cold water. 'But you only lost the top of it, stupid,' someone shouted angrily from the shore. And then, of course, I was trying vainly to struggle up again through the ice.

When I woke it was dark and the Indian hostess had changed into a sari. The VC 10 was going on to Bombay and Singapore. We few who were getting off at Cairo weren't important it seemed; the real excitement and purpose of the trip lay beyond the first stop. We were being dropped in the desert, in that powdered sand and air like a hot cupboard that kept things the same for ever: hate and love, boredom and exhilaration, beauty and horror; Egypt dealt only in extremes, her weather extended the same charity to them all: to the flies and the maimed beggars on their trolleys in the cities; to the temple at Karnak and the tombs in the Valley of the Kings. It was a place where nothing ever died—where death was always visible.

In memory at least, one quickly learns to avoid the tedium and failure of the past, as I had done whenever I had thought about Egypt, and one can far more readily avoid the actual circumstances of a previous unhappiness. Yet here was a country where, in returning, one might easily be forced to live it all again. It might well have preserved the disaster intact: the heavy Edwardian bedrooms, grubby, steeply raked pre-war Peugeot taxis, the smell of crushed sesame and lime dust and paraffin blowing up through the bedroom curtains in the empty afternoons when there had been nothing to do except the one thing we had done so willingly and well then. That strange weather of the place might have secured all the props of my short marriage to Bridget ten years before just as surely as it had preserved the golden evidence of Tutankhamen's tragedy for three thousand years longer.

It was not a country, I supposed, from which once having lived there one could ever really escape—no more than one can avoid the nightmare return of childhood in the dreams of later life.

BOOK TWO

CAIRO, MAY 1957

IN those early days in Egypt, when I was teaching in Heliopolis and before I'd met Bridget, I spent most week-ends and holidays in Cairo at the Oxford Pension at the top of Soliman Pasha Street and at the bar of the Continental Hotel in Opera Square, with a listless existence in between at one of Groppi's cafés, various cinemas and the Estoril Restaurant. I can only think of the heat as reason for my not going further afield—the stupefying blast of muggy summer air, rising from the flooded river and the delta and saturating every pore of the city—so that one found respite, if at all, only in those few public places which had air-conditioning. One lived a sort of cave life then, surrounded by the dark panelling of the Estoril or the Regent Bar, the black mirrors in the Continental, the drawn curtains of one's room—emerging only at night into the open, looking for variety and pleasure, with all the suppressed energy and appetite of an animal in search of prey.

Herbert Cherry—Williams's Cherry, there couldn't be another and he alone had stayed on in Egypt after the rest of us had left—was one of our group who taught mathematics in another school in Heliopolis. He was stout and nearing middle age and spent a lot of his time vigorously avoiding the implications of both facts. To do him justice—the way he would have seen it anyway—I suppose I should describe him as being young at heart. Much more, he reminded me then with his oblique humour, his ubiquity and his studied concern for the flesh, of Leopold Bloom. Certainly he knew as much about Dublin. He ought never to have left that city really, it was the true centre of his existence, and his life in Egypt then seemed to be no more than a series of defensive engagements—hopeless skirmishes designed to protect the lines of memory which led back to his native city and his real consciousness against the marauding sounds and images of Cairo. In this wasteland I was his only sounding board.

He had a cherubic glitter, an intensity of recall, that turned him, in long nights over Stella beer, into a clown and character

assassin; a Robin Hood of memory, robbing the past to pay for
the present. Thus he would describe in detail various journeys
made about Dublin—wordy encounters and drinking Odysseys
conducted in earlier days—the flavour of the wet Georgian
architecture and the slang of the city tumbling into, transform-
ing, the present aridities. 'I saw him on the steps of the National
Library—of course he thought he had the job but the
unfortunate thing about him was—that affair with a greyhound
in the back of the taxi . . .' And so it would go on late into the
evening. His gossip was not malicious but rather a form of love.

Because of all this shuttered longing, and the heat which
irked his great bulk—and because too he was merely shopkeeper Protestant-Irish (not Anglo-Irish as he often described
himself) and therefore covertly British—Mr. Cherry failed
conspicuously to get on with the Egyptians. He would adopt in
his dealings with them an hauteur which would have seemed out
of place amidst the worst excesses of colonialism in that
country sixty years before. The Egyptians failed equally to
understand him, though this perhaps was because they never
bore the brunt of his dismissive cynicism—as I did—since he
didn't at that point speak any Arabic. None the less, in a
succession of violent gestures and abusive gutturals, he would
incite the locals to within an inch of his life at most
opportunities. Late at night, when repeated moves from one
night club to another had forced him off the Stella and on to
whisky, he would sternly introduce himself to the doorman or
head waiter as 'Lord Salisbury and party. And hurry about it';
which usually, and quite properly, resulted in our paying double
for everything before being thrown out.

I suppose it was his marriage that eventually reconciled him
to the place—or perhaps it was the rather sinister attraction
Arab countries can have for people with an authoritarian view
who have somehow not managed to express that aspect of their
personality adequately at home: Egypt had reconciled Cherry
to the mild tyranny of his nature.

Angelo, a Greek Jeeves, ran the bar in the Continental and
there was a small Italian orchestra that played 'Ciao, Ciao,
Bambino' over and over again in the evenings. Between the two
it was the most enjoyable place in Cairo at the time. In the
mornings, before things got going, when Angelo was getting the
bottles out and clunking the ice into silver thermos bowls, I

would sit at a table in the corner correcting exercise books or writing letters in the cool shade. By lunch time Cherry had usually turned up and the real shape of the day would begin to emerge.

It was during the early part of my first summer in Egypt that we met Bridget here—a tall, dark-haired girl with a confident, provocative look about her. Years before, when the English had run things in Egypt and one hardly ever came across an Egyptian in the centre of Cairo, it wouldn't have been unusual to meet someone like her, so 'English' looking, in the Continental at lunch time. It was now; since Suez there were no more than a handful of British people left in the whole country.

She was with her friend Lola from Beirut so that at first I wondered if they might have been two high-class tarts looking for Europeans since even in those days Germans and Scandinavians had started touring Egypt in high summer. In fact they were both working as secretaries, doing a job with an airline, and this being a Saturday they had the afternoon off. Bridget of course wasn't entirely English but as a product of the old English school in Heliopolis she might as well have been. Her mother had come from England before the war and had married a Copt who had later become an under-secretary for something in Farouk's government. Recently—and prematurely—they had retired to the suburb of Maadi outside Cairo. None of this was apparent initially as we chatted about the city and the heat—politely, inconsequentially—like tourists comparing notes. But it wasn't long before we realised we had much more in common—that this was a meeting in a desert, a miraculous coming together of true minds and shared assumptions in a savage outpost. As soon as it became clear that we were all genuinely foreign (and being the daughter of a Christian in Farouk's old government made Bridget more of an exile than any of us) the personal data of our lives became an open secret among us and we fell on each other with a thirsty, incestuous release.

Later, after a number of drinks, Bridget decided we should all have lunch together at their apartment and we travelled there in Lola's car, going by a market they knew of where we loaded up with a colossal meal, including great slabs of steak, a thing I'd not seen since my arrival in Egypt.

The heat had emptied the streets, the trams had stopped;

even the beggars had gone to ground while the rich had all left
for Alexandria. Only at garages where men sprayed weak
rainbows of water over the underground petrol stores was there
any activity. In the car, even with all the windows open and
bowling along, there was still only the feeling of moving
through a scorching vacuum. Draped about with our bags of
food and muzzy from the iced Zibib which Angelo had specially
recommended as a foil against the heat no one spoke as we
glided across the city.

Perhaps by now Cherry and I had anticipated something of
the nature of the afternoon ahead of us. Remembering our
initial meeting and that stifling journey—with its too polite
opening movements, its menace of animal restraint—it seems
impossible now that we could have been completely unaware of
the outcome. But I think we were, or at least I was, for Cherry
never spoke of it afterwards.

The two girls had a small apartment at the top of a ten-storey
building by the Nile in Garden City. And the lift was out of
order. While the girls went to their bedroom Cherry and I
patrolled the living-room—nervous, exhausted, unable to sit still.
There was a small Victorian chaise-longue in one corner, a
collection of brass and leather ornaments scattered about the
place—the Arab equivalent of flying china ducks on the
wall—and a tiny velvet-green card table in the middle. It was like
a room in a dolls' house, an oven perched high against the sun,
and I felt like a cumbersome tenant inspecting something I
knew already I didn't want.

Turning from a photograph of Bridget on a beach I saw her
come out of the bedroom, naked, except for a trail of light
cotton flowing from her shoulders as she moved across the
room, struggling into a day-gown on her way towards me.

'Wouldn't you like to dress more lightly? It's very hot here
I'm afraid. We have some gin but no ice.' She moved across to
the chaise-longue. Cherry had briefly noticed her arrival but had
then resumed his gaze out over the city, more intently now, as
if he had spotted an accident in the streets below or a
thunderstorm on the horizon.

From beneath the sofa Bridget dragged a cardboard crate of
Gordon's Export gin—the one with the blue sloes down each
side of the label, like an English hedgerow in autumn, and the

red boar's head in the middle. Real gin had been unobtainable in Cairo since the British had left and this, I supposed, was a memento of their departure. Lola had gone across to the kitchen and had returned with glasses and water. The mixture was warm but strong.

Bridget faced me: 'We have so much of it and we never really drink it. We should shower in it.' She smiled seriously. 'You really ought to take some of those clothes off. You'll expire.'

Lola, who didn't have the same command of English, looked at Cherry by way of similar encouragement—Cherry, with his coat off now and the pained expression of a housemaster trapped amidst a riot in the boys' dorm.

'Will you help me in the kitchen? We will beat the steak,' Lola said and Cherry was led gently away.

Nothing seemed really to have changed. The polite tones of our rapport hadn't altered, nor the casual indifference, as though all of us were really absorbed in other matters. Yet I was aware at last, now that a choice had quietly been made, that the significant side of the day had finally emerged: I was to have Bridget and Lola wanted Mr. Cherry.

We heard them going to and fro in the kitchen, thumping the steak, but without any accompanying voices—as if the two of them were involved in a limbering up process preparatory to some mysterious rite. Bridget and I looked at each other for a moment—she on the chaise-longue, the trails of her gown now sprawled high over the rise at the end of the couch, and I, still fearing to sit, assuming a negligent pose by the window opposite. Her skin was the palest sort of yellow, darkening towards the years of sunburn round her neck, with the still darker flow of her hair above that. A round, monkey face—like a schoolgirl's, with a sort of permanent impertinence about it; a face made attractive through its failures—the abrupt turn of the jaw so that her mouth seemed unnaturally long, the misplaced nose that suddenly occurred between the eye line and lips before curling gracefully into a snub like a petal, breasts that were just a gesture, no more than small undulations of skin, and hips that splayed dramatically out of true below her waist.

She said nothing but looked at me with a smile of assent—as if agreeing with these wordless comments of mine about her body—seeing in her flaws and my appraisal of them a potential which delighted her. Then, as if bored with the idea and I were no longer there, she stood up, throwing her gown behind her, and with a fresh bottle of gin, cutting the foil with her nail on the way, she moved towards the bathroom. There was a splash of water for a minute or two before she called me.

She wanted to make love there and then as we mingled beneath the trickle of warm water—she in a bathing cap and I dodging awkwardly beneath the rusty surround of metal. I countered with the imminent lunch and the cramped circumstances. Instead we compromised—poured the gin over each other, drank some of it and kissed.

Cherry meanwhile must have accustomed himself more to the surroundings. I'd heard him laughing—his sudden manic shrill as he and Lola went to and fro arranging lunch on the card table. But when we all sat down together, crouched around the little velvet square like gamblers waiting for the ace, he was still firmly in possession of his clothes. Now that the overtures seemed to have been successfully concluded Bridget and Lola talked quite a bit in Arabic, as if we'd simply been friends of theirs who'd dropped by for lunch. And later we talked again about our life in Egypt and theirs. But it wasn't the light, excited chatter of introduction any more; it was the prelude to an act.

The sun had dipped in its arc over the roof and slanted now directly into the room. But it was far from evening and the moment's wind which sometimes came then, up the delta from the sea. We finished lunch with Turkish delight and coffee and some more gin. With its elaborate preparations, its confused chatter in different languages, its barriers of communication—it had been like a Sunday lunch in childhood years before; a ritual with strange guests talking incomprehensibly after which everybody would have to 'do' something. Cherry and I both managed to prolong it, alternating requests for more coffee with small frenzies of chatter between ourselves. We had even embarked on Cherry's Dublin—a famous row between two professors at Trinity College which he began meticulously to reconstruct—in order to stay the proceedings. But Lola and Bridget mistook our subject for small talk and the eagerness in our voices for impatience and started to clear the decks. We had a last gin quietly together while they were out of the room.

Cherry, as though bent on some high and arduous purpose, disappeared with Lola through the big double doors of the bedroom. Bridget and I made some highly unsatisfactory love together, balancing precariously on the chaise-longue. Moaning afterwards, but catching some broken sentences in between, I realised she was regretting Lola's use of the double bed next door as much as my own precipitate performance. Charitably she saw in our discomfort the reason for my failure—saw too, perhaps, that I was not really up to the sexual obstacles, the 'flaws' she had contrived for me in her idea of the shower together and her choice of the awkward chaise-longue. She changed her mood, became gently impatient.

'See what they're doing in there. If they've done with the bed we could use it. It might be easier.'

At that moment Cherry's bare arm slid through the doorway and he shook a towel at us. He called to me, softly, and clutching another towel I hurried forward to the mid-wicket conference.

'It hasn't worked,' he whispered. 'Lola says we should try the chaise-longue. Are you done with it?'

Lola and Bridget were never satisfied. The afternoon dragged on in a series of blows and parries, from room to room, place to place. Fortified, in our separate ways, with gin and desire, Cherry and I gradually faded while the girls redoubled their attack. Lola took to berating us in long storms of Arabic, her mouth forming immense shapes as the normally relaxed syllables of her tongue rose in angry and vicious gutturals towards us. 'Ya-a-a-LAH'—the last three letters coming upon us like a thunderclap. Now that the pretence of communication, the polite exchanges, had been thrown away—we laughed in return, masking our impotence with roars of indifference, as if we understood her every word.

It was then that Lola embarked on her belly dance—the Trojan horse in the proceedings, as she must have seen it, which would surprise our lust behind the fort of our fatigue and indifference.

She rooted vigorously in cupboards about the bedroom, throwing a vast hoard of tempting apparel about the place. It piled up around the bed on which Bridget was now lying back naked—these diaphanous colours of previous battles—like salad round a dish. Cherry and I watched the preparations carefully, in our underpants, from two small occasional chairs by the card table. Bridget took no interest at all but stared at the ceiling, her eyes fixed intently on a point above her, as if she expected to see in it the explanation to a mystery.

The garment which Lola eventually strapped herself into had an operative rather than a seductive quality. It was heavy and came down from her waist in a series of leather petals, embroidered here and there with the dull wink of cheap jewellery. It was a little like the skirt of a Roman legionnaire and had the unreal, unused air of a Hollywood prop. There was an attachment above it, starting with a veil over the midriff and ending in a sequinned harness about the bust. But she dispensed with this, casting it aside dramatically, making an overture out of what I suspected was simply a faulty clasp.

And then a clap and a change of eye and a strange harsh expression, fixing us with a stare that never left us, her big bones moving rhythmically, delicately, Lola started her dance around the bed—trampling with each sudden shiver of her body the finery of her wardrobe into the floor. Soon she started a song, a viciously accented accompaniment, throwing her voice passionately between the thwacks and twists of her body, working herself into an angry frenzy without a smile. She had moved far from the dull coquetry of the form and before the end she had turned the dance—hands moving tightly across her body—from a symbol of the act into the act itself. Exhausted she hurried away to the bathroom through the wide doorway and we sat there saying nothing.

Bridget had long since turned away from us and from the dance, her face to the wall, and while Cherry went into the next room to get dressed I moved across and sat beside her, against the long length and pale yellow skin of her back.

The evening had come up outside as we left the silent chaos of the flat. The expected wind stirred, shutters opened, white figures padded towards a mosque on the corner and the trams clanked again in the distance. Like signals from different parts of the city, the sounds rose one after the other on the air around us, breaking the vacuum of the afternoon, opening up the night, as though it was the beginning of another day.

2

BEFORE the start of the autumn term that year most of the overseas teachers, except Cherry and myself, had left. Home leave was due every second summer but apart from ourselves none of the others had managed to survive the punishments of the first.

Two of the women in the group were flown back from the Valley of the Kings with sunstroke while a third, a woodwork teacher from a vocational school near Limerick, distinguished himself by running foul of the very lax Moslem attitude towards pederasty. The remainder squabbled for weeks with various uncomprehending juniors at the Ministry of Education about transferring their piastres into pounds and their tickets back home before Cherry and I, deciding that we might as well stay on in Egypt and dissociate ourselves from our hysterical colleagues, took a taxi to Alexandria for the rest of the summer.

We stayed at the Hotel Beau Rivage near the beach at Sidi Bishr—a splendidly off-hand sort of place with a terraced garden at the back with little wooden pavilions for the guests looking down over a great carpet of crimson flowers and buzzing blue insects. Here, towards midday, we had 'English' breakfasts and fresh mango juice, and the summer passed quickly enough; there were only the afternoons and evenings to fill. A vegetable life.

In the afternoons I swam off the 'Cleopatra Beach'—a private strand near the hotel where that lady was reputed to have once taken a bath—while Cherry paddled in the shallows, flirting with the elderly latter-day *grandes dames* of the city, so that out at sea his voice echoed to me over the water, the shrill of his hopelessly immature laugh, as he clowned about their deck-chairs.

'Tee-hee. Ha-ha . . .'

Like a child being tickled.

'Oh, comme vous êtes méchant, Monsieur Chéri!'

The dialogue came across the flip-flap of small waves like snatches from a Restoration comedy.

'Quel esprit! Et vous êtes hollandais—incroyable!'

And Cherry, already exercising the beginnings of that language which he was so quickly to become adept in under their tutelage, would howl triumphantly, wagging his finger at the ancient crones:

'Pas hollandais—*irlandais*!'

And there would follow a barrage of squeaks and twitters and oh-la-las.

For these ladies, the last of the city's fabled courtesans, in their dark billowy silks and the remnants of their jewel cases, nailed to their chairs and their memories—Cherry, with his profligate eccentricities and attentions, must have been a happy reminder of their youth: when the government and the Embassies took their intrigues to Alexandria for the summer, shot duck on the lakes in the autumn—and between them all the ladies had played a vital role in the careless history of the times.

In the late afternoons, during those few moments before dusk when in better times the ladies had 'taken the air' of the city before dressing for dinner, Cherry would stroll back with Eugénie and Clara and Mathilde and sometimes I joined them, walking slowly behind the little troupe, down avenues heavy with flame trees and the smell of jasmine, as one by one the ladies dropped off into their crumbling villas which lay behind the sea front.

'Vous savez—comme c'était beau ici avant la guerre . . . Maintenant les domestiques sont impossibles. Elles ne savent rien: même faire du thé . . .'

The metallic rattle of their voices had softened now under the heavy canopy of trees.

'Eh! Les "spare parts"—ils n'existent plus. On ne conduit pas aujourd'hui . . .'

'Ah, mais oui, je me souviens très bien, des voyages qu'on a fait au Lac Mariout. Et les fleurs là-bas—des asphodèles, des mignonettes, des anémones. Et des autres—des fleurs tout à fait uniques. Ca n'existe plus bien sûr. Il y a un dépôt du gaz là-bas maintenant. Un odeur tout à fait différente, je vous assure!'

Like trembling excited birds they vied for Cherry's attention. And Cherry with a pained expression would turn and stare at

each of them in turn, his eyes wide open in mock astonishment—a face of incredible seriousness and unbelief. And then
with a special twinkle lighting up the whole football of flesh:
'Mais je peux vous conduire . . . Je connais le chemin!' And they
would wave shaky fingers at him—'Oh! Comme vous êtes
méchant!'—before breaking into enthusiastic cackles.

As we approached the gates of their villas wizened arthritic
porters rose up from the dust like old newspapers in a light
wind, saluting stiffly as the ladies crossed the threshold, giving
Cherry and me the wary hopeless glance of crippled protectors.
The broken arm of a lawn sprinkler clanked somewhere in the
twilight and a Daimler lurked in a garage without wheels. I had
no wish to go back to Europe.

3

'THERE is a train of course. The Helwan train from Bab-el-Luk.
Every ten minutes. Get off at Maadi. But I imagine you'll be
taking a car.'

The Headmaster's voice on the telephone was assured, rather
condescending and impeccably English. I was surprised for his
name was Dr. El Sayid and when we met he was certainly
Egyptian. With the departure of so many of our group I had
managed to get transferred to the El Nasr school in Maadi,
previously Albert College, Cairo, and the Eton of the Middle
East until a year before.

The Doctor clicked his fingers suddenly and several porters in
grey serge *galibeahs* grabbed my luggage and disappeared into a
long low prison-like compound with small windows.

'I'll have them put your things in your room. You'll be a
form master. Fifth I think. Your rooms are above class.'

He had darted on ahead of me after the porters.

'Let's hope you like it better here. What with the English—
and I may say the Irish more recently—we've been having too
many changes. It's been rather unsettling—'and he added,
looking straight ahead so that I hardly heard him—'for a school
like this.'

There was an edge of dangerous efficiency in the Doctor's voice which I didn't like, a call to order much at odds with my previous experience of the country. We had reached the door of my room on the second storey of the compound, along a low corridor reeking of that peculiar suffocating smell of baked concrete and plaster which one gets in desert countries. One of the porters produced a key and opened the door.

'Your predecessor here—a countryman of yours, I believe— kept alcohol in his room. A Mr. Simmonds. We had to lock the door. I'm sure this won't be necessary in your case. It's not only a matter of Moslem tradition, this isn't Al Azhar after all, it's a matter of policy here as regards staff. I'll send Bahaddin up in half an hour, to show you round. He's Captain of school. Oh and by the way,' he'd turned from the door and was rubbing his long fingers delicately together—'we don't tip the *suffragis* or *boabs* here. There's a fund for them at Christmas which you may want to contribute to.'

The Doctor moved briskly away down the corridor as if he'd just had a cold shower. The porters saluted dully and were about to move off when I startled them with a ten-piastre note apiece.

My room looked out over a large scabrous playing field—odd tufts of bleached grass and the rest a sandy loam with distinct intimations of the desert beneath. Maadi had been built by the English at the end of the last century along a feeder canal from the Nile ten miles south of Cairo as a sort of suburban arboretum, an Egyptian Bagshot complete with every sort of exotic shrub and tree and civil servant. Now, with the fading advertisements for soda water, Virol and Stephens' Ink which peeled from the walls of the small row of shops by the railway line, and the departure of the men whose lives revolved around those products, Maadi was slowly withering, eroding under the desert winds, sinking back into the sand.

Bats began to flip and turn in the stillness and insects squeaked their knees together in the remnants of the herba- ceous border outside the window. The sun dipped into the line of pine trees which flanked the canal at the end of the playing field—a great crimson chunk of fire spreading from strawberry into pink and finally a very pale blue over the sky above. A cricket ball, it must have been, clunked somewhere and three *suffragis*—skullcaps awry, their *galibeahs* tucked up into their pants—struggled in a manic dance in one corner of the field with the crossbar of a soccer goal.

Bahaddin seemed to be at least in his middle twenties—a minute, perfectly round face, dark, but with traces of yellow, like a ripening blackberry. In his cream school blazer, flannels and a silver name-plate around his wrist he gave the impression of a dentist in a hurry—constantly moving key-rings, nail clippers and other pieces of metal from one pocket to another. He stared at me carefully, as if wondering how best to proceed with the extraction, and then offered me a Player's cigarette.

'My father makes them.'

I looked at him carefully in return.

'I mean—he has the Arabian concession. Sheik Bahaddin . . .' He didn't finish the sentence but with an expansive gesture left the rest of his father's identity hanging in the air as a glittering image of unlimited power and riches.

'One of the Trucial States?'

'Yes. He's with the Head now. I don't think I'll be staying on. At least if I do, only till I get enough 'O' levels. London University, I hope. My sister lives there. South Kensington. Do you know it? She's doing political science.'

'I see . . .'

Bahaddin started to clip away at a portion of loose skin above his thumb.

'Of course I don't really take classes here any more. I've been going through the material privately.'

'What—with Mr. Simmonds?'

'No. With Mr. Edwards. He does senior English here. You'll meet him. A very decent fellow. English—or rather, White African. What does one call them from those colonies? Did you know Mr. Simmonds? He was from Ireland.'

'No. I understand he spent most of the time here locked in his room with a bottle.'

'The Doctor has a thing about that—he's been on to you about it? Well don't worry. I can get you all the drink you want from the Club in Maadi, I'm a member. The Doctor is mad.'

'And his leather elbows and tweed jacket—that's part of the madness?'

'That's the previous Head's jacket. He had to leave nearly all his stuff here—twenty-four hours to get out of the country. So Sayid took the lot over, silver spoons, golf clubs, everything. The Head gave it all to him in fact.'

'I don't suppose he had much alternative.'

'I don't think it was purely, or even partly, a matter of alternatives.'

'Oh?'

Bahaddin looked at me with the confident pitying air of a judge about to pass a final and savage sentence.

'If you really want to know—I think that's the answer.' And he'd sprung up so quickly and gone over to several old school photographs by the door that I thought for a second that he was about to unmask an eavesdropper. The Doctor himself perhaps. 'There. That's El Sayid in the back row. And that's the last Headmaster in the front. He wasn't the Head then of course—junior Divinity I think.'

I looked at the jolly young Arab faces in their high collars and Edwardian blazers, their dark woolly heads sticking up like ninepins along the back row—but merging at once into four more rows of solid young Empire-builders beneath.

'You see,' Bahaddin said triumphantly, ' "Albert College— 1928". Some years they let more Arabs in than in others. It depended on the riots in Cairo, on how the Egyptians had been behaving to their Lords and Masters. That was a good year, quite a few wogs in the back row . . . They used to be called "Belcher's Boys", he was mainly responsible for their entry— had some idea about training them to be the future leaders of their country. Well, El Sayid was his particular cup of tea that year. That's the story.'

'Not an unusual one in this part of the world I'd say. Has it done any harm?'

'Wait till you get to know the Doctor better—you can judge for yourself. I'd better go now. My father must be about ready to start his caravan. May I show you round the place later?'

'I'm worried about Bahaddin. I think he smokes.'

Dr. El Sayid was putting away a pair of laboratory scales when I arrived in his study and there was a package in front of him neatly wrapped up in tissue paper.

'He must be as old as I am.'

'Indeed?' The Doctor looked at me quizzically as if the fact of Bahaddin's age had never struck him before.

'Yes. I suppose he is a little elderly for this place. But what can one do? Quite a few of them don't pay at all now since Suez. Let alone in advance. And in gold.'

He fingered the tissue package on the desk and then thumped it against the wood a few times like a bar of chocolate.

'Desert Gold. Desert Gold . . .'

He murmured the words like an incantation, as though they evoked in him some deeply pleasurable memory, something which he had lost.

'Besides, he's doing his 'O' levels again this year,' Dr. El Sayid went on very much more briskly.

'He told me.'

'I'd like him to get a few of them this time. Show them we aren't quite off the map out here. We'll just have to persevere with Bahaddin for the time being.'

The Doctor, his hands braced against the table, looked at the tissue package sadly and then he sprang up suddenly and locked it away in a large safe in the corner, shielding it clumsily with his body so that I wouldn't see the combination.

'Well now, Mr. Marlow—to give you some essential background to the school, a little bit about our routines and ideals—the two so often go together, don't you think?—in education. There have been changes of course. We're not a Public School any more but the College is being run on exactly the same lines, just as it was before this recent trouble. The Minister's very much behind me on that. Take this College for instance: the English were very good at schools like this—the great Dr. Arnold . . . it's a very old tradition and we can make use of it out here today. The College can play a vital role in the new Egypt. I'd like you to see it that way in your work here.'

'I can see it's an advantage to have people go on learning English but surely the rest of it's just perpetuating privilege— and somebody else's privileges at that. Was that part of the revolution?'

'I fancy that's part of every revolution, Mr. Marlow. There has to be an élite—and nowhere more than in the sphere of education. That's where it all begins. We have a great responsibility. One has got to be able to offer people something a little over their heads—there'll always be a few who are tall enough, as it were, to benefit from institutions like this.'

'I should have thought it was simply a question of their being rich enough. Still.'

The Doctor seemed to consider my point with great care, furrowing his brow and looking down intently at his fingers on the table. Then, almost in the movements of a pianist embarking on a delicate and well remembered passage, he looked up slowly, his face quite cleared of any distortion or emotion, his voice carrying all the pain of both.

'I hope that before too long we may get some of our *English* staff back here, when things settle down. Meanwhile we shall just have to make do as best we can.'

He spaced the words out quietly and very precisely, like a nanny giving a last warning, then turned, literally, to other matters—swinging his chair round and gazing at a heavy bronze statue of a Greek discus thrower on a corner cupboard.

'As regards policy here, the rules and so on: I'm sure it won't take you long to familiarize yourself with them. Our attitudes here are much the same, I imagine, as they were in your own school. There's only one other thing—in which schools like this in Egypt, being a Moslem country, differ from similar ones in England. Some of the boys here, a very few I'm glad to say, are inclined to strike up associations—well, outside the norm. I suppose one might say that it's perfectly understandable within a general context out here, we're a friendly people after all—but I can't have them doing it openly in the corridors in front of the others. I'm afraid to say there's been rather too much of that in the past. I'd be glad if you'd keep your eyes open. I want to put a stop to it entirely.'

'A stop to what? I don't understand.'

'To their *holding hands*! Good God, must I spell *everything* out? To their holding hands—and worse!' And he got up very suddenly, rising straight up into the air as though weights had been taken off his feet, and walked rapidly over to the window, slapping his hands together with insane vigour.

'I see. I'll keep an eye open then.'

'Well, did you get the Gospel—the Book of Rules?'

'Yes. Is he really mad?'

'Not at all. Just more English than the English. The Doctor

knows what he's doing, he frightens the wits out of them down
at the Ministry. Practically every Sheik and Emir and Arab
tycoon in the Middle East sends his sons here—even since Suez
and just because of the Doctor. They think they're still getting
the real British thing here—Eton and Harrow and toasted
muffins; those leather patches and the accent—it gets them
completely. The propaganda value for Nasser is enormous, not
to mention the gold. As long as Bahaddin and the other Crown
Princes stay on here the Doctor can do as he pleases.'

The Staff Room was empty. The other Egyptian house-
masters had long since taken up their various positions in the
dormitories; I'd seen their cubicles at the end of each of
them—'Port Said', 'Ismailia', 'Suez', and 'Port Tewfik'—like
stations of the cross the four houses in the school had been
renamed after the ports on the canal in honour of the great
Egyptian victories that had occurred there. Henry Edwards sat
at a long ink-stained table sipping Turkish coffee and reading
the *Egyptian Gazette.*

'I'm surprised he had any more of you Irish back here. They
had job enough at the Ministry getting the Doctor to take
Simmonds and he was out quick enough.'

'What did Sayid want to get rid of Simmonds for? He wasn't
Egyptian at least and isn't that what the Sheiks want—anything
but an Arab education?'

'The Doctor wants to force the Ministry to get the English
back here as soon as possible. You Irish are—or were—in the
way. He wants the old sort of staff back if he can get them.
Duds from the home counties with the right accents. Egypt still
reminds a lot of people in England of turbanned servants and
gin and tonics on wicker chairs looking out over sunsets on the
Nile. And for an ill-paid, overworked usher stuck in somewhere
like Reading it must seem quite a paradise out here. Especially
with those traditional British inclinations, if they have them.
That's still rather an inducement out here you know—the
chance of getting your hands on that sort of limitless sexual
provender.'

'The Doctor seems to want to put his foot on all that.'

'Does he, indeed?'

'He told me to keep my eyes open.'

'He just wants you to pimp for him, that's all. Have you seen

the Maadi Club? A fine piece of End of Empire with the local
fellows beating hell out of the *suffragis* instead of the English.'

The old taxi swerved violently round a circle of cracked earth
that had once been a lawn and deposited us at a little sentry
box, brightly lit by a sort of concentration camp spotlight
overhead. Henry greeted an ancient retainer dressed half in a
very old cord jacket with 'Maadi Sporting Club' across the front
and half in a ragged *galibeah* a size too large for him.

'Goo' evenin', Mr. Henry.' The old man gave us a tired salute
and I saw that he had some sort of military badge on the lapel
of his coat.

'Queen's Own 11th Hussars. Ahmed used to feed the horses.'
And we were walking towards a long yellow building, surrounded by shrubs and trees, which looked like a sizeable public
lavatory in the undergrowth. The main room was packed tight
and very busy; a record player ground away at full volume in
one corner—'I have often walked down this street before . . .'—
and a selection of bronzed, rather bored young people were
pushing each other self-consciously round the floor.

'The original cast recording . . . I saw it last week in New
York . . . *Marvellous* . . .'

Some others were chatting next to the record player, led by a
sallow middle-aged Egyptian in a sharkskin suit which glistened
like jaundiced flesh in the hard light.

'Dear me. Gala night. They have one every month in the
winter.'

Henry pushed his way to another room beyond. On one side
was a long bar and the other was crammed tight with horsehair
sofas and leather armchairs and tightly knit family groups—old
mothers-in-law dressed completely in black and screaming
five-year-old children running amok with Coca-Cola bottles and
straws. Sweating, beady-eyed *suffragis* pushed and cursed their
way among the crowd with beaten copper trays piled high with
whisky-sodas and tall icy bottles of Stella on their way to a
third room beyond. From here came the click of billiard balls,
and sometimes a silence followed by a terrible gale of gruff
laughter as a ball bounced through a doorway followed by a
suffragi, laden with a tray of empty glasses, to pick it up.

Over the bar were two large yellowing photographs of the old
Shepheard's Hotel and the Cairo Turf Club and between them a

gilt and mahogany panel inscribed with the names of past Club Presidents and Secretaries: a splendid roll of Anglo-Saxon names and ancient dates which I thought at first must be a war memorial until I realised that someone called Dalton-Smith couldn't have been killed in nine successive years.

There wasn't what any of the old Club members would have called a 'European' in sight. Except Bridget who was sitting with Lola, and I presumed her parents, at the far side of the room.

'That's the Girgises over there. With old Lola. You don't often see them all together. He was a Minister with Farouk. You'd like them. We'll go over later.' Henry waved at them but I'd turned around quickly and started to order.

'What would you like?'

'No, let me. Your first day. Let's have some champagne.'

4

'HOW long have you known them?'

'The Girgises? I knew Bridget at the University here. She was a student of mine. Her parents live round the corner. She's English—Mrs. Girgis. She came out here before the war. Why? Have you met them—I mean Bridget?'

'I don't think so.'

Henry looked at me in mock astonishment, his head thrown back quizzically, smiling. He had the knack of making one lie—and then making it obvious.

'Perhaps . . . Bridget. I met her—I'm pretty sure—in the Continental several months ago.'

'I thought so. Most people out here now run across them at some point or other. With Lola?—at the bar.'

'Yes, I think so.'

'More than likely. They used to go to the bar in the Cosmopolitan in the old days.'

'They just move around the bars, do they? I thought they were secretaries.'

'Bridget had a fellow who lived in the Cosmopolitan. An Englishman, something to do with soda water. Chucked out

with the rest of them. They were to have been married, I gather.
Rather tough.'

Henry's hair had begun to ruffle, almost to stand up on end
as he ran his hands through it, and his glasses had steamed up in
the heat as he quaffed great mouthfuls of the Asti Gancia.
There hadn't been any real champagne but there were still some
Italians in the country.

'And Lola?'

'She just shares the flat. She was a belly dancer in Beirut. Got
landed with a non-existent film contract here with a nonexist-
ent producer. She wants to be an actress.'

'They all do, I suppose.'

'No, Lola's quite a good actress. Too good really for the
song-and-dance sort of thing that goes on around here.'

'Why does she stay then?'

'She's happy here. A lot of people are, strangely enough.
Except Bridget.'

'Mrs. Girgis—a new colleague, just arrived. An Irishman if you
please, but better than nothing, a step in the right direction—
Mr. Marlow.'

Henry introduced us and I shook hands all round like
someone at a funeral, leaning over Lola's shoulder so that I was
aware only of her thick bluish hair and a heavy, sweet smell like
old honey. I tried hard not to look at Bridget at all. But she
took the initiative, as she'd done before and was so often to do
again.

'Where's your friend Cherry?' she said brightly.

'You know each other then?' wondered Mrs. Girgis. 'Sit
down, do.'

'But there are no chairs—Esma!' Mr. Girgis turned and
bellowed at a *suffragi* who came dancing across towards us
gesturing hopelessly.

'Ma fishe chairs, Effendi—ma fishe!'

'Yallah, yallah ala tennis court,' Mr. Girgis advised him
loudly. ' "Ma fishe" chairs indeed. It's "ma fishe" everything
here these days. Since the English left. There's a dozen chairs
outside—just too damn lazy. So you've met my daughter then.
And who is this Cherry? I knew an Irishman once, out here with
the irrigation people, tried to blow up a sluice gate at Aswan. A
revolutionary! Can you imagine—as if we hadn't enough of our

own. Well, it's good news to get some of you people back here anyway. What do they say?—"The Best of British Luck"?'

He raised his glass in a cumbersome arthritic gesture. Mr. Girgis obviously missed the British. He had a heavy, bruised, old man's face—sad and peasant-like and Balkan, with a droopy moustache and a white film of spittle at each corner of his mouth. He was wearing frayed dancing pumps and an Edwardian smoking jacket and might have been a waiter at the old Carlton Grill. The *suffragi* returned with two decrepit deck chairs which he at once got in a fearful tangle over before I straightened one of them out and put it down firmly next to Mr. Girgis. Whatever I might have to say to Bridget that evening could wait until I'd had a few more drinks. On the far side of the table Henry had placed himself between Bridget and Mrs. Girgis and had embarked on an account of the royal caravan that afternoon at the school.

'What are you drinking, Mr. Marlow? Not that fizzy Italian stuff—we can do better than that. There's a crate or two of Haig left—not quite off the map out here yet! Esma! Esma!' He shouted wildly and clapped his hands above the din. 'We'll have a bottle.'

To my surprise the introductions had gone off with great brio, without any embarrassments. After the vegetable summer I'd obviously come back to some sort of life again. The previous disaster with Bridget hardly seemed to matter. I leaned back happily and the deck chair collapsed beneath me like a rifle shot.

Henry and Mrs. Girgis were caught in mid-sentence, like lovers, and the entire club came to a halt, except for the record player.

'*That ohh-ver-pow-er-ring-feee-ling . . .*'

Bridget laughed and I managed to raise the broken stem of my Asti Gancia glass to the company from a completely recumbent position.

For some reason, after I'd fallen over, things became easier between us all. It was as though, quite by chance, I'd fulfilled some arcane social obligation by collapsing amongst them and could now properly be admitted to their circle.

Mr. Girgis took my shoulder.

'*Well* done, well done! Nothing broken, I hope? That's the

spirit. No fault on your part—we can't have deck chairs in the lounge—have to bring it up at the next meeting. Now you'll have a decent whisky.'

He and I were suddenly friends of a casual sort, as if we'd just met again after a war spent together long ago, and I felt like a prodigal member of the Club who had returned and disgraced himself in a mild, appropriate, well remembered way as evidence of my continued solidarity with Mr. Girgis and the other stay-at-home members. I drank my whisky. Bridget had got up and was dancing with Henry. And I remembered it was Gala Night once a month so I danced with Lola.

She murmured, 'You're better at dancing . . .'

I smiled vaguely, brought her to me a little, and looked beyond her sly, cherubic face, her dark scented hair tickling my ear, to where Bridget and Henry, passing in their dance, had suddenly emerged from the crowd. Henry had his back towards us; they were together as closely as Lola and I, but in a way that spoke of great ease and familiarity and not embarrassment, so that I couldn't immediately understand the sudden calm expression on Bridget's face as she looked at me, a calmness in her eyes that was for me and not Henry.

In the second as she passed she was not, as she had been for me before, an unfortunate experience, a nonentity that one had picked up, forgotten and had happened to meet again, but she took on the form—as though we had both been prompted by a thought, I of loving: she of being its object—of someone who, because of this intuition, I was certain I would one day possess. And because of this, seeing in her glance a definite promise for the future, I paid no more attention to her all evening.

It would be ridiculous, I suppose, to imagine that there existed between us that evening—in that moment when we really knew nothing of each other—a sort of correspondence, an element of acceptance and understanding which, though neither of us was aware of it then, was the beginning of that conscious state of trust which later, in the short time we loved each other, made it equally unnecessary to ask questions, to put things into words.

In fact it must have been my obvious indifference towards her that evening which set the fuse alight and led to the opening bids of what was to become a long, rarely happy, and finally disastrous struggle to possess—subdue, dominate, exploit, hurt . . .

When we have to find an alternative to love it is not, unfortunately for us, hate; it is any of those other words which we choose to enact—which we know will tie us to the other, so that we won't lose them but remain together in anger, ensuring that if the love was not mutual the punishment will be.

But the words have gone now, along with everything else: the rather awkward, widely spaced eyes—so large that one might have thought them the result of some deformity or illness—the small, sharply triangular face, the thinly disguised curiosity which lay behind her smile—her sexuality. Above all her regard: her way of looking—prompted by a thought, which became a way of thinking, and then suddenly like an explosion became an instantaneous expression of her whole life at that one moment which would never afterwards be repeated at any other.

It was a part of her living through a fraction of time which she cut away from all the surrounding facets of her existence and which, in her expression, she offered me. Smiling, looking out on the river from her room, reading a magazine, making love—those idle or intense preoccupations of hers which went on quite above language, which were nowhere concerned with words—this is what has gone. And afterwards, just before we'd left each other, all the words returned: the saying of things, that desperate telling, questioning and explaining with which, when we have lost a true language, we debase the words that are left to us so that they can do nothing but denigrate or destroy, where they will serve only as carriers of the pain which has overwhelmed us and which, like an infection, we are determined the other should catch . . .

I watched her dance with Henry. Why does our sixth sense not warn us at such times?—instead of drumming into our heads, 'This will be happy. This one is for you.'

Henry brought some whisky home and we drank it in my room, sitting on the ugly little dormitory bed like prefects at the end of term.

'Did you make love to her then—the first time you met?'

'After a fashion.'

'Oh, why? She's very good at it you know.'

5

'WERE you with Henry—before?—I mean—'

'Why didn't you tell me you were a teacher?'

It was a week afterwards, another Saturday, on the terrace of the Semiramis looking over the river. She had wanted to meet as soon as I had telephoned her; not later or some other time but then, that morning, *now*. Already we were involved in the urgency of an affair, that extraordinary impatience in love which begins by making every meeting possible and ends by making them all impossible—'I have to go to the hairdresser, to see my aunt, my doctor, dentist.' We were a long way from the impatience of departure but we had started on it.

'A teacher? I thought it would have sounded rather a dull occupation—in the circumstances.'

'That meeting in the Continental—you thought it was just a pick up? I suppose it was.'

'There's nothing wrong in that, is there? It was what I wanted. I don't know about Cherry.'

And we laughed at Cherry. Already, too, there were the appropriate things in common: the beginnings of that obsessive regard for each other, the confident immunity from other people, the small jokes at their expense; the unique and secret marks we make in even the most casual relationship.

I said, 'You wouldn't have gone for a pair of dotty teachers.'

'Yes, I would. That's why it happened. I wanted you. It was as simple as that.'

'Were you with Henry then?'

She looked at me patiently, plaintively, rubbing her nose with the glass, as though I'd asked her whether she could tell the time.

'Of course. Didn't he tell you?'

'I didn't ask.'

'At the University here. You're getting the impression of a vagabond. But what's the point of being sly about it?'

'Isn't it rather strange?'

'You're the schoolmaster. Aren't children like that? Doing

what they want. Isn't it supposed to be good for them?'

'Come on . . .'

She frowned. 'Well, anyway, there was what's called "another man" . . . Christ.'

'I know. I've heard.'

'Henry told you. "The man in the soda-syphon" he used to call him.'

I had got up to order another drink.

'You don't have to. They'll come if you just look at them. Let's have some more *sudanis* as well.' And we ordered another lot of the little papery brown nuts in a saucer, squeezing them out of their shells through our fingers, and washing them down with the gin and tonic.

'Henry seems rather a postman these days, the way he passes on everything. Still, it doesn't matter. There's only been him—and the soda-syphon.'

'And the others?—you just made love with them. There wasn't anything else to it.'

'Why? Why should there be "others"?'

'Why make love with someone you hardly know? I'd just assumed there were.'

'Fool.'

A BOAC staging crew came in behind us and made for the bar, demanding loudly their pewter mugs which they kept there, and half a dozen bottles of Stella, and talking about a party in Uxbridge the previous week. The great lateen sail of a felucca reared up over the terrace, bleached dead white in years of the same weather, the curved mast rising again having passed under the Kasr el Nil bridge just below the hotel. The ropes squeaked sadly across the heat on the water like a small animal dying in the sun.

'Fool.'

And she took her drink up to the bar where someone called Roger, with much facetious encouragement from the others, made a great fuss over her and gave her a carton of tax-free Player's.

She phoned me next morning at the school. Mahmoud, who dealt with the coffee in the staff room, took the call and through force of habit gave the message to Henry.

'She wants to speak to you,' Henry said flatly when he got back. And I supposed his passion for her to be as dead as mine was.

'I'm not sorry,' she said at once, her voice ringing down like the start of a song. 'And you're quite right to be offended.'

I said nothing.

'So where do we go from here?' And then, fearing the answer might go against her, she rushed on without waiting for a reply. 'What's Henry answering the phone for? I asked for you. Does he live in your pocket—messenger boy as well as postman?' And then, the wind gone out of her bravado: 'Can you be separated? I'm with my parents down the road. Can you come round?' And again, like a ticker tape that won't be answered, which tells the rise and fall of fortune in the same second, in the same hurried accents, she went on: 'I *am* sorry. I am.'

'There's soccer this afternoon. I've got to look after it.'

'Can I come round *there* then?'

She walked along the touch line with Henry, looking at the game every now and then, catting with him, laughing. They might have been parents up from the country, come to see their child score the winning goal. Two of the four school houses were playing—Port Tewfik against Suez I think it was; I'm not very clear as most of the boys still called the houses by their old names—I think that afternoon it was Trafalgar against Waterloo. The ball bounced around uncertainly on the hard, cracked soil and once it disappeared into the murky canal on one side of the field.

'Send Fawzy after it, sir, he's got bilharzia already.'

It was very hot and at half time everyone collapsed and drank Coca-Cola and pushed the tops into the large cracks in the soil.

'Sir! They're putting the tops into the ground.'

A tiny figure with a serious adult's face in an immaculate soccer outfit rushed up to me as I joined Henry and Bridget.

'Are they? Who are you—you've not been playing have you?'

'I'm El Sayid, sir. Hamdy El Sayid. The substitute, sir.'

'Substitutes aren't allowed in soccer.'

'Yes, I know. But I'm the Headmaster's son.'

'Oh. Well go and tell them to take the tops out again.'

He ran back to the others, shouting as he went, and they dug the tops out of the ground and threw them at him.

Henry turned towards Bridget. She was wearing a white cotton outfit with a small gold cross round her neck—like a nun in a sleeveless dress—her dark hair tamed neatly round the back of her head in a circle. There was something prim about her—prim but uncertain; a nun in the Dark Continent.

'Here comes that troglodyte Bahaddin,' she said.

Bahaddin in his blazer, with a friend in a shiny business suit, was coming towards us along the trees by the canal. Both were gesticulating violently.

'His stockbroker, I should think. Not much on the exchange out here these days. Cotton's dropped right out of the market. They've mortgaged the lot to the Russians.'

'Good afternoon—Miss Girgis, Mr. Marlow.' Bahaddin bowed slightly towards me, fingering his silver wrist tag and eyeing us all very seriously. And then, with a big puff of breath and putting both hands across his chest like a man about to send a message in semaphore, he launched himself into what was obviously the real matter in hand.

'May I present Mr. Sofreides, Auctioneer.' He added his profession awkwardly, as though it were a title like Esquire. 'There's a sale tomorrow. Some sequestrated property. An English family. Mr. Sofreides is handling it and I thought perhaps you might like to come along and have a preview. There are some rather nice things, I understand—perhaps to enlighten your room, Mr. Marlow.'

'*Enliven*, Bahaddin. Not enlighten.'

He bowed again, very slightly, in Henry's direction, but his eyes remained fixed on the piece of metal at Bridget's neck.

'I'm glad to see my small gift so beautifully displayed.'

'Not at all, Bahaddin. It was a beautiful gift.' They bowed to each other again. A strained formality had come over everyone.

'You'd like to look at the things then? They're just down the road. In Garden City. And perhaps you might do me the honour of dining with me afterwards? I've reserved a table at the Estoril.'

'Yes. Shall we do that, Bridget?' Henry said as though she were his wife.

'Why not?'

I tried to catch her attention but the sun had fallen in the sky behind her, blinding me as I looked towards her.

'Sir, they've had ten minutes.'

El Sayid's long face pushed its way into the circle around our waists and he held out a gunmetal fob-watch towards me with a triumphant look.

'And Mr. Marlow—will you be joining us?'

Bahaddin didn't look at me, as if my answer couldn't be of any importance, but had turned and was examining El Sayid's watch very carefully.

'Certainly. I'd like to.'

Bahaddin was now completely absorbed in the watch, putting it to his ear, shaking it very gently, stroking his cheek with it, cosseting it in his hand as I'd seen him do before with every piece of metal that he came across or had about his person. And then at last he said, looking at his own gold Rolex, 'But why is it two hours slow, El Sayid—why is that? Exactly two hours.'

'It's Greenwich time, Bahaddin. From Big Ben. The Greenwich Meridian, the zero line of longitude.'

Mr. Sofreides—who had very soon asked to be called George—had a large, pre-war Packard and we drove back to Cairo along the river bank just as the sun began to dip behind the pyramids on the other side of the water. An absolutely still evening, the smoke from George's Gauloise swirling slowly back to Bahaddin and myself, the others chattering away like a family in the front.

'Major and Mrs. Collins,' George was saying. 'He was retired. One of the military attachés, I think, to Farouk's father. An old man. He didn't want to leave. Very bad luck really.'

We had reached the outskirts of the city. The pressure lamps above the brightly decorated barrows selling rissoles and beans flared at street corners and there was a smell of paraffin and urine when we stopped at the traffic lights, drifting in from the sidestreets below the Citadel, completely obliterating the burnt French tobacco.

The flat was on a lower floor of Bridget's apartment block in Garden City, looking out over the river across the corniche: there were the usual collection of *boabs* in the long hallway making up their beds in preparation for their night's vigil and a drowsy, ill-kempt soldier with a sten-gun who got up from a chair next to the door of the flat and saluted George in a muddled way as we arrived. The remains of a clumsy wax and ribbon seal which had been over the lock hung down now like a tattered Christmas decoration.

George opened the door with a proprietary flourish, turned on a large chandelier in the middle of the hallway and gave us all a stencilled catalogue with the pompous formality of an immigration official. It was a large, high-ceilinged apartment done in expensive bad taste; half a dozen rooms leading off the central hall and drawing-room, the furniture a mixture of pseudo Louis Quinze and dowdy Home Counties without dust covers; there was a curiously lived-in feeling about the whole place though the owners must have left a year before. I noticed a package of Gauloises under the huge gilded mirror over the mantelpiece. George had gone to a cabinet in the corner and was mixing whiskies, clunking in the ice from a silver bucket which had a polo pony and rider as a handle.

'Yes, I will be sorry to leave. It has been good here,' George said when we'd sat down in chairs looking over the river. He raised his glass to the furniture: 'We've had some good times here together.'

'You live here then?' I asked.

'It was best to be sure of the things. Best way. There are some valuable pieces . . .' His heavy eyes twinkled as he looked at Bridget. He had the traditional sallow, suspicious good looks of a Levantine *commercant*—a condescending way of looking at people, as if he had already used them or was about to consider doing so. There was an air of tired success about him, of deep boredom with life. One felt that even before he was born someone had been in his debt.

'George has been having some trouble with his wife,' Bahaddin put in slowly, dragging out the sentence, relishing the idea, as though it were the one pleasure lacking in his own abundant marriages.

George acknowledged the fact with a gesture of mock despair and a slow smile.

'I am helping Major Collins too. There are a few pieces here and there, some silver, which he's anxious to get back to England. By the law, of course, he can't touch them. But I think I can help him out. So it suits everyone.' Again he glanced at Bridget—casually, confidently, as a cat reminds itself of the mouse still in the corner.

'Well, let us take a look at the list. There may be something—even for you, Miss Girgis. Mrs. Collins had some rather—*jolie*, how do you say?—yes, some rather *jolie* things.'

I looked down the smudged sheet and could see nothing at all in what I imagined to be Bridget's taste; yet I was imagining, perhaps George knew.

> *Louis XV style Salon furnishings, gilt and carved wood. Aubusson tapestry upholstery. Console with mirror and silver-gilt wood. Bokhara and Scutari carpets. Antique clock. Oak Secretaire. English Silver tea service. 'Singer' Electric sewing machine, (DC) . . .*

The list went on interminably. There were no nylon stockings, something which would have been useful in Egypt at the time; perhaps George had Bridget in mind for the sewing machine.

We wandered round the rooms, drinks in our hands, looking at the bits and pieces without enthusiasm. There was a small bookcase in the study; two volumes of Cromer's *Egypt*, Meinertzhagen's *Diaries* and a number of regimental histories. Bahaddin had gone into the kitchen and I could hear him shuffling his hands about in the silver drawer and then the sudden whirr of an electric blender—his metallic obsessions being given full rein. Henry was looking at the oak secretaire in the study, opening each of the minute drawers. He took out a pile of visiting cards. I looked over his shoulder at one of them:

Major Edward M. Collins, M.C.
Military Attaché
to
H.R.H. KING FUAD I
Abdine Palace
Cairo

And there was an old Kodak folder with some yellowing prints inside: a thin unsmiling woman in a solar topee on a camel in front of the third pyramid at Giza.

George had gone into the bedroom with Bridget. I could hear his voice in the background—soft and insistent, a caricature of the Greek manner in such circumstances.

'Now what do you think of this? ... Not quite of the moment, it's true; but the material is superb. It's going as a "lot", all the dresses, but I could make an exception. In your case—'

'I'll have to try it on.'

And in a moment Bridget was in front of us in the drawing-room wearing a long velvet wrap with a hem dragging along the floor in mottled fur; a sort of skating dress, something, perhaps, dating from the period of Major Collins' attachment to the last Czar.

'I like it. Let's live here—why don't we? Couldn't we take over the lease—if we *all* paid something?'

And she swirled about on her toes, glaring at each of us in a mad way, the ghastly fur hem rising from the floor and spinning round like a ring of old ferrets chasing each other.

'Better than that dreadful monastery of a school. Better than my dingy bird's-nest upstairs. Couldn't we, George?'

George said nothing, but stood behind her like a satisfied ringmaster. Bahaddin had turned on a small portable radio and some dreadful squeaky Arab music emerged and he started to wiggle round Bridget, thrusting his backside violently about in time to the music, clapping his hands.

I poured myself another whisky.

'It's a pity Lola isn't here,' I said. 'She's rather good at that.'

George took his coat off and joined Bahaddin in paying court to Bridget, except that he circled round her in the Greek fashion, both hands arched above his head, kicking alternate legs and flapping a silk pocket handerchief. Both of them had already begun to sweat in the humid night air, patches of dark moisture spreading in great stains beneath their armpits. I supposed they would all be showering in the whisky soon.

Henry had gone out on to the terrace.

'Why does she do it?'

'She's unhappy, I told you. I think it's rather splendid.'

'Unhappy about what—about not getting enough men to go to bed with?'

Henry took off his glasses and rubbed them on the tail of his shirt. He spoke as if he were explaining an important point of syntax to his class.

'You must remember Cairo's pretty well been cleaned out of her sort—of our sort that is—in the last year. She hasn't had much fun, and we've not all got your self-control. Anyway you had a go at her yourself. Why should it bother you? When the English were here it was fine. She had all the "right" connections then. Now she has none. I suppose she feels now she has to take her chances, the chance to live it up like before.'

'But those tykes—in there—they're not exactly Brigade of Guards, are they?'

'And they're not Egyptians either. She draws the line there. Force of habit I suppose. Foolish of her; I don't. But I agree it's rather a bore. Let's go and eat.'

Bahaddin appeared in the doorway, flapping the tail of his dripping shirt and mopping his brow. He'd been drinking as well as dancing.

'My dear sirs, I shall have to change before dining. George has offered me a choice from Major Collins's wardrobe—shirts, trousers, dinner jackets, decorations, everything. Come and help me choose.'

'Take Bridget. She knows what you look best in. We're going on to eat.'

We came indoors. Bridget had collapsed on the sofa and was running a piece of ice from her whisky over her forehead.

'What have you two men been at—making out a report on me? Can't leave being schoolmasters, can you? Peter, come with me, will you?' She got up and I joined her in the bedroom where she picked up her dress. 'I know. I was supposed to meet *you* today, not all the others. And I *will* meet you. We will. Don't you understand?'

She had so many ways of looking serious, one could never tell from her expression what degree of any feeling she intended to convey.

'It doesn't matter.'

She went on into the bathroom and had started to undress when I arrived. I sat on a metal laundry bin by the lavatory.

'What's wrong if I dance with them?'

'There's so many of "them"—so few of "us". We have to meet in bathrooms.'

She turned the shower on. Again, the pale body, the darkly

sun-browned circle round her neck, the water cascading over her arms, patterning itself, dividing, merging into different whirls and eddies as it ran off the oils of her skin—not just standing under the shower, but giving herself to it, eyes closed, head tilted back, arms crossed over her breasts, like a martyr at the stake suffering a delicious agony in the fire. She opened one eye at me through the water.

'We ought to have made love properly, that first time. That's all. Then you wouldn't be so worried. You have this possessive thing. I know.' She opened the other eye, looking at me charitably, as if that were all I possessed.

'You think we just want each other,' I said, 'in that way.'

I lit a cigarette, twirling it casually in my fingers, and she stepped out of the bath and bent down and kissed me intensely.

'You worry so much. Yes I do think that. I do. Is there anything wrong?'

The water dripped down from her hands about my face, over my collar, and I looked at her rather glumly. *I do, I do* . . . her trick of repeating a phrase like this was what really worried me. She seemed to emphasise the physical part of our relationship because she saw no additional parts to it, either then or in the future. And yet it was there, in that clinical, white-tiled bathroom with its bidet and a great round faded box of Mrs. Collins's dusting powder which smelt of old oranges, that I first started to love Bridget, beyond simply needing her, being jealous of her. And she must have sensed this, and wanted to encourage this new emotion, for the next thing she did was to look at me with embarrassment, with an expression I'd never seen on her face before, as if I'd suddenly broken in upon her, the first man ever to see her naked. She stood there, perturbed, with an unhappy face, like a schoolgirl stuck with her prep.

'Aren't you going to get dressed? What's wrong?'

'Nothing. Throw me that towel will you, Peter.' And she draped herself carefully in it from head to foot. It was impossible to kiss her in return.

I thought at the time that our relationship had simply become more appropriate, more real; in fact it was I who had become more appropriate in her eyes: not a Guards officer or a third secretary at the Embassy, true, but something in the same line of country: an English teacher at the snob school in Cairo. Unsatisfied in sex, and therefore temporarily disapproving of it,

I had drawn from her an old memory of the proprieties of love,
and the ways in which it can become a means rather than an
end. I had reminded her of something her mother had once told
her about men—or perhaps it had been a lecture to the sixth
form after class from a spinster housemistress.

I started to love her at a moment when she had ceased simply
to need me, as someone to make love with, but saw in our
association a less tangible, more important outcome. And that's
what it became, as it never should have done, that evening in
the bathroom: an association and not an affair—a liaison with a
respectable future without the limitations which pleasure for its
own sake might have imposed on it. I had become something
too good to waste on pleasure alone. So that now, in trying to
remember when we'd been most at ease, most honest together, I
think of the beginning of it all, before there were any special
advantages for her in our being together: I think of our casual
failure on the chaise-longue in the little room against the sun as
the happiest time. Certainly, from then on, we were a success in
every conventional way.

It was Bahaddin, a little drunk and wearing one of Major
Collins's boiled shirts, who first noticed the change. We were
walking towards the Estoril which lay half way along a small
alleyway between Kasr el Nil and Soliman Pasha. Before, the St.
James had been the best restaurant in Cairo but it had closed
and the weary little flower lady with her dark shawl and
someone else's child had moved her site from there to the
mock-Spanish doorway of the Estoril and was now berating the
customers in a wailful voice, thrusting white carnations in their
faces, while the child slowed them up by their coat tails.

'Sir!' Bahaddin had given her fifty piastres and had bought us
all a flower. He gave me two. I looked at him. 'Sir, it is for you
to give to Miss Girgis.' He was impeccably polite, bowing
slightly, his feet together, his boiled shirt glistening in the lights
from the restaurant, like an Edwardian stage-door-Johnny.
There was something ridiculously gallant about him so that I
thought at first that he was embarking on some subtle joke.

'Why Bahaddin, have you given her too many flowers
yourself already?'

'Not at all, sir.' He was almost offended. 'Simply Miss Girgis
is with *you*. It is manners—for you to do the honours.'

The flower was the beginning of all those many formalities

which were to plague us later but at the time I lent myself to
Bahaddin's gesture with perfect ease and just the right amount
of ceremony; I lent myself blindly to the conspiracy: I pushed
the flower behind Bridget's ear and kissed her lightly. It must
have been exactly what she wanted in the new roles which she
had cast for us both; the evening passed without her looking at,
or hardly speaking to, anyone but me. Only George was visibly
annoyed. At odd moments between courses, when we had come
off the tiny dance floor by the bar, he would pull himself away
from some intense conversation with Henry or Bahaddin about
Egyptian affairs and look reproachfully at us with his watery
eyes. After all, he had made a bid for Bridget earlier which had
gone unnoticed in a subsequent overwhelming suit from
someone whom he could never have contemplated as a rival.

But his was a momentary shadow, his greedy disappointed
attitude an encouragement even, and I completely forgot my
worry about why Bahaddin and Henry were so correspondingly
uninterested in Bridget that evening and how she had come
about the small gold cross, Bahaddin's gift to her. For the
moment, for the first time, I felt no need to wonder about her
past, her lovers, for she had, as I thought, added that extra
dimension to our relationship, which I expected then of any
affair, which would set me up above any mere lover: the
dimensions of care and trust and permanence. The trouble was I
thought such things could co-exist with passion; while she had
learnt to expect them only in the context of marriage, when the
passion had quite disappeared. For her passion would always be
a thing on its own, something she could only give to a stranger.

Luckily I never got to know Sofreides well enough to ask him
if Bridget had slept with him that night, as Henry told me she
had long afterwards in England. And she denied it vehemently
when I asked her just before we split up. Certainly she and
George both left us at the entrance to the block of flats at the
end of the evening and went inside together. But then, of
course, they both lived there.

6

CHERRY seemed to have disappeared—at least he was never
around the Continental bar at week-ends, where normally I

would have expected to see him. And when I telephoned the Bursar at the school in Heliopolis where he'd been teaching I was told he'd gone to Alexandria.

'To Alex? But he's only just come back from there.'

'You know him better than I, Mr. Marlow,' the pernickety old Copt who ran that side of the school's affairs replied. More than likely, I thought.

'He has been transferred there temporarily as I understand it. You should be able to reach him there—the El Nasr College.'

The El Nasr College in Alexandria, a co-foundation with our own institution in Maadi, had been the most spectacularly British school in Egypt before 1956—and a spectacular neo-Gothic building in red brick with turrets and cloisters. Even after the English had left it had managed to maintain most of its ridiculously Anglophile attitudes and I was curious to know how Cherry had contrived to break into its cloistered calm.

'I don't much fancy meeting your Mr. Cherry again,' Bridget said to me when I suggested taking the next half term off and visiting him. And I would not have thought of it myself had not the idea of our all being together again suggested a return to a less formal relationship than ours had become. We were as intimate as it's possible to be without going to bed together, met as often as we could and she kept suggesting I go with her to her parents' house for Sunday lunch. If I'd had a small sports car and a taste for warm bitter we might just as well have been living in Surrey as Cairo. But I loved her. We had even stopped going to the Semiramis, or any of the other bars, and were sitting that morning at Groppi's sipping lemon tea.

'Anyway you'll have to phone him first and we don't get any half terms at the office.'

'What—are you *ashamed* of our love?' I said mockingly.

There were the bad jokes of love then too, that only love allows. There was everything except the chaise-longue.

As it turned out the matter of my seeing Cherry was decided for me when he wrote from Alexandria saying he was getting married in the new year, to a 'Mrs. Larousse, like the dictionary', whose husband had once been French Consul in Dublin and had died recently, 'at an advanced age while carrying out the same function in Alexandria'.

I met him by myself when he turned up in Cairo before

Christmas at the start of the holidays. It was a baking hot, ninety-degree day, completely unseasonable weather, and for some reason, perhaps because of its frosty, tinselly associations, we went to a Bavarian restaurant off 26 July Street, not at all in line with our old haunts in the city, but then Cherry was turning over a new leaf. And perhaps, too, he saw that blatantly stolid hostelry as a sort of secular retreat, a denial before marriage, the beginning of redemption for all his imagined sins of the past. We were not disappointed. It was a grim, dark, empty room done in imported pine with heavy gothic furniture and velvet drapes over all the windows, the light coming only from the little folksy wrought-iron table lanterns. There were notices everywhere, done in an elaborate ornate script, like a Book of Hours, which might have been directions to the lavatories but in fact were hearty German sentiments of good will and other compliments of the season. A radiogram churned away in one corner, charging the air with Strauss and memories of snow. I was here, over sauerkraut and Niersteiner—an awkward mixture which Cherry insisted on ordering—that I heard the story of his demise.

'She'd been teaching music after her husband went, piano to the Junior School. I'd seen her of course before, in the common room, on the Wednesdays when she came—and it was a Wednesday I remember that I became unwell. Anyway, one day she saw me with a copy of the *Irish Times* that I get. She was very fond of Ireland—and, well that was it. She's middle-aged but not unattractive. One must think of oneself.'

'How do you mean?'

'Well I won't be going back to Ireland.'

'You mean there's work in the old one yet, she'll teach music and you'll take it easy in the Cecil Bar?'

'Not quite . . .' Cherry was put out by my levity. 'Anyway you'll come to the wedding. It won't be a big thing . . .'

'Of course we will, Herbert.' And he paid the bill, already the responsible paterfamilias, and we bowed out through the dark drapes and into the blazing weather like a pair of cotton brokers up in town for the day.

'Not quite like it was before—"Lord Salisbury" and all that,' I said as we emerged. But Herbert didn't seem to hear. He was thinking of something else.

'What do you mean "we" will be coming to the wedding.'

'Bridget and I. I haven't told you about Bridget. Where are you staying—the Continental? Let's have a beer anyway.'

A look of horror spread over his face, that same wide-eyed clown's stare with which only months ago he had teased the old ladies on the beach at Sidi Bishr, except that now there was a completely serious intent behind it.

'You mean—Lola and Bridget? Those two. *That* Bridget?'

'Yes. It's no more surprising than you and Mrs. Larousse—less so by your account of it.'

We got no further than one of the small Greek bars behind the High Court between 26 July Street and Soliman Pasha, a place given over to desultory chatter and tric-trac games between dissolute lawyers and tailors and small businessmen of the community who came there to drink watery Metaxas throughout the afternoon siesta instead of going back to their fearful wives on the outskirts of the city.

'The scandal, the scandal,' Cherry muttered as we stood against the bar. 'Imagine it. If that got around Alex—my being with Lola.' He was sweating. The ham actor who has completely lost confidence in his role.

'Nonsense, Herbert. Alex has known far worse than that. You mean Madame would throw the dictionary at you. Well we won't come to the church. Just the drinks at the Cecil—or will it be at the Beau Rivage?'

He was clearly appalled now at the whole idea of my attending his wedding—seeing me as the jester, sprung from a raucous past, come to split the ceremony apart with laughter; the bawdy, boozy skeleton in his cupboard who would do nothing but fall over the altar chasing wine and wife.

It was Cherry's unexpected, saddening conformities that afternoon, allied to Bridget's, that made me think my own innate sense of the vulgar was disappearing as well. The chatter of legal business and shipping orders and spiteful marriages had reached a crescendo around us, the small merchants of the place getting in the last word before going back to their offices for the evening's work. And I saw in them, and in Cherry, the casual hazardous joys of the country—and all the other small ways I'd learnt to be happy in the city—becoming predictable as bales of cotton: the city had become like any other, a place where people worked and had dull marriages and drank to forget both. And I was very nearly one of them.

'Get me a brandy. I'll be back. I'm going to phone Bridget.'

Cherry laughed for a moment, the old manic whistle, as shrill as ever but with a new nervousness, and then tried to stop me. I suppose he thought I was going to suggest we go along for another set-to, a threesome in her flat.

'Don't do that. You're out of your mind! They arrest people for that sort of thing out here you know.'

I got through to her office. It was four o'clock. She had just come in and was out of breath and distant.

'What do you mean we haven't *done* anything. We're seeing each other all the time. Tonight—aren't we meeting tonight?'

'I mean making love, that's what we haven't done.'

'Not on the phone. For God's sake. This is an extension. You're mad. Go away. I'll talk to you later.'

'You may not. Cherry's getting married. I may go back to Alex with him.' There was a pause, as though she thought this might be true.

'You're drunk.'

'I can still climb on a train.'

'Aren't you coming round this evening? Can't we talk about it then?'

'No. I'm going out with Cherry. You don't want to be with him.'

'Tomorrow then. Sunday lunch. What about that?'

'Oh God, we'll talk about making love with your parents— over the rice pudding. Oh God, no.'

'Well, what else? Why not? The house is big enough. I have my own bedroom. There's the afternoon.'

Thinking of Cherry's odd middle-aged passion, his loss of nerve with the music teacher, I wanted her then, on any pretext, anywhere, before it was too late. So I said yes. Sunday lunch. When I got back to the counter Cherry, as though he'd overheard these coarse thoughts, had disappeared leaving me a Metaxas. I drank the mixture with its flavour of a vanilla cake-mix that's been kept in the cupboard too long, and ordered a whisky.

7

THE Girgises' house was a mile or so away from the school in Maadi, shut off from the road by a mass of flowering trees—jacaranda, bougainvillea and others I didn't know the names of—and the air around the place was as damp and sweetly oppressive as a ladies' hairdressers. A young *suffragi* with a brilliant green sash at his waist and the deep velvet black skin of his Sudanese ancestors let me in. He moved his head half an inch, a minute, utterly distant bow.

He was the last of the properly Arab world that I was to see until, hours afterwards, he bowed me out of the house again. From the drawing room to my right came the confident bumpy tones of a Victor Silvester quickstep; music being poured over cobblestones: the Sunday morning overseas request programme from London. An old grandfather clock made in Bath with the quarters of the moon and the four seasons picked out in flaking colours about its face ticked in the dark of the hall. The leafy, fruity smells outside had been replaced by a suggestion everywhere of dry cedar and in the cloakroom next to three pairs of old gumboots were a pile of *Country Life* and *Illustrated London News* tied up with string and addressed to the Anglo-American Hospital.

Bridget came down the dark stairway in a grey pleated skirt, flat-heeled shoes and a boy's tennis shirt.

'Dear me. I didn't bring my gumboots—or a racket. I'm sorry.'

'Don't be silly. You'll want gumboots for the garden. They flood it every morning. Alexander's very keen on it—you'll be shown round—and *do* be a bit interested.'

We moved into the drawing-room where her parents were—a room littered with silver-framed photographs of friends and relations and interminable children, including the mandatory image of Mr. Girgis—Girgis Bey—in full regalia as an Egyptian civil servant thirty years before, looking more than ever the Turkish peasant in a tarbush, decorated sash across his breast and a bushy moustache.

They stood up and smiled graciously, distantly—as though gently emphasising the distance between their home and the Maadi Sporting Club—and Mrs. Girgis turned the radio off.

'No—please. Don't turn it off for me.'

'But Mr. Marlow, we want to hear about *you*. And anyway,' she went on in a lower voice, gesturing towards a bundle of old Army blankets in a chair near the radio which I hadn't yet noticed, 'it's for her. Mamie. Alex's old nurse.'

A woman of incredible age, almost completely swathed in a coarse threadbare blanket with just a wisp of white hair falling from beneath the cowl which the material formed over her head, looked at me carefully and rather malevolently from behind a pair of gold-rimmed spectacles. It was an old face, grey—almost indistinguishable from the colour of the blanket— withered, shapeless as folds of sand, except for the open eyes, magnified by the glass, which were pale blue, large and fresh as a child's. I had the impression that although I was supposed to accept her as a senile harmless old party, mentally in her dotage and physically far beyond greeting me, this was not the case—an assumption that soon proved correct. I had turned away and having finished my greetings with the Girgises was about to sit down when a squeaky, crystal-clear announcement emerged from the bundle.

'Would not Mr. Marlow shake hands with me? Would that not be manners?'

With its repeated negatives, its reproving, petulant insistence, it was an ageless, endlessly practised injunction: honed in wars of attrition against countless bygone brats it came now over the air, a message from the past, a call to order from the nursery, a reminder that however far afield we had gone in time or place that dictatorship was ever at hand. The words were vindictive, in a way I had long forgotten; they had been put not as a question but as a sentence handed down from a court without appeal. I wondered for a moment if all of us would have to have lunch in the pantry without any pudding.

Mrs. Girgis was the first to recover herself.

'But, Nanny, I thought you never shook hands. You never have.'

And indeed there were no hands to shake. The grey blanket remained folded over the chair, completely covering the minuscule body, like the bark of a strange tree.

'I shall have my lunch upstairs as usual.' The tree came to life. Mr. Girgis in a pair of old check carpet slippers helped her to her feet with the air of a man attending a grave accident, giving her a malacca cane with which she walked slowly but firmly across and out of the room.

'I *am* sorry.' Mrs. Girgis was truly upset in an awkward way. 'She never wants to meet anyone. She just comes downstairs for the Sunday programme—you must have come a little early. She was Alexander's nanny. She came from the Residency. She'd been with one of Kitchener's aides before that. I simply can't understand it.'

'I can,' Bridget said. 'It's quite simple. You ought to have introduced her to Peter.' And Mr. Girgis looked at her in astonishment.

Lunch, which was a too mild curry with an assortment of bland chutneys and chopped fruits, was rather strained. And I did nothing to add to the gaiety by preferring the local Egyptian cheese—the strangely smoky, acrid *gibna* of the delta—to some yellowing, sweating cheddar which I knew had been imported through a firm in Denmark by the Embassy people.

Afterwards Mr. Girgis came to life. 'Come and see the garden. You'll need a pair of gumboots. I've got an old pair, I think. They flood the place at midday so it'll still be pretty wet,' and we went out into the cloakroom. The boots didn't fit so I took off my shoes and rolled up my trousers and he gave me a tiny straw hat and took a long pruning staff for himself and we went outside like a pair of mad fishermen.

Huge trees completely circled the acre of garden and beyond the small square of lawn which led out from the terrace the undergrowth was as dense as a jungle.

The little garden, between the lawn and the jungle, was like a willow pattern saucer, complete with two willow trees leaning over an ornamental pool, water lilies, clumps of papyrus with their feathery white cockades and a crooked wooden bridge. Raised duckboards, like a miniature railway line, threaded their way through these studied effects, and all around them an inch or two of water giving the whole place the air of an exotic paddy-field under the blazing sun.

Mr. Girgis splashed off across the lawn and prodded some scented flowering bush with his stick, detaching a few of the petals which rose a fraction in the air around the plant, drenching the damp atmosphere with sweetness, like a woman drying out against an electric fire in a small room.

'It needs some more water,' he said to me confidentially. 'Ahmed!' He bellowed in the direction of a small hut in the trees and Ahmed, a disgruntled, sleepy gardener, appeared and was given detailed instructions about the hose and the plant.

There followed a manic dance about the garden as Ahmed, mishandling the appliance, doused the three of us in a warm jet of water. He dropped the hose so that it thrashed around at our feet, the water splashing in small waves over the top of Mr. Girgis's gumboots.

'God damn him.' Mr. Girgis picked up his pruning staff and we paddled back to the terrace where the others had arranged the coffee.

'Nescafé is ready!' Mrs. Girgis sang out, as if heralding some incomparable nectar. 'When you've dried yourselves.' And the two of us trooped upstairs.

'Here, I can lend you a shirt and trousers,' Mr. Girgis said when we'd dried ourselves and were in his bedroom, and I decked myself out in an old pair of flannel yachting trousers which reached half-way down my legs and moth-eaten turtle-neck pullover—part of the same outfit with the name 'Cleopatra', one of Farouk's smaller boats, on the front of it—the only thing in his wardrobe which remotely looked like fitting me and even then it stretched tight across my chest like an old sock so that it itched fearfully.

'Bridget had better show you the rest of the place,' Mr. Girgis said rather huffily, as if I'd turned the hose on him. 'I shall catch my death.' And then, as an afterthought, he made the strange inquiry—'Did you have some rum? Let's have some rum with our coffee.'

His choice of this particular drink as a reviver seemed to have been taken quite unconsciously, without reference to my nautical garb. Perhaps my clothes may have jogged to life again some deeply buried maritime experience of his long ago, a careless shipboard party off Alexandria, with the young Farouk and his English friends—perhaps a naval squadron from Malta was visiting at the time—for rum is not an expected drink in Egypt.

Downstairs he poured out two glasses of rum in his study and we sipped them in the dry air like men taking disagreeable waters.

'Some ice perhaps?' he said hopefully, after I'd lowered a second mouthful less enthusiastically than the first. And then he thought better of the idea, looking around him. 'There isn't any. It would only mean another disaster with the *suffragi*.

Shall we join the ladies?' But Bridget had appeared in the doorway without our noticing and was smiling quietly at both of us. Mr. Girgis looked at me.

'My old summer togs—eh? Rather a sight I suppose. Well, I must get back to Ahmed. I expect you've had enough of the garden. I shouldn't walk about outside in that jersey in any case—mightn't be taken in the right spirit. Show him the paintings, Bridget.'

She moved across the room towards us, looking at me carefully, taking the damp clothes from my arm, as though she'd not heard her father speak. We finished off our glasses in one go, as if the outcome of this ridiculous charade lay in some pressing business offstage, and moved into the hallway. Mrs. Girgis was laid out on the terrace, fast asleep on the chintz-covered steamer chair. A cat I'd not noticed before, a large over-fed tabby, was up on the small trestle table among the coffee cups lapping carefully from the silver milk jug.

'Good Lord—Mamie's cat has got out. Down the creeper. I thought it was past it. We should have had it put away—but what can one do? She got it as a present years ago, one of the under secretaries in my department—currying favour, British love of animals and all that. Sly fellow. He wanted a trip to San Francisco, I remember. It was the start of the UN. We called the cat Hopeful—in memory of that event—and my colleague's diplomatic ambitions. I had him posted to Addis Ababa instead. But that's another story. Don't wake Mamie upstairs. With any luck she'll sleep till supper. Like a child, you know. She needs her rest.' He had put on his gumboots again and now he tip-toed away from us, hitching his dressing-gown tight about him, past his sleeping wife, lifting the cat off the table—it kept its great grey muzzle embedded in the milk jug until the last possible second—and on out to do battle with the luckless Ahmed.

The grandfather clock in the corner of the hall chimed softly, four bell-like notes in a scale. Part of a full moon, with a face like Humpty Dumpty, was creeping over the horizon of stars at the top. And at the bottom, on a corresponding scale, the month of February in a gothic script, garlanded by two plump salmon, the fish of Pisces, was coming to an end. Only the time—a quarter past three—was very nearly correct.

Bridget came up behind me and stretched her arms over my

shoulders, her fingers picking at the dark cotton letters of
Farouk's ship on my chest.

'It's a mad-house,' she said slowly. 'What a stupid, marvellous
thing.'

'What?'

'I love you.'

'It itches like hell.'

'What does?'

'The jersey.'

'Take it off then. But not here. Upstairs. We can "look at the
pictures".'

In a boxroom, wedged under the eaves, beneath the burning
rafters, we made love again. There were two narrow dust-
covered windows looking out over the garden and we could see
Mr. Girgis dictating to Ahmed, the two of them moving
painfully from plant to plant like men walking a punishment
course across a swamp, the rough Arabic syllables falling upon
Ahmed like a succession of curses.

We lay on our clothes, her tennis shirt and her father's
yachting trousers as a pillow against the dusty floor, that small
body constantly changing position, moving beneath me, locked
in mine. There was an Egyptian flag in one corner, the old one,
three stars and a crescent moon against a green background, and
the remnants of a Hornby train set in another—a still-bright
black engine lying on its side with the legend 'L.N.E.R.' on the
coal box.

'He plays with trains. He used to.'

In other corners of the room trunks and suitcases were piled
on top of each other, and wicker boxes with P & O labels
directing them to Port Said and Tilbury and the Metropole,
Monte Carlo.

'Doesn't this answer your phone call yesterday? I mean it's
better than talking about it. Making love is better.'

'Yes.' We had stopped for a moment, and lay next to each
other, sweating.

'I was angry—because you wouldn't do it the past few
months, when before, the first time, it was so easy for you.'

'It's *not* as easy now, that's all. My wanting you now—it isn't
in the same way.' She looked at me, perplexed, a glance for a

tiresome child. 'But why is it so important for *you*? It is for me, I know. But for you? That possessive thing? How can you love like that? Don't you know?'

'Yes, it is the possessive thing and I don't know.'

'God, I've never talked so much about making love—and done it so little, with someone I wanted so much. I *want* you now because I *love* you now. But don't be held by it. I don't want to—possess, be possessed, all that. So why talk, argue? Make love. I need it, mean it, want it.'

Mrs. Girgis had joined her husband outside and was following him gingerly along the duckboards, treating him in much the same way as he had dealt with Ahmed, except that, with her, the continual comments and criticisms drifted up to us in the purest tones of Refined-Surrey.

'Really *far* too much water, Alex . . . it's not a paddy-field you know. Is it *impossible* to get Ahmed to understand *anything*? Are any of the figs ripe? Can we get some for Bridget to take back with her? Alex! My border is *quite* water-logged . . .'

'We'd better go. They'll start to call. Make love again. Please.'

There was a noise outside on the stairway, a quick deter-mined step on the creaking wood, and the door opened. Mamie glanced around her vaguely, with the numbed look of someone unhappily released from a deep sleep.

'Hopeful? Hopeful?'

The ridiculous name squeaked out as she peered around the trunks. 'Puss, Puss!'—and she moved towards us and away again so that I thought for a second that she hadn't seen us. And then, with the same look of perfect understanding that I had remembered from before lunch, she noticed us, peering down her nose as if she had suddenly seen some terrible, ineradicable stain on the floor.

'I thought Puss might be here. I'll ask your father, Bridget, if he's seen him.'

She spoke in the sad way that one speaks to a child who has done something beyond any scolding, whose crime only some infinitely high authority can now judge.

8

I MET Bridget at the Semiramis a few days later. We had gone back to drinking in bars again.

'It doesn't matter. It just means you won't be asked for Sunday lunch again.'

'What did she say?'

'That I'd been "playing" with you—you know, like children under the dining room table. The only thing is he may try to interest your Dr. El Sayid in the matter—"not the sort of thing one expects from a guest, Doctor—in one's own house, and in *front of my old Nanny*"—I can hear him.'

Which matter Mr. Girgis duly proceeded to interest the good doctor in.

Henry and I were staying at the school during the holidays and a day or so afterwards as we were passing by the side window of El Sayid's study on our way for a game of table tennis in the basement of the Old School, there came a violent rat-a-tat-tat as he machine-gunned the window pane with a coin, as he did every day in term time, signalling in his wildly imperious manner the start of afternoon classes. A long finger beckoned me.

'We are a small community out here in Maadi, Mr. Marlow, a small but honourable one, of which this school forms very much a part. We rely on each other for our good name about the place—indeed about the whole city and the country. And even further afield. We bear a responsibility to each other for our behaviour—corporately and individually. So I am not in the least surprised, as you may be, that one of our neighbours, with whom until recently you were acquainted—Girgis Bey—has seen fit to ''tell tales out of class'' as it were. I am very obliged to him. A matter as I understand it—and I shan't descend to details—of "abusing hospitality" as he put it, in a manner quite unbecoming to your status as a guest in his house and member of the staff here. Not a legal matter, I gather, but really—and I think this far more important in view of your responsibilities to the young here—a matter entirely within the moral sphere. To

cut a long story short it would be completely unsuitable for you
to remain in your present position with us. You appear, to put
it bluntly, to be lacking in even the very rudiments of physical
control. The dangers of allowing such licence in a place like this
must be obvious to you.'

'It was a woman, Doctor. Not a boy.'

And he rose from his desk in a fury and walked vigorously
towards the window, slapping his thigh repeatedly on the way.

'I don't care *what* it was!—man, beast or ripe melon—I insist
upon your resignation. You may take two weeks' notice from
the beginning of next term—an arrangement, I think, entirely
generous in the circumstances.'

'I'm sure it's more than I deserve.'

I went down to join Henry in the basement of our 'house' in
what had been known as 'Old School'. He'd got the net up and
was talking to Mahmoud, the little janitor and odd-job man who
had his closet down here, full of brooms and dusters, a
collection of dirty coffee cups, a primus stove and a bed—
though he didn't sleep here officially. Mahmoud had quite
taken to Henry and me for some reason—as opposed to the vast
majority of other Egyptian teachers now employed by the
school—although neither of us could follow his strangely
accented Arabic and he spoke no more than greetings in
English. He—or his father, one could never tell from his attempt
to explain the genealogy—had been with the school practically
since its foundation and perhaps he saw in Henry and me the
last remnants of a preferred regime, an appropriate link with his
previous masters; we must have given him, through our inability
to understand each other, a comforting sense of continuity.

'I've been "asked to leave".'

'Oh.'

Henry didn't seem all that surprised. I suppose now that
Bridget had already told him everything that had happened.
Certainly he must have seen her then, without my knowing,
almost as often as I did.

'Don't worry. We can get you private lessons. Everybody
wants to learn English. We'll have a game and go down town.
What does it matter? I hope you gave him hell.'

When we had finished Henry went back to his room to

collect his wallet—even in those days he never seemed to have what he needed about him—and I stayed on with Mahmoud over another coffee with which he punctuated our every day like a clock.

In the old days, before Suez, this lower part of the old school had been used for all those extra-curricular activities so dear to English educational tradition, those rugged pursuits through which character is supposedly moulded and happiness usually crushed: Scouting, P.T., Amateur Dramatics and so on—and in shuttered rooms leading off this central hall were stored the instruments of all that pain, the littered remains of the white man's burden: old footballs, punch bags, dumb-bells, chest-expanders, smashed cricket bats, a number of bruised bowler hats and tattered copies in French's Amateur Acting Edition of *The Monkey's Paw*. The new regime, not yet fully aware of these riches beneath them, left the basement area entirely to the shufflings of Mahmoud; this was his dark, cool domain.

So while Henry was gone I took another, perhaps a last, look round.

In a cupboard at the end of one of the rooms—together with a lot of broken laboratory equipment, old gauzes, test-tubes, retorts and encrusted Bunsen burners—was a broken film projector, some rusty cans of film—'The Three Counties Agricultural Show 1937', 'The British Police', and 'The Port of London Authority'—a number of well rubbed copies of a booklet published in Fenchurch Street in 1939 called *Wireless Telegraphy for Beginners* and a radio receiver or transmitter, I couldn't make out which.

'Come on. We'll miss the train. I'm not paying for a taxi—yet.'

Henry stood in the doorway, oddly impatient.

'They never use any of this stuff here?'

'Never. Suez was the End of Empire. Didn't you know?'

We went to the Fontana and another club on Roda island. And the Perroquet on Soliman Pasha, ending up just before dawn in a gharry at the Auberge des Pyramides.

'Where are you going to go?' Bridget asked.

'A hotel—why not? Henry has ideas about private lessons.'

'Yes, Henry said there's all those girls from my old English class at the University. Some of them still think they can get an external degree.'

'You could advise me on—what do they call it?—syntax. Yes, English syntax,' Bahaddin added. 'And I could get you a maid's room at the Cosmopolitan. The manager's a friend.'

'You could live with me. Lola's finally decided to go back to Beirut,' Bridget said lightly. And apart from that idea it was rather a grim little Christmas dinner that Bahaddin had arranged for us all on the roof restaurant of the new Shepheard's Hotel.

A week later I moved in. The lift had been repaired.

The weather had cooled appreciably by now. It was the start of that month or so of winter in Egypt; soft, almost damp grey mornings by the river and streaky clouds far overhead and odd vicious dusty winds—intimations of the spring khamseen from the desert which swirled the low water by the corniche into momentary thrusts and eddies and clouded the sun with a fine gritty haze. And once, at the end of January, it rained for the first time since I'd arrived in Egypt, an afternoon of velvet grey clouds rolling up the delta from the sea—and then for ten minutes or so before dusk, just a few drops, like someone shaking wet hands at you.

Lola had stayed on in Beirut and we shared the big double bed at the back of the apartment and Bridget went out to work every morning and came back at lunchtime, when we often made love. I had never been happier. There was an ease in our relationship for those few months which neither I, nor I think Bridget, had ever thought possible. We loved each other and we made love, and there was nothing left to be said.

It was a marriage, I suppose, but without obligations or rights, without the possessiveness she feared—without any of the things which were to make the marriage itself, when it came, such a disaster. Even the fact that my private lessons never came to very much and that after the first month Bridget had to pay most of the expenses didn't seem to matter. Or so I thought then. With no more than the usual egoism felt in such circumstances I saw an indivisibility in our love, and a corresponding unimportance in the details of life. Afterwards I had assumed that things had gone wrong simply because Bridget had been less of an egoist, a much more conventional person than I'd imagined; the sort of woman who, at the end of the fun, finds her deepest needs in the traditional supports. Now—there are so many other questions involved that one has stopped, thankfully, looking for answers.

Henry had put me in touch with Samia—a nice dull elderly girl with a wiry cloche of hair and a green dress—the younger sister of someone he had taught at the University, who was unaccountably attempting 'O' levels. Twice a week I trudged through *Macbeth* with her in a back room of her father's office in the old part of the city beneath the Citadel—down alleyways small and dirty as gutters, completely overhung by shabby wooden houses with balconies that almost linked overhead so that it was dark even at midday. Her father had his place at the end of one of these crammed passages; he was a huge mediaeval figure with a boxer's face and the devout air of a prosperous, deeply traditional Moslem; with his rolling moustache—and without his immaculate *galibeah* and green turban—he might have been a Victorian paterfamilias. He ran a small export-import agency so that the whole place smelt strongly of sacking and dried beans and the sweet stench of Turkish coffee. At whatever time of day I arrived his friends were always gathered in a circle round his desk, a cabal of wizened cronies sipping from thin cups, and I would be given the inevitable cup myself before being led through to the tiny office beyond a curtain by one of the clerks, entering upon Samia, distractedly fidgeting with her notes, like a lout broaching a harem.

Her father and his friends guarded the approaches while I imparted the mysteries; their soft chatterings moving in counterpoint to my weary explanations about the three witches, which Samia followed not at all. Her attention would drift outwards, beyond the curtain, to the talk in the next room—of ships and bales and bad weather, I suppose, and foreign places, while I—in my own distraction—would remember what I'd had for lunch that day with Bridget: beans cooked in oil with lemon juice and wrapped in thin crescents of dark sour bread which she'd picked up from one of the cafés on El Trahir square and left in the oven too long while we made love.

At the end of my hour with Samia I would emerge thankfully from the closet and there would follow a lengthy exchange of 'salaams' and cluckings and smiles and salutes with her father and the others before I disappeared down the backstreets again, coming alive now after the still of the afternoon—paraffin pressure lamps hissing urgently above the stalls and barrows as they were pumped up, like animals provoked beyond endurance, before breaking into innumerable flares all along the passageways.

I suppose it was this background of the grubby winter city—far from the sad arrogance, the BBC request programmes and the ancient Hillmans of Maadi—a background pared of all inessentials, which gave to what happened in those months a definition, a quality of hope, which a similar time, spent say in Paris or Venice, would not have had. The grubby and unpromising can only suggest promise; at least, we persuade ourselves, they cannot disappoint. So we are prompted to beliefs which in other more favourable circumstances we would never have contemplated. I believed that I was happy; that Mamie and the folly of Dr. El Sayid had led me to my proper station in life, that everything had conspired in my favour. Only now am I aware of the proper nature of the conspiracy.

When it is over, we look back vehemently for that moment in a particular experience when the first flaw appeared that led to the end; quite perversely, like geologists tapping their way about volcanic rock, we seek the first intimation of the explosion, running our minds savagely back and forth over the affair: late mornings looking out over the river from the open window of her apartment, the bitter smell of the low water, coffee together on the Semiramis terrace on Sunday mornings; the old men flushed, with bloodshot eyes, in tarbushes and white duck suits wandering aimlessly around the pillars in the huge hall behind us, flicking their whisks dispiritedly at the few winter flies, offering elaborately formal greetings to acquaintances before moving on as though to some pressing affair; early evenings hurrying back along the aromatic side streets, from Samia or some other luckless student, towards the river again, with the sun behind the pyramids now—spreading a veneer of rose and purple over the town, cutting out the huge triangles of stone in soft charcoal from the sunset behind them . . .

In all the happy manoeuvres of that calm winter—when did it begin?

We'd had lunch one Sunday at Mena House and had walked

up the hill afterwards towards the pyramids. It was late February and the hot weather was already in the air. We sat on the terrace of the old Viceregal kiosk at the foot of Cheops, sipping colourless tea, beating off the shoe-shine boys and camel drivers like any tourist.

Suddenly, a tiny dark bean of a child appeared from nowhere at my feet and started to clean my shoes furiously, rubbing away at them with a kind of foamy black paint. They were suede, not leather.

'No!' And then the same word, louder, in Arabic. But he went on eagerly as if he'd heard nothing.

'Tell him to stop for God's sake. He'll ruin the shoes.' I had got to my feet, appealing wildly to Bridget.

'Oh, what does it matter—what does it matter? They're horrible old shoes anyway. I was just longing for them to be finished with. You can get another pair.'

The child in his ragged blackened nightshirt, one eye closing with trachoma, had stood up now, unsure of what to make of our outburst, and had begun to slink away before Bridget called him back and gave him five piastres.

'You're so mean—those rotten shoes. My God, you can still get *shoes* out here at least.' She spoke quite calmly now and had turned away to look at the pyramid.

'I don't have all that money.'

'No.' She sipped at her tea without looking round, quite uninterested in my statement so that I felt I had to force her attention.

'Fifty piastres an hour is what I get at the moment and I can't ask for much more, that's pretty well the top rate. And the flat is seven pounds a week.' The annoyed, querulous tones of the forgotten remittance . . .

'What does the flat matter? Are we just living there together for sheer convenience?'

'No, I hope not. Just I've not got the money to start buying new pairs of shoes, that's all.'

'You could earn the money if you wanted to. You've still got your work permit—to teach in the English schools. And there are more of them besides Maadi.'

'They wouldn't have me. We've talked about that.'

'Oh Lord.' She drew the words out in a sigh. 'You sit around all day in the flat. You're always there when I get back. You could do some sort of job couldn't you? Where's this all getting us—you, me? What do you do here, after all? You go to the Council Library, Groppi's, you meet Henry for lunch at the Cosmopolitan and drink in the bar there all afternoon with those awful Greek lawyers—and you come back at four in the morning from the Fontana or somewhere and expect to make love with me. And it goes on and on. And then you say you can't buy a new pair of shoes. That sort of life suits you—and it suited me too—but does it suit us both together? I mean, why be together—if we just go on behaving in the same old way? Shouldn't there be something—else?'

'What else?' I was thoroughly annoyed.

'I don't know. Work perhaps, regular work—something to interest you. Aren't men supposed really to need that, not just the other things,' she said lightly, bitterly.

'What "other things"?'

We had become children, quarrelling over words, throwing them heedlessly about.

'Love? Is that what you mean—that sort of thing? That's what I *don't* need—I just need the drinking with Henry and a good job in some wretched boys' school?"

'Don't be stupid—you're not going to spend the rest of your life just loving me—and nothing else. What *else* are you going to do?'

'What do you mean—"what else"? Do you expect me to join the Army or something, become a lawyer, "settle down"? I'm just a teacher. Or was. Rather dull, I suppose.' She said nothing but looked at me blankly. 'What "else" is there, from your point of view? I'd like to know. It's becoming a bore really, isn't it? Just loving me, with nothing else in sight? None of those extra things that you might properly expect from a relationship of this sort; none of the things that came with the men you had before—martinis on the terrace at six o'clock, yelling at the *suffragis*, trips to the Gezira Club in the afternoons and summers on the beach at Alex: you're looking for a future. I know what you mean.'

'You don't. You're just stupid.'

'She wants to marry you—what's wrong with that?' Henry had ordered another bottle of Stella and it was dark at the end of the bar in the Cosmopolitan. It was another of our 'afternoons' as Bridget called them. 'You could do it at the Embassy—you were born in London, weren't you—dual nationality. No trouble—if that's what you want. Though I'd say you wanted a job really. No point hanging on with those private lessons if you can help it. Do you know Crowther at the Consulate here, commercial attaché? He might have some ideas about work. Go and have a word with him. He's a friend of mine.'

'Don't just marry me—because of that talk at the pyramids.'

'Of course not. I was mad. I'll get a job. Henry has ideas, someone at the Consulate. I *want* to marry you.'

'And not just because it's giving you something definite to do—marrying me instead of getting a job, because it'll make you feel better?'

'You're mad now. No. Though it does make me feel better. Why are you so cagey about it? Aren't you sure?'

'Yes, I am. Just I'm surprised—now it's happened.'

We'd walked over the Kasr el Nil bridge to the Gezira Club and across into the middle of the race course towards the huge baobab tree that stood in the centre of the park on the island. It was a Saturday, the last meeting of the season, I think, before the horses all moved to Alexandria for the summer. The bell clanged in the distance before each race, every half hour or so, and the tiny horses thundered round the perimeter, taking the curves flat out against the fence in a line, like animals on sticks in a child's game.

'Let's do it soon, that's all.' There was an urgency in her voice as if she were talking about our making love and saw our marrying simply as a legal means of ensuring that end on a permanent basis.

9

MR. Crowther had the features of a frightened weasel; an unbalanced face: a broad flat forehead narrowing sharply to a point in a minute chin, eyes close together in a setting of continual alarm, fox-coloured moustache and the stringy, lazy body of someone who years before had made a habit of bowling

two fast opening overs before retiring to matron with a twisted
ankle. Thin silvery hair, a bow tie and a rather crumpled linen
suit completed the impression of a last delicate flowering before
the light desert airs blew him completely to seed.

He waved me to a sofa some way from his desk and then
hurried back into his chair—as if to lessen some expected impact
in what I had to say.

'*Married*?' he said with exaggerated concern when I had
explained my business. 'But that's surely something for your
Church. You should see the Provost at All Saints' or—'and he
looked at me like a doctor deciding on a diagnosis—'Father
McEwan at Heliopolis.'

'No, I—we don't want a church. I thought it could be fixed
up at one's Embassy.'

'It might be—if there were one here. But there isn't. And no
Ambassador either. In any case I understood from my friend
Mr. Edwards that you were Irish—?'

'Yes, but born in England—dual nationality—'

He didn't seem to have heard; brow furrowed, looking deeply
into his desk, running his finger along the woodwork, he
appeared quite given up to the struggle of marshalling his own
arguments.

'I'm afraid there may be difficulties, you see. Your fiancée is
Egyptian you said. And you are Irish. Now, if both of you had
been *British*—then I think something could have been arranged.'

Satisfied that he could now rest his case Mr. Crowther—*Basil*
Crowther as I'd seen on his office door in the Consulate
building behind the main Embassy—got up and moved warily
towards me on the sofa, his linen suit, smudges of darkness
spreading under the arms, suffering, like himself, agonies from
the heat. He looked wearily at a photograph of Queen Elizabeth
trooping the colour in the fresh brightness of a London summer
on the wall behind me.

'The Guardsmen always used to faint, didn't they? I
remember in the old newsreels. And they just left them there.
That was before Suez of course. Now they cart them away. *Sic
transit* something . . . of course, your being Irish you
wouldn't—really appreciate . . .' He left the idea hanging in the
air, as if in a mental faint, and mopped his face.

A little elderly lady had appeared and Mr. Crowther ordered

tea in such graceful tones that I wondered if there might not be cucumber sandwiches as well.

'No, it's difficult. And very bad luck. I'd like to be able to help. It's not that I'm overburdened with work at the moment either. But I've remembered now—it's the *Italians* who deal with the Irish here. There was a nun in here last month. From Aswan or somewhere. She'd left the order. Something about a policeman—whether in Aswan or Tipperary I couldn't quite gather. Anyway, we sent her on to the Italians. You might have a word with them. Though now I come to think of it they don't marry people in their Embassies, one of the few countries that don't. And you're not Italian.'

I thought perhaps that I must have caught Mr. Crowther at a time of immense personal pressure—'my wife or something' as he might have put it.

'What about the Cathedral—All Saints'? You could get married there, couldn't you? Have you thought of that?' He seemed particularly pleased at the idea as if he'd solved the problem. 'The Cathedral, yes. Now that would make a splendid setting. You couldn't do better. But perhaps—' he looked at me suddenly—'that might be a little too public for you, what? One wants a decent privacy in these things. One is not marrying one's mother-in-law after all.'

'No.'

'Ah, our tea. Thank you, Mrs. French. Lemon, Mr. Marlow?'

Mr. Crowther's face cleared. He smiled for the first time, an awkward grin, like a dusty accountant who has got the figures out of the way with a wealthy client and feels the need to embark on brief innocuous banter to suggest his position as co-equal, if not in the social hierarchy, at least in matters of the world.

'You've been teaching out here, haven't you? Edwards told me. At Albert College in Maadi—what's it called now?—I can never remember.'

'Yes, but I've stopped. I'm giving private lessons.'

'But you could go back to teaching—I mean, if you wanted to. You've still got a resident's permit—and a *work* permit, much more important?'

'Yes. But I'm not too keen. I may have to, I suppose.'

'Hmmm.'

Mr. Crowther paused and blew gently over the top of his tea, cup and saucer lifted to within an inch of his chin, little finger slightly extended, like a dowager at a tea party.

'There's an ex-British school at Suez, isn't there?'

'I think so. Yes. But I wouldn't fancy going there—was that what you meant?'

'Possibly. Edwards mentioned something about your looking for more congenial work. I've not been down to Suez yet. My assistant goes there sometimes, when there's trouble on one of our boats. We used to have an honorary Consul there of course. A Greek gentleman, unfortunate business—I was just thinking. It probably wouldn't suit you.' He fingered vaguely through my passport which had been lying on the desk in front of him along with my other papers; and then he stopped abruptly at a page near the beginning. 'Born in London?' he said in astonishment. 'I hadn't realised that. I mean, that gives you dual nationality, English as well as Irish, if you wanted it. We could marry you then—you'd be a British subject, quite within our province. All we need is another passport for you—and a word with London.' He ran on in jubilation, stood up and looked through the first page of the passport against the light. 'Another passport. That's it of course! That's the answer. Here, I'll give you some forms to fill in.'

He seemed quite irrationally pleased with this outcome, as if it were he who had been trying to get married and not I.

'Ah! I see you went to Springhill,' he said glancing at my answers to the questionnaire under the heading 'Education'— something which the wretched minor public school I'd been to in North Wales had conspicuously failed to give me.

'Yes, for a while.'

'We used to play them at cricket . . .'

A long time afterwards Mr. Crowther pumped my hand enthusiastically at the door, barely able to get to the goodbyes.

'You must come to our reception. Queen's birthday. Very small do, I'm afraid. Not even official. Just a few of our friends in Cairo. After all you should be British by then. Half British anyway. You may even be married.'

We were—twenty-one days later. Henry and Bahaddin were the witnesses and Mr. Crowther officiated. The only thing I

properly remember about it all was Crowther's locking the door
of his office during the short formalities . . .

Afterwards he smiled affably, and took us all to lunch at the
Estoril. Henry, I remember, drank a little too much and spilt
half a bottle of wine.

We sent a telegram to her parents and that evening went to
Luxor for a week which used up the last of the money that I'd
saved. It was the end of the school year too, exams were in full
swing and my private lessons had dwindled to nothing.

10

JUNE 13, the Queen's birthday: the maple leaf over the British
Embassy buildings wrapped around the flag post, a mourning
drape in the still air, the heat rising like a smack in the face
from the yellow, burning streets; kites motionless in the sky far
away, specks in the distance, like aeroplanes, until they dipped
suddenly, swerving over the trees on Gezira Island: the old
Peugeot taxis braying across Kasr el Nil bridge, and the
Mercedes, gliding by, curtained against the glare: a group of
farmers, up from the country, with sheep and goats and huge
shallow metal dishes of simmering beans, camping under sheets
of corrugated paper against the corniche in front of Shepheard's
Hotel. The harsh amplified prayers from a mosque at the corner
of El Trahir: June 13, the Queen's birthday.

We slunk into the Embassy grounds through the old ballroom
at the back of the Residency which had been turned into the
British Council's library. Crowther's Mrs. French took our cards
at the desk for returned books, the muted crackle of Dim-
bleby's commentary on Trooping the Colour coming from a
portable radio behind her. Henry had come with us and we
went on into the gardens in front of the Residency which ran
down to the high wall which now formed one side of the
corniche; before, the lawns had gone right to the banks of the
river; before Suez.

It was late afternoon and the heat was dying a little and it
was just bearable if one didn't move around too much, and
stayed under the flowering trees—flame trees and bougain-

villea—which bordered the lawn on either side. Henry caught a
suffragi in a red sash rushing past us with a tray of martinis and
we gulped the warm mixture.

'Mr. and Mrs. Marlow!'

Mr. Crowther detached himself from a group of elderly ladies
who were sitting on little gilded chairs at trestle tables and sped
towards us with remarkable purpose—quite out of keeping with
our importance as guests. A Sudanese bishop and an American
in huge brogues and a Cabot Lodge tropical outfit just in front
of us turned quite huffy as he passed them by with only the
most perfunctory greetings.

'How nice to see you. And you've got drinks. How was
Luxor? You stayed at the Winter Palace I hope? Not the best
time of year really, though one does avoid all those awful
German tourists.'

And we told him about the Valley of the Kings and Queen
Hatshepsut's temple among other inconsequential bits of
chatter. But Crowther had something else on his mind; fidgeting
and slightly red in the face, he seemed only to be waiting for a
decent interval to pass with these opening formalities before
broaching something much more important.

He didn't get the chance until much later when Henry and
Bridget had become embroiled in conversation with a professor
they'd known at the University and I'd wandered off to one
side of the lawn and gone through a hedge and into a little stone
plaza with a minute swimming pool in the middle. I was
surprised to see a very portly, benign-looking gentleman asleep
in a deck chair under a sun shade at the far end of the pool.
There was a red carnation in the button-hole of his immacu-
lately cut white linen suit and a half empty bottle of champagne
on the table in front of him. I turned to leave thinking perhaps
that it was the Ambassador being kept discreetly under wraps
until diplomatic relations between the two countries were
resumed. But Mr. Crowther, who must have seen me going
through the hedge, was right behind me when I turned.

'Ah! Marlow—just the man I wanted to see. There's someone
here who I think may be able to help you,' he said with urgent
discreetness. 'I'd like you to meet. Dear me, he's gone to sleep.'

'Help me? How?'

'About work, my dear fellow. About work. You remember—

Henry told me all about it. About your looking for something to do out here.'

Crowther's persistent interest in my well-being puzzled me at the time. I put it down simply to a concern on the part of Her Majesty's Government for all British citizens abroad, even quasi-citizens, and have since had ample occasion to revise that opinion.

But then, I followed him willingly as he stalked quietly towards the recumbent body, jumping neatly over one corner of the pool, as if intent on cornering a thief and shaking him till he woke. He did nothing of the sort; instead, he leaned over the gross, dandified figure, close to his face, like a lover.

'Robin—*Robin*?' he murmured. 'I've Mr. Marlow to see you. Mr. Marlow.' He dragged my name out very slowly in the way that one explains something to a child.

The figure stirred and then sat up, slowly, painfully, as though the least movement of the immense torso was an agony. But he was quite awake. He looked at me, a look of decided interest, with huge watery blue eyes; a look of kindness as well as interest—a twinkly animated look as though, like Crowther, the eyes alone had survived intact in the wreck of his body.

'Oh. I dropped off.'

He twirled the champagne glass in delicate withered fingers, the skin barely covering the bones; his hands in fact looked like someone else's, tacked on, so at odds were they with his general corpulence and air of excessive good living. He drained what was left in the glass and poured some more.

'Mr. Marlow—this is Mr. Usher.'

'How are you, Marlow? You've not a glass and indeed I see no chance whatsoever of your getting one without attracting "unnecessary attention" as Basil would put it, although I might add that's something I've been doing very happily all my life. That's why I'm stuck here round the corner like a poor relation, pretending I've got a "bad leg"; rather unimaginative that idea of yours, Basil. Anyway, I can't see why I shouldn't have seen Marlow in the Residency, all that nonsense about the place being bugged; Egyptians aren't up to that sort of thing yet, hardly learnt how to use the telephone.' He looked at Crowther mournfully and cast a reptilian glance in the direction of the privet hedge, listening to the excited chatter beyond.

'All those young voices . . . and I can do nothing whatsoever about it.'

'Very few young people about in Cairo these days, Robin. And no one of that sort here today. Just old Lady Goodridge and a Sudanese bishop. And you wouldn't want to meet them. Not your style at all,' Crowther said quickly, hoping perhaps to suggest that Usher's interest in the young of the city, foreign or domestic, was entirely avuncular and that what he really missed were the great days of the Capitulations and the witty adult company of the old British Raj.

'You do go on so, Basil. You really do. Mr. Marlow knows very well what I'm talking about. What I miss are the young—the young everywhere. And there's something compelling about voices behind hedges, don't you agree, Marlow? Not just the idea of something clandestine but something positively obscene as well, something quite uncalled for. I suppose I shouldn't complain of my station this afternoon; there's something to be had on both sides of that hedge. Titillation for a jaded eavesdropper. The trouble is that I've found my imagination inclined to flag lately whereas my other appetites grow apace . . . A coarsening of the spirit in a body more than ever willing, a common thing among the old I believe. The dangerous age, not far from death.

> *The grand old Duke of York*
> *He had ten thousand men*
> *He marched them up to the top of the hill*
> *And he marched them down again . . .'*

Hesitating over the words he hummed the rest of the verse in a jaunty growl.

'How does it go, Crowther? I feel in that sort of mood myself: an overwhelming sense of irresponsibility.' He poured the remainder of the champagne into his glass and raised it to within an inch of his long bulbous nose. 'I don't really like it, you know; the chill's quite gone. The trouble is once I get the taste of it in my mouth I never feel like stopping.'

He thrashed the liquid about in his mouth for a moment so that I thought he was about to spit it out. Crowther had brought up two more deck chairs and we perched on the edge

of them. Some rust-coloured petals eddied slowly round in one
corner of the pool, moved by the breeze that had come up the
river and over the wall. It was nearly evening and we sat there in
front of Usher like an audience waiting for the start of an open
air performance. Mr. Crowther took his cue.

'I think perhaps, Robin, we might start. We can't be sure of
our ground out here for too long.'

Usher gave a last lazy sigh and then embarked in a brighter,
more formal tone.

'Ah, yes. Crowther tells me you like it out here but haven't
got any decent work. Well, we need a man—at Suez. We've no
one there now and I gather there's an ex-British school in the
town where you could teach. We don't need very much, just
details to keep us in touch with the mood of the place, till we
can get one of our own staff men back there. Details like—well,
Russian tankers at the refinery: how many, how often. Who's
running the Greek Club now, morale of the Egyptian canal
pilots, troop movements and emplacements on the Cairo
road—and a hundred and one other small points you'll learn
about by just living there which we'll quiz you about from
time to time. Oh—and there's an American living in Suez,
working on some UN programme or other, we'd like to know
about him—sounds most dangerous. That sort of thing. We
could offer you the work on a contract basis—what is it,
Crowther? The equivalent of a P_3 minus on the permanent
rate—about £80 a month after UK tax, apart from what you
earned yourself of course, the money payable in sterling, in
London, or in any other currency you chose except that of the
country you're operating from. Security measure that. There
wouldn't in your case, I'm afraid, be an overseas allowance,
locally recruited staff don't qualify, but on the other hand we'd
be most lenient about any out of pocket expenses; we have a lot
of blocked piastres out here. Crowther can give you the rest of
the details—a year's contract in the first place, with thirty days'
notice on either side and with possible Establishment later.
That's about it. Like to get the boring part over—what do you
think?'

'Rather dangerous—'

'Not at all. It's not an active position. We call this an I O
Posting—"Information Only"—information you'd come across

in the ordinary course of your work, nothing extra. No snooping around dark alleyways with revolvers, nothing like that; no radio work, messages in code—none of that nonsense. No exposure of any sort. You'd report verbally to us, that's all.'

I laughed. 'One could get caught easily enough doing just that. The Egyptians probably know I've come here today and they'd certainly think something was up if I kept on seeing people here.'

'You wouldn't—or necessarily see either of us again. You'd deal entirely with your friend Mr. Edwards. It was he who suggested you to us—you hardly think we'd have advanced this far in the matter without establishing the most comprehensive bona fides as to your character and so on. What else did he say, Basil?—that you had an "insatiably curious approach to life"—just what we need, a sharp pair of eyes.'

'Even so—I mightn't like the idea and you've told me rather a lot for someone who might refuse your offer and disappear— over to the other side, who knows?' The martinis had begun to sink in.

'That's always a risk—and a much more prevalent one, I may say, among our permanent staff who know far more about us than you do. No, once we're certain about someone we prefer a completely open handed approach.'

'How can you be "certain"—about me?'

'Well, to be blunt, we thought it suited you—in your present circumstances. With a wife to support and all that. You don't want to lose out on that—on her, I mean.'

'What do you mean?'

'Well, you don't want to be the odd man out. I don't see you going over to the "other side", as you rather melodramatically put it, without your wife. And I can't see her going off on such a caper. She's with us too. An I O posting actually. Not active, but completely reliable, been with us some years now. So you see our offer to you is really in the nature of a safety measure—though I'm confident you can be of value to us in your own right. You'd have probably found out about Miss Girgis—Mrs. Marlow, I beg your pardon—in due course; marriage leads to so many sorts of intimacy, God help us, and this is a way of ensuring a sort of mutual security in the matter. It's better having everyone in it together. Loose ends in this sort of operation are the only really dangerous thing. Once you married Miss Girgis we had to do something about it; you see our point, either dispense with her, which might have been awkward to say the least, or take on you—which I'm sure you'll agree was much the more civilized response. I'm confident you won't let us down—your marriage may depend on it.'

I looked at Usher in astonishment, yet savouring the beginnings of that elegant considerate double talk which was afterwards to become so familiar to me. Part of what he had said was true, certainly. But which part—and for what reasons? And why the need for lies and truths in the first place—and why those *particular* lies and truths? I hardly know now what I had no inkling of then.

'Do think about it—think about what I've said. We're not scoundrels, old fellow. We didn't hire the Embassy for the afternoon, you're not being invited to join some illegal organization, a lot of gangsters; this is all perfectly above board—relatively speaking.'

He ended the sentence in high good humour, accentuating the idea of a gang being involved in this charade as a ham actor might play up the role of a wicked uncle in a Victorian melodrama.

'And now, Basil, would you help me indoors before that inquisitive Bishop finds me here. Though perhaps,' he said, turning to me, 'only the *truly* inquisitive could have found their way into this privy. You've really invited this on yourself, Marlow. Uncanny really, we thought we might have to use some pretext . . . it shows very suitable initiative on your part, if I may say so. Just what we want.' And he bowed slightly in my direction, inclining his great white head just a fraction in a gesture of patriarchal assent; and then an equally limited flicker of his eyelids, the skin passing very rapidly up and down over the watery blue orbs, like a coquette in a silent film. And he was gone, propelled by Crowther on what I now saw to be not only a deck chair but a deck chair on wheels.

It was impossible to say whether he really had a bad leg, was pretending to have—or had no legs at all. Henry didn't seem to know either.

'I couldn't tell you about it. They had to make their own minds

up. I put you in touch with them—they knew about you
anyway, through Bridget. I told Crowther I thought you could
work for us—and what he told you about ditching Bridget was
perfectly true. It may seem nasty—I mean underhand in a
personal way, from your point of view, but the alternative
could have been worse—'

'Christ Almighty—how could it be worse? Marrying someone
who doesn't tell you what they're doing, what they're really up
to. What could be worse?'

I'd left the Embassy, furious. 'You'd better talk to Henry, I
can't explain,' Bridget had said. 'Obviously not,' I'd added, and
Henry and I had gone once more to a corner of the bar at the
Cosmopolitan.

'What sort of lark is this anyway? If it was anything serious
you can be sure they wouldn't have let me in on it—those two
pooves. That reptile Usher—does he really have a bad leg, or no
legs—or what? It's a lot of utter nonsense. Cloak and dagger
nonsense.'

'I don't know how many legs he works on. I deal with
Crowther anyway.'

Henry smiled wearily and shuffled his hair about with
unusual timidity. I wondered how much of his explanation had
been prepared, for he must have been briefed about, expected,
this confrontation for some time. Were there to be lies from
him as well?—lies one would never know of. Henry had always
seemed to me congenitally blunt and straightforward; it was
difficult to see in his character any sort of restraint—least of all
a discretion imposed on him by others.

'Yes, it *is* a bloody lark,' he went on. 'And cloak and dagger.
The lark part—is Usher and Crowther. But remember, they're
only "countrymen"—liaison with London. And at that end it's
all perfectly serious. The more so now since the serious gents,
the hatchet men, who used to be here, they've all been chucked
out. Crowther and Usher are the only two left here with
what's called "open cover"; they can live here under quite
proper bona fides—Crowther in the Consulate and Usher in his
Mameluke house by the Citadel. He's an Arabist, a Moslem—and
God knows what else in that line. The place is crawling with all
sorts of youngsters and desert knick-knacks. The fact is the two
of them can behave pretty much as they like, for the

moment—drum up every schoolboy fantasy, since they're the only two senior people left in the circle out here. They're indispensable from London's point of view—and they know it. Hence their rather unorthodox approach in your case. It's also true of course that they really want someone in Suez. They tried to send me. Anyway, that's about them. In fact they must have complete confidence in you, or else, as you say, they'd have hardly embarked on the details today. Usher would have just weighed you up and I wouldn't have been saying all this.'

The son of an Egyptian landowner, down to his last million, and a regular at the Cosmopolitan at this time of night, struggled up to the far end of the bar, swinging his arms about and shouting, in a wave of lonely bonhomie. Henry returned his greeting diffidently, only raising his hand towards him, palm outwards, in a way they had always acknowledged each other's presence. On other nights Henry would have joined him, or he us, but tonight something kept us apart: again, that unexpected restraint on Henry's part—like a drunkard far gone, embarking unwillingly and for the first time on a cure. Henry had a job to do with me. I wondered what it was.

'I suppose they think they've got me in some way—that's why they're confident—through Bridget: that I'm bound to work for them since I've married her. What have they got on her?'

'Isn't it obvious? Her parents. They'd blow her and that would be the end of them in Maadi—and Bridget. It's an old hold—and there's no use arguing the morality of it because there isn't any in this sort of snooping and there never was. It's just a job. You can kill people with just a wrong word down the telephone anyway.'

'No morality, all right. But belief surely? Usher and Crowther, they believe in it. And you?'

'Oh yes, they believe in it,' Henry said, easy suddenly as though giving the response to a well-known riddle. 'And that's more than enough morality for them. Crowther and Usher, they believe all right. In different things. Usher has the old Anglo-Arab approach, Lawrence and so on; the Englishman and his desert: the delicious punishment under the stars, the mystique of the empty places, the ritual in everything; the extreme concepts of honour and pleasure—honour among men

and pleasure with the boys; the tough, sink-or-swim male
society with its inexplicable, cruel, deeply pleasurable rules—
like school. In fact for people like Usher the Arab world is just a
great big public school, with the deserts for playing fields and
Mohammed as the mysterious Headmaster, where they never
have to grow up. And Usher hates Nasser for doing away with it
all, for closing the old place down. Crowther's just a Tory civil
servant who believes in the Englishman and his castle, that the
Suez Canal runs through his drawing room on the way to India
and so on. He believes in the toy soldiers aspect of it all—and
giving the wogs a lesson. And he likes the mystery and the
rumour and the deceit of the job as well—the hiding from
Nanny before bedtime. That's how he never grows up. They
believe, and I understand it. It's the romantic attitude.'

'And you?'

'I don't believe. I took the job on years ago, at a low ebb.
Money, interest, adventure even—perhaps I wasn't able quite to
throw over the *Boy's Own Paper* stuff—but I don't believe in it.
Perhaps that's the pity.'

'But they don't have anything on you—you could get out.'

'Perhaps I'm fitted for the job. People are, you know. It suits
them to do certain things, it's good for them even, like a regular
bowel movement or an apple a day.'

'And you'd "blow" someone—you wouldn't worry—if you
were told to?'

'That would be London's decision—area committee or head
of section—'

'But would you *do* it—do away with someone, which is what
it amounts to? Bridget for example—if you were asked to
"blow" her, as you call it, or if you even knew about it, what
would you do?'

'See that it didn't happen, that it never got to that stage.'

'If you didn't know it was happening?'

'That would be awkward, certainly. Except that I think I
would know about it—unless they wanted to blow me as
well—since I run her. I'm her "operator", I'd *have* to know,
unless, as I say, they wanted me for the high jump as well, since
I'd have to get well clear of her before that happened. Bridget
and I have open contact as well as cover—our circumstances
happened to have allowed for that. If the Egyptians got on to

her I'd be the next most obvious link in the chain—or you—even if she didn't break down which she probably would. That's the way we have to work it out here now—open cover, open contact, almost nothing clandestine—which is another good reason why they want you involved. You're one of us. Married to Bridget. There'd be something suspicious if we *weren't* all together a lot of the time. But for Christ's sake don't take it all so seriously—this business about blowing people out here—it's not going to happen, there are far too few of us. They want to *get* people, not blow them.' He grabbed a handful of *sudanis*, threw them into his mouth, and finished his gin. 'Come on, let's go back to Bridget and have some food. Don't be so glum about it, you're with us now. At least we won't have to pretend any more.'

'That's charming, I agree. One doesn't want to deceive one's wife more than is absolutely necessary. What would you call our arrangement now? An "open troika", I suppose?'

Henry smiled briefly, warmly; the smile between friends when one of them has said something quite without consequence. He got up and left the barman a ten-piastre note in a busy fashion and we went down the steps of the hotel and into the night, like a steam bath now and loud with the racket of the tric-trac boards in the small cafés which bordered Soliman Pasha, and the wail of music from the radios on the shelves beneath the portraits of the President: photographs, garish oil paintings, posters—in whatever form, a reminder everywhere of a disputed Saint; a saviour or a rogue—or simply an object of indifference? I had never thought about it: that ubiquitous, tigerish face, like an ambitious barber's with its darkly brilliantined scalp: caught in the unflattering glare of the coloured neon so that it readily assumed all the lineaments of 'the enemy'.

Suddenly I felt as though I'd just arrived in a different, well remembered country and despite the overwhelming presence of the street—the smells of some sharp spice, ginger or nutmeg or copra, riding on an air of paraffin and old leather above the cooling dust—I felt there should be train whistles and snow and soot in the night air, the sense of something unwanted and forgotten, and not any of those other marks of the city that I'd become so familiar with.

'The train now standing at platform seven is the 8:45 *Irish mail for Holyhead, stopping at Rugby, Chester, Crewe . . . change at Rugby for North Wales . . .'*

I remembered. The damp, cold succession of Septembers and Januarys, seven-and-six for the taxi and the first month's pocket money, the doors slamming all along the train, greyhounds whimpering in the guard's van, the condensation already thick on the view of Chester Cathedral: the end of every summer and Christmas—the beginning of a journey to a bell at seven next morning, to a life where life would be out of my hands. That was what I remembered—what Henry and Bridget and Crowther and Usher had reminded me of all day.

'Damn it—this bloody place.' Henry was struggling with his shoe which had stuck in a patch of moist tar on the pavement. We'd stopped at the Soliman Pasha roundabout waiting for the run of traffic to pass.

'Perhaps not a "troika", Henry—aren't we all "double agents"? Isn't that the term you use? After all, you and I and Bridget—we don't really believe in any of it, do we?'

Henry walked out from the pavement suddenly so that I had to grab him off the wing of a taxi.

11

BRIDGET was laughing the moment she opened the apartment door, rushing forward to kiss me, as if there had been guests and jokes behind her and we'd arrived a little late for a party. On the sideboard were several bottles of wine and a bottle of that Gordon's Export gin which I'd thought we'd finished long ago. This was to be a celebration of sorts: a private affair, not in any of our old public haunts, but behind curtains with the lights turned down and the radio tuned to the BBC, like proper conspirators. She'd arranged the table in the living room—an intimate dinner for three: a red tablecloth, which we never used, and a silver candlestick, a cherub supporting the bowl, a present from someone which she usually kept out of the way on the top of the bookshelf.

And it was a new Bridget; a *public* Bridget, no longer

petulant, diffident, but liberated, now that all three of us had
been joined in a secret: a woman perfectly released by the
outcome of a professional arrangement, not through any private
association, not by love, not by me. For the first time since I'd
met her a year previously in the Continental she had assumed
again, freely, willingly, that true intensity of character which
had first attracted me to her and which I knew now she had
withheld from me ever since.

There was a vast pleasure in her face, her bearing, in the way
she looked at both of us, touched us casually as we moved
around her—a fierce coquetry, as if, in amazement at the
chance, she were starting an affair again with two old lovers
simultaneously. She seemed to want this to be a joyous,
irresponsible, loving homecoming, in which every failure and
disappointment of the past, hers and ours, would be forgotten.
As an echo of this happy determination, perhaps, she was
wearing the same cotton house-coat that I knew from a year
before and I remembered the casual, clumsy beginnings of our
relationship which I had shared with Cherry in the same room
the previous summer. Yet Cherry, at that moment, with his
bumbling passions, his innocence—seemed part of a far more
happy and irresponsible world than this.

'Dear Peter.' And I was kissed again, while Henry poured out
the gin and went into the kitchen for some ice. This time, I
thought, there's ice. In just a year we'd passed from awkwardness to respectability.

'You seem happy.'

'I *couldn't* tell you. Didn't Henry explain?'

'Yes. That he was your "operator". It all seems so childish.'

'Perhaps.' And she sat down on the old chintz chaise-longue,
head in hands, collapsing like a puppet, a sad doll. 'Surely it's
better though? That we all *know* now. Now that you're *with*
us.'

'Oh yes. That's what Henry said. It's all much better, now
that I'm on "your side". But you see I thought I was already. I
didn't know I had to go through a second initiation with you.
And another with Crowther. And Usher. *And* Henry. It's like that
game—tugging children across the drawing room over a handkerchief at Christmas—what's it called?—"Nuts in May". As
childish as that. And not as fun. I thought I was part of the fun
already.' I went over, drew the curtains back and looked out

towards the Kasr el Nil bridge and the lights of one of Farouk's
old boats on the far shore which had been turned into a night
club. 'Not that I was given much choice in the matter—whether
I played the game or not. You don't mind my opening the
window? I mean, you're not expecting an air-raid or anything?'

It was hotter with the window open. The day's heat, rising
from the streets, finding no escape through the dense furnace of
air which lay above the city, fell back in one's face, with a sour,
rotten smell of dust and urine. Bridget had leant back against
the end of the chaise-longue, hands clasped behind her head, her
back towards the window. One side of the cotton house-coat
had fallen away from her body on to the floor.

'Take your coat off or something, for God's sake. You'll
expire.'

'You said that last year.' I turned and sat down at the dining
room table and fiddled with the wooden corkscrew which had
been neatly laid out between the two wine bottles. 'Were you
preparing for all this? The dinner and so on? Was it all arranged,
as a sort of grand finale to our going to the Embassy and my
being conscripted? Or would there have been two places laid
and not three if things hadn't gone off properly? And which of
us, Henry or I, would have been left out? I mean, if they hadn't
liked the look of me, what then? How were you so sure there'd
be three of us for dinner this evening, that I'd be here?'

'Henry was sure.'

'Were you?' I turned. Henry had come in from the kitchen.

'Pretty certain. I told you. They need people here. Badly.
Your credentials were impeccable and now let's stop going on
about it.'

'What happens if I decide to go back to England?'

'That's up to you.' Henry squeezed a quartered lemon into
his gin, then made one up for me.

'Oh God.'

He walked over and put the glass of gin and tonic very
carefully on the table beside me like a doctor leaving medicine
for a patient after the bad news. I drank half of it down,
looking at Bridget over the rim of the glass, quite still on the
sofa—fear, nervousness, in her face, love perhaps—as if she saw
completely my predicament and had no idea for the moment
how to deal with it.

Then she came across and knelt in front of me, arms on my knees, hands in mine.

'Peter, it was because of this, my work with Henry, Crowther and the rest of them, that I didn't want to get involved with you in the first place. So that you thought me a sort of whore when we were first together. But with you, eventually, I told Henry I couldn't go on, with *not* telling you. It was my idea that you go to see Crowther, that you become involved in all this—because that was the only way you could know about me. I couldn't live with it, the idea of losing you.'

' "Losing me"—how? You'd have stopped your goings on with Crowther, with Henry, if I hadn't been "acceptable", wouldn't you?'

Henry started to open one of the wine bottles officiously behind us, the cork squeaking fiercely against the glass.

'Of losing you, yes,' she went on hesitantly, ignoring my question, seeing no help from Henry. 'Because you can't stop in this business, whatever they say. There's no getting out—if they don't want you to get out. And they didn't, with me. So it was losing you—or giving it all up, and losing my parents. Or getting you in—and its being all right.'

'What sort of madmen are they? You mean they said "Square Marlow or else—" Get me in on the deal or else get me out of your way? And if you did neither they'd blow you—let the Egyptians know you'd been involved with them?'

'Yes.'

'It's true,' Henry said, and he popped the cork and sniffed the top of the bottle. It was a French burgundy, rarely obtainable in those days, a Pommard. I wondered where she'd got it from. Henry, I supposed—or Bahaddin or the Greek auctioneer. I felt as if I'd crashed a bottle party, without a bottle.

'I told you, the two of them have a completely free hand here. They can do what they please. They're fanatics. They *are* madmen. That's the danger. They mean what they say; they'd certainly shop Bridget—if they'd thought there was any danger in her being with you. But they haven't, they took a liking to you. We've been lucky. Now for God's sake realise the situation. It could have been quite hopeless—Usher could have said "get rid of him"—he didn't.'

Henry moved away to the window, waving the bottle gently in his hand.

'Bridget, there's no food. I forgot to pick it up. Let's drink the wine and go out.'

'Let's finish the gin first.' Bridget got up, kissing me briefly again—as if these small repeated contacts might somehow convince me of her good intentions in the whole stupid matter—and went back to the sofa. We finished off our gins, vehemently, quickly, like strangers suddenly trying to be friends.

'We can go to the boat,' Henry said hopefully. 'There's food there. We can dance.'

'Bahaddin'll be there. He usually is. Bahaddin.' Bridget repeated his name abruptly, almost with disgust. 'He's part of the whole thing as well. He's with us. Henry was going to tell you.'

Henry nodded his head sadly, as if embarrassed by this further complicity, this additional character in the charade.

'Oh—what is he? "Active" or "passive"? Or "Information Only"—or is he the gunmetal man, stalking the alleyways and embassies with a .38?'

The whole thing had begun, faintly, to amuse me; Bridget and Henry's seriousness—in minutes they had become dull and unhappy and I felt it was my fault, that I had broken a pleasant day and evening, wrecked the homecoming. I smiled and they looked at me hopefully—a well-disposed audience desperately hoping for relief, looking for a laugh in a bad comedy.

'All right, it's making us all so boring. Let's forget about it for the moment. I'm sure you're right, there's nothing to it, Usher just wants me to give him a bit of gossip about the morale of the canal pilots, and I'm being obstructive, pedantic. Just I never missed the toy soldiers thing as a child. And I don't miss it now. It all seems rather mindless to me.'

The farmers had settled down for the night underneath their corrugated paper huts against the river wall and their evening fires crackled with light all along the far pavement as we walked towards Kasr el Nil bridge. The smell of sesame, and beans cooking, and desert tinder drifted over to us, mixing with the terrible sweetness of jasmine which groups of Pyjama boys hawked around the hotel entrances, the great garlands looped around their arms and necks turning them into Michelin children.

Since afternoon the taxis had redoubled their attack, charging to and fro along the corniche, picking up and depositing groups of chattering frenzied people bent on the same pursuit as ourselves. And above all the heat, rising from the darkness, embracing everything, like a huge steaming towel: a breathless, moist evening in which everything seemed just about to suffocate and then to survive, with an immense gasp, at the last moment: everything poised for the relief of a storm which one knew would never come. Ten o'clock, June 13, the Queen's birthday.

The boat, the *Nefertiti*—one of Farouk's Nile steamers, a long graceful Edwardian affair—was moored on the far side of Kasr el Nil bridge near the main entrance to the Gezira Club. Its aft promenade deck had coloured lights along the rails and streaming down from the mast, and a small Italian orchestra was tuning up, plucking dissident strings, underneath the funnel.

In what had been the Royal Lounge under the bridge there was another orchestra, a restaurant and a bar, and here we had a drink before going out for supper on the fore deck. It was early and hardly crowded. I recognized Farid, the manager of the boat, with a party of friends at a large table outside near the rail. Some of his guests hadn't turned up, there were empty spaces here and there, but he was in high good humour—jumping up and down, toasting and being toasted, a little scut of a man, bald, with a half rim of hair going from ear to ear round the back of his head. It was his birthday too, apparently. Giant pitch-black Nubian waiters in blues and golds, like coloured pictures from a child's Bible, padded aloofly round their table, pouring out whiskies and dumping ice from great silver bowls, strangers to this tribal feast.

'Bahaddin! We thought you'd come. How are you?'

Bridget was the first to see him as he ambled up to the bar in a crisp white jacket, slacks, frilly Italian dress shirt and a bow tie. In the light of her earlier bored attitude to the possibility of his being on the boat that evening she seemed unaccountably pleased by his arrival.

'Good evening.' He kissed her hand, bending down much lower than necessary, more than usually punctilious in these gracious formalities which he so enjoyed.

'What are you doing? Have dinner with us.'

Perhaps it was just the day's drinking that gave such extraordinary warmth to Bridget's invitation.

"I'm very sorry—I'm with Farid and his party. I wish it were otherwise.' Still holding her hand they looked at each other for a moment with an awkward knowingness, like two people in a wedding photograph, before he turned away.

'How are you, Henry?—and don't ask me about my "O" levels. I've given them up for the summer. I'll try again next year, if you're still around to help me.'

And he laughed easily, as if these exams were an old joke between them, worn thin with use, a cover for quite a different pursuit, as I now knew them to be.

'What, you didn't get them then?' I asked.

'I'm afraid I didn't sit for them, sir.' And he took out some money and began to play with it on the counter, looking at me curiously, and then at Henry behind me.

'Don't go on calling me "sir", Bahaddin. I'm not a school-master any more.'

'I'm sorry, sir. I had been wondering how things were with you—about work. I'm sure I could help you out—' And he added, as if the fact were proof against all mortal difficulties: 'My father is coming over from Aden next week . . .'

He looked at me with genuine concern, running what I now saw to be a Maria Theresa dollar between the fingers of one hand like a conjurer.

'It's all right, Bahaddin. We're getting Peter a job. He's with us now,' Henry broke in quietly. 'We're all together. Are you going to buy us a drink?'

'I won't congratulate you—I won't take your hand, too obvious—but I'm very glad. Most happy.'

And he was. Like everything he did or said, he meant it. He nodded his large head slowly at me several times, like an old cricket coach from the boundary, determined to offer some acknowledgment of my honour, albeit clandestinely. He was a person, I realized afterwards, with a far too highly developed sense of the proprieties for the job in hand.

'Yes—a drink. By all means,' he continued. 'A quiet celebration, a decent drink, before I have to fulfil my other objectives.'

'Obligations, Bahaddin, not objectives,' Henry said. And

Bahaddin ordered champagne from Mustafa, the squat Sudanese barman.

We lifted the tall tulip-like glasses—which Mustafa said he'd rescued from Farouk's pantry, keeping them for just such an occasion as this—and drank a minute toast to each other. From a distance, if anyone had been interested, our little group must have appeared suspiciously subdued. I was beginning to feel drunk and didn't like the taste; the champagne fizzed in my mouth, reanimating all the other tastes of the day, with a stale nausea. Bahaddin drained his glass.

'Well, I mustn't stay—but very good wishes.'

He bowed again, picked up his cigarette case and gold Dunhill and made off, pushing his way delicately among the crowd of people who were rapidly filling up the room.

'Everyone's pleased. It's as if I'd just got engaged—though I can't remember anything like this when I was . . .'

'Let's not talk about it here.'

'Come on, Peter. Dance with me—before you fall off the stool. Get some air.'

'I'll join you.' Henry went off towards the lavatory. Bahaddin meanwhile had joined Farid's party amid scenes and shouts of great welcome. Their long table faced over the small brightly lit square in the centre of the foredeck where couples were trying vainly to keep up with the measure of a new Italian number. The orchestra, a recent import from Milan, and perhaps unaccustomed as yet to the fiery Egyptian nights, were themselves showing signs of fatigue in sustaining the fast rhythm, and had it not been for the sudden and unexpected arrival of Bahaddin on the floor they would, I'm sure, have quickly changed to something slower in tempo. As it was they were forced to keep up the murderous pace for a good five minutes more, going full blast, as Bahaddin and a woman careered over the boards in a frenzied, kick-stepping dance, half Charleston, half twist, clapping their hands, separating, coming together again and even squirming around each other's backs, arms linked overhead, their hips and feet retaining the furious beat of the music.

I'd not seen the woman before. She must have arrived by the front gangway, one of several latecomers to Farid's party. Perhaps she was Bahaddin's new girl or something and yet, besides the interest which Farid, like everyone else, was taking in this wild dance—which had really become an act, clearing most of the other dancers off the small floor—there was as well in his wrinkled urbane face a distinct measure of distaste as he watched their antics; Farid looked at the woman as if she, as well as her dancing, were out of place. There was no good-humoured understanding in his consideration of the spectacle—an attitude he might well have taken, as he had before, in the high spirits of his birthday guests; she might have been an unpleasant stranger to him and I thought simply, remembering Farid's real proclivities in sexual matters and Bahaddin's good looks, 'He's jealous of her. She's snapped up Bahaddin before he'd got his hand in. He's the angry suitor. He shouldn't have asked her.'

The woman—girl really, she hardly looked twenty—could have been Italian or Greek, not Egyptian, with her long, sharply triangular features and dark hair parted down the middle; a classic strangely formal face, childlike and unmarked, bland and empty in a way, like a photograph taken before first communion or a Renaissance virgin in the Uffizi. And yet it was she who led the dance, encouraging Bahaddin to ever greater flights, always one step ahead of him.

Henry had joined us and we sat round the table we'd booked on the opposite side of the deck to Farid's party, next to the river wall.

'Who is she?'

'No idea. Not one of Farid's friends. He'd never risk inviting someone so attractive. One of the girls with the orchestra perhaps. She's quite something.'

People had come out of the bar and had crowded round the floor, several deep, thinking the cabaret had started early, so that we had to stand up to see the last tumultuous flourish of the dance. Their hands linked across the floor together, the girl was spinning Bahaddin round in circles like a weight at the end of a piece of string—his face quite without expression, his body so relaxed, inert, that its animation seemed due to centrifugal force alone and not to any muscular process. The music finally exhausted itself in a long crescendo of chords and drums. But the two figures spun on in silence afterwards, only gradually losing momentum, unwilling to release themselves from what appeared now as an intensely private affair, not connected with the music or the place. At last they stopped, faced each other for a moment in surprise, like strangers, standing quite still—and then, taking no account of the applause which broke over the deck, they disappeared among the press of people on the far side of the floor.

'What on earth got into Bahaddin? Was he drunk? He didn't look it,' Bridget asked and the people drifted away and the band mopped their faces, looking pleased and supercilious as if they, and not the girl, had been the reason for this outburst of enthusiasm.

'Who is she?' someone asked at the next table.

We could see Farid's party now but she wasn't there. Bahaddin had his back towards us and was sitting next to an elderly European lady who seemed to be congratulating or berating him without receiving the smallest flicker of a response.

The orchestra broke into a ragged version of 'Happy Birthday' and everyone at Farid's table stood up, glasses in hand, and toasted the beaming figure at the end, now fully restored in his traditional self-satisfied humour. They mouthed the ridiculous words with embarrassment, for they hardly knew them, so that the old lady had to lead the song, like a matron at Sunday school. I supposed that Farid had once had some service of her—as an entrée to a sexual opportunity among the English community in the old days perhaps—and that thus, unwittingly, she had been numbered among his guests this evening. And I was wondering about this when I saw her trying to manhandle Bahaddin to his feet.

For everyone had stood up except Bahaddin.

Instead, with the old lady's prodding, he fell across the table like a happy drunk. And because we all thought this to be the case, that drink and exhaustion had taken him, and seeing the waiters help him indoors, we thought nothing of it until fifteen minutes later.

Henry and I were with Farid when Mustafa came up to tell us that Bahaddin looked more than drunk. And he did. When we got to the cabin amidships he was quite obviously dead.

'My God. At my birthday party. Are you sure?' And Farid

looked at us all hopefully, humming something lighthearted under his breath, as if there were still some small chance that the evening's entertainment might yet be saved.

'How can you be sure?' he continued desperately. Henry told him to shut up.

They had opened Bahaddin's frilly collar and he lay on the bare coiled springs of an immense brass bedstead with Farouk's initial worked in gilded metal above his head. The cabin had been part of the king's private quarters and was now used as an office and a store room so that Bahaddin lay surrounded by crates of whisky and wine and piles of tablecloths which had been thrown off the bed on his arrival. One of Farid's assistants sat at his desk, talking to the police, apparently unaware that Bahaddin was dead, for he kept on mentioning the word 'drunk'.

'Yes, completely drunk, passed out. Can you send someone round to take him off? Yes—the Prince. Bahaddin. Yes, I'll be careful. No. Just too much to drink.' He turned to look at the little group round the bed as if to confirm this last point but Henry had moved to block his view. He looked at me briefly and then nodded towards the door. Farid was still fussing round the body, pinching Bahaddin's cheeks, slapping his face, vigorously massaging his chest—as if his life, and not Bahaddin's, depended on it. He was almost in tears.

'My God—what will I do? He cannot be dead!' He might have been his father.

'Just stay here, Farid. I'll get a doctor.' And we left the room.

'Get Bridget off the boat. Go to the Gezira Club. I'll join you there. Don't wait. Hurry—*move.*'

I picked up Bridget and we got off the boat moments before a police car swung off the bridge behind us and turned into the Gezira corniche.

'What's happened to Bahaddin? What's going on?'

'He's dead. I don't know how. Henry's going to meet us at the Club.'

'No. That's nonsense. Let's go back.' She spoke seriously, precisely, as if I were drunk and playing some stupid prank. She turned and we both looked back at the boat. Already the police had barred both gangways, a second car had arrived with plainclothesmen and the music had stopped: there was a confused angry murmur of voices, the sounds of orders and imprecations. We walked on briskly towards the Club.

It struck me how quick and efficient the police had been in getting to the boat—just for a drunk. And then I remembered that it was a dead drunk and the implications were suddenly clear: I'd come to see Bahaddin in several ways: as a friend, as an engaging part of the city's décor—the eternal playboy always doing his 'O' levels, suitably weary, almost middle-aged; as head prefect at Maadi, taking assembly, going in first to bat, sharing his endless packets of Player's with me late at night in my room; Bahaddin with his suite on the top floor of the Cosmopolitan and his many wives back home. And that was the clue, the thing about him I'd quite forgotten: Bahaddin, the scion of one of the great families of Islam, heir to one of the richest thousand square miles in the world, to an ancient kingdom whose strategic, financial and moral position in the Middle East was of vast importance to Nasser in his bid for leadership of that world.

To have such a figure publicly drunk as a guest in one's country was bad enough; that he should die apparently as a result of that excess suggested an embarrassment to Egypt so monumental that I could only guess at its political implications. But that was what it amounted to. And the next step was easy enough. What if someone had contrived such an embarrass-ment?—and there were many who might have—the French, the Israelis, the British; they had done their best to get Nasser off the map a year previously; how better to continue their efforts than by eroding Nasser's prestige among his Arab neighbours— by knocking off one of their Crown Princes? And finally there was Bahaddin the British agent, his last role, which everything else had been a cover against, and perhaps the one that had killed him. It hardly seemed credible, least of all when Henry explained that he'd had a heart attack.

We'd met later on that evening in one of the Club lounges looking over the cricket and croquet pitches, the last few elderly members folding up their bridge games under the table lights so that we were almost in darkness.

'Yes, I got a doctor. And there was another who came from his Embassy. A coronary.'

Bridget had been numb with some sort of emotion and had hardly said a word in the half hour that we'd waited for Henry. Now, her fear or nerves quite gone, she levelled a barrage of impatient whispered questions at Henry.

'How? A heart attack? He was perfectly well. They must have got on to him, that he was with us. I thought they'd got you too.'

'No. There was no question of that. It was the dancing, I suppose. It must have been. Some people just go like that. Suddenly.'

I remembered the girl with the dark hair.

'The girl then. What about the girl?'

'What about her?' Henry said. 'Unless she knew that Bahaddin had some sort of heart condition. What's she got to do with it?'

'They'll do a post-mortem?' Bridget asked.

'I doubt it. His father was coming over here anyway next week. They'll take the body home. Untouched. Like the Jews, these families don't go in for the idea of cutting up their relatives. I can't see why it wasn't just an attack—why do you think it wasn't?'

'I can't see why you're so sure it was. It's too convenient. People of Bahaddin's age, whatever it was, don't drop dead after a few drinks and a dance. He'd been doing that sort of thing most of his life.'

'Perhaps that's what happened. It finally hit him.'

'The point is, Henry—and you're being very thick about it—surely he was murdered in some way: if they weren't after Bahaddin because of us, then what could they have been after him for—and *who* could? Anyone who wanted to do Nasser a very bad turn. And who would that most likely be?'

'A lot of people—'

'But *particularly* who?'

'The French, the Israelis—' Henry paused, resenting the logic of Bridget's questions.

'And the British,' she added. 'What about them? What about London?'

'Don't be mad. I'd have known about it.'

'They could have sent someone in.'

'*Why* would they? He was crucial to the circle out here.

London knew that perfectly well—worth far more alive, for his work, than as a pawn in any power game. The main thing is they're not after us.'

'How do you know? Security here may have had a lead on Bahaddin—which would have led to us—if he hadn't had his "heart attack". That would have been reason enough to get rid of him.'

'You mean Crowther and Usher? They had something to do with it—and didn't tell me? Hardly.'

'You said they were madmen, quite fanatic about the whole thing out here—that they'd do anything,' I added. 'If they'd heard something about Bahaddin . . .'

'I don't know what you're going on about. There's a chance he may have been killed. All right. It's a possibility. Some personal trouble or jealousy back home—one of his numerous uncles or brothers wanting a crack at the throne, it's happening all the time where he comes from. But the idea that he was part of some international plot is absolute conjecture. I don't go for theories. Until I know any more I'll settle for what the doctors said it was—heart failure.'

And so his death was described on the back page of the *Egyptian Gazette* the following day. What wasn't reported, on that day or any other, was that the Sheik's Mission to Egypt was withdrawn by the end of the week, along with thirty-eight million sterling held on deposit with the Bank Misr as part of a development loan to Egypt, and that the Ambassadors and other senior officials of three other Arab states had left the country by the end of the month. A good part of the Arab world outside Egypt was aflame with indignant editorials though no breath of this appeared in the Egyptian press and no other papers which dealt with the topic got further than the censor at the airport. None the less these facts and rumours— this scandal, along with its glittering centre-piece—quickly spread among the bars and cafés of the city: that Bahaddin had been poisoned. By whom? Unlike Henry, the Cairenes were much given to theories and Bahaddin's death provided them with an orgy of speculation.

Incidental to all this, everyone who had dealt with Bahaddin at the school, or who had been in any way connected with him in the city, was closely questioned by the police. It must have been a long job, which in my case, at least, was conducted with meticulous thoroughness.

'Yes, I was on the boat that night. We spoke to Bahaddin just before he joined Farid's party. I was a teacher at Maadi, out here on a contract, yes, you know about that. With the ex-British schools . . .'

I rambled on through the details of my connection with Bahaddin and my presence in Egypt. And Colonel Hassan Hamdy, from the Army's special security branch, I assumed, made a pretence of noting these facts although I could see that he had in front of him my file from the Ministry of Education and must have known nearly as much about my activities in Egypt as I did.

For some reason I'd been called not to the main police building up by the railway station in Ramses Square but to an office at the top of a new twelve-storey apartment block which housed the Ministry of Information in Soliman Pasha. And then it struck me that, of course, with anyone who'd been as closely involved with Bahaddin as I'd been—and likely to give a lead—this part of the investigation would have been passed over to the Army who ran everything of importance in Egypt in those days—then as now.

'Forgive me for pressing these details but you can see our embarrassment in the whole affair. We have to go into everything very carefully. You've heard the rumours of course?'

'I've heard a few, yes.'

'You don't have to worry about incriminating yourself, Mr. Marlow, this isn't Scotland Yard. I mean, that he was murdered, poisoned?'

'I'd heard that, yes.'

'Of course there's no proof. They wouldn't let us touch the body. But the police doctor thinks it wasn't a heart attack, some sort of quick poisoning. Of course normally we would have thought that he'd been killed by one of his own people, a relation, a rival for the succession. But that's not the way his family see it. And I must admit that nothing's happened in his own country since to suggest that any sort of *coup de palais* was the reason for his death. So we have to look into all the other possible motives.'

Colonel Hamdy was unlike the usual Egyptian army officer at

that time in that he spoke English perfectly, with barely any accent, and was middle-aged—early fifties, I'd have said. He might have been a British colonel really, with his little half-moustache, his tired, civilized features, his lanky frame and air of casual lack of interest in everything. He seemed to have finished with his wars long ago; there was no sense of urgency or viciousness in his approach, which I had expected. We might almost have been chatting in a London club, except for the heat, which the tiny fan on his desk did nothing to alleviate, and the baking smells of refuse and hot tar which rose from the street engulfing the small room. He pressed a buzzer on his desk and ordered coffee.

'How do you like it—*mazbout*?'

'Please.'

He came out from behind his desk and we sat down at a table with a tourist map of Egypt embedded between two sheets of glass on top of it. He must have taken over the office from someone in that division of Egyptian Information and I noticed an elaborate legend on the map, surrounded by dolphins and a mass of coloured fishes, south of Suez town, advertising a new underwater fishing resort on the Red Sea.

'Suez,' Usher had said. 'We need someone in Suez.' But I wasn't worried that the Colonel knew anything of this. I'd not yet come to think of myself as being on the far side of the law.

'You like it here, don't you, Mr. Marlow? I suppose most people in your position would have gone home—having lost their job. Most of your colleagues have left, haven't they? When their contracts ran out.'

'Yes, I like it. I'm married to an Egyptian.'

'Oh? At All Saints'?'

'No. The British Consulate.'

'Mr. Crowther?'

'Yes.'

'But you're not English.'

'No. But there's no Irish Consulate here. And I was born in London. They can do that sort of thing—you take out dual nationality.'

'Yes, I suppose so. It just seems strange—your being Irish. I thought you people didn't get on too well with the British . . .?'

'That was years ago.'

'So you intend staying on here then?'

'Yes, for the time being anyway. I was hoping for another job. Teaching.'

'Well, I wish you luck.'

The Colonel switched the conversation rather awkwardly, as if, having done his duty in putting me at my ease, he had now, regretfully, to embark on the real purpose of our meeting, a more delicate topic.

'You knew the Prince pretty well—didn't you?'

'He was a friend, yes. I liked him, we got on well together. I suppose you could describe him as being rather mature for a schoolboy. We got on as equals. I can't see why anyone would have wanted to kill him,' I added without thinking, as if the dialogue we were having was part of a play.

'Can't you?'

'I mean—apart from one of his relations, as you said.'

'You mean he wasn't the sort of person to be mixed up in these sort of affairs, these political intrigues?'

'Yes. What intrigues—?' I stopped short. The dialogue had suddenly gone wildly astray from the text.

'Well, he was a British agent, their Middle East Intelligence. The Cairo-Albert circle. Called after the school I suppose. Rather a hopeless outfit, though of course they're short-handed at the moment. Even so, it was extraordinarily amateur. I hope you may do better in it. Add a little sense to the whole thing. You're not a fool.'

The Colonel looked at me with an easy, appreciative expression and went over to his desk where he picked up a pipe and a flimsy sheet of paper which he brought back and handed to me. It was a copy of some sort of Intelligence report, with the heading *United Arab Republic: Ministry for the Interior.* It was in Arabic except for the anglicized names which were written down in a column mid-way through:

Usher
Crowther
Edwards
Girgis
Prince Bahaddin

And then with some sort of explanation in Arabic before my own name:

Marlow

'I see our Security people here assume that you've already joined them.' The Colonel lit a pipe. 'Their usual optimism. You're still thinking about it, aren't you? And Miss Girgis—she's your wife. Isn't that right?' There was a polite tone of enquiry in his voice, almost of condolence, as if she'd had an accident. '*Mrs. Marlow* it should be now of course. A husband-and-wife team. That was rather an ambitious ploy of Usher's, wasn't it? Getting you involved with them in that way. I wouldn't have credited him with it. How would you describe it? Investing in the private sector?'

'You see, Usher found out that we were on to Bahaddin—and had him killed. It suited him rather well really. Apart from stopping Bahaddin talking, and I fancy our people here would have got him to do that, there was the bonus, the quite substantial bonus, of the embarrassment he knew his death would make for us. And he was quite right: one of the few professional things Usher's ever done. Quite in line with the accepted principles of this sort of work—a pawn for a queen. What puzzles me is how Bahaddin ever got involved with them in the first place, what they had on him, how they got him in. In his position I'd have kept a mile away from Usher and his friends. He must have realized that he was a more than usually valuable property in the game, marvellous potential as a sacrifice, not so much for his work but because of his political importance. He must have known they'd get rid of him if his cover was ever broken, if not before, for the sake of the capital gain.'

The Colonel's voice took on a chatty, enquiring tone. He seemed genuinely curious about the whole matter and to be inviting my comments on it. I said nothing.

'Perhaps it was all just part of his Anglophilia—like Hussein of Jordan, walking around without proper security and shopping at Harrods; a sort of dare-devil foolhardiness. I suppose that English school at Maadi bowled him over with those old-fashioned ideas, about adventure and empire and the lesser breeds. He may have seen himself as a sort of Lawrence of Arabia in reverse—"Bahaddin of England"—I've seen a lot of my contemporaries go like that out here. I can't see what's wrong with being an Arab. He was a real one too. You'd have understood that surely? Being Irish. And married to an Egyptian. Don't you find it all rather tiresome? This wanting to be something else, somebody else, in life—and not what you are?'

'It's the curse of the profession, I should think. But I agree. It is stupid. I said so at the time.'

'You've not joined up with them yet then—have you?'

'No.'

I knew already what Colonel Hamdy had in mind: the same sort of blackmail that Crowther and Usher had used, except that he would introduce it more discreetly, in the same agreeable manner that he'd brought to our conversation since the beginning.

'Can you have lunch with me? I must just change my clothes.'

When he came back, the Colonel was in almost bell-bottomed slacks, a yellow cotton shirt and faded silk cravat.

'I have a room in the Semiramis—a dining room. You go on. The first floor, at the end, number 136. I'll meet you there.'

We had lunch on the terrace of what must have been a sort of senior security men's dining club, under a parasol, looking over the river. There were grilled steaks of Nile perch to start with and a bottle of white Ptolémées on ice.

'From the old Roman vineyards outside Alex. Have you been there? A Greek gentleman—there he is, Gianaclis, on the bottle. I used to know the family—he started it up again in the last century. I rather like it. In fact, unlike some of my colleagues, I've never doubted the civilizing influences of all the many cultures who've found a place in this country over the centuries. Though I must admit I never expected to see the Irish as part of that great tradition. Your health.'

'What do you want me to do?'

'I want you to take the job you've been offered, Mr. Marlow. That's all. If you've been in any doubt about it let me tell you it would be the best course open to you—for you and your wife. And your friend Mr. Edwards. And I want you to tell us all about it.'

'I thought you knew all about their operation here. You seem to.'

'In Egypt, yes. But I'm sure you won't be spending all your

life here. If you do well, and I think I can arrange things so that you will, you'll be promoted, sent back to London, where some of the real news about the Middle East comes from. We'd like to know about that. Obviously. Does the whole thing shock you? I mean, you don't seem to have been very enthusiastic about working for Usher and you may not be for us either.'

'I don't think I have much choice—from either of you.'

'On the contrary. You do have a choice. You could go and tell Usher what's happened and he'd have to pull you all out of here—including himself. We could put that to some advantage. We could make something of that.'

'You could round us all up and give us thirty years apiece too, couldn't you? Or shoot us. Wouldn't that be even better?'

'Yes, we could do that. If we had to, if it were forced upon us. But it's a much better idea, isn't it, now that we know about you all, so that your outfit is harmless to us anyway, to turn the screw the other way, to make it a long-term operation, find out how your people manage things at the centre, in London, as I was saying.'

'Why me? Why didn't you go for Crowther? Or Edwards? You could have got a lot more from them.'

'We wouldn't.'

The Colonel eased his cravat, ventilating his body against the heat, and looked out over the river. He drained his glass with an expression of kindly patience.

'You're a beginner, not marked yet. Not trained. The others would have shut up shop at once, wouldn't have given a thing away. They'd have had their thirty years rather than let out a squeak. And it would hardly have done to bring your wife into the matter.' He smiled, not facetiously, but in a way that made me think he meant this. 'But really, what I'm getting at is if you thought it worth your while working for Usher—then why not us? Apart from the accident of your birth you've no special connections with Britain. Just the opposite in fact, I'd have thought—being Irish. You should ask yourself again—*why* work for Usher, why consider him and not us? What are you having next? There's a set lunch or would you like to have something from the *à la carte*? There's not a great deal, I'm afraid. Perhaps a salad and a steak. And some of Gianaclis's Red? The Omar Khayyam. That's rather good too.'

He rang a bell for the waiter who didn't recommend the

steak. We had Kebab Semiramis instead: the pieces of lamb and red pepper cold, on a skewer, in a marinade of oil and lemon; and Gianaclis's Red.

'Personally I've always thought it madness to go round threatening people—prison sentences, shootings and so on— unless you have to. Think about it, be rational. What we'd want from you would be no more than Mr. Usher wants of you. And if you can in any way justify his needs in the matter above ours I'd be pleased to hear how you do it.'

'I can't. I don't see any justification for either point of view. And that's the trouble surely—to do this sort of work properly you have to believe in it. And I don't. I prefer looking out over the river, being here, in the world, drinking the wine. I've never taken to those hard-bitten frontiers of right and wrong—in nationalisms or private affairs; a sort of *tabula rasa* of belief, I'm afraid. I came too late to see countries in a pecking order, one above the other, one against the other, too late to see people as toy soldiers. I never played that game.'

I looked at the Colonel's striped cravat, like a regimental tie, and thought: he has. And he's tired of it in some way; the slacks and the chatter about wine; toy soldiers and some army's colours; they suited him once, they were part of an obsession— but not any more.

I felt that I had talked to him in the way I had because some great disenchantment in his character had allowed it, encouraged it even; because he secretly agreed with me. There was none of Crowther's cunning or Usher's flamboyant theatricality in the Colonel. And I felt suddenly that Egypt might well be my home, as Bridget was my wife, and that between the two of them perhaps, if anywhere, lay the kernel of the only sort of belief I was capable of. I was beginning to like Colonel Hamdy.

'Yes, perhaps you're right,' he said. 'Toy soldiers. A younger generation, fed up with the mess; the kind of world we've left you with. I can see all that. You're quite right to want no part of it, to get away from something that we're trapped in. But you see—I can't escape it—'

'—Then what are we worrying about? You agree with me. I'm not your man.'

'I said I could *see* your point of view, Mr. Marlow; not that I could agree with it. That's always the tragedy, isn't it? Seeing but not believing, not being able to. You see, as far as we're concerned in Egyptian security you *are* one of Usher's people. There's no going back on that. I may believe otherwise, in fact I do, but the others never will. And that being so the rest follows. What I said earlier.'

'That I work for both of you?'

'One without the other wouldn't be much use to us.'

'And if not?'

'I'd prefer not to go over it all again. Believe me, I really don't choose to use threats. I'd hoped to appeal to your logic, to suggest to you where your real interests might lie—and I still do: I want you to see the thing in reason. And I think you will. But the real point I was going to make before you interrupted was that you're trapped, just as much as I am. With the toy soldiers. You're completely compromised. And that wasn't us, remember. That was Usher, Crowther, your friend Edwards. Your wife even. You were compromised by your friends, Mr. Marlow; you became part of their circle. They had no alternative but to include you in their real affairs. Nor have I.'

12

WE met that afternoon at Groppi's and had lemon ices on the terrace. It was July and the heat had become unbearable.

'Did you have lunch?'

'A sandwich.'

'Well, tell me all about it. What did they say to you?'

'Nothing much. Routine. They don't have anything on us.'

I was lying to her, at last. I knew something which she didn't. But I felt no sense of responsibility, of doing the right thing, the only thing; for her good and Henry's. The Colonel's secrets ran about in my mind, oppressive, inescapable, like the weather—an almost physical presence, I thought, which anyone could have recognized if they'd looked at me, like a tic or a bad haircut.

Bridget sat there easily on the little garden stool, the line of her body arched over the table, elbows on her knees, hands clasped around her face; there was an air of comfort and trust about her. She was like a tired child looking into the fire waiting for a story.

I thought: I could tell her now. Tell her all about the Colonel: get it over with. Aren't we more important than their games? Even than her parents, even Henry . . . Couldn't we accept the consequences, ride it out together?

The consequences. Surely, if it were ever discovered by Usher or Crowther, there could only be one consequence in working for 'both sides'. They didn't retire people in the middle. They would have something quite different in store: like burying their mistakes. A house in Wimbledon or a dacha in the Moscow suburbs? For the lucky ones, perhaps, yes. For the really valuable men. I wasn't one of them. I was simply an inconvenience—unmarked, untrained; involved simply of necessity, through the accident of friendship, as the Colonel had said. I certainly wouldn't be missed. For Crowther it might even be a pleasure. He wouldn't hesitate in getting me out of the way if he thought I'd been near Colonel Hamdy. And Bridget was one line of communication to him.

Bridget was a tired child that one couldn't trust. Children told stories out of school. And Henry was no use either. For there was another Henry, not just the friend whom I was protecting by keeping silent. There was the Henry who'd known Bridget long before I had, whose past with her—days and nights together, things said and done—was still a mystery to me because I'd left it that way. There had been arrangements between them; and there still were. He was her operator after all. They had their secrets too, I felt, which I wasn't to know simply by being in their 'circle'. It was simple enough: neither of them was to be trusted.

And I thought with clarity, the idea standing out sharply as none other did: this is what it's really like. The game. This is how it touches you—in everything, each detail of life, not just the job itself which by comparison I could see becoming a source of release, as something quite prosaic. I had come into a narrow world suddenly, made up of secrets and deceits, traversed by long and careful lies, defended everywhere against trust. And I would have to remember this each time I said anything or looked at anyone in the future. I would be reminded of it everywhere, as an endlessly repeated feeling of nausea.

This was what stretched in front of me: a disability—as if I'd emerged from the room in the Semiramis, as from a car crash, without a leg and a crutch for the rest of my life.

Bridget lit one of my cigarettes.

I said, 'Let's have a drink,' needing it now in a way I'd not done before.

'What did they ask you? Who did you see?'

She appeared so calm.

'Just my connections with Bahaddin. The school and so on. I told them the truth—as we agreed. That we went on to the Club, that Henry joined us there.'

She drew deeply on the cigarette, sipped the whisky the waiter had brought us and said hopefully, with relief, as if she too felt that our life was beginning all over again, but in a happy way: 'The thing now, surely, is to continue as if nothing had happened. Get the job in Suez. Apart from Crowther—it would be something for you to do. Some work.'

'Why do you suppose I would get work there? I've been thrown out of one ex-British school here already.'

But I knew there would be no trouble. When I'd put the same point to the Colonel he'd smiled and said it would be the easiest thing in the world; they actually needed an English teacher in Suez, apart from needing a double agent there as well. It was something which he'd hardly have to 'fix' at all. Once I'd made my decision I was to apply to the Ministry of Education in the ordinary way. The application would go straight through, the place would be kept open for me.

'You could try it, go and see the Ministry. We could go to Suez now in any case. There's a new resort down the Red Sea. Underwater fishing. Couldn't we do that—and get out of here?'

'Money?'

'We've got it. I got it this morning, through the Council library; that's the way we're keeping in touch now, through books, I'll tell you about it later. It's your money, from Crowther. And I'm due two weeks' leave from the office. We could leave the place altogether . . .'

She was happy, enthusiastic. It seemed a sensible change, a move from the unbearable city that Cairo had become, something which, in ordinary life, we would probably have done in any case: a few weeks by the sea, lying in the sun, and looking at the fish. In fact it was a cliché, perfectly translated into action—it was the point of no return. Once on the road to Suez I was in Crowther's hands, the Colonel's. And Bridget's. They came together in a package; the professional, the personal, obligations. The alternative was an exit visa. Or a boat coming through the canal. And both were as unlikely a means of escape as a trip on foot across the Sahara . . . It hardly mattered now. I would have to work for them. The Colonel had made that decision. But again, the feeling swept over me, one had to pretend; if one spoke at all one had to lie; that was the other side of the coin, the second secret of survival: only pretend.

And I thought, we blame life for our disillusion whereas much more it's the trespass we make away from it that sends us over the precipice.

13

NO one has written a true book about happiness, so they say. But that fortnight was happy. So perhaps it alone, among the incidents of this story, may not bear description.

We lay on the beach under a long canvas awning that had been put up over the sand and we swam with goggles over the coral that sloped gently out to sea, and among the coloured sea plants and strange fish. At night we slept in a small wooden cabin at the end of the line, naked in the dry air of that burnished marine sandscape. The cabin was like a cell; just a chair, a medicine cupboard with a mirror and two army camp beds which we strapped together with an extra sheet that Bridget had wheedled out of the manager. The resort had only just opened and apart from the goggles had no other underwater facilities. None the less it was full up and the other guests never lost an opportunity of telling us how unlucky we'd been in getting one of the end cabins that hadn't been 'properly finished'. We didn't listen. We were living again in the present, after so much that had been unreal; living in that uncomplicated adventure of the moment, caught for once in the fabric of life where we saw or felt nothing except with the eyes and heart. We looked at each other again; and it was that *regard* which played by far the biggest part in our loving each other then: her face, moved into so many patterns by her thoughts—thoughts, I know now, she could not admit and others she was barely conscious of—which rose up, like the tide filling the indentations of a strand, flooding her face with desire, humility, sadness—with all that she really felt, so that her real words, when she spoke, seemed no more than apologetic, unnecessary captions to a series of unique photographs.

We invent passion: so that it can become a thing in itself, without past or future. It has to be invented. We made love then, we lived, so fluently that I can only see that passion as a quite separate creation, as something which had nothing to do with our real selves, and which died when those selves intruded and demanded the same accents.

I had spoken to her one day about our staying on in Egypt, not going back to England, of my making a career there in some way. And she had said doubtfully, 'You mustn't cut off the approaches, *your* approaches, to yourself. This country won't always satisfy you.'

'Us, I meant. Won't it satisfy us? Don't you want to live here?'

'How can I tell anything now. What should I say?'

'Why are you so doubtful?'

'I'm not.'

But she was.

On our last day she sent a postcard to Henry.

'What's the point?' I asked. 'We'll be seeing him when we get back to Cairo. Or you will anyway.' And she said seriously, 'How do you know?'

In the middle of September we went to Suez. The school was a tiny yellow building with a corrugated iron roof at the other end of the main street from the Bel Air Hotel where we lived. It sat right on the edge of the desert so that on coming into the town from the Cairo road it loomed up before the other buildings of the place came into sight like a small fort, an abandoned outpost from *Beau Geste*, with a wall round it, a tall flagpost in the concrete yard at the back and a lifeless flag.

Mohammed Fawzi ran the place. 'Fawzi Esquire' as he liked to be addressed. I imagine he considered the suffix as an important Anglo-Saxon title, resting somewhere between plain Mister and being a Lord, so that he became known to us all as 'Esquire'.

There were two other teachers there who, like me, had been sent down from Cairo, Cassis and Helmi, and the four of us spent most evenings together, sampling the few pleasures of the shoddy little town; the second show at the Regal Cinema, cards, drinks at the Refinery Club outside Suez, or the French Club at Port Tewfik, and odd trips to the Casino, a strange little night club five miles up in the Attaka hills to the south. At other times we had supper with Cassis and Helmi looking out over the Red Sea from rooms they had taken high above the oily waterway.

' "Neither the Arabian quarter, with its seven mosques and unimportant bazaar, nor the European quarter, which contains several buildings and warehouses of considerable size, presents any attraction." ' I read them the passage out from an old Baedeker I had brought with me one evening.

'It's not changed much, has it?'

And Cassis, who taught English, had said, 'But it has a Biblical importance, or perhaps,' and he looked at Helmi who taught geography, 'perhaps one would put it better by saying that the place has a certain geophysical interest.'

'Oh, yes.' Helmi took the allusion confidently and more bluntly. 'If you stepped from a boat out there, way out there, you would only be above your knees.' And he went on to explain the Bible trip, how the Israelites had crossed over the Red Sea because they knew the line of sand bars which ran right across the neck of the bay and how the wicked Egyptians, who didn't know the route, had been swallowed up. Helmi was a Copt.

'Before they made the canal you could walk right across the bay—if you knew the sands. They were very various. Even now you can walk right up to the canal channel. And that's what happened. The first group knew their way across. And the others didn't. Or got lost in a sandstorm maybe, that often happens here. Quite suddenly. Phut! Whizz. Finish!' Helmi moved his arms in circles vigorously about his eyes. 'You see nothing and the boat can upset. Here, take a look through these

glasses. You can just see where the sand bank ends and the
channel begins.'

I looked through the binoculars, scanning the bay from the
headland at Port Tewfik right down to the red and violet haze
which hung over the horizon far down the gulf. Twenty or
thirty ships lay at anchor in the roads, waiting to go up the
canal in the night convoy. And to the right, along the coast, in
the shadow of the hills, two Russian tankers were berthed at the
refinery jetty. I could even make out their names. If that was
the sort of information Crowther really wanted, getting it didn't
appear too difficult.

And in due course I was able to inform Henry of these
shipping movements, the frequency of buses and trains to Cairo,
the name of the secretary of the Greek Club and the time of the
first house at the Regal on Sundays. Henry reported that he was
perfectly satisfied and Bridget agreed that Crowther seemed
even more of a fool than I'd taken him for.

My relations with Colonel Hamdy were equally uneventful
and satisfactory. I passed on to him exactly what I gave Henry
for Crowther. And every so often I'd get a message in return:
'Very glad to receive your good news. Look forward to meeting
again.' This correspondence was conducted, whenever we came
to Cairo for week-ends, through Rosie, the Greek telephonist at
the Semiramis Hotel, and through the receptionist at the same
establishment. I used the letter rack behind his desk, dropping
an envelope in the compartment marked 'H' for Hamdy on my
way to the gents while the Colonel left his messages with Rosie;
which I later picked up from the large assortment of similar
billets-doux on blue paper which were kept for customers on a
board outside her booth. A great many people used the hotel in
this way, as both post office and telephonic *poste restante*, the
official channels in Egypt for such communications being
notoriously uncertain.

14

BUT I stopped working for the Colonel, as I did for Crowther
and Usher, for by the end of the spring term I'd stopped living
with Bridget, had left Egypt and and returned to London.

Our marriage, like the events consequent on our first meeting, went through appetite, satisfaction, farce and enmity; it ran a fixed course for the rocks, the two of us struggling gamely at the wheel to keep it steady. And soon enough we had reached that point where words became as useless and unnecessary as they'd been in the times when we were most at ease and happy. We were genuinely incompatible. It was a classic journey.

Bridget resigned herself to the fact that whatever I might become, or might be 'underneath'—in more favourable circumstances—I was not the person she thought I was, expected me to be. She had been mistaken. I was not the 'right' person, and there would be therefore, at some future date—she didn't know when, for she would not precipitate it—an end to it all. Meanwhile she would close up shop.

I, on the other hand, seeing her running, hiding in this way, the words drying up like a guilty witness, dropped the role of lover and assumed that of detective. I became a genuine agent—proficient, ruthless, imaginative—in a way I never did with Usher or afterwards with Williams. A St. George in dark glasses and shoulder holster. The battle was on: I would save love.

Why we play this game, to which we lend a passion we never quite give to loving, I don't know; unless it be just one more of the unconscious steps we make towards our real ambition, evidence of our secret craving, which is to end love, to be released from it.

Bridget would be disappointed, of course, in having to assume again that truth which is implicit in all affairs—except the one shared with the 'right' person—that love does not last. But to offset this there would be room for congratulation: she would have faced this demise with me—and survived; and she would have learnt something for next time, for the next person. And there would be that, wouldn't there?—another time, someone else; in a bar or at a party, the friend of a friend. Above all she would be free again. Once more she could pick and choose from all the huge promise of the future; the charm of the unexpected, so long withheld, would once again be lying in wait for her—the unknown passions she would embrace, which already existed in the form of someone who even now was rising towards her, along the lines of destiny, to that future point where their paths would cross.

It was a girls' story, something from a popular magazine. I thought Bridget was like that—though not at heart; I was the literate man who would bring her to better reading, wreck her conventional assumptions, explain a serious love in a long book.

Neither view was real. I was the agent running to the crime, the man from the gutter tabloid on to a good story, forcing the pace, getting a foot inside the door, flourishing the cards of desire. And it cannot have surprised Bridget; it was quite in keeping with the form these protracted endings take. It was natural that I should become the inquisitor, pondering the clues of a vanished emotion, marshalling the evidence, with which, when I knew everything else had failed, I would indict and slander her, so that we should both part satisfied, that is as enemies, happy in the knowledge that all the proprieties had been observed. It was natural, because only in being arraigned and accused in this way could she rise guiltless and clear above the sordid argument I had reduced our association to.

It ended. A simple failure of the imagination. I came to inhabit the cliché: I couldn't accept another man's future with her, someone unknown, the stranger who would climb on my shoulders into the light, smiling, after a strong gin and a romp, appreciating the river view; the man who would replace me in those empty afternoons when there was nothing to do except the one thing we had done so well. I shouldn't have worried about strangers; I knew the men well enough at the time, and came to know them even better. In other circumstances I should never have charged Bridget with infidelity. Fidelity was really her strong point.

The three of us had a drink in the Continental the day I left to get my plane to London, Henry with us, as I thought, in the guise of a friendly receiver for a bankrupt. It was early summer, with the usual warnings of savage heat to come—the crowded first class carriages to Alex, the flocks of shimmering cars on their way out over the bridge through Dokki to the desert road, while those who remained in town became animals, searching out intuitively the darkest corners, the deepest shade, emerging only at nightfall to feed and ravage. We had Zibib and talked about the weather; polite inconsequential chatter. We left each other as perfect strangers.

Henry had said he would get Usher to recommend me for a job with Mid-East Intelligence in London, something quiet, 'Information Only'. I told him not to bother, that I was thinking of something else altogether. 'Besides,' I'd said, 'you don't know about it, but I met someone, a Colonel Hamdy . . .' And I told him what had happened six months before. He laughed.

'Hamdy? Military Intelligence? As long as it wasn't the Political Intelligence, they're more serious. But Hamdy, he's doing that all the time. It's happened to most of us out here at one time or another—happens to almost everyone in this business; subversion, blackmail, infiltration—we played a game with each other out here, his set-up against ours. I shouldn't worry about that.'

I didn't. I never mentioned the fact when Williams first interviewed me. But of course I joined headquarters establishment in London before the rot set in, when there were still things to hide, secrets to betray, and little or no screening. I got in just before the vets arrived, before the doors were finally bolted on the deserted stables.

Why? Why did I bother with a pursuit that had already wrecked one good part of my life? In those weeks in Cairo I had acquired a taste for conspiracy and deceit, almost a craving, a loyalty towards betrayal. This ridiculous sense of vengeance didn't last but it was enough to carry me to Holborn, to make me almost a professional in a trade I had scorned before. One speaks of 'turning' a man in our line of country—turning him into a double through psychological or physical pressure; of making him deny his own 'side'. But the expression is misleading in that context; one is 'turned' in this way from the very beginning, through some reverse or imagined slight, or some long-nurtured sense of injustice; it can start in childhood, or later, through a childish response; the seed blooms in secrecy that is the nature of the business, doing much ill; one is 'turned' only from the business of sensible life.

BOOK THREE

LONDON AND CAIRO, MAY 1967

1

WILLIAMS was talking to Marcus, his deputy and head of the new security bureau within the section. Marcus, though only six months started on his career as ferret in Mid-East Intelligence, already had a nickname throughout the department—'The Grip', the one who didn't let go. They were in Williams's small office at the back of the tall building in Holborn, which he preferred to his quarters at the front, looking over the courtyard and the huge Hepworth abstract which he couldn't abide. Contemporary sculpture sent him into a fury, ever since he'd first gazed at Reg Butler's 'Unknown Political Prisoner' in the Tate.

'Our only problem is that *we* don't know—do we?—if Edwards and Marlow know. We don't know the real nature of our "agreement" with them. Still, it won't much matter. That's the beauty of the plan.'

Williams took up the file which lay in front of him and ran his fingers gently over the red cardboard folder as if there'd been dust on it—the file marked 'MOUSE'.

Williams had never been one for code names; it had been Marcus's idea. He was new to the business. If he wanted it that way—why not?

Williams put the file away in his safe, got up and walked over to the hatstand where he fingered his hat and coat absent-mindedly for a moment, looking out of the window towards the glimpse of St. Paul's between the tall white buildings which threw back the early May sunset in a blaze of light. He turned away from the vision with bored resignation.

'I suppose I shall have to put in an appearance at the liaison meeting downstairs. The Americans would take it badly if I didn't. The usual lot this time, are they? Dutton and Elder— "the callous gentlemen". They're so keen on protocol. Like we used to be. Care to drop by with me, Marcus?'

The two men left the eighth-floor office. The lifts were busy so they walked down the stairs to the liaison annexe three floors below.

'I never asked you, Marcus—why "Mouse"? Why that for the code name? The usual connotations—"cat and mouse"?'

'Partly. It's the poem by Burns.' And Marcus recited a verse as they moved through the dusty shafts of sunlight from the stair windows between the floors, his dull, classless accent massacring the original lines:

> 'Wee, sleekit, cowrin, timirous beastie,
> O, what a panic's in thy breastie,
> Thou need na start awa sae hasty,
> Wi' bickering brattle! . .'

The tread of their feet echoed down the vault of the stairwell, the slow irregular smack of leather on concrete, like a horse dragging along a road at the end of the day.

'Yes, I know. I'm not quite sure I see the point though.'

'Edwards is the mouse, isn't he? It's obvious, isn't it? When you come to look at the plan. Because he doesn't see it. He can't.'

'Yes. Yes, of course, I wouldn't have thought of it. The title, I mean.'

Williams suddenly remembered the Russian doll his mother had given him to play with as a child—the brightly coloured barrel-like figures all with the same frozen expression, one inside the other, and another inside that, getting smaller and smaller. And he remembered the feeling of despair that had come over him whenever he played with the toy, the fearful idea that real children, too, went on for ever, one inside the other, in the body of their mother, for he had been an only child at the time: the knowledge, which must have been born in him then, of the endless ramifications of deceit, the tricks which lay up every sleeve; the voices beyond the nursery at the end of the landing, the doctor's voice, the nurse's, someone else's—his mother perhaps, a shout of pain, and the screaming infant; the feeling that you could never be sure of anything, returned to him now for an instant before he heard the bland accommodating drawl of Dutton speaking to McCoy at the entrance to the liaison annexe. And his cold memories of the past were washed away in a tide of even stronger resentment.

2

THE United Arab Airlines Comet had stopped at Munich on its way to Cairo and for the first time in years Edwards felt near panic when he was in a position to reflect on it.

He didn't mind that Williams might now know that he was a double—or that perhaps he'd known for a long time; that could have been so and he would have survived, as long as his account had showed a profit and he'd seen to that, he knew it had. What worried him now—as it had since he'd first been asked to go on this mission by Williams a week earlier—was his complete uncertainty about the purpose of the plan; it didn't add up. It might make sense to someone who'd never been to the Middle East, but that person wasn't Williams; he knew the situation there backwards. The man in Cairo would never look at the plan, Edwards knew his background and his real inclinations fairly well—Mohammed Yunis, mildly 'left-wing' and secretary of the only legal party in Egypt, the Arab Socialist Union, 'political rival to the President' as Williams had naïvely described him at one of their meetings over the plan together. That didn't mean much in Egypt these days; every putative Marxist there, both in or out of jail, saw himself as a potential rival to Nasser—just as most of the leaders of the right-wing Moslem Brotherhood did, not to mention some of the younger army officers. Nasser himself stood firmly in the middle of these warring ideologies, supported fervently by the great public who cared little for alternatives; they never had—the army of bureaucrats and farmers, ninety-five per cent of the population, who saw nothing beyond their next pay chit or weevils in the cotton crop. Political rivals, in these circumstances, were a drug on the market in Egypt. They didn't have a chance and the idea that Yunis, helped by Britain and America, might stir the country to a new revolution and overthrow the President seemed impossible in the first place and in no sense an advantage to the West, if it happened, in the second. And anyway, he thought, Yunis was so much the last man in Egypt to get himself involved in this sort of thing: Yunis had once harboured vaguely Marxist ideas it was true, but he was a very conservative socialist now. He had come to an age and position in life where he could personally reap the benefits of the first Egyptian revolution and the idea of creating a second, Edwards thought, couldn't have been further from his mind.

The plan was so palpably unrealistic that Edwards not only saw a trick in it but saw as well that he was *meant* to see this in it, which was something quite different, quite new in the history of his relations with Williams who until now had always given him definite, realizable aims—operations where success or failure could be accounted for as meticulously as figures in a ledger.

If only he could have approached Williams as the others in his section did, the ones who genuinely worked for him, he thought, how easy it would have been to say to him: look, this won't work and this is why . . . And he longed for that sort of trust, knowing it was the one step he could never take, the step which broke the gentlemen's agreement he had with Williams— broke the rules which governed the game and which for so long had ensured his survival as a player on both sides of it. In his position he could never query Williams's directions, alternative suggestions from him could only be taken as evidence of bad faith, of the wrong kind of double dealing, favouring one side more than the other; one had to go through with the instructions, to the letter, and he always had.

But now, with this plan—here was an operation that could never show a profit or a loss—to anyone—for it could never succeed. And the logic then was inescapable: he was being dropped. He was a tight-rope walker who went to and fro between the poles, and there was trust at either end as long as he managed the feat, as he always had. And now, here was Williams at one end shaking the wire vigorously, knowing that he could do nothing but try and weather the storm, that he couldn't move to safety in one direction or the other. And that was the only logic of it all—that he had to fall.

But why?

He decided to stay on the plane during the half-hour stop at Munich, noticing the sharp east wind which blew the mechanics'

overalls into vicious flapping shapes about their legs. He knew
the airport anyway; there was nothing to be got out of
stretching one's legs, or even a café-crême and a cognac with the
weary commercial travellers at the horseshoe bar. He'd done it
so many times before. Until he thought suddenly, ashamed at
his fear, that it wasn't the cold wind that kept him in his seat,
but the idea of something lurking for him outside: someone
behind the swinging glass doors of the terminal building, a car
waiting for him on the tarmac, a marked transit ticket. All the
traditional fictions of his profession surged into his mind and he
realized he was a complete stranger to them, that they had
never impinged on his professional life, and they were as unreal
and frightening to him now as they might have been to an
outsider, a happy man in the back row of the stalls.

He was quite unprepared for this sense of mystery; the idea
that these fictions might suddenly become facts had never
occurred to him. Until now he'd played the tune, from the
middle as he'd seen it, and all three sides—Moscow, Cairo and
London—had been happy. He'd always known what was
happening and had been quite prepared to see himself as a
huckster who gave full value for money; and he'd justified his
behaviour in terms of maintaining what he thought of as his
'primary interest'; his Russian connections, his *belief*, for it was
still just that. But if he went, if Williams were getting rid of him,
he knew his other interests would vanish as well. It was a cat's
cradle; one tiny movement of a string and the whole intricate
pattern of trust would collapse. And Williams had made that
move by involving him in this hare-brained scheme.

Why?

He thought carefully over the events of the last month—the
last year perhaps? Blake's escape? Blake had worked out of
Williams's Middle East section and there had been some uneasy
times after his arrest and during his imprisonment. But Blake
didn't know of his involvement with Moscow—as he hadn't
known of Blake's. They were careful of that sort of thing in
Moscow these days. No KGB double knew the identity of any
other in the same position—not after the disasters of the past.
Unless Moscow had arranged to shop him? The permutations,
non-existent a month ago, were endless now.

Edwards tried to isolate and catalogue them for the hundredth time, yet in the end only one thing was really clear: London wanted him to do something which they knew would result in his immediate obliteration if he attempted it—so they must have known too that he would never attempt it. At the same time they'd surely not gone through all this elaborate charade for nothing; they had something else in mind, something which he hadn't seen, which he couldn't see. It almost began to amuse him, the clues were so obvious, like the values for a simple equation . . . yet he couldn't work it out. And he'd been good at that sort of thing in school.

3

THE passengers came back from the transit lounge. Edwards could see them through the cabin window, forcing themselves into the wind, whipping the puddles into blisters on the concrete apron, clutching their hats, their faces wrinkling painfully, and he was glad he'd not gone with them. He stretched his legs down beneath the seat, yawned, closed his eyes. He gave himself over to the feeling of warmth and safety which the cabin induced in him. A weakness, he thought, but this was a place, probably the last place, where he could safely indulge it.

There were a dozen or so new arrivals, half of them Egyptians, too sharply dressed in Italian-cut suits that hadn't been made with quite enough cloth; returning from some trade or government mission, Edwards thought, when he opened his eyes cautiously and looked at them flapping about the aisle, pushing for seats, making a nuisance of themselves like men who don't travel often and are determined to make the most of it.

He had taken a place at the very back of the plane, where he always sat, next to the cabin staff, hoping that none of the new arrivals would get that far. To discourage the possibility he put his briefcase and a pile of newspapers on the two vacant seats to his left and looked determinedly out of the window like a stuffy woman travelling below her class.

He'd always had an obsession about sitting by himself on

journeys; he couldn't bear enforced company, being with anyone, in fact, whose presence he hadn't actively encouraged. As a child—it had begun then, at the end of term: the vicious, howling cabal of schoolboys savaging each other with their peaked caps and bunching in the corridors on the train away from Capetown—the sense of release he'd craved then, as he did now, and had only found when he'd changed at the junction and was sitting alone in the rackety wooden carriage which took him along the branch line to his uncle's home up country.

'May I.'

Edwards nodded distantly, barely turning his head, as the small, perky, almost balk figure in a glistening Dacron suit moved the papers diffidently and sat down on the far seat from him. Nodded, and closed his eyes again. But he couldn't avoid hearing the storm of Arabic which followed from the man—the brusque, admonitory phrases of someone too long accustomed to giving orders, as he shouted for the steward. Apart from the rough country accent—from Upper Egypt, probably Aswan—the voice might have belonged to some petty court functionary from Farouk's time and not Nasser's. But then Nasser had been in power now for as long as Farouk had, Edwards thought, and one regime is much like another as far as the functionaries are concerned. When they get into their stride you couldn't tell them apart: obsequiousness by the well-heeled, with the well-heeled, and stuff the people; the secret society of boot strappers: the new rich, and the 'government class'; and between them the shared nightmare memory of a mud village lost in the delta two decades before, when the night came down in black frustration and you were the only person in the café with trousers, talking revolution over the sizzling pressure lamp.

And the revolution had come; others had brought it, sought death for it, defined it—you were buying stamps in the General Post Office at the time. Never mind. It was just what you'd always talked about in the village café, it had come to pass exactly as you had said—it was yours, your number had come up at last. You were out in the streets for the rest of the week, you yelled more than anybody and looted a little. And later you bought a jacket to go with the trousers and had a word in someone's ear—a friend of your uncle's who had actually been seen with a stick in his hand on the first day.

Now the ranks had closed again after the whirlwind, you met the fixers again, the ones you'd rallied against in the village, only they wore suits now—you met them again, came together like long-estranged and passionate lovers: the ten per cent men; the kick-back, as violent and profitable as American football; government by baksheesh: the call from the hotel lobby before the tender is put out, the piece of marshy land beyond Ismailia bought from a small family for £200, already surveying it in the mind's eye, seeing the graceful curve of the new road, the tall chimneys of the chemical factory. . .

The trouble was he'd gone on thinking there *was* a difference, between one sort of government and another, for too long. The man's arrogant, peremptory attitude came to him as a shock, he realized—as another indisputable sign of something he'd long wanted to avoid recognizing: that the things some people fought for didn't make the rest any better, that if there were improvements in their life they took them as being no more than their due; that was the accepted order of things—personal advantage, material gain—these were the things that came first whichever side you were on, whatever you had fought for. Edwards wished that he could start now like everyone else, dreaming of a colour television set and a second car, that he'd never come to believe in sides.

The man was loudly demanding the basket of sweets before take-off, like a fractious child, and when the steward came he grabbed a whole fistful, and then another, and stuffed them in his pocket, some of them dropping down between the seats.

'Please, Your Excellency,' the steward fawned in Arabic, 'I can arrange for you to take a bag of them with you, before we get to Cairo.'

His conciliatory, false voice—how quickly the steward had changed from privileged official to grovelling servant. It reminded Edwards of his father's basement office next to the cellars in the old Shepheard's Hotel in Cairo and the monthly agony of paying, and docking, the servants' wages. Edwards had worked there for a few months when he'd left school at a time when his parents still hoped he'd follow them in the hotel business. 'Please, Effendi—*Please*, Mr. Edwards—' when some floor waiter had broken something or had had a complaint laid against him. And he remembered the repeated pleas of one

particular servant who had smashed a decanter, an elderly
Nubian who spoke like a child as his father calculated the
three-month deduction from his salary: 'Please, Effendi, I'll
never do it again, I'll never do it again.'

He'd wanted a world then, really ever since he could
remember, where saying things like that would never again be
possible. That was when the vehemence had begun, the anger
that had lit all his life, and which seemed to be dying in him
now.

Sweets, he thought—that's what it all comes to. That's all
they want. That's all the anger has really been about.

'Sweets,' the man in the seat next to him said affably,
sucking and chomping on one loudly. 'You can't get them like
this in Cairo these days, I'm afraid. My grandchildren love them.
What can one do?'

Edwards had to turn now and was about to nod his head
again in vague assent when he saw that it was Mohammed Yunis
who had spoken. His Excellency Mohammed Yunis, Secretary
General of the Arab Socialist Union.

For a moment Edwards thought he saw the answer to
London's riddle: that Williams had organized some kind of
incredibly subtle end for him, whose instrument was to be
Yunis. The first stages were already under way.

Or perhaps the plan was that he and Yunis were to go down
together, literally, on the flight to Cairo. But it couldn't have
been planned like that, nothing could have been organized so
that he should meet Yunis in this way: he'd changed his flight
himself at London Airport, as he often did, from a BOAC one
to another an hour later on United Arab Airlines. Still, there
was an advantage in seeing Yunis—it confirmed his only course
of action. Yunis, he saw now so clearly, was nothing more than
the largest cog in what they were pleased to call the 'elected
government' of Egypt—the Arab Socialist Union which was
simply a rubber stamp for the President's intentions. He might
have been somewhat to the left of Nasser but not nearly
enough, and quite without sufficient support in the country, for
anyone in the West ever to think of approaching him with ideas
of a counter-revolution. Yunis was just a dapper, greedy old
socialist, anxious for trips to Berlin and London, for good
English sweets, properly boiled, and long-playing records of

Jewish musicals. Edwards thought: anyone who could see him, as Williams apparently did, in battledress master-minding a coup, didn't have Nasser's end in mind but his own. Yunis would have him in the hands of the police the moment he suggested such a scheme.

It was a fortunate coincidence in fact, Edwards thought again, this meeting with Yunis. It had come as a last warning, a clear sign pointing to sanity and survival: he would have to disappear; into Egypt or further south, from where he'd come. Williams had burnt his boats on one side and he couldn't see Moscow taking him back.

The currency he'd worked with for so many years would be discredited at once, he realized—the moment he tried to work outside the peculiar circumstances which alone gave it a value. No *single* organization could trust him now, not with his long history of work with that organization's enemies. Each side had trusted him so long as he remained in the middle, like a reliable news agency, giving them all the news. But for one side to give him sanctuary would not only be valueless to them, it would be dangerous too. For how could they be sure it wasn't a trick, that he wasn't a Trojan hen come home to roost? Williams had put him quite beyond trust and he cursed him for it. His deceits in the past seemed like honesty now—by comparison with the future, which he'd thought of as the beginning of that state at last. The dacha in the Moscow suburbs wasn't really on, he saw. Or the hot toddy.

4

WILLIAM'S dinner with his mother had gone off rather well in his house in Flood Street: they'd reached the coffee before she'd embarked on the condition and position of her daughter-in-law.

'How is she—where is she, Charles? I never hear of her. Why all this mystery?'

'Alice is in Devon. You know that perfectly well. There's no mystery. She's been there since Christmas.'

And just then the telephone had thankfully gone. It was

Marcus. 'Just to confirm his movements, I've had word from Heathrow: he's on his way.'

'Good, Marcus. We're under way then, too. Now there's only Marlow to send packing.'

'We're seeing him tomorrow afternoon. It shouldn't be too difficult. They were close friends after all.'

Williams put down the receiver and blew his nose. A minute sliver of the chicken fricassee they'd had for dinner had lodged somewhere in the back of his throat and he felt the need to clean his teeth.

He'd like to have left his mother at once and gone back to the office. There was so much to do. There was no denying it—his plan was shaping well.

5

EDWARDS assumed there'd be one of his section officers checking on his arrival at Cairo. There usually was, though he never knew who, and certainly Williams would want to know in this case, so he left the aircraft with Yunis, ending a conversation with him about Egypt's balance of payments problem as they walked down the steps to the apron, before Yunis was swallowed up in a crowd of party hacks and photographers who had come to meet him. The thing was to keep London happy for as long as possible, let them think he was going through with their plan, whatever it was, until he could get his bearings in Egypt, decide what to do and then dump the whole thing.

And surely Bridget would have some ideas, he thought.

Things, in fact, worked out rather better than he'd expected. He must have made more of an impression on Yunis than he'd realized, with his talk of World Bank loans (he'd said he was going to Egypt to do some articles on their hard currency crisis) for from the middle of the crush of well-wishers Yunis turned back towards him and offered him a lift back into the city—turned round like a friend recognizing him in a crowded street and suggesting lunch. How easy it was, Edwards thought, to lead an ordinary life, to make up one's day with meetings

and activities that one enjoyed. He thought of Yunis's sweets
and found he didn't resent his greed any longer. The two men
pushed their way through the crush to the passenger exit. A big
government Mercedes was humming by the kerb. They got into
it like minor royalty and drove off towards the city.

6

THE rather distinguished-looking Egyptian eased the collar of
his old-fashioned linen summer suit in the moist air of the
airport's main lobby. The lapels were far too wide. He knew
that. The air-conditioning plant had long since broken down
and he had spent some uncomfortable minutes pretending to
make a phone call from a booth which looked out over the
main passenger entrance before coming out on to the concourse, mopping his brow, breathless and perturbed. He nodded
absent-mindedly towards a man in a suit of grubby blue cloth
on the other side of the hall who at once left the building and
disappeared after Yunis's cavalcade in a small Hillman. An angry
squabble of passengers were shouting and waving their arms on
the baking pavement outside. The airport coach either wouldn't
start or, by arrangement, wasn't leaving then, and they'd been
left to the mercies of the rapacious taxi-drivers who had started
to move in among them, hawking their broken down American
cars for a trip to the city. An American woman it was who had
supposedly been raped in one of these taxis several months
before, the man in the summer suit remembered, at night on the
old road back into Cairo past the City of the Dead; appropriate.
The incident had come up to him in Military Intelligence:
someone in the city police, as a way of avoiding responsibility
for the investigation, had suggested that the woman was an
imperialist spy and the taxi driver had only really been doing no
more than his patriotic duty.

The man in the summer suit dealt with spies, as head of
Egyptian Counter-Intelligence. He finished tidying himself up,
tucking away a large spotted handkerchief in his breast pocket.
It was frayed at the edge, but you'd have to be close to notice
it. Too much laundering, for too long. That's the only thing

they're really good at. Nothing else works here, he thought, with unusual impatience. Everyone is a liar, all of them—absolute rogues. But then that was exactly what he had always liked about the country, he remembered, trying to calm himself: he'd never cared for efficiency or skill in those he worked with; it cramped his own effectiveness in that sphere. He could pretend, as he had for a long time, that he was slipshod and vain like the others, knowing that he wasn't. That was his pleasure, which Egypt gave him every day of his life: the confirmation of another secret, inside the secret of his work.

But now someone from outside had come up with a mystery, something he wasn't in on, and it had thrown him completely. Until then he'd known about everything, everybody else—he had been in the middle of the web—but what was Henry Edwards doing with Mohammed Yunis? Nothing, nobody, had prepared him for that.

Colonel Hassan Hamdy thought about it all over a cup of sweet coffee with the airport's Chief Security Officer in the stuffy little room on the second floor of the passenger building. He hadn't in the least wanted to see Selim but it might have looked odd if he'd not put in an appearance. Home Security expected that sort of condescension from the senior military branch of the service and the Colonel had never failed to supply it—to play the arrogant role whenever necessary, as it so frequently was—in his twenty-three years with Egyptian Intelligence.

Selim was both annoyed and pleased to see the Colonel—unable to decide whether the honour of seeing him at the airport outweighed the implications of his having felt it necessary to come there in the first place. Had not His Excellency's arrivals always gone off exactly to plan?—without interference from the military branch? Unfortunately, though Selim continually thought about such real or imagined slights, he knew he could never voice them, so he proceeded instead to welcome the Colonel with an effusive, elaborate courtesy.

'Salaam alaikum . . . 'am di'illah, Colonel . . .'

The Colonel listened to the usual succession of God-be-with-yous and other invocations to the deities while carefully adjusting the small fan on Selim's desk so that it favoured him rather than Selim. They expected that sort of thing too, he reminded himself, they really enjoyed being cast down, and now of all times it was important to behave just as usual. Was he behaving a little nervously? Selim's next words made him think he might be.

'I hope His Excellency the Secretary General had a successful mission. I believe our security arrangements for his arrival were satisfactory?' Selim made his inquiry with just a hint of directness and dissatisfaction, as though he'd suddenly become aware of a certain unusual vulnerability in the Colonel.

'Yes, Selim, they were *all right*,' the Colonel retaliated, emphasising the words so that they suggested a doubt rather than a recommendation. 'I think the car should have met His Excellency on the apron and not at the passenger exit. There's a risk—in his walking between the two, through the corridor, other passengers and so on. The press and film people in the main lobby, like chickens round a corn sack. Anything could have happened.'

'But His Excellency insists on meeting them. And the film people told me they don't have enough cable to reach the apron for their cameras—the power connections—'

'Don't they have batteries?'

'Ah, not these days I'm afraid, Colonel. As you know yourself we can get very little imported material now. And our own batteries, I'm afraid . . .' Selim shrugged his shoulders, raised both hands briefly, policing the air, and began to chatter again about the Will of God and about the lack of even the smallest comforts in Egypt today, and the Colonel nodded in agreement, thinking what a liar Selim was, knowing that he and all his more cherished friends got everything they wanted from the tax-free airport shop downstairs. When would they stop lying? the Colonel thought again. When? But then he remembered his own life-long deception and tried to think of something else. He couldn't.

How and why had Edwards met up with Yunis? This meeting was just one more query in a succession of inexplicable events which had plagued the Colonel for the past twenty-four hours, another part of the mystery, which was something he had always rigorously avoided in his work. When he sensed it he was like an animal downwind of the gun and he had to fight the panic that came over him, the need he felt to run.

Someone, for once, knew more about what was going on than he did—was arranging things behind his back, manipulating people, had *him* in his sights perhaps as well. He had to force himself to stay where he was, do nothing, behave normally. And Selim's grubby, anonymous little office was the ideal cover for his mood. He could bury himself in the idle bureaucratic chatter, use it as a camouflage. Selim's venal pursuits, which he had despised before, were part of a safe world he wanted to belong to now.

'They've recently had a very fine consignment of Japanese transistors downstairs. I've put in for one on our allowance. You might like to look at them . . . My wife wants to go to Ras el Bar for the summer . . . Hate the place myself—the girls, you know, they put the price up . . . It's impossible. Yes, I'd like to see him get promotion but his father's a complete farmer . . .'

The Colonel nodded his head and said 'Yes' and 'No' and 'Of course' and sipped his coffee. And he thought about Edwards.

Where was the trick? There must be one. What was it? The first part of the problem made sense, or might do: the message which he had received the day before from his Control in Tel Aviv: that Edwards, a British SIS man in their Mid-East section, was a KGB double and was on his way back to Moscow via Cairo, with the names of a group of Israeli intelligence men in Egypt. And the message had been crystal clear: stop him *immediately*, at the airport if possible—kill him with the utmost dispatch; the security of the entire Tel Aviv circle in Egypt depended on it.

There was a slight problem in this, of course, which Tel Aviv didn't know about: Edwards was one of his own men, an Egyptian agent, doubling in Holborn—had been for seventeen years. It was an essential part of the Colonel's cover with Egyptian Intelligence that he form his own quite separate network of people working genuinely for Cairo and that these people should never be known to Tel Aviv. It was a problem he could rise above, the Colonel thought. It was easier after all to kill someone face to face, rather than at a distance, with pills or silencers: the close approach—sighing in the man's ear, turning the knife delicately between the ribs—that was far easier. But Mohammed Yunis had got in the way of all that.

How—and why—had Edwards met up with him? the Colonel

wondered again. What purpose could they have had other than that of swapping notes? The puzzle began to fit then: Moscow would give Yunis the names of the Israeli circle in Egypt in return for his co-operation in toppling the President. With those names Yunis would be in a nearly unassailable position of power: he would be able to expose the President and his intelligence services as bumbling fools, save Egypt from dishonour and emerge as the natural successor and hero—and Soviet puppet.

It was for just such reasons that Yunis at this moment, on instructions from the President, was on his way to an unexpected appointment in Heliopolis: he had been chattering too much in Moscow already. And it was no more possible to stop him talking now than it had been to do away with the messenger who had accompanied him. The two men had taken the precaution of sticking together all the way, one protecting the other, on the plane and through the airport welcome. The only way of separating them was to risk going to Heliopolis himself, hoping that neither of them had talked yet. Edwards, after all, was his own man—with Military Intelligence, not Home Security. There was just a chance he hadn't opened his mouth about the Tel Aviv circle in Egypt. If he could get him away, he would ensure that he never did.

'Tell me, Colonel, would you like to take a look at one of these transistors? They fit in your pocket . . .'

Selim interrupted the Colonel's calculations so that he looked up and said 'Yes' before he knew what he was doing.

7

EDWARDS began to enjoy being with Yunis, not so much for his chatter about Egypt's economy—he couldn't, in fact, understand why, after so many visits to the country in the guise of journalist and the fruitless attempts to see people like Yunis for his articles, the man should suddenly now have taken an interest in him—but because he knew that as long as he stayed with him he was safe. No one was going to pick him up—or off—in the big black Mercedes with its electric windows, glass partitions and bullet-proofing.

It was a pity though, he thought, with the windows shut, in

the false air—there was not that real sense of his coming back to
the country which he always looked forward to, the sudden
overwhelming indication that he had really come home: the dry
chalky smell of baking concrete and lime dust, the sharp breath
of paraffin and rotting newspapers swirling up from the rissole
carts in the back-streets of Heliopolis which they were passing
through. Before, on every other journey, this had been the
unmistakable evidence that he'd come back into his own
world—that, and seeing Bridget again. The two had so often
gone together in the past, when she'd met him at the airport
and they'd driven back, taking the old road into the city past
the City of the Dead, to the warm cedar smell of the house in
Maadi where she lived alone.

This time she hadn't come; he hadn't told her. He was
supposed to be defecting. If only it had been as simple as that.

Yunis had been talking all the time—about Egypt's economic
problems and the price of rice and what the Arab Socialist
Union was going to do about it all if they could manage another
loan from the World Bank—and Edwards had barely heard him.

'. . . I'm afraid the economic outlook is not bright—a hard
currency crisis . . . I feel our real hope lies with Moscow.
Unfortunately they are not prepared to consider any more
barter deals. They want something better than that, nearly all
our cotton, which of course would give them a financial
stranglehold, something which the President naturally is not
prepared to consider. The canal and tourist currency . . .? No
one knows where it goes to—to the Army in some shape or
form, for sure. They get everything in Egypt nowadays. We are
in trouble . . .'

Edwards nodded his head sagely, still thinking about other
times, as if he were chatting with some knowledgeable but
boring economist from the *Financial Times* in El Vino: until he
realized that no Egyptian, least of all someone in Yunis's
position, had ever talked to him with such bluntness, and would
never do so, except for the most appalling reason.

He looked round at Yunis sharply, sensing in his words, not
the scoop that would have otherwise occurred to him, but
something dangerously candid, a frantic upset in the whole
temper of Egyptian official life, in the rigidly secretive attitudes
of Cairo officialdom with which he was so familiar.

Yunis looked at Edwards quizzically, as though he'd failed to understand something very simple, something obvious, behind his words.

'What do you mean—"*We're* in trouble"?'

Edwards was calm, but only through an effort born of long practice; the empty, windless feeling in his stomach and the sudden consciousness of sweat rising up the back of his neck giving him sure warning before his mind had told him anything.

'Just what I said. The doors are locked. I'm sure they are. They do it from the outside.'

The questions in Yunis's face disappeared in crinkly lines which spread up his cheek and over his eyes, just the beginnings of a wan smile, as though he were congratulating himself on having at last made himself clear to Edwards.

When thought flooded back a moment later it was about Williams. Why had he arranged for Yunis to pick him up? And he saw Yunis in a policeman's uniform for a second, as a London bobby in a tall black helmet: it wasn't possible. And then as the car drew in past the main gates of the Armour depot and barracks in Heliopolis and Yunis was frog-marched in front of him towards a group of old Nissen huts, he realized that Yunis was the victim, not he, that he'd just been taken along for the ride.

Certainly Edwards was more than an embarrassment to the Major who met them at the entrance of the building, which must have been exactly Yunis's intention, the partitions in the hut were far too thin to allow any immediate rough stuff to go undetected.

'Who is he?' the Major spoke abruptly in Arabic to one of a group of men in civilian clothes who had drawn up behind them in a car a few minutes afterwards. Edwards had noticed the man among the crowd of journalists who'd flocked around Yunis's car at the airport—a particularly compact, tough little man with an acid expression and tooth-brush moustache: an upright swagger—one of the President's personal security men, Edwards thought, an élite corps of some fifty or so people, most of them junior colleagues of the President during his Army days, and now his Praetorian guard.

'Well? Who is it?'

'A British journalist. We've got his papers.'

'What's his connection—with—' the Major paused, but admitted—'His Excellency?'

'I don't know.'

'Who does he work for?'

'There's no mention of any paper. Visa through the Press section of the London Embassy. He's been here often before. Arab affairs, Middle East expert . . .'

The officer looked across at Edwards with a completely blank expression, as if attempting some complex mental arithmetic which would connect Edwards with Yunis, and failing to add up the figures he became angry.

'A *journalist*? Middle East expert—but *how*? Why *here* at this moment? Explain.'

'Yunis joined him on the flight. After Munich. Wanted him along for protection. He must have known we were going to pick him up. It's obvious.'

The swagger man licked his moustache and pursed his lips aggressively, pulling his rank in Nasser's secret army; he wasn't going to be browbeaten by any mere officer in uniform.

'There was nothing to do about it. Yunis offered him a lift back to the city. We had to let him go along with him. There would have been trouble—passengers, the press—he was surrounded; we couldn't have pulled him at the airport. You knew that. And it doesn't matter. Just a freelance. They won't be looking for him in London. We can keep him. We'll have to.'

Edwards looked across to where Yunis was standing by the opposite wall, between two officers, his neat black briefcase by his feet, mopping his face, still holding a copy of the *Economist* under his arm like any weary stockbroker waiting for the 5:25 at Waterloo. A weary but somehow contented man as he returned Edwards's look with another of his brief miniature smiles.

Behind him was a window and through it Edwards could see a group of soldiers in singlets and black underpants playing soccer in the first coolness of the day and some others hanging up their laundry and boxing each other good-naturedly about the ears. It was evening and in another half hour it would be quite dark with stars, and Edwards longed with sharpness for the bath and the terraced room smelling of hot plaster looking out over the river in the Semiramis, and the meal on the roof

restaurant later on, at one of the small tables with their
Edwardian lamps next to the parapet: the first taste again,
which he missed even after a few weeks, of the spongy flat
bread, the moist tartness of the local cheese which he ordered
specially, and the purple Omar Khayyam from Gianaclis's
vineyards outside Alexandria—wanted it sharply, for he knew it
wasn't going to happen that night and, like sex, he wanted it
then, right away.

He thought how he'd tailored his pleasures in life to the few
he knew without question he could always have, to unadventur-
ous things he could rely on: not happiness or girls in night clubs
or the long-awaited letter. He'd accepted long ago that these
things didn't work: the letter never came, the girl had someone
else. And it was happiness enough just to know that these things
were so, to be sure of them.

The intense flavour of certain tastes and places—and the
feeling of ease in a strange land, these were the diversions he'd
come to take for granted, which depended on him alone, which
were really his life, and he cursed again the profession which
had encouraged such dilettante pursuits in him over the years
and had now, just as haphazardly, withdrawn them.

His mouth was dry and salty and he felt dizzy as if he'd
swum a long way without pleasure. He began to wonder what
role he should play now and the thought made him feel sick. But
when he spoke it was with bruised conviction, an actor coming
midway into the lines of an old and well-remembered character.

'Do you think I might have a drink of water?' His tone was
pompous and old-fashioned and very English, jumping a class
into the outraged accents of someone who believed wogs began
at Dover and had never known another tongue. It was as well to
preserve that fiction as long as possible. The Major turned from
the doorway and gestured to the man next to Yunis.

'Take him.' Yunis was led away down a corridor.

'I'm sorry. There has been a mistake. Come.' The Major
pointed to a seat in his own room, without ceremony or
abruptness, but mystified, thinking.

'A mistake . . .' He pushed a bell on his desk.

'That's what *I* was going to say. You've taken the words out
of my mouth.'

'I don't understand . . .?'

And he didn't, Edwards thought. He was dealing with a senior man. He'd used the colloquialism intentionally, to see where he stood, to gauge the officer's importance in Egyptian military security. One could place a man in this hierarchy almost exactly by his knowledge of English. Knowing too much of that or any foreign language had always been regarded with the greatest misgivings in their service. It dated from the time of Nasser's original *coup de palais* against Farouk when almost everyone concerned had been junior officers who had never had the opportunity of learning a second language, and in the security divisions at least this linguistic frailty had since been encouraged; it was thought to be a guarantee against outside infiltration or influence while at the same time it had made Cairo a haven for every sort of penetration. Egyptian security there—eavesdropping or interrogating—often didn't really understand what their target was saying.

'You would like a Coke or some coffee?'

'I'd like to know what I'm doing here.'

'I'm sorry. You ask for something to drink. That will come now. But no questions. You must wait for some—for another man before you ask questions. There has been a mistake.'

He repeated the phrase as if his future safety depended on the words being fully understood.

They left him alone in the office with a warm Coca-Cola. Edwards swallowed a mouthful and then rubbed the lip of the bottle carefully with his cuff.

Colonel Hamdy, out of his linen suit and in uniform now, came into the room an hour later. He smiled at Edwards and glanced at the three empty Coke bottles on the desk.

'You're drinking too much, Henry. Relax.'

8

'MARLOW'S coming at three. You've seen his preliminary report? Rather cagey, I thought. How close was he with Edwards?'

Williams sat down and looked at Marcus through his 'In' tray. There was nothing there; it was just after nine o'clock and none

of the secretaries had arrived. He and Marcus had come from
breakfast at Carlton Gardens.

'They were close—very close as far as I can gather. It was
when Crowther was Principal Officer in the Cairo circle, so one
can't be too sure about anything. The files are very skimpy over
that period. But they were close, certainly. That's one of the
essential factors in the operation after all.'

'Homosexual?' Williams inquired brightly.

'No. Marlow was married at our Consulate in 1958. Apparently it was part of some deal we arranged—to get him to work
for us. It gave us a lever. His wife was with us too at the time as
a stringer. She'd been Edwards's mistress—and that was part of
the deal we had with him. Edwards said she was necessary cover
for him—he was a real whore-master then. As well as everything
else. But the woman did a good job, as far as one can tell from
the files. The marriage broke up, dissolved some years later, and
Marlow was put on the strength in London. Recommendation
from the Cairo Resident. Marlow seems a decent enough fellow,
quiet, fall guy material I suppose, though even so there's a
chance he may not go along with all this.'

Williams looked at Marcus walking in and out of the morning
light that flooded through the bright shaft from the half-drawn
curtains.

'He'll agree. He's agreed to everything here in the past eight
years, as long as I've known him. Civil servant material—the
same as "fall guy" material, as you put it. A good fellow,
certainly—and very good on those Arabic rags too. I'll be sorry
if I have to lose him. But he'll agree all right. It will be a matter
of honour for him. He'll want to prove something—either my
stupidity or his friendship for Edwards. Or both. He's a reliable
fellow.'

Marcus nodded, privately unconvinced, and walked across to
the window which looked over the car park at the back of the
building. Cars were popping in through the control gate, one
after the other, stopping and starting at the barrier with hideous
regularity, as though automated and not driven. On-the-dot,
conscientious people in little Heralds and Minis, twenty-nine
miles an hour all the way in from Croydon and Barnet with
their mild tweed jackets and a copy of last week's *Sunday
Express* in the rear window. Yet in half an hour they would be

sorting cables in the cypher room, decoding reports from the field, culling through the Beirut and Cairo pouches, handling people's lives—and Marcus's reputation.

They looked so very safe and dedicated and English, Marcus thought. And stupid. But one such person had been Philby, a second Blake, another Edwards. And perhaps Marlow? Williams was too beguiled by him, too soft. Marlow was so ordinary it worried Marcus. And it crossed his mind if, in these stringent days, a certain degree of flamboyance in a spy might not be a better guarantee of security and trust—rather than the anonymous characteristics of these people who locked their cars in a top security area and streamed in through the back of the building with such an air of probity and dedication. You couldn't tell a thing from their faces. It made Marcus uneasy.

Still, with Edwards, there would be an object lesson for them all at last. He would never again have to doubt those inscrutable morning faces. Edwards's total demise would put an end to it all, make up for it all: there would be no dacha in Moscow or forty-two years in the Scrubs for him; the deceits and betrayals of the past, the good men in so many sectors who had simply disappeared and the rest who were nursing ruined careers on cut pensions in small houses in Sussex.

Marcus thought about their various fates with an overwhelming righteousness, as though in multiplying the pity he brought to bear on their individual misfortunes he could justify his own insensate vehemence in the matter of defectors and double agents.

He knew Williams didn't share his vindictiveness, indeed that he was far more concerned with his own rider to the plan of disposing of Edwards. He wanted to use Edwards before he 'disappeared' whereas Marcus just wanted to see him dead— something which he could no longer arrange for him through any British court. And he saw just a chance that in being tied in with Williams's scheme Edwards might get away. That was the flaw in the plan—simply that there were *two* plans. Edwards was being given an alternative, albeit an impossibly dangerous one, which Marcus would never have allowed him: a narrow exit which, if he were foolish enough to take it, could get him clear of them.

Marcus's plan for him had been straightforward enough:

Edwards had gone to Cairo and his own department had already blown him to Israeli Intelligence in Tel Aviv as the Russian agent he was. They had said he was on his way there with the names of a group of Israeli Intelligence men stationed in Egypt—names that he had picked up in the course of his work for Holborn—and that he was about to pass this information on to Egyptian Security before beating it back to Moscow. On this impeccable advice Tel Aviv's men in Cairo would pick Edwards up at the airport—or the moment he got to his hotel—and kill him. The Israelis were tough about that sort of thing. Necessarily tough. Unlike Williams.

The operation had every chance of success—until Williams had imposed what seemed to Marcus a quite unnecessary handicap to the scheme: the ostensible purpose which Edwards had been given for going to Egypt was to contact Mohammed Yunis and stir revolution within the Arab Socialist Union. Williams had justified this as a 'necessary *reason*' for sending him to Cairo, without which he would immediately suspect something. Marcus, on the other hand, had argued that Edwards went to Cairo every few months in any case, as a matter of routine—and wasn't that sufficient reason in this case? But he had been unable to dissuade Williams.

Why had Williams wanted to jeopardise the plan? For that's what it amounted to, Marcus decided. Was he getting too old for the job, too cautious, past making an unequivocal decision, intent always on creating innumerable 'standbys' and 'provisos'? Was that it? And if not was it possible that somehow, for some reason, Williams *wanted* Edwards to have a get out, wanted to warn him that the whole affair was a trap by offering him the clearly impractical idea of subverting Yunis? And who would *want* to let Edwards off the hook? Unless, like Edwards, he worked for Moscow?

It was a quarter past nine. Someone opened the door in the next room and the two men looked up, almost apprehensively, and then continued talking, but in lower, more careful tones, like conspirators. But were they both involved in the same conspiracy? Marcus wondered.

'Edwards may break,' Marcus said. 'I mean not *after* the Israelis get him—but before. I can't believe that anyone with his experience of the area would fall for that plan about contacting Yunis. And if Edwards has any suspicions don't you think he'll run the moment he hits Cairo? Or before—on the way. He'll know we've cooked something up for him. A trap.'

Williams knew that this was perfectly true, just as he'd known long before anyone else that Edwards was a double, working with Moscow. He'd realized it finally when, out of the forty or so British agents in the Middle East whom Blake had shopped, only Edwards and half a dozen other minor figures had remained with their cover intact.

All had been well until Marcus had been moved from the Scottish Office and appointed as an internal watchdog by the new Minister to look into the whole question of security in the Middle East section—from then on the sands had begun to shift awkwardly.

Marcus had got to the point about Edwards with uncomfortable rapidity. He'd hit on the fact that Edwards's cover had been left intact after Blake had shopped everyone else, he'd combed his files, turned his life inside out, grilled Crowther in retirement. He just couldn't accept that Blake could have overlooked one of their key men in the Middle East section— and he'd been right.

Petnicki, the defector the Americans had got hold of a month before, had confirmed it all. And Williams had been unable to do anything about it—except ensure that Marcus's investigations didn't percolate up to him, and try to get Edwards out of the way, which he couldn't do directly, or through Moscow, since he'd cut every contact with them once Marcus had begun his ferreting. As far as Moscow was concerned Williams was 'buried' for the time being, which meant he didn't exist for them, was not to approach them in any way, warn them, or tell them anything. That was the arrangement. It was his only chance of keeping his cover intact. After Philby and his two friends, whom he'd recruited in the early 'thirties—and then Blake and now Edwards—he was the last, the most important man left in the Citadel. It wasn't a question now of being caught without a chair when the music stopped; he couldn't afford to play the game any more at all. It was a matter of sitting tight and never taking one's eyes off the orchestra.

He looked at Marcus firmly. 'Edwards may run. But if he does they'll be with him. The Israelis were going to have a man at the airport.'

'But the whole *idea* of his contacting Yunis—it seems to me an excellent way of warning him—no? If he has any sense, and he has, he won't go near Yunis and he'll know something's up. We should have had him in the Scrubs by now, with another forty-two years, and not given him the chance, however slight, of getting back to Moscow.'

Williams smiled slightly and created a sigh. 'Forty-two years doesn't seem to do much good. They don't seem to last the pace these days. And the hanging judges have all gone. This is the way to do it. Edwards won't be many days on the Nile—and he'll never see Moscow. The Yunis alternative is perfectly sound—perfectly in order.'

Williams lied comfortably, a slow pensive authority in his voice—the voice and the authority born of many years dealing with over-conscientious, pushy subordinates—underlining his real knowledge of Middle Eastern affairs which he knew Marcus, for all his other skills, didn't possess. He'd been involved with the Scottish Office for too long and in negotiating that devious terrain he had found little time for any wider geography.

'We've gone over it all. Goodness me. And Edwards is already there. We've talked it out together, you should have voiced your doubts at the time.'

'I suppose so. I wasn't so familiar with UAR affairs then. But it's clear enough now to me. We're *warning* Edwards . . .'

Marcus looked directly at Williams for the first time that morning: a sad look, the small blue eyes admitting failure for a moment, Williams thought. Or were they questioning him, connecting him directly with this idea that Edwards had been warned?

For that had been exactly his intention—to alert Edwards. He hoped what he'd done would be sufficient, that Edwards would get himself safely to Moscow. He would leave the Cairo flight somewhere along the line, at Rome, or more likely at Munich where he could slip into Berlin, contact the Resident there, cross over into the East city and on to Moscow. And that would be the end of it all; Edwards would go home; he would never get near the Israelis at Cairo Airport, let alone Mohammed Yunis. Without any direct contact, Williams would get him out of the way under Marcus's nose. The message and the warning would be implicit in his directions to contact Yunis and infiltrate his Union—for nothing could be more obviously suicidal: he was waving red flags all down the line at Edwards. He couldn't fail to notice them.

After all, thought Williams, if he put himself in Edwards's position, as he'd often done recently . . . it was surprisingly easy, professionally they were the same sort of men. And Williams reminded himself once again of how many professional characteristics they must share: the development to a fine pitch of all those senses beyond the fifth—those which created confidence and attracted luck in the worst corners, the others which warned or encouraged, pushed or stalled one, at just the right moment, so that even in the most hazy circumstances where logic was useless, one felt impelled towards the right decision. Thus equipped it was possible to survive indefinitely in two worlds, for these added dimensions of the deeply committed liar, like any gift of genius, had the effect of creating a patina of trust around one which the merely honest rarely possessed.

In these circumstances one paid court to the dissembler and mistrusted steady virtue. A licence for deceit was like cut garlic in one's pocket: one stank of belief.

And Edwards must still have all these gifts, Williams thought. He would not have lost them—the confidence and the skills and the early warning systems born of a lifetime's necessary disloyalty would now be more acute than ever: Edwards would run for his life. There was little to worry about there.

But there was Marlow to think about; the other half of the plan called MOUSE: the official Holborn plan which would now have to be put into operation when they met Marlow that afternoon. He was an important lever in the machine: if Israeli Intelligence in Cairo, once they got hold of Edwards, were to believe that he was a genuine Soviet defector and not just a plant, London would have to appear much more concerned at his loss; someone from the Holborn section would have to be sent chasing him, to try and stop him before he got over to the other side: a bona fide spy-catcher, a warranty of the goods being supplied; Marlow was to be that man.

Of course, it would never come to that, Williams realized; since Edwards would surely never get to Cairo Marlow would never be needed to guarantee him in this way as a defector: certainly not; Marlow's visit to Cairo would be for another purpose altogether, something which Williams had planned and arranged long before with Moscow.

Suez had given him the idea; Eden's muddled 'collusion'— they would do it properly this time: a scheme for Moscow which would once and for all bring about a complete Soviet grip on the Middle East: the subversion of the Nasser regime by creating a war for them against Israel, which they would necessarily lose and which would subsequently allow for a massive Soviet military and political build-up in Egypt, which in turn would lead to their virtual control of the country and the other Arab satellites—a position Moscow would never achieve as long as Nasser remained in power.

The steady, honest, loyal Marlow was to be the man who took the fall here, the 'plant' who carried the virus, the British agent dealing with Israel, to be unmasked by Egyptian security in Cairo with a secret memorandum, a forged copy of an Israeli Ministry of Defence document from the Chief of Staff General Rabin to General Elazar, Commander Northern Front, outlining details for an advance on the Syrian border—troop dispositions, attack schedules, primary targets—orders, in fact, for an Israeli preemptive strike against Syria.

With a message of this sort, found on a genuine British agent, Nasser would have his MiG's and Sochi bombers over Tel Aviv within forty-eight hours, and Israel would have shot them out of the sky and been on the canal by the end of the week.

The Moscow Resident's department in London had had Marlow under surveillance for some time and as soon as he packed his bags for Cairo their plan with him would come into operation: the hidden document which Egyptian Security would 'find'—on a tip-off from Moscow.

Williams had chosen Marlow as the carrier of this virus because he had initially agreed to his recruitment into the service, years before, for just such an eventuality as this. Every Intelligence Department needed people like Marlow on hand— men in whom nothing had been invested and whose account could only show a profit when it was closed. And that, after all, was the proper use—the only positive justification—for an intelligence service, Williams thought: to make war for a country that didn't want one, and couldn't win it, in order to bring on better times . . .

Marcus turned away from the window, sat down and stretched himself amiably, easing his muscles, tilting his head back, in a happy cruciform.

'You're right. There's no real warning for Edwards in the Yunis plan. It's reasonable—or as reasonable as some of the other schemes I've come across in the files here. It takes time to accustom oneself, that's all—from the Highland Development Authority to Cairo back alleys—it's a different sort of intrigue. It was just a thought about Yunis.'

Williams suspected the intrigue was probably identical.

'We've all had too many second thoughts. The ones we started with are all right. You can depend on it. Let's get some coffee. The trolley must be about by now.'

Williams got up, looked into the still empty room next door, and went now to the window, pulling the last bit of curtain back firmly to the edge of the casement. The secretaries were flocking in through the back entrance—Navy Recruitment used the front one—and he looked at the bobbing scarves and heard the click-clack of small feet beating on the concrete like a football rattle and found that he could no longer interpret what his senses told him about the view in any meaningful way. Abruptly, there was no *name* which he could give to what he saw; the idea that the 'things' crossing the car park could be described as 'women' or 'secretaries' or by any other word was ludicrous. It was like looking at a fork for so long that it lost its identity, its forkiness. It sometimes happened to him, this: it was a rapid sensation, hardly more than seconds, like brief concussion, during which everything lay suspended.

But as soon as he managed to put words back to his vision—'those are the secretaries in scarves and stilettoes arriving for work'—he knew that Marcus was lying. That querulous Scottish logic of his that had eased up so many stones in his department, smashing the insects, had now suddenly disappeared. He had not climbed down in the face of Williams's explanations about Yunis, he had argued all the way and had then suddenly fallen headlong backwards. He had accepted everything, given up the questions.

'Of course there's no warning implicit in Edwards's directions to contact Yunis. Of course not. It was sound thinking, so that he won't suspect his trip has any other motive ...' Marcus might as well have said the words there and then, Williams thought, sitting back, arms triangled behind his head, like someone who has at last seen the light in an argument and taken pleasure in the admission. Williams had been prepared to argue the case for subverting Yunis—as he had done, convincingly, in the face of persistent arguments against the plan from Marcus. He was not now prepared to accept the man's capitulation. There was something completely out of character in it.

And that was what disturbed Williams: the break in the logic, in the slow precise meanderings which had always before got Marcus out of the maze and into the truth; Marcus had broken off too soon. Now there was a real threat to his own long sense of security in his cover in Holborn; he could feel it, like a proffered knife. He had come to depend so much for his safety on intuition, on the sense which he had developed which monitored every detail of his work and office routine: the low-grade memos and files he was passed and the others he received on a strictly limited circulation: a new secretary in the next office but one, a different messenger in the corridor, a click at the wrong time on an outside call: he had come to assess all the minute paraphernalia of his work as a single picture, which he glanced at every hour of the day, and which, if it changed even in the smallest detail, like a degree on a barometer, alerted him like a gun blast. He had been safe for so long; the picture had remained exactly the same for thirty-five years. And now Marcus had turned it upside down, in seconds, while his back was turned.

He knew now that Marcus had finally agreed with him because in some way he *had* seen the light; he had seen exactly what was going to happen: Edwards *was* going to give them the slip. He would never get near Cairo—or make contact with Mohammed Yunis; that ridiculous rider to the plan would warn him and he'd run for Moscow long beforehand: Marcus had seen all that. And the next thing Marcus would see, or confirm—how long had he?—days or hours?—was that the man who had carefully rigged this red light for Edwards was himself.

Williams looked out at the last of the girls, a few tall stragglers in silk scarves and twin sets, crossing the rear car park; the 'better class' of girl who still lived with Mummy and Daddy in Tunbridge Wells and never made it on time. Marcus was on to him—or dead set in the right direction for him at least; there was no doubt about that. His ordinary senses had failed a minute before, like that passage of time on a train ferry when the carriages pass from one gauge to another, but he had come now into full possession of those other senses, every one beyond the fifth—the ones which warned one, at just the right moment, so that even in the most hazy circumstances where logic was useless, one felt impelled towards the right decision . . .

A woman knocked and came into the room.

'Morning, Rosalie. Two coffees, please. Both with. And sugar.'

He would have to break cover, contact Moscow. There was nothing else for it. It was not Marlow now who had to be dispensed with, it was Marcus. And there weren't many ways to do that, without inviting more suspicion upon himself. It wasn't going to be easy. Yet in thinking of Marlow he had the clue already, saw a way out.

Marcus—the lawyer, the interrogator, the counter-intelligence expert; the wily Scotsman who missed nothing, the Russian speaker who'd been the terror of every Soviet trawler skipper in the North Sea when he'd been in the Scottish Office: very well then; he would secure for him a quarry worthy of his talents, somebody possibly even more important than himself: an investigation that would result in his going under for a long time.

Williams left the office at exactly his usual time that evening. His two meetings earlier with Marlow had passed satisfactorily. The man had voiced a number of perfectly reasonable doubts about the scheme to 'look for' Edwards, and he had seemed to think that Edwards was in Cairo already, without actually being *told* that this was so, but otherwise there had been few bad moments. Marlow was a loyal fellow. If only it went as sweetly with Marcus, Williams thought.

He had always walked some distance from the office, before catching a bus or tube to the King's Road—always had a drink at any one of a number of different pubs on the way and gone on to buy an evening paper from an equal variety of news stands. It was a haphazard wandering which he had built into his routine years before—a proviso for just such an occasion as this, when he had to make contact: if he was already under surveillance he would be doing no more than he did every night, going in and out of various pubs, crossing from the saloon to the public. But tonight he would do much more—getting on to the Waterloo tube at the last possible moment, getting off and coming back to where he started, on to the street again, walking, then the same process on the Central line to Oxford Circus, engrossed in his paper, jumping off just as the doors were closing, waiting on the stairway for any footsteps behind him.

He was tired an hour later, his back against the sweaty phone box in the ticket concourse upstairs, the last of the rush hour crowds swarming past him.

'Mills here. Who's speaking?'

Williams had almost forgotten the Cockney-Jewish, White-chapel Road voice. It wasn't the sort of mixture one heard often nowadays, with its echoes of a Russian émigré past in the East End, so that the 'Mills', in the way he pronounced his name, became 'Meals'—which wasn't, of course, his name at all.

Williams gave his code phrase by way of reply and asked for an urgent meeting. They wasted no words on the phone.

'Come to the office then; the usual routine.'

Williams had a whisky in the bar of the Grosvenor House Hotel, left a second one unfinished, went to the gents and from there to the penthouse elevators at the rear of the hotel. He turned his back to them, pretending to look for someone, waiting for an empty car. He got off a floor below and walked up.

Mills opened the door. He was in his sixties and had the rouged and toupéed features of a man who had tried and failed to escape from the mould which nature had cast him in: that of a caricature Jew—a large nose, bulbous and hooked, wide forehead and narrowing chin, hooded eyes close together: a Disraeli from a nineteenth-century cartoon who had done his best to iron out the trade marks of his ancestry. He looked now slightly rubbery and false, like a half finished wax-work or an idea in the make-up department for a horror film. He has survived, Williams thought, because he looks so obviously devious.

But there was nothing the least shifty in his manner. He had a busy, straightforward, almost overbearing attitude, like a man who had little time to spare and took salad and a glass of milk for his lunch.

Mills ran a small film company from the office—('Marlborough Films—a ring of confidence, don't you think?')—and there was recommendation from the Cork Film Festival on the wall behind his desk—'Carrot and Donkey' it had been called, a documentary about a red-headed child in Connemara. Williams had seen it once in the King's Road Odeon. It had been better than the feature.

They sat together on a sofa under Cocteau's poster for the Edinburgh Festival.

'There's some soda water in the fridge?'

'Without for me.'

They drank their whisky in large Waterford glass tumblers (another award from Cork) and Mills listened to Williams's story of his meeting with Marcus that morning.

'Well, what do you suggest then?' Mills looked upset, as though he were being put upon unnecessarily. 'A fast car going down his street? We can't risk that sort of "incident"—doing in your deputy. It would certainly find its way back to us, and *you*. And kidnapping, you surely don't—'

'No, of course not—'

'We can't really do *anything* to him here without risking more suspicion falling on you. He'll almost certainly start voicing his theories about you—'

'That's the whole point. I want to arrange for someone else altogether to settle him—before he makes his mind up about me. I want you to bait him. Listen: he's a lawyer, his reputation is as an interrogator; counter-intelligence—that's his métier in our section: quizzing possible doubles, defectors: ferreting. That's what he was brought in for. Now I want you to get Moscow to lay on a defector for him—in Cairo. Urgently. And someone important, not some station slogger. Someone he'll want to go for. Get the man to ask for asylum at the British Consulate in Garden City. They'll contact the Chief of Service here and he'll ask for Marcus to go to Cairo to check the man out. That's his job. Our Mid-East section would have to deal with that sort of thing in any case. I won't appear to have had anything to do with it.'

'And how will that silence him?' Mills sniffed and pulled his nose, quickly and vigorously between thumb and forefinger, as though intent on plucking it away from his face without his or anyone else's noticing.

'Marcus won't ever get to the Consulate. He'll be carrying the goods we've arranged for Marlow. We just change the two of them around: the word from Moscow to Egyptian Intelligence will be *Marcus*, not Marlow. Marcus will be carrying the memorandum instead; I'll see to that. I expect he'll get fifteen years for his trouble. Marlow we just leave to look around Cairo for Edwards, as planned; we don't break him to the Egyptians. As for Edwards, he should have come home by now. Has there been any word?'

'No. But I wouldn't have heard yet in any case.'

'Well, get over to the Embassy straight away. Line up your defector in Cairo, have him approach the Consulate at once, and wait till I call you to say Marcus is on the way. Then bounce him to Egyptian security there. That should be in two—three days at most, if you work fast.'

Mills was worried. He didn't like Williams and he cared less for his plan. But there was nothing he could do about it. Williams outranked him; he was the man at the top of the pile in London, the one they could never afford to lose; and certainly he didn't want to be the man responsible for that: all the others who'd been lost to them over the years had been pawns by comparison to this queen.

'Right then. I've been here too long already.'

'I'll have to clear this with the Colonel here. Vorishil—'

'Clear it with the Politburo—if you think you've got that sort of time. But *do it*; otherwise I'll have to break—*now*. Moscow won't like that. And there's no reason for it: Marcus *suspects* at the moment, he may have me under surveillance, that's all. He'll be working on it—and me—for the next few days. He'll want to be sure, absolutely sure, before he comes out and says anything, before there's any serious investigation. So we have that time, we have forty-eight hours start on him, at least. Make the bait ripe enough—and he'll go for it. I can guarantee it. Take his mind off me: give him a real peach to get his teeth into. And by the way, don't swamp the air waves on the Moscow circuit up at the Embassy—that's how they first got on to Philby. No arguments, no long correspondence with mother—just *one* message, help you to make it all the sharper.'

Williams avoided the lifts, walked down the stairs and back into the gents on the ground floor next to the bar. He tidied himself a little and then returned to finish his whisky. He'd been gone more than five minutes. Too long, but he was sure no one had got near to following him, even if they had already started to tail him. It would have been almost impossible to pick him up in the crowded bar and lobby in any case—if they'd ever got that far: the place was full of stuffed shirts for some ball, in scarlet cummerbunds, lowering quick brandies while their women prepared themselves in the ladies' cloaks.

. Williams envied their vulgar ease, their next few irresponsible hours, before he decided he might as well match it. He ordered himself a third whisky, an expensive Malt which he took neat. He didn't want to go back to Flood Street. Not yet. For the moment, like a child playing truant, he felt safety lay in luxury, anonymity, distance—being far from school, leaning over the rim of a Knickerbocker Glory.

Then he went home, walking briskly across the evening park, glancing at the pickups—an exaggerated blonde on a bench—an exotic flower in the night; the commoner strolling troopers looking for beer money and a bed till reveille—inspected them professionally with perfectly concealed interest. Yes, but not now. Not yet.

He poured a small glass of sherry for his mother. He couldn't bear the stuff, even the smell of it; yet he'd liked it long ago. Something to do with his father? Another way of getting at him? The locked tantalus in the Thames Valley library; the butler had a second key and they'd taken gulps at it together; another conspiracy, not long after the Russian doll. Or was it just that, with age, one required the ultimate refinement of the grape: fine, mellowed brandy? Williams amused himself with these sybaritic reflections on long-ago tastes and present passions—fiddling with memory, the panorama of his life, to no purpose—like an idle man on a pin-ball machine: dabbing in the shallows of thought.

He'd done his thinking for that day, he decided, come clear of the dangerous passages. Now it was time to merge into the background again. You had to know when to switch off. He'd have a drink round the corner in the Wellington: there was a new Guards battalion in town and rumour of two Swedish frigates on a courtesy visit just berthed below Tower Bridge . . .

The great thing to remember, he thought, if they were on to you, was to keep the pattern—exactly; no panic, do the things you'd always done, stick to type. That was what saved you. When the others lost their heads, broke faith and started running for the night ferry—you just carried on as you'd always done, doing the obvious thing. And then, if they were looking for you, they looked right through you. They never saw you at all.

9

COLONEL Hamdy shook hands with Edwards and then took a seat next to him on one side of the desk. Major Amin, who had first questioned Edwards, joined them.

'I am sorry, Mr. Edwards. An unfortunate mistake.' The Major spoke in Arabic. Edwards sighed, ruffling back his hair. Fine. He'd have to have the ritual cup of coffee with them and then he'd be on his way.

'I'd no idea you were with us,' the Major continued, 'until Colonel Hamdy told me. I'm with Home Security as you've probably realized. We don't always know what our Foreign section are up to. My apologies.'

Colonel Hamdy nodded a happy confirmation of this, eased himself in his chair.

'How are you, Henry? I didn't expect you back so soon. What have they sent you on?'

Edwards looked at the other officer.

'Go ahead. You can speak quite freely.'

'Well, I don't know what's going on with Mohammed Yunis. The thing is that I was sent out to make contact with him. We met on the plane quite by chance . . .'

The two men seemed to look at him more closely than they listened, as though his face might give them more of a clue to what had been going on than his words, which already sounded hollow and unconvincing.

'I was to approach Yunis, sound him out on his real views about the President and the possibility of my section infiltrating his Union—the idea was to form a fifth column around Marxist dissidents in the UAR—'

'With the idea of overthrowing the President?'

'Yes. Though of course it hadn't got beyond the early stages—of finding out what way Yunis might go. That was my job. A wild idea, I thought. But I had to pretend to go along with it. I'd no intention of contacting Yunis. As I said, it was quite by chance. He got on at Munich and took a seat next to me. What have you picked him up for?'

'He's been chattering, talking with Moscow, making "unauthorized arrangements".' The Colonel looked at Edwards closely. 'After what you've said about being *told* to contact him, you don't really expect me to believe you met him quite by chance on that plane, do you? The two of you seem to have been involved in exactly the same scheme—an ASU takeover here, a Moscow puppet government.'

'How could Holborn be involved with *Moscow* in a plan like that?'

'Because they see things the same way over this. East and West—they'd both like to see Nasser fall. Their interests are identical there. Another bit of collusion, I'd say. You'd better think up a stronger reason than coincidence, Henry. What were you *really* doing on that plane with Yunis? Oughtn't we to talk about it?'

He glared at Henry, and then at the Major. Getting Edwards away from him was like taking sweets off a child.

They drove to the new Military Hospital outside Cairo on the Nile road that led to Maadi. Colonel Hamdy sat in front, half turned towards Edwards, his arm stretched behind the driver's back.

'Why the Hospital, Hamdy? What's the point? Truth drugs or something? I've told you the truth already.'

The Colonel looked out into the darkness, at the yellow light flickering here and there on the water from small fires built in the sterns of feluccas going southwards, their huge lateen sails just visible against the sky as they moved with infinite slowness upstream.

'This isn't a matter for the ordinary police, or Home Security. It's just between us for the moment.'

They pulled round to the back of the main hospital building and walked away from it to a group of smaller, half-finished buildings which ran down in two lines to one of the many irrigation canals which drained the area: a flat landscape of berseem fields and market vegetables, as far as Edwards could make out, a mile or two before Maadi, laid out beneath the white pile of the Mokattam Hills just visible with the lights of the Casino high up in the far background. Edwards knew exactly where he was; the canal almost certainly was the one that followed the Bab el Luk–Helwan railway, which went past the station at Maadi, bordered the playing fields at Albert College and dipped round half a mile to the west of Bridget's house.

Edwards and the Colonel went inside one of the new buildings, with light flexes hanging out of the plaster and a smell of limewash everywhere. Two expensively dressed men in the hallway stood up, led them to a room more finished than the others (they'd already managed a photograph of the President on one wall) and coffees were ordered.

'Well, you're out of Major Amin's tender care. Now, tell me, what *did* Williams send you here for?'

'To see if Yunis would jump. I've *told* you, for God's sake. A mad idea. I knew Williams was on to me—'

'But if he was on to you, he'd hardly have let you go like that, straight back to your friends. Unless he wanted to be *rid* of you—I mean, dispose of you, kill you—if, as you say, he'd found out you were really working for us. That doesn't make any sense.'

'Perhaps he expected somebody else to get rid of me. The Israelis perhaps. He could have blown me to the Israelis—they have their men in Cairo after all. They'd have willingly done the job for him—if he'd told them I had their names here or something.'

'So, what happened?'

'I met Yunis, of course—or rather, he met me, latched on to me as a kind of hostage, arranged to stick with me all the way: on the plane, at the airport, then the bullet-proof car to Heliopolis. They haven't had a chance to get me yet.'

The Colonel nodded his head, thinking how exactly that had been the plan. Edwards had been the target all right; the Holborn defector with the names of his circle in Egypt, the tip-off he'd had from Tel Aviv. And he was playing it well now, suggesting the truth in the most off-hand way imaginable so that it would appear entirely unlikely. He still had those names and even if his involvement with Yunis had been pure coincidence, it meant simply that the names were for someone else.

Perhaps Edwards, staring with such a bewildered look across the table at him now, had his own name, trembling for utterance on his lips. And then again, the Colonel thought, perhaps he's given Yunis my name already. One should always assume the worst in this business. And the immediate corollary was that he should get clear at all costs, this instant, run for his life out of Egypt.

And then he knew what had been in the back of his mind all the time, what he hadn't been facing: he didn't *want* to leave Egypt, and the logic of that followed equally quickly: he was a bad double. Tel Aviv wasn't getting value any more, the goods they'd agreed on years before were shoddy now, not the same quality. He hadn't changed sides; he hadn't betrayed Israel, he just wasn't really interested in it any more and he felt he'd only managed to betray himself with any real skill over the years.

It simply hadn't been worth it, he thought. In his sort of work you had to have an anvil of belief—in a people better than others, in one country above another, in a first idea against a second. But one could lose faith in a country like a dripping tap and find the tank quite empty one morning. Whatever was fine in it hadn't helped you—as an exile, living outside its borders, its spirit hadn't come across to make one day better than another; the days had got worse and you knew the land you worked for wasn't in your bones.

He'd worked for the British, as an intelligence officer attached to the Eighth Army. He was Jewish, he'd been born in Egypt and after the war he had worked for the Israelis. But he'd spent his life in Egypt and had never ceased to enjoy the place: the people and the river, the remains of so many empires, so much crumbling thought. He'd liked it better, far better, than the few glimpses he'd had of his own adopted country—which he remembered mostly as a new and raw place, full of emptiness and ambition. The land had reeked of fresh concrete: the fine grey powder blew everywhere around the new buildings. It grated against one's hands when one washed them and left a tide mark round everything. It was uncomfortable and disconcerting, like a pair of spectacles worn for the first time.

He believed in his own people all right, in their belief and their suffering, but he enjoyed the other things, in Egypt; he loved them, he realized—why pretend otherwise?

The whole business was a bad book about history. Belief required something better than an ideal, or a story they made up about you after you were dead. It was the drink before lunch with friends—something in that direction at least. It was a selfish, deprecating thing—not this crushing self-importance which was the only return he had got from the necessarily secret nature of his work—work which he knew now was simply a foil against loneliness. It was better not to be lonely, if it was at all possible to do anything about it, he thought.

'How did you leave things with London—what about the others in your section? They'll be wondering about you. Marcus for example, the new man you told me about. No one else knew of course—that you were coming here—besides Williams?'

'No. Not as far as I know. I only dealt with Williams.'

'No friends . . .? The grocer—the milkman? You still have your milk delivered in England, don't you?'

'I buy it from the corner shop—and cream, for horseradish sauce. You know all about that too, I suppose . . .'

'Nobody? You were just going to leave London forever—and you told nobody?'

'What are you getting at? You mean I'd have risked telling someone in the face of an "overwhelming temptation"—wanting to leave some memorial behind me?'

'That sort of temptation goes with a bad conscience, after all. Let's get back to the beginning—you may have run too soon. That's what I'm getting at. It's possible Williams wasn't on to you at all.'

'Of course he was. You know the Yunis plan would never have worked. It was a trap.'

'So you were going to "retire"—come home to Mama? You were *running* surely? Isn't that all?'

'Not running away. I was running towards something.'

'Here—in Egypt?'

'Yes.'

'Your friends are all here, you mean—and there's nobody in London that would miss you. You reckoned on just walking out of that life as if it had never existed?'

'People tire of their jobs, you know. Others in the London section talked about it. About getting out. It's a fiction—that bit about never being able to leave work like this. I talked with Marlow about it the other day, said he ought to get out, that the whole thing was a toytown.'

'You what?'

'A toytown—a pretence—for children.'

'No, you talked *to* someone. Who did you say—?'

'Marlow—you remember Marlow. He's in Library. You approached him once, to work for you. He was worried about it.'

The Colonel remembered Marlow. Or rather he remembered him through Bridget. She had loved him and left him, like cheap fiction; they had even got married. He had never understood how she had become involved with him in the first place, what she had seen in him. And here he was again, waving his arms about inexplicably in the firing line; the Jester or thirteenth guest, fate's toy who upset every calculation. You could never make sufficient allowance for people like Marlow; their innocence was the most dangerous of all imponderables. It gave them a talismanic gift: no matter how distant, they could ruin your own careful dispositions, as polar storms affect tropic weather.

With Edwards, for example: Edwards had told Marlow he was getting out of Holborn, or as good as told him, the Colonel was sure of it. Thus, among all the others and against all the laws of probability, Marlow would be the one chosen to look for him, to stop him before he got to Moscow. And with Bridget; Marlow's relationship with her was not necessarily dead, but sleeping. The Colonel resented Marlow ten years before; a case of sheer envy at his marriage to Bridget—even though it hadn't lasted, and their own affair had begun again soon afterwards. He had as well, he remembered, tried to break up their relationship by implicating Marlow with Egyptian intelligence, and having him packed off home as a result.

And later, when it was all over, and Marlow had gone home in any case, he had resented still more Bridget's compassion for him, the responsibility she felt for the disaster, which had worked itself to the surface long after she had ceased to have anything to do with him, which had soured some of their own days together. It was the quality in Bridget which he most feared—these obsessive residuals, which could flare again. If Marlow ever did come back to Egypt, he thought . . . The nostalgic temperament which he recognized so well in her, could fall in love with remembered passion just as easily as falling off a log.

Marlow would be the least expected person in Cairo, yet it was exactly his nature to come untimely. And so, the Colonel argued, with that certainty of intuition that comes of loving, fearing loss, Marlow would return—just as surely as if he had bought the ticket for him in London himself.

He feared Marlow. He was another of the signs of the last twenty-four hours; they were not messages of logic but a kind of magic which until now had preserved him in his profession and protected his passion—signs, there was no other way of putting it, given in tents, heard on the wind, written on sand. But he could no longer interpret them. He feared his luck had just started to run out.

The Colonel thought of his long affair with Bridget Girgis as if it were already finished. It had begun when she was hardly twenty, and he nearly twenty years older, just after the war. It had started so easily in those fluent days of parties and dances before the British had left; it had been an affair of light, carried forward effortlessly on a tide of dazzling linen tablecloths, sheets, glazed martini glasses, picnic hampers. She had taken to him without a murmur, had become a perfect part of his conspiracy.

Perhaps she had found out that he had once been with British intelligence in Egypt from her father, with whom he'd had professional contacts during the war. And the rest had followed without any strain: Bridget had gone on assuming he was with the British, working now as one of their men in Egyptian security. It had been a joke between them on the few occasions when the subject had come up; he had warned her never to talk about it—and they had both subsequently contrived to forget their knowledge of each other's work, when they were apart—or together. It had been a matter of no importance, a detail which, though acknowledged, had nothing to do with their real focus of intent, their ambition as lovers.

And yet she had gone on seeing Edwards whenever he came to Cairo—in the same generous, impossible way that she had taken up with Marlow. He knew that; he'd had Edwards followed, though he'd never mentioned it to her. That had been the one proviso in their love—never to question trust. And she had been trustworthy, certainly: to him, to Edwards, even to Marlow. She had been more than kind to everyone. While he and Edwards, and no doubt Marlow, nursed uneasy consciences, she seemed to ride high above doubt, living with suspicion and dissension as happily as she did with the men who brought these things to her.

But Edwards had more than a bad conscience now; he had come to the last peg as an agent: Edwards was beyond trust, therefore he was as good as dead. And in any case one never picked women up on the way down, on the run, even if they were old friends. A passion to save yourself—your neck or your conscience—stopped the kissing like bad breath. Henry was finished with loving too.

The Colonel thought of Bridget again with sudden hope, as something vital still within his grasp; for her sake alone, perhaps, he had not yet tired of conspiracy; because of her he still had armour, could bring foresight and professional skill against disruption or whatever the signs held for him. He would hold her as long as he never came to pity himself—that was the way to look at it.

Edwards had been chattering away about 'devious plots'. The Colonel was bored out of his mind by his theories. He knew the facts now: Edwards was going to double-cross him, expose him and the other Tel Aviv men in Egypt. He would kill him in the morning: not now, but tomorrow. He was late already now.

The ceaseless questions which had raged through the Colonel's mind for the past twenty-four hours drifted away as he remembered his appointment with Bridget that night. He was due to pick her up later at Maadi. They were going on to dinner afterwards on the Semiramis terrace.

The Colonel turned to Edwards. 'Look, you'll have to stay on here for the moment. I can't immediately countermand Major Amin's orders. It's his show—this business with Yunis, and you're involved with it one way or another. I believe what you say; there's been a mix-up, we'll get it straightened out. I'll see Amin tomorrow and we'll talk about it then. The quarters are comfortable enough here. I'll have them send you some food.'

'Yes. Certainly.'

Edwards spoke with the good nature of someone trying to ingratiate himself, having decided some time before that he would get himself out of the hospital at the first opportunity and make his way—by whatever means, the canal seemed promising—to Bridget's house in Maadi.

Edwards was quite determined to escape for he was certain now that he was involved, not just in a trap, but in a trap set to kill him in the morning. He couldn't understand why the Colonel hadn't got under way with it that night. Perhaps he was in a hurry, was late already for an appointment with a woman or something.

10

AFTER the Colonel had left, Edwards sat in the office and listened. Now, twenty minutes later, he was in complete darkness. All the lights had gone out just after they'd brought him some food—a plateful of mushy courgettes and some stringy meat fried in breadcrumbs. It was the last he'd see of it, thankfully.

They hadn't locked the door. They had brought blankets and shown him a bed in the next inter-connecting office. But the entrance to the low building would still obviously be guarded on the outside. Before the lights went out there had been a noise too, Edwards remembered now that it had stopped: a generator or a boiler, an insistent powerful humming noise. What was it? And now the room was getting warmer, the whole atmosphere of the building becoming slightly muggy and velvet, like any other Egyptian night, while before there had been a slight crispness.

Minute beads of sweat began to form around his hairline before Edwards understood: the Colonel's office was next to the hospital's refrigeration plant—the cold rooms where they kept drugs, food and obviously the bodies as well. Presumably the humming would start again the moment power returned, or the emergency generator was activated.

The lights came on. The soft purr from behind the walls returned. A power failure; as regular and certain an occurrence in Cairo as the weather. But there had been several minutes during which the whole building must have been in complete darkness. Which meant that the emergency generator didn't cut in automatically.

Edwards looked around the office and noticed two strands of exposed cable above the Colonel's desk, the beginnings of a light fitting which hadn't yet been installed. Both ends of the flex had been bound up with tape, something they'd have hardly bothered to do, he thought, if the wires had been dead.

He got a chair, stood up and wound the tape off each strand of wire. He took a coin out of his pocket, an old copper piastre with Fuad's head almost rubbed away, and pushed it into the plastic clip of his pen . . .

In the first moment of blackness Edwards ran as fast as he could down the corridor towards the entrance, shouting in Arabic:

'Quick, quick! The foreigner—he's broken through the window. Out the door—quick!'

He avoided the approaching beams of torchlight, which now swung away from the corridor towards the main door of the building. He actually opened the door himself, cursing and shouting at the other two figures by his side, and the three of them raced out into the night, two to the left of the building where his window was, and the third to the right, making eastwards towards the white spurs of the Mokattam Hills which showed in the faint light.

Edwards crashed straight into the fence in the darkness and wondered how he'd got to the far side when he picked himself up, gasping for breath, his face covered in soil, spitting grit and something that tasted like spinach. He must have caught the top wire, chest high, and somersaulted on to the other side.

He had, he calculated, at least fifteen seconds start on them, and double that time before the lights came on again in the compound: about two hundred yards start, but across completely flat, open countryside.

For the moment there was no sound of a chase behind him and by the time he had got to the canal, and the lights had come on again, he saw why. The two smart men had stopped by the fence. They stood next to one another now, as though holding each other up in shaky indecision, before one of the men turned and ran back towards the hospital. The other fell to the ground, perhaps with a rifle, his body flat out in a line facing the canal.

Edwards ducked beneath the shallow bank and was twenty yards down the water before he realized that one of his pursuers had been electrocuted.

His feet sank deep into the mud each time he moved, the water rising and falling over his mouth, soft and tasteless as rainwater, and it was a sudden old-fashioned fear of bilharzia or a monstrous go of Gyppy tummy—more than drowning, or cut glass or his slow progress—that made him scramble up on the bank a few minutes later. Fifty yards to his left, between the feeder canal and the Mokattam Hills, there was an embankment and on top of it the double railway line which ran from Bab el Luk to Helwan. When he got to it he saw the lights of Maadi station winking through clumps of palm half a mile away to the south. And beyond the station he could just make out the glare from the croquet floodlights at Maadi Sporting Club. That strange Egyptian passion for the game, which they played late into the night, meant that the locker rooms would still be open.

He came in over the sagging chicken wire beyond the last tennis court, walked past the deserted pool, into the gents, across the showers and from there to the locker room beyond. He knew this moist geography of the Club almost as well as he knew his own bathroom in Kentish Town.

Abdul Khaki, under the letter K, was his benefactor. He had known him ever since he'd first come to teach at Albert College—a witty, careless, overweight man who had once, in slimmer days, played squash for Egypt before making a fortune in real estate—and he had left his locker open. There were a reasonable pair of plimsolls, Slazenger shirt and pants, an old blue blazer and an even older squash racket: Abdul's second division equipment. Edwards transferred his money, his damp cheque-book, passport, and a book of English stamps and threw his own clothes into the laundry bin. He would get them back in twenty-four hours, beautifully done, if he wanted.

They were playing bridge behind the glass windows of the terrace—beaky, white-haired ladies and crop-headed old men in Rex Harrison cardigans, utterly absorbed. And he could hear the furious clonk of wood on wood as other older and even more vehement members dispatched each other to the nether ends of the croquet court on the far side of the building.

The minute porter in the ragged corduroy jacket who had once looked after King Fuad's stables at Abdin Palace saluted Edwards carefully as he passed the little sentry box by the main gate of the Club.

'Good night, Mr. Edwards, sir. Taxi?'

They never forgot you here, Edwards thought, and he put his hand down the vest pocket of Khaki's blazer and found a few coins there—the little essential baksheesh that every good club member kept in store for such contingencies. He gave the old fellow a five-piastre piece.

'Thank you, Ahmed.'

A taxi pulled out from the station rank, swung round the sandy circle in leaps and bounds, carburettor stomping and spitting vigorously, and pulled up at the entrance.

'Thank you, sir, thank you,' Ahmed said, opening the door. 'Your bat, sir! Don't forget your bat!' And he pushed the mysterious instrument through the cab window.

He left the taxi at the end of the dusty street, the arch of evergreens stooping overhead all along its length, and came to the house by its back entrance which led to the garden—past the *suffragis'* quarters in a thicket of bramble and flowering laurel, through the wilderness of papyrus on the damp margin of the lawn and over the willow pattern bridge.

The lights were on downstairs and on the terrace but all he could see was Bridget's feet stretched out on a sun chair behind the parapet and its tumble of orange flowered creeper. She was reading probably, as she often did late at night, and Edwards wondered what it was: a travel book from the Council library, a new biography perhaps. He had often brought her out the latest

success in that line when he came from London. A surprise . . .
And he wished now that he didn't have to surprise her, that
she'd known he was coming, as he walked up the terrace steps,
broken racket in hand, in his billowing shorts. That was surprise
enough. A joke as well. Perhaps that was the way to handle it.
Anyone for tennis?

Bridget wasn't reading. There had simply been a silence
between them, the empty stillness after a row—as though she
and Colonel Hamdy had just had a flaming row: that was it,
Edwards was sure of it.

The telephone, taken out on a long extension from the
drawing room, was on a table between them. The three of them
glanced at it, like a gun, before it started a long, stumbling,
jittery ring.

'Aiowa,' the Colonel said. 'Aiowa,' between pauses, impatiently, as though confirming a grocery order with a tiresome
merchant.

'Well, the man isn't dead.' The Colonel put the phone down.
'Just burnt. The trouble is they think you're going to blow the
Yunis business to the press, that you really are a journalist.
That's the problem. We'll have to get you out of here.'

Edwards put the racket on the parapet and took a cigarette
from a pack on the table. Bridget leant forward, handing him a
lighter, taking one herself. He realized he was shaking now, the
cigarette bouncing around in his hand. Not from the cold, the
terrace was warm from years of continual sunlight. Bridget had
never looked like speaking. There was surprise, certainly; the
incredulous lines on someone's face before one laughs.

'Before I came,' Edwards said, looking at her intently, as if
searching for a vital response, 'what were you fighting about?'

'We weren't fighting. Hamdy just told me you were here.
That you'd been arrested at the airport, being held by security.
We were thinking.' She looked at the Colonel. 'Now that you're
here you might as well know,' he said. 'Why not?' And Bridget
went on quickly, as if making up for something, making up for
years of necessary lies: 'I'm sorry you didn't know about
Hamdy before. I couldn't tell you.'

'What?'

'That he's with us. That he's always been.'

'With Holborn?'

'Yes.' Bridget got up and went to organize a drinks tray in the room behind.

'How the hell is it *you're* the only one to know about it then?' Edwards shouted after her. 'That's a likely story.' He was trying to be angry. 'How come I've never heard of it? With twenty years in the same section.' He was about to add 'With twenty years working for the same man' but stopped himself in time.

'Don't be stupid.' The Colonel came over towards him. 'Of course you never heard about it, *could* never hear of it. Do you think my position with Egyptian intelligence here would have been secure if I'd ever been an *official* part of the Holborn circle in Cairo? No one knew. Except central office.'

'And Bridget.'

'Yes.'

'But she was just sustenance. Lemons at half time. To keep you going. I know. But what about me?' He lowered his voice. 'I've been working for you for twenty years, for your *Egyptian* office. Why did you never tell them that in London?'

'Because it didn't matter. Nothing I got from you ever went beyond me. I *needed* you for my own cover with the Egyptians. Don't you see? I had to be able to show them that I had control of at least one man in Holborn, that I'd turned him. It was a crucial point. That way they were never likely to suspect that I worked for Holborn too. But I shouldn't talk about it. She doesn't know.'

Bridget came back with a tray and some whisky. Edwards sighed. It made sense, like so many things did which you'd least suspected: it was the longest shot in the world, that the Colonel worked for London. But that was what the whole business was about; seeing who could be the cleverest.

And he realized how it explained Bridget's ease, even her light-headedness, over his arrival: it wasn't the danger of the situation which had occurred to her, it was the fact that the three of them were now being 'true' to each other at last, in really *knowing* about each other. And just as she'd welcomed Marlow into the 'British camp' ten years before—with a sudden overwhelming joy because the pretence of their threefold relationship was over, so now she was inviting Edwards to join the celebration of a similar 'truth' which she had obviously enjoyed for a long time with the Colonel. This time Edwards was the guest—at a reception of a marriage that must have occurred years before.

She handed Edwards his whisky- almost formally, smiling hugely, as though he was the first man in a receiving line at a lucky late wedding, the Colonel behind her, flapping about the place like an embarrassed groom.

For Bridget the grubby, deceitful days were over and she was celebrating.

Celebrating what? That the Colonel had been a loyal British agent all along and that he'd just been used to give him cover, while really believing Hamdy was working for the Egyptians. That was worth a drink. And perhaps if one day the three of them really got to know each other, Edwards thought, he'd tell them he actually worked for Moscow.

The telephone rang again. Bridget picked it up.

' "A message from Hassenein," ' she repeated the words at the other end. ' "Would I tell my friend he can pick up his car *now*. The brakes have been fixed." Right, I'll do that.' She put the receiver back. 'Someone from the Semiramis. Who's "my friend"? Is that your car, Hamdy—is that you?'

So Henry had done for him after all, long before, on the plane, with Yunis. The Colonel wondered why he didn't go for him there and then, kill him, wipe him out—wondered why he just stood there patting his pockets absentmindedly. Because of his togs, he thought—the ridiculously billowy shorts and blazer, the Chaplin plimsolls, the rakish clotted hair and mended spectacles: one didn't go for a man so obviously down. There wasn't the air of a traitor about Henry, it was useless. He looked, he had been behaving, like the second lead in a marital farce, the cuckolded husband, bursting through the French windows, intent on hopeless revenge; so it was that the Colonel couldn't contemplate a similar role. He thought of the message from the Semiramis instead.

The suffix 'now' meant just what it said. 'The brakes have been fixed' stood for 'get clear at all costs' and 'Hassenein' was the code name for a man he'd never met: one of the other men—he'd no idea how many there were—who, like him, worked for Tel Aviv in Egyptian intelligence. He had never been given any method of contacting these people; they were pilot

fish, infiltrated into various sections of the Cairo *apparat* over
the years—as cypher clerks, secretaries, telephonists, messen-
gers—almost solely for the purpose of warning him of impend-
ing disaster. They contacted the telephonist at the Semiramis
who had his home number, and Bridget's, and she had passed
the message on.

The form of the message had been agreed many years before,
the Colonel remembered, just after the war when the British
Army had still been in the Kasr el Nil barracks and he'd
managed to buy a pre-war Morris 8 with perfect brakes from a
major of a returning regiment. The major, a Jew, had been his
initial contact with the Israeli underground. Subsequently he
had left the army and gone to Palestine. The Colonel had
worked for him ever since. They'd drunk themselves silly
together in Shepheard's all afternoon before he got the train to
Port Said to join his men and the ship home. Gin and limes. Gin
and everything. 'Let's hope your brakes never fail,' the major
had said, and he'd stumbled into a gharry, the harness bells
tinkling away into the flare-lit alleys beyond Opera Square.

Well, the brakes had gone now, and with them twenty years,
many more than a thousand and one nights. He'd betrayed a
country and he'd come to love it—to love it greatly in exact
proportion to his treachery. He was bored by the grip this cliché
had had on him, appalled now that it had held him in Egypt so
blindly, for so long. He ought to have seen from the beginning
that he would one day have to accept an equally banal ending:
that he wouldn't get away with it for ever. If he'd come to hate
Egypt he would almost certainly have survived, he thought.
Hate protected you from clichés.

'It's a "get clear" message, Hamdy, isn't it?' Edwards said.
'No one's really phoning you about your brakes. And you can't
have much time if they're prepared to use an open line to you.'

Bridget didn't wait for him to answer.

'What is it, Hamdy? What's happened?'

The Colonel had only moments to make up his mind. He
could agree that it was a code message, but simply from his own
section in Cairo—leave them, and try and get clear. Or he could
take them with him. The first choice was the obvious one. Yet
he prevaricated with himself for a second, found himself arguing
the toss against his will. And the moment he began that he

knew he was finished. He might get clear of Egypt with luck, as an ordinary man; he would never again survive as a professional. He didn't mind. He argued; he delayed; he thought of Bridget. It was impossible to get clear of Egypt without going through a number of elaborate pre-arrangements, he reminded himself—which needed time to organize and a place to do that from. He had the place, the top floor apartment in Gezira. It was where he took Bridget when they were in town together, when they 'had a moment' . . .

It was really only a matter of whether he brought Edwards with him too, he thought, since he'd now established that he wasn't going to leave Bridget behind. And then he realized that he had no alternative but to take Henry—if he wanted Bridget. From her point of view, after all, they were now three British agents on the run: like an old British film.

'Henry's right, isn't he?' Bridget said. 'Intelligence here has found out you're with London. Someone from the Consulate—or that man at the airport—they've warned you?'

The Colonel nodded. 'Come on. Don't pack. But get Henry one of your father's coats or something. And a pair of trousers. It's not the moment for squash.'

The house was a dry oven smelling of orange blossom and cedar when they left. The clock which had been made in Bath chimed the first quarter after eleven slowly, four bell-like notes in a scale, the bull of Taurus moving round a semi-circle at the bottom, and a large Humpty Dumpty moon bouncing over the blue-starred horizon above. Bridget took a couple of copies of *Country Life* with her as she went.

Was that what had kept her going in Cairo all these years, Edwards wondered: the idea of returning eventually to England once with him, once with Marlow, and now with the Colonel? When the story finally broke, and all their cover gone, she might, if they were very lucky, achieve a lifetime's ambition; come into her due reward: something small and half-timbered in Sussex, a paddock and a fast midday train to the London shops, with Hamdy sipping gassy bitter in the Wheatsheaf at week-ends. 'Tea planting, don't you know. Back from a little trouble in Ceylon.'

Was that the dull reason for her attachment to the Colonel? In his twenty years as a double in Egypt he must have outranked everyone except Williams in the Holborn section. Perhaps, she may even have reckoned, Hamdy might be in line for a manor in the Cotswolds—if they ever made it home.

Intrigue, Edwards thought, what a lot of bloody intrigue. He took the bottle of whisky with him. He would have to look to his own intrigues from now on. Moscow perhaps. He too needed time to make preparations; the only sort of house he wanted at the moment was a safe one.

They turned left at the T junction from Maadi on to the Helwan road, swung the old Chrysler round facing Cairo three hundred yards away under some trees by the river, and waited. There was only one road back to the city on the narrow stretch of land between the Mokattam Hills and the Nile, the road they'd have to use if they were coming after the Colonel.

Fifteen minutes later they came, not fast and not all together: a Mercedes and then two jeeps, recent Russian models, without markings. They turned off into the clumpy velvet evergreens of the estate, one jeep stopping to block the road out, and the other two vehicles turning round the circle by the Club and going on towards Bridget's house.

Edwards and the Colonel crouched down in the back seat and Bridget, waiting another minute for some other cars to pass, drove quietly after them towards the city.

BOOK FOUR

CAIRO, MAY 1967

I DIDN'T try to remember anything as the taxi jumped and swerved along the airport road into the city: either remember or compare. I told myself—all that was ten years ago, this was now. There were few cars on the road and fewer lights, just the swishing shadows of airline billboards and half-completed buildings on either side of the highway. I might have been driving along the airport road of any warm, desert country. I was a traveller being taken to his hotel with a decent enough suitcase, a change of linen tropicals, a carton of Philip Morris, a bottle of Haig, and an allowance of £11 a day made up in £200-worth of American Express travellers' cheques, to include expenses . . .

I had simply a business connection with the city: Edwards was supposed to be somewhere in it. And perhaps, in the unlikely event of my finding him, we might have a good meal together at the Estoril, a lager at the Regent, an afternoon at Gezira, and then come back to London and no more would be said about it. And if I didn't find him I'd do these same things anyway, make a few discreet inquiries and get back home.

I was as tired of intrigue, suspicion and difficulty as I'd ever been in my life—and I'd tell Henry so if I came across him: that was the purpose of the trip, to find him and tell him he'd been right. There was nothing else, for I'd exhausted my past in this city as well—on the flight over with too much burgundy and too little sleep.

All I needed was to finish off this business as quickly as possible, with some pleasure perhaps, and get back. Then, with or without Henry, I would decide whether Williams and the Arab press still claimed me—or whether there was any real alternative in the Olive Grove Syndrome, the song-of-the-man-at-forty, the village in Galway.

I turned the window right down. There was just a smell of burnt newspapers and urine riding strongly into the car on the night air. Had there ever been the drift of sesame and spices, cloves and brick dust, through open windows here?—or the one thing in the empty afternoons we had done so well?

They gave me a room on the top floor of the Semiramis looking out over the river. Nothing had changed in the hotel, but there was no one I recognized. It was past midnight; the huge Edwardian shell of the building seemed not so much asleep as deserted. There was a new electric map of the city by the reception desk with coloured lights behind the various tourist attractions, and buttons that you pressed underneath to identify them. One of them had stuck and a light was flashing on and off half-way up Soliman Pasha Street. I looked at the label on the button: 'Ministry of Tourism and National Guidance, 12 Talaat Harb.' The old name had gone but not, I noticed, the Perroquet Night Club in the National Hotel further up the same street. I pushed the button for it, so that a green parrot started to flash on the map and not the Ministry of National Guidance.

Cherry, Herbert Cherry of Greystones, Co. Dublin, had once attempted to play the trumpet in the orchestra there and they'd taken a month's wages off him before they'd thrown us out. I would look for Cherry in the morning. The ubiquitous, fleshy, nervous Cherry. Cherry, our man in Cairo.

The English language magazine that Cherry worked for was edited and printed from the offices of the *Egyptian Gazette* off 26 July Street on the road up to the main station. They'd had an old copy on the hotel bookstall and I'd looked at it over breakfast. It was called *Arab Focus* and was done in a print and on a paper which quite belied its title. I tried to detect some of Cherry's idiosyncratic Dublin-English in the mass of translated articles from *Al Ahram* and the Cairo weeklies, but I could find nothing of him at all in the arid prose about the High Dam, the stories about the last—and the next—Arab summit. I suppose the magazine wasn't the best market for stories about grey-hounds in the back of taxis on the way to Mullingar.

'Twenty-four Sharia Zakaria Ahmed,' I'd said to the cab driver outside the hotel and he'd then repeated the address to a policeman at a kindergarten table by the head of the rank.

'What's that for?'

'Tourist police. We have to tell them where we're going. With foreigners. Though you don't speak Arabic like a foreigner.'

'I used to live here.'

The driver grunted and barged the car through a crowd waiting to cross the main El Trahir Square, before swinging

round, bumping within a foot of a tram, and then going up Kasr
el Nil to the centre of town.

Already, at ten o'clock, the Midan was a cauldron, well on
the boil: scribes and photographers under black umbrellas,
gesticulating with envelopes and from behind velvet drapes,
were manhandling petitioners in front of the huge Education
and Home Affairs Ministry on one side of the square; hefty
galibeahed and skull-capped farmers tore round the central
island, *Ben Hur* fashion, in huge-wheeled ass carts like gun
carriages on their way back into the country from market;
children in oversized, stained pyjamas were selling ballpoints
and grubby trinkets at every corner; soldiers with a day's leave
gazed blankly at the mysterious improbability of the flower
clock next to the oily waste of the central bus stop; while the
disintegrating maroon buses themselves, with dozens of people
hanging on with toes and fingers to the outside, heeled over
gracefully on the roundabout like fishes, the tips of the
mudguards scraping up the soft tar.

Nothing had changed on the Midan in ten years: this arid,
scrubby, filthy, dangerous hodge-podge of baking concrete—the
'Hub of the City' which had repulsed so easily so many
attempts to 'integrate' it, or 'improve' it since the British had
left and the old Kasr el Nil barracks on the same site had been
destroyed. It remained a no man's land between the bridges
over the river on one side and the town proper to the east.

I had lived here. In the blazing light with the sweat bubbling
already under my arms, there was no chance of denying it now.

On Kasr el Nil, moving up the old European centre towards
Soliman Pasha roundabout (he had been replaced by the hero
Talaat Harb, bird-limed in his cocky tarbush), things were more
shabby and broken down than ever. The once pompous
Haussmann-plan streets, the ornate French-Levantine-style
apartments with their excessive curly stucco, decorative rue de
Rivoli arches, balconies and roof balustrades, were all rubbing
away, splitting, in the cracking, hot-cupboard air. The pavements were an obstacle course of blistering, volcanic mounds;
the traffic lights broken coloured spectacles winking a pale
white light; a plate-glass window had gone in Au Salon Vert and
sand blew in through every doorway.

True, it was May and the end of the Khamseen winds—that
part of the year when the city, in the best of times, very nearly

gave itself back to the desert—that scorching, gritty breath
which now, without money and the foreign adventurers long
gone, made it seem as if all the buildings had been detonated
and were simply waiting to be pushed over, like trees standing
firm as ever after the blade has passed, the moment before the
fall.

'Ah,' El Khoury said, 'Mr. Cherry has had—an accident?—no. A
trouble?—yes.' Mr. Khoury's English stumbled and doubled
back in much the same way as the language did in his magazine.
He led you on with it in sudden leaps through horrible
misunderstandings only to dump you, equally ignorant, in the
waste spaces among 'abbreviations' and 'recent additions' at the
end of the dictionary. His office for *Arab Focus* was in a
corridor of the *Gazette* building, at one end of it in fact, so that
we sat opposite each other, pretty close to, with a few feet to
spare on either side of our chairs, Mr. Khoury with something
less than that for he was a large man with moist locks of dark
hair round his ears, broken yellowish teeth and very bloodshot
eyes—eyes which seemed to have looked long and without
reward on some sunspot nirvana.

'An accident? Trouble?' I queried.

'A wife—*his* wife,' Mr. Khoury responded vigorously, suddenly hooking on to the right words with a huge smile. 'She is
not very well. In fact—' he paused, massaged his stomach under
his shirt, then wiped the sweat off his hand on a blotter, '—she
is very bad. You will like to see her? Yes?'

'Yes. I'm sorry. I remember her when I was last here. She's
French, isn't she?'

'Franciowey. Aiowa.' He broke into Arabic. Then he glanced
doubtfully down at his fly. Then the hand went under again.

'And you are here to do some stories,' he continued after the
moment's repairs. 'The *New* Egypt. The new UAR as we call it.
We can reprint them. The new High Dam, the new Arab
summit, new pyramids from the World Bank—we are very keen.
We will talk for a long time about it. You will have food with
us. I am very glad to see you. There will be much talk about it.'

'I'd thought really of doing a fairly simple colour piece—
"Life in Cairo Today", that sort of thing—'

'Of course, of course,' Mr. Khoury interrupted. 'We will do
that. I will show you the new hotels—the El Borg, the Cairo

Tower, the TV centre at Maspero, one of the very best—I think we have some English equipment—bathing, holidays, Nile cruisers. We will do everything. My wife will be very pleased to help.'

'And perhaps something on the antiquities, I'd thought. You're doing something new at Sakkara, I understand. Looking for Imhotep's tomb—'

'Mr. Marlow, I tell you frankly, everything is new. With the antiquities we are doing many new and wonderful things. Very up to the minute. And I am doing a drama myself. In four acts and a prologue.'

Mr. Khoury shuffled among the crowd of typescripts and paper rubble on his desk. He produced a small booklet, a play in English by Taufiq Al-Hakim, a well-known Egyptian writer.

'There.' He handed me the play in triumph. 'Mine is so much different. This man is talking about townspeople, Cairo people, talking and having their coffee in Groppi's. I am writing a story of country folk—the world of the village, the man who comes to the city. The *pressure*—' he raised both arms in hold-up fashion and then brought them together about his head, a cage of fingers over each ear '—the pressure of urban disturbances on the rural mind. The millennia of the past—' he opened his arms out again '—faced with the millennia of the future!' He opened his arms wider still so that his fingers bumped the walls on either side of him. 'These are the things of most importance. I am calling it *Yesterday and Tomorrow*. We will talk about it.'

'It's most kind of you—'

'You say ten years before you were here—teaching at Maadi?' I nodded. 'You know, *three* times I have been in London since then. Three times. The Strand Palace Hotel, I always stay there. You know Mr. El Bakri at Chesterfield Gardens? He has an apartment now near Kew Gardens. Very strange luck—no? You are knowing him, I expect. We were always eating at Lyons restaurant in Piccadilly—you are knowing that place too, I am sure. What good times we had in London—what a place! Well, we will be arranging things for you here, Mr. Marlow, I can assure you. You are at the Semiramis? At what time are you free tonight? You will meet my friends and we will talk seriously, most sensibly. And I will prepare a programme for you between time. Six o'clock at the hotel then. I will be awaiting on you.'

Mr. Khoury stood up in a hurry.

'May I confirm that with you?—I have to see if I can find Mr. Cherry. Where do you think I might get him now?'

'Ah, of course, your friend Mr. Cherry. I have not seen him for some time. He writes English for us now and then. His wife is very—not well . . .'

'In hospital?'

'I am afraid yes.'

'Where?'

'The Anglo-American in Gezira. She's French, you know,' he added regretfully. 'Behind the Cairo Tower, you can't miss it. A most unfortunate occurrence, I'm sure. *A toudaleur* then, Mr. Marlow—and I must say I can't say how nice . . .'

A ragged porter, who insisted on carrying Khoury's gift to me of the last twelve issues of *Arab Focus*, saw me down the dark circle of stairs smelling of machine oil, and, having had his five piastres in the hallway, ushered me out on to the boiling street.

I took a taxi back to the Semiramis and lay down at once. I'd felt very queasy in the cab and now, on the bed, the room started to tilt and veer around me; the ceiling moved. I must have had a temperature, it seemed too soon for a go of Gyppy tummy. There was a nineteenth-century Italian print on the wall: a ruined temple on a hill, with shepherds and flocks of assorted animals in the foreground. A classical landscape. It twisted slowly on its axis, goats walking up one side of the frame, the ruined temple sliding down the other. I was unable to take my eyes off it. Pain shot up the back of my neck and I realized I was twisting my head violently trying to steady the picture and get it level again. I gave up and left the frame to slide around as much as it wanted. It proceeded to spin and flutter like a wagon wheel in a Western.

The terrace doors were open and the remains of the Khamseen wind kept the muslin curtain steadily flapping against the glass. I seem to have been quite conscious of the noise it made—and of the cries drifting up distantly from the corniche outside, the water lapping against the embankment, the slowly circling ray of sunlight passing over the end of my bed—throughout the rest of the morning. All the same, during some of this time, I must have dropped off to sleep more than once. For the dream I had, in reconstructing it immediately

afterwards, was half fact, half fiction—the first commenting on
the second, as I fell in and out of consciousness.

I had started to think about my last day in Cairo ten years
before. I was catching a TWA flight that evening back to Paris
and the three of us, Henry, Bridget and I, had just left the
airline office in Opera Square where Bridget worked and she
had given me a folder with my ticket in it.

'A drink in the Continental?' Henry suggested. And we had
gone there and sat up at the dark, mirrored bar and Angelo had
served us *arak* in tall whisky glasses, ice-cold water circling
down the outside. The bill had been forty-five piastres, plus the
service, and Angelo had put the strip of paper in Henry's little
glass behind the bar, on the first shelf of bottles. Henry was
staying on in Egypt, his credit was good. But my own sherry
glass was there as well, full of previous chits, at least two
hundred piastres worth. Was Angelo going to ask me to settle up
with him now?—had they told him I was leaving? Or didn't he
know? I'd have to tell him I was leaving myself, and pay up.
But when? Now—or at the end of the session? However I
handled it there was going to be an awkward break—this saying
goodbye to Angelo, paying my bill. It would be the beginning
of the end, a public acknowledgment of my departure—and I
was absorbed in wondering how to face it. I was determined not
to get involved in any goodbye business.

We drank on at the Continental for an hour, swapping polite
inconsequential chatter—English teachers taking the morning
off with a girl in town . . . We'd arranged to go on for lunch at
the Estoril.

All this was fact; it was exactly as it had happened. But in the
moments after remembering it, when I'd fallen asleep, the
dream came which was quite different. Instead of going to the
Estoril we were driving down Soliman Pasha in a taxi, to
Bridget's flat in Garden City, the heat lapping round the car in
waves.

The lift wasn't working and when we'd climbed to the top of
the building we had gin from the cardboard crate which Bridget
kept under the chaise-longue—the three of us romping around
the small burning room, throwing our clothes off, laughing and
chattering like bright sparks at a cocktail party.

And then Henry had suddenly gone into the bedroom with
Bridget—as simply and naturally as though it was an arrange-

ment, an appointment they'd had together which we'd all been aware of for a long time.

I stood at the window, my back to the bedroom doors, chuckling, sipping more and more gin, looking out over the river, perfectly happy, until Bridget called me, her head half-way through the glass doors.

'It won't work,' she said. She seemed to be shouting at me, her sun-burnt face showing up like a full stop against the yellow whiteness of her body. 'We can't get down. We're trapped.'

'Why ever not?' I said casually. 'The door isn't locked.' And I moved towards it. It gave easily in my hand, swinging inwards, and the afternoon sun dazzled me. Instead of the door-mat and corridor there was a small window ledge where my feet were, with some withered plants in pots, and below them the outside wall of the tall apartment block, a sheer drop of twelve storeys to the corniche below.

When I woke, I had opened my eyes several times, thinking about this, but had closed them again, drawn back each time by the memory of the dream—trying to re-achieve it; its light-headed, smooth dazzle, its sex, its extraordinary reality. And for moments I was part of it once more, could feel its exact shapes and sizes, but soon there was nothing left; I had exhausted it. I kept my eyes open the next time. The landscape on the wall was rock-steady, frozen goats and broken grey columns.

I got up and went on to the balcony and looked to left and right along the rooftops of the buildings on the corniche. I could just see the top of Bridget's apartment block in Garden City beyond Shepheard's Hotel. She was probably still here, living in the city. She might even be in the same place. Her parents were dead, I knew that, and in the years afterwards, when Henry and I had met again in London, he had never told me that she had left Egypt. After the first bits of news he had given me about her and her family, and after our marriage was dissolved, we had dropped the subject altogether.

But now it was different. Henry was no longer my only consideration in the city. For the first time in years I was thinking of Bridget again, thinking intensely, trying to imagine where she was and what she was doing, wondering whether I might not simply go up to her old apartment and ring the bell, or phone her. The dream had suddenly freshened everything about her, the details had re-created her completely: I had seen her face again, the dark triangular features, the eyes so far apart and the nose turning slightly upwards like a petal. And in the glass doorway of the bedroom the same barely formed body, the narrow shoulders and wide hips. A woman in her late thirties now, somewhere in the city. I was sure of it.

2

BRIDGET had gone out each evening for food, but Henry and the Colonel had not set foot outside the apartment in Gezira for more than two days. They were by now nervous and short-tempered and all of them were thankful of the three separate bedrooms which the accommodation offered. It was an old turn-of-the-century block on the island and the apartment ran right across the building, fronting on to Gezira Street and the river on one side and, from a covered terrace, looking out over the playing fields of the Sporting Club on the other.

The place had belonged to an aunt of the Colonel's, distantly Jewish and aristocratic—a minor *grande dame* of the city during Fuad's and Farouk's time—who had spent her life there and died just before the revolution when the Colonel had quietly taken it over as a possible bolt-hole, a 'safe' house. The furnishings were immensely heavy and portentous: pseudo gold-caked second Empire mixed with a few genuine oriental pieces—a wooden filigree harem screen by the drawing room door, a silver hookah with passages from the Koran finely inlaid, and some Persian lambswool rugs, barely trampled, deep and splendid as a snowfall. All the rooms were dark; there were few enough windows in the apartment in any case and over those were hung tall velvet curtains which, when they were fully opened, let in no more than just a central A-shaped panel of light.

The three inhabitants seemed to move on perpetual tip-toe over the heavy carpets. One of them would enter a room on some casual errand only to find that, without intending it, he had frightened the wits out of someone else already there. There was a telephone in the hall which they had moved on its long extension to a heavy armchair by the drawing room window, putting cushions round it, stifling the very possibility of its ringing. And it never did.

The Colonel had made two calls, both to someone in Athens—a coded message dealing with the export of so many kilos of dried fruit. He had explained that it was his contact with Central Office in London and that all they had to do now was wait.

Henry wasn't convinced. He had never heard of any Cairo-Athens contact in his experience with the Holborn section; on the other hand, it could have been uniquely a Central Office link. In any case he wasn't prepared to run for it on his own just yet. The only contact he could make would be with the KGB Resident in Cairo. And he hadn't made up his mind about what welcome he might receive there. He was 'resting'. That's what the house was for, he told himself: a 'safe' house.

Bridget listened to their tiresome conversations about British Intelligence, about how and when they would all get out—an English boat passing through the canal, the same thing at Alexandria, disguises at Cairo airport, or as BOAC freight. There was something false and constrained about their talk, she felt, because they wouldn't get out, would they? The Russians—and even the Egyptians too—managed these things with ease, to spirit people away in foreign places, in trunks and packing cases with chloroform over their noses.

But not the English.

They no longer had the bite in their intelligence service for that sort of thing; their men got caught in Prague with false-walled caravans or distributing religious tracts in Red Square. And how, in the best of times, was one to leave Egypt covertly? Through the Sahara on foot with a compass or a walk on the waters? Its land and sea frontiers were as open and harsh and empty and as easily controlled as the lines on a hard tennis court. They were trapped, were they not? It was as simple as that.

They talked these things round and about in low voices, drank beer at six o'clock that, without the refrigerator which had broken, now tasted dull and watery. They listened to the hourly newscasts on Cairo radio, shredding the dull communiqués for some sign of their pursuers, a sign that they were actually on the run—a feeling which the heavy soporific

apartment completely denied them. They wanted some confirmation of the action they had taken, which had pulled them
forever from a familiar world but which had not yet brought
them any other life.

And they felt impelled, against their professional judgment
and training, to stick together as much as possible now, each
watching the other. For in a life of disloyalty which had just
ended, mundane personal considerations were all that was left
to them for the moment—the private concerns of ordinary men
and women.

Thus they were careful in everything they did and polite to
each other, taking on the colourings of their bourgeois
surroundings: Bridget laid the table studiously for every meal
and the men didn't drop ash on the carpet. And at night they
took to their separate beds like the inmates of a monastery and
tried to read French popular novels of the utmost decorum and
triteness which the Colonel's aunt had collected in profusion.

The real strain in the ménage, of course, didn't come from
their predicament, or from the loss of a happy past; it came
from the fact that neither of the men dared tell each other—or
least of all Bridget—that despite all the confessions and dramatic
disclosures they were not what they seemed, that there was in
each of them a final layer of deceit which they had not
revealed. The two men weren't prepared to risk the consequences of displaying their real allegiances, not merely for
professional reasons, but because they didn't believe their
relationship with Bridget would survive such a confession.

'I am an Israeli agent.' 'I work with Moscow.' The phrases
themselves would sound ridiculous in the present circumstances,
they thought. And they would not be said, or acted upon,
except in the last resort, for to assume their final identity,
although it might mean individual salvation would also mean
losing Bridget. Whereas for as long as both men held to their lie,
both were trapped, both were secure, with her.

So the two men watched each other, and wondered, hiding
their real absorptions, while the Colonel talked of the merits of
Oxfordshire or Northamptonshire as counties to look for houses
in, and said he'd square things with Williams when they got
back to Holborn. Henry would be all right, the ridiculous
business with Yunis would be forgotten; he'd see to that. As for
the fact that Henry had been a double, really working for the

Egyptians—the Colonel said he would forget about that too. In the circumstances. And in the circumstances Henry agreed with him, describing his offer as a reasonable return for the cover he'd given Hamdy over the years.

The two men lied to each other, comfortably, secure in the knowledge that each of them would have to make quite different moves in the end. All that worried them was when.

3

I HAD dosed myself, and slept all afternoon and it was after five when I left the hotel to look for Cherry. The Khamseen, the fifty-day desert mistral, had practically beaten itself out and the city had an air of empty battered fatigue: resting for a moment on its knees, after the wind and before the oven of summer. Or so I thought: it might well have entered on its last rest for all the activity about: the City of the Dead beyond Mokattam seemed to have moved into the real city. The feluccas and barges had disappeared from the low sand-filled water and a soldier dozed, nursing an ancient sten-gun beneath the bronze Trafalgar lions which guarded the entrance to Kasr el Nil bridge.

A new network of streets had been built by the exhibition ground on the far side of the bridge, the Cairo Tower sticking up from somewhere in the middle of them, and I couldn't make out where the hospital was in this ugly, half-built scatter of roads. I walked through the remnants of an arboretum, part of the old Gezira botanical gardens, with lines of broken Edwardian green houses on one side, down through an avenue of magnificent, towering Emperor palms. At the end was a long low wooden building, with a terrace and doors all along its length, overhung with creeper; a rackety, impermanent affair—a memory now, from the *Illustrated London News*, of one of the new hospitals in the Crimea.

'Mr. Cherry?—I understand he's staying here. With his wife.'

A young man had come into the hallway, a stethoscope in his pocket, wearing plimsolls and a long white coat. A boy stood behind him in an open doorway which led to a dusty courtyard, throwing a ball impatiently from hand to hand. The man took off one of his shoes and thumped the sand out on the floor, knocking the heel vigorously against the reception desk.

'Yes. Yes—*Dr.* Cherry,' he said. 'Dr. Cherry and his wife are in number 9. I'll show you.'

The glass doors of the room were open, a length of dark muslin hanging between them, so that I had to bend down and struggle with the sand-coloured material to get in, like passing into a fortune teller's booth. There was a smell of sugar and burnt milk inside. Cherry was sitting on a kitchen chair facing the bed reading the *Egyptian Gazette* and the woman in front of him seemed like a child who had been tucked in and gone to sleep for the night, the sheets pulled right up against her ears, lying flat out without a pillow, neat and still and straight and precisely rounded under the bedclothes—as lifeless as a roll of linoleum. There was a four-pound tin of Nescafé on the chest of drawers, some imported tinned milk and a primitive paraffin burner. Many elderly British people, governesses and the widows of civil servants on minute pensions, spent their last years permanently in this hospital, and Mrs., or Madame Cherry must have taken over one of their rooms without bothering, or having the energy, to change the ancient Empire decor.

She must have been an old woman, I thought, whoever had occupied the room previously, her roots in Egypt stretching back to before the turn of the century, married to a soldier by the looks of it—he'd probably been taken off with cholera in the Sudan forty years before—for the walls were covered with military photographs, yellowing in cross-cornered frames: a regiment of lancers lined up on some nude provincial midan, a formal group of officers sitting on elaborate garden furniture in front of their mess—thin faces and moustaches and scabbards scraping the dust. And there was a sampler which had been made into a screen on the far side of the bed; row on row of faded stitching in different Gothic lettering commemorating odd skirmishes in that part of the Empire: Omdurman, Tel el Kebir, Khartoum.

There was a bamboo bookshelf next to the window with broken struts all down one side, so that the shelves had collapsed over the books: a row of Victorian adventure novels in coloured pictorial boards—*Cleveley Sahib*, *A Tale of the Khyber Pass*—holding up another row of less inspiring books—Bishop Butler's *A Tour of the Shire River*—which held up a third collection, a line of sporting memoirs—*The Turn of the*

Wheel, MCC in Australia 1928 and *Gilligan's Men.*

Cherry was sitting on a pile of thick blue books, so that he could get on a level with the closed eyes on the bed—two volumes of Arthur Mee's *Children's Encyclopaedia*, I saw, when he stood up. The doctor had gone back to his soccer and I could hear the thump of leather on a wall and odd, quick cries in Arabic.

Cherry didn't say anything. He might even have been crying. He put both hands round mine and pumped them slowly.

'Well, I'd never have believed it,' he whispered at last. And his face confirmed it. He was like a remittance man suddenly confronted with the one relation from his past who had borne with him, vaguely understood his follies and given him lunch in his London club every July: a thinner figure now, sunburnt with bad eyes, squashed linen trousers and a red Irish tweed tie that had completely faded; the flesh in the face and neck just clear of the bones, falling away in small dewlaps, the air imperceptibly, but definitely, leaking from the inner tube. The moon face was on the wane and his hair had thinned out into one or two black strands which ran across his bald' head sideways like earphones.

'What are you doing here, in God's name?' He smiled and there was the old put-on glare in the eyes for a second.

'Looking. Just looking.'

'What?' he said in a roaring whisper. 'You're not playing cops and robbers, are you? For God's sake! They arrest people out here now for that sort of thing. Nasser'll bang you into the Siwa oasis on beans and water, you know . . .'

I looked at the wisp of fuzzy grey hair on the sheet, the dark coal-scuttle eye-lids, the pointed, slightly dilating nose: the doll's head by the Omdurman sampler.

'I'm sorry to hear—'

'Yes. Madame . . .'

He furrowed his brow and pouted his lips judiciously. A boy had done something serious at the back of the class.

'Yes, we're waiting. Not long now, I should think,' he said, as though when his wife 'arrived' we would all go off somewhere and enjoy ourselves for the evening.

'Is there another room? I don't want to wake—'

'She can't hear a thing. She's on the drugs. She was deaf lately as well. I'll leave the radio on in any case. She always used to be able to hear that, so she said.'

Cherry turned on a small transistor by the bedside and an orchestra crackled out, and a voice—a Neapolitan tenor it sounded like, something from Puccini perhaps. The music surged and faded from its distant station as we clambered under the muslin and out of the dark, sweetly smelling tent, and took seats on wicker chairs on the terrace.

The late sun streamed through the vine-like tendrils that had grown up over the balcony and Cherry flapped about on his neat small feet like a waiter.

'Tell me—wait. I'll go and make some coffee first. There's a night nurse who comes on at six and I usually go to the Gezira Club for a drink then. It's near enough for them to send a message. We'll go on there.'

Cherry went back into the room and I stretched my feet out over the terrace and listened to the squeaky opera behind me. They were coming to the end of an act, a pair of voices tearing at each other in explosive counterpoint. Madame Larousse making an exit. Or was she? There had been no sign of illness or pain in the tiny features; the pencil of flesh beneath the bedclothes had been as calm as a small wave. The devoted Cherry—and Cherry the stringer for our Mid-East section. And Cherry the man who had once driven a taxi backwards over Kasr el Nil bridge, sitting on the windshield, his feet on the steering wheel, with the driver and myself navigating from the rear window. And Williams's Mr. Cherry—'Don't trust him—he doesn't, and he mustn't, know what you're doing in Cairo.'

Cherry was the sort of person I should have gone on trusting—Williams the kind I should never have become involved with: a wrong turning made long ago; expectations lying in the gutter: that was what I'd believed of Henry, thinking myself tougher and less sensitive in accepting it all. I wondered about that now. The hell with Williams, I thought.

Cherry came back with two glasses of milky Nescafé and we stirred the mixture slowly like chemists.

'My God, when I got the message that someone called Marlow was coming out here . . . I thought you'd gone back to Dublin when you left here. And now it's the bloody cloak and dagger stuff. You must be out of your mind.'

'And you? You're in the same line of business in Cairo, aren't you?'

'Not full time, not really. Not a London man on Establishment. What are they paying you? Four grand plus?'

'What does it matter? A sheep as a lamb—and you're actually in the firing line. I've just been stacked away in a cupboard in Holborn with a lot of Arab newspapers. If they catch you they'll really make you jump. Why—what made you do it? Greystones is pretty British and you used to wallop the wogs out here. But—?'

Cherry said nothing, sipping his coffee, enjoying the mystery.

'What was it? Playing a role or something, the satisfaction of doing something exciting which no one ever knows about? Or did you have genuine "ideological" motives?'

'Nothing as grand,' Cherry said. 'You're the first open contact I've ever had with London. I just give them the mood of the place, background stuff, cocktail chatter.'

'Give it to who?'

'To Usher of course. You must know about him. The Mameluke house beneath the Citadel.'

Usher. The ancient gentleman by the swimming pool at the British Embassy ten years before—carnation and spotless sea island cotton shirt. Crowther and Usher and the Queen's birthday.

'Usher? Is he still here? He recruited me. I'd forgotten.'

Cherry looked pained. Someone from London should have known all about Usher. I think he almost began to mistrust me.

'But aren't you setting up something new here? Or have I got it all wrong—and you're really working for the Russians?'

'I'm looking for Edwards. Henry Edwards. You remember him from Maadi—or had you gone to Alex by then? He was going to run the circle here and now he's disappeared. You never had any dealings with him?'

'A short fellow with glasses and a haystack of hair?'

I nodded.

'I've seen him several times at Usher's place. A journalist.'

'That was the cover. Like mine. Yours too, I suppose. What a lot of writing gets done on behalf of Her Majesty's Secret Service, a real patron of the art. Anyway, he's gone off somewhere, possibly out here. He was a friend of Bridget's too. You remember her?'

Cherry smiled willingly enough. 'I'm sorry I didn't get to the wedding.'

'I didn't manage yours either. Did you have a good time at the Beau Rivage?'

'We had the two days. She was quite old you know.'

'Yes.'

'I suppose you wondered.'

'A little.'

'She was a good woman, though. Amusing. Good company. She talked her head off, sensibly. There was nothing crumbling or faded, until quite recently. Ten good years, marvellous really. I was at the college in Alex, she took the music; a lot of laughter. Then we came to Cairo—Alex became barbaric. Then this.' He turned towards the bedroom. 'Bone cancer. What happened to your wife?'

'I don't know. She's probably still here.'

'I meant to say—I knew you'd left her. I saw her once about three years ago, a party at Usher's, she was with your friend Edwards, I think. The haystack.'

'Three years ago?'

'Yes. I'm not likely to forget her. I kept clear.'

'She bites, you mean? You've become very proper, Herbert.'

'Settled down, that's all, I suppose.'

'It wasn't like you though.'

'I know. It won't be for much longer.'

He stirred the sugar at the bottom of his glass and spooned it up like strawberry jam, mouth wide, eyes agape in the old staring way. He might have become a proper man, I thought, but the old matrix, the innate rumbustious folly was not quite dead.

'Are you going to look for her as well—your wife?'

I shook my head. 'Not my wife now. But I might look her up.'

'For old times' sake, you mean? The old Marlow. At the rodeo again. Into the ring . . .'

' "Lord Salisbury and party and hurry about it", you mean? And a taxi backwards over the bridge.'

'You won't get anything of that sort of thing around here nowadays. That's all gone. All deadly serious now. You wouldn't recognize it.'

'What is the mood here then, Herbert? That's your department.'

'There'll be a war. Third round. Seconds getting out of the ring at the moment. People are jumping round the place right now, vile tempers and bad hangovers. You won't notice it at once. Battle fever—but no battle; that's what irks them. They'll be slaughtered if they start. Nasser knows that, but the others don't; and not the Army. They're going full belt over the cliff. There's trouble at the top too. Yunis of the ASU was talking out of school in Moscow last week. Now he's reportedly under house arrest. Moscow wants to keep things on the hop here, keep their finger well in. That's the mood—just a matter of waiting for the bell to go.'

'I'd rather the old times.'

'We'll look for this fellow Edwards then—and your wife? That's just like old times—nothing serious. Nothing about your setting up a new circle here, that was just cover?'

'That's what they want in London. "Find Edwards," they said.'

'And how have they *lost* this fellow—if they know he's in Cairo? You mean he's gone under—or over?'

'Possibly. But I don't know if he's even here. It was just an idea of mine. We had a meeting—'

Cherry let out a dreadful bellow of laughter.

'That's really serious. We need a bit of that out here. Happy days again all right: you just dropped by to see if he was here, like you'd drop into Davy Byrne's on a wet afternoon looking for the price of a drink if Harry was there. And if he isn't, well, I'll drop over to McDaid's later, he might be there. Or the Bailey. That's how it is, isn't it? But they shoot people out here for that sort of thing, didn't you know?'

Cherry, with another bark, had woken up into some kind of form.

'Jesus, nothing serious all right!'

The little opera had come to an end in the bedroom behind us. Cherry got up. An elderly country woman in a baggy black cotton dress and cap flapped along the terrace in plastic toe-hold sandals, and Cherry spoke to her in Arabic, enumerating various details on his fingers, counting out the things that would have to be done for his wife that evening, like teaching a child on an abacus.

'Come on, we'll have a beer at the Club. I've got to meet Khoury there in any case. My "editor".'

'I was supposed to meet him back at the hotel at six.'

'You must have got it wrong. Khoury practically lives in the Club. That's where he meets everybody.'

4

BRIDGET said, 'I don't damn well care. No one can see me on the balcony, unless they can look round corners. And there aren't any buildings opposite. It's crazy being stuck in here.'

She opened the French windows, took a paper and a drink with her and lay down on a wicker garden couch, opening her house-coat at the neck and flapping the lapels, trying to move some of the evening breeze about her damp, hot body.

They had been there three days now; nothing had happened, the papers hadn't mentioned anything of them, nor the news. The telephone hadn't gone. The resigned immobility of the two men was beginning to annoy Bridget. They sat around the place, talking and smoking endlessly, doing various chores in the mornings like housemaids. She had expected more urgency; she wanted something to *occur*. But Hamdy was damp and lethargic: 'We mustn't do anything, don't you see? Mustn't upset the arrangements. Just wait for them to call. It'll take *time* for them to organize things. We can't get out of here on our own, you know that . . .'

But she'd had her own way about going out on the balcony; the Colonel hadn't stopped her. And now he went back to the bathroom and began to shave, as he did every evening, as if expecting an appointment or a party an hour hence.

Henry was in the kitchen tinkering with the fridge. Warm Stella drove him wild and he'd been trying to get the thing to work ever since they'd arrived.

'She doesn't like being trapped, Hamdy,' Henry called through the doorway.

'It's us, isn't it? Not so much her. She goes out, after all. We're the ones who're stuck.'

'That's what she doesn't like.'

'So what does she expect me to do—call a cab to take us all out to the airport?'

Had he lost some weight? the Colonel wondered as he looked at himself in the glass. Sweating? Fear? Hardly that. There'd been a moment's panic at Bridget's house, but not fear: he

couldn't somehow feel that emotion about a country, about a
people and a security organization he was so familiar with,
whose ways he knew so deeply. It was having Henry with them
that made it so difficult. If he and Bridget had simply been
together . . . They would have slept in the same bed, the
cumbersome affair with its silk hangings and hardened mattress,
that she alone now occupied. That was what was wrong. He
could have tended her, consoled, comforted her. He could have
loved her and perhaps smothered her impatient fear. For she
was frightened, he thought; simply that.

But now the situation was a French farce, with the three of
them manoeuvring round the set, suspecting false doors and
waiting for their trousers to slip. And he had to deny her the
one sort of attention, his obsession for her, which he knew
would calm her. He had to keep to the rules. And the only
encouragement he had was in knowing that Henry had to keep
to them as well.

He pulled the razor round in a neat half-circle between ear
and chin, did the same for the other side, then soaped his face
again. He remembered all the other times he had done this,
preparing to go out with Bridget. He would have to do
something, take some action, if only for her sake.

The Colonel wondered what their reactions would be: if he
told them that the call, when it came, was for him alone, that
he was not with London but with Israel, and was going back
there. What would they do? They wouldn't like it. That's what
it amounted to. Before he finished shaving he knew he would
have to get out on his own without telling them anything. And
yet . . . There was still time before a final decision. He hunted
around for Bridget's rose-water which he'd used since his own
cologne had run out.

The refrigerator started to purr. Henry wobbled it and it
stopped. Another jerk and it was on again. He turned the
freezer carefully up to 'high' and put half a dozen bottles of
Stella on the top shelf, along with some local cheese which had
gone like dry putty, and an oil-stained paper bag of olives. He
didn't bother about the milk or butter or the other food. He
felt in better shape already. The heaviness of the past few days
lifted—the depressing inactivity and befuddled thought. He had
achieved something, started to work himself out of the

situation, and he felt as relieved about the beer as a traveller come to an oasis having seen it hover for many days in the sky.

For those three days he'd been prepared to believe that the Colonel was one of Williams's private appointees in their Mid-East section—or someone who had been placed in Cairo years before when the British Army still occupied the city. And that—in the secretive way of things, the bluffs and double bluffs of his Holborn department—he'd never known about him. It would have been a natural course to take with someone so highly placed in Egyptian intelligence, keep him buried completely from everybody, even to the extent of giving him his own completely separate 'supporting staff' in Cairo and elsewhere—men whose job it would have been to 'service' the Colonel, warn him of possible breaks in his own Cairo *apparat*—and get him out of the country in the event of his being unearthed: his 'ticket men'. At his level the Colonel would have had all these ancillary services, just as he'd had them himself in better days in London and New York from his Moscow source.

All that was perfectly possible. But the one thing that made no sense was that a man in such an exalted position would have run from them long ago, left them and made his own way home. Whatever his personal affections, and the Colonel obviously had these for Bridget, such a man would have bolted from the word go. And the way to do that was to do it alone, not with two other people hanging round your neck.

The information gathered from twenty years with Egyptian security, and latterly as head of counter-intelligence, would have been invaluable to Holborn and no man would risk the chance of getting it home by hanging round with friends, or even his colleagues, and least of all his mistress.

The Colonel would never have taken the risk: affection, love, personal loyalties—whatever it was—didn't arise in a situation like this; not for someone with his professional skills.

Who was the Colonel with then—and where was he running? Henry hardly cared; he would have to run for it on his own, that was his only clear thought. London was over, and Cairo. And Bridget. The places where he wanted to be, and the people who lived there, were gone. Affection, love, loyalty—whatever it was—didn't arise in a situation like this . . .

There was only Moscow and that wasn't certain: the long

de-briefing, a badly-heated apartment, unintelligible rows with a provincial housekeeper, a job in some backwater of the service, ghosting books with the others of his kind, getting drunk with them on Christmas Day: airmail copies of *The Times* when everybody else had thumbed through them: a life within a belief he didn't believe in any more. It lay over the bridge, all this—the scrubbed subways and too much vodka—over Kasr el Nil and down to the hospital where the Moscow Resident worked, just a short walk away. He began more and more to think he didn't want it; now that the fridge was going again.

Bridget finished her drink and looked across the cricket pitch to the entrance of the Club in the distance. It was six o'clock, just starting the half-hour of twilight. The day had cooled, the wind was finished: there would be a few weeks now of perfect weather before the summer really started, tearing everything to shreds. People, other friends of hers in the city, would be doing things: she'd arranged some time before to go down with a doctor's family she knew to their farm in the delta, the remains of a once large estate: a few days walking about the dovecotes and banana groves, watching the grain being forked from pile to pile, the chaff blowing away in the north summer wind from the sea. The creak of Sakias, Shadufs, Archimedes screws; the endless lapping of water. The blanket of night. Card games.

And there were others she knew, comfortable casual acquaintances, probably some of them were walking up the drive of the Club at that moment, if she could have distinguished them, between the squash and croquet courts, on their way for an evening drink.

She wanted to be one of them; quite plainly and vehemently and suddenly she wanted to be done with all this. She wanted to walk out of the flat, down the corniche, up the long drive of the Club and into ordinary life. It was as simple as that.

Behind her the telephone started.

She heard the muffled buzz beneath the cushions in the armchair next to the window. Henry was clattering the last of the bottles into the fridge and the Colonel was dousing his face repeatedly in a flush of water from both taps, screwing his ears out with his fingers, plastering back his thin hair.

She let the phone go on ringing until it stopped. Then she got up and went to get her headscarf and shopping bag.

5

WE turned up the drive to the Club with Cherry stepping along briskly in front of me—a goat on his small legs and grubby suede shoes, red tie and dirty linen coat flapping out around him and his beer belly pushing out over his trousers. He had the pedantic, bear-like, weather-beaten air of some minor British Council official who's been thankfully out of England since Munich, traipsing round the grubby corners of the Levant on the same small salary and in the same clothes: the sort of rundown happy academic who 'keeps in touch with things' at home, and ministers to the locals, with a box of lantern slides telling 'The Story of Parliament' in one pocket and Desmond MacCarthy's last book of *Critical Essays* in the other.

He smelled vaguely of old beer and long siestas; of ink and chalk and small evening classes on the Lake Poets in some baking upstairs room above the tramway, looking out at a statue of Garibaldi—or Ataturk, or Soliman Pasha: a bare trickle of sense seeping through into the willing, mystified faces of refined old ladies and the secretaries who dreamed of a season at the Berlitz in Oxford Street. Cherry, the genuine expatriate with his weekly copy of the *T.L.S.*—the sort who'd never even thought of getting a job on the Third Programme.

Cherry was full of certainties; he'd found his mark in this isolated, crumbling city: it was exactly his weather. He was someone here.

The cars and taxis swirled past us on the drive, full of flannelled, blazered men and girls of 'good family'. The slow 'thunk' of the croquet, and the vicious 'snap-FLACK' of the squash, resounding from the courts on either side of us—and Cherry strode along towards the entrance with the vigorous impatience of a child on its way to the nursery. He was someone here; yes indeed. It made all the difference.

'Yallah, Mohammed!' he called to a waiter at the top of the steps. 'Entar Mabsout? Quais Ketir?'

'Aiowa, Bey! 'Am di'illah.'

The man saluted and we walked through the small hallway and out on to the covered terrace by the small pool beyond.

I said, 'You weren't a member here before, Herbert. Rather overdoing the Raj thing, isn't it—for a good Dubliner?'

'Nonsense, Marlow. This is for Egyptians now.' And before he went over to the table on the far side of the pool where I could see Mr. Khoury sitting, he had started to clap his hands impatiently at another waiter.

'Dine etnine Stella, fi cubia,' he shouted, as we threaded our way between the tables where the smart set in polo necks and armless cotton frocks were gathered in huge circles, the men, in groups, lying back with their feet up on opposite chairs, spinning rackets in their hands, looking serious; the girls in just as easy, confident, though much straighter, positions, skirts sometimes an inch above the knee. Before the British had entirely left Egypt ten years earlier, an Egyptian had publicly relieved himself in the Club's small pool by the terrace. 'It's Egyptian water now,' he'd said. 'Like the canal.' It was a famous incident. But in these days there was no need for such insecurity; the smarter Cairenes had replaced the English exactly in the hierarchic ecology of the Club, were indistinguishable from them in their proprietary and superior airs.

Mr. Khoury had stood up long before we reached his table, wreathed in smiles, his mouth a twinkling hollow of black gaps and gold fillings, already waving his arms and giving his companions a running biography of us and our affairs before we were near him.

'. . . and Mr. Marlow from London who is doing some programmes and we are going to help him.'

There was a woman near him in the latest saucer-like sun glasses and half a dozen others round the table: middle-aged, intellectual, young-at-heart. Two wine coolers with bottles of Stella rammed neck first into the middle of them stood at either end of the table.

'We don't see many people out from England here these days,' the saucer-eyed lady said to her companion before Mr. Khoury had finished with the introductions.

'. . . Mohammed Said, Ahmed Fawzi, Morsy Tewfik, Ali Zaki, Mrs. Olive Moustafa . . .'

Mrs. Olive Moustafa. I leant across the wine coolers and shook hands. She took her glasses off. A sunburnt, small, hard-worked sort of face, neat brown hair with threads of red in it, the remnants of freckles showing through a tanned and oily forehead. She might have been Scots or Irish.

'Mrs. Moustafa works for the International Press Agency here—that right, Olive?—you'll get all the news from her, what you won't read in the papers. That right, Olive? Is Michael coming down?'

Olive smiled lightly, perhaps even bitterly, at Khoury.

'He might. He's very busy right now.'

Cherry had gone over to the other side of the table and was leaning over a young American, berating him vigorously, clapping him repeatedly on the shoulder to emphasize a point.

'. . . and why *can't* we read what you write about the place? Why can't we get your bloody paper out here—eh? You tell me.'

'You ask Morsy that, Herbert. He's Press Censor. He never gets out to the airport to check them through, that's why. They just lie there, I think. That right, Morsy?'

Morsy Tewfik was sitting next to him—a soft, round, pulpy face, a very well-kept fellow going to fat in a silk shirt and gold cuff-links, with what used to be known as a 'brilliantined scalp': each hair flowing straight back over his head like a petrified oil slick. When he spoke it was in a perfectly enunciated, top-drawer, Oxbridge drawl.

'I don't stop your paper, Jim. You don't send any—except the ones for the Embassies. And the Ministry copies we get. Who is there could afford fifty piastres on the streets out here anyway? It costs too much, that's all. That's why Herbert doesn't read it.'

Mr. Khoury butted in—'Jim Whelan, *New York News* correspondent out here. Mr. Marlow, from London . . .'

'Pleased to meet you, Mr. Marlow.'

Whelan had a tennis shirt on, with a green laurel garland embossed over the heart, fine but profusely growing hair all along his forearms, a pair of colourless spectacles—of the old-fashioned Bakelite sort that you see in photographs of Harold Ross—and behind them a slight squint. He had a bounce of flaxen hair that stood up and shivered when he spoke and was one of those ageless young Americans. He might have been anything between fifteen and forty and his permanently quizzical, disappointed expression suggested that he'd never been able to find out how old he was himself; a serious man on an even more serious earth, one felt, and by God he was going to find out the truth about it all if it killed him.

'Mr. Whelan writes about us *every* day,' Mr. Khoury said, as though Whelan was working out a prison sentence.

Morsy Tewfik and Whelan and Cherry embarked on an argument about the price of rice in the delta as opposed to Cairo—Whelan's piece for the next day apparently—and Olive Moustafa leant across to me.

'Could I get some lemonade to mix with the beer?' I managed to say to Mr. Khoury, before she pinned me down.

'What are you doing . . .' She started off like a greyhound out of a trap.

What, where, why and for whom. She was a persistent party. I wondered who Mr. Moustafa was and how she'd come by him, but didn't have the chance to ask. She quizzed me studiously for several minutes without getting much back.

'You ought to meet Pearson, Michael Pearson, our correspondent here. He'll be able to fill you in,' she said, rather aggressively, I thought—the physical connotation more in my mind than the journalistic.

'Oh, I'm not doing any news stories. More background material, colour stuff. I used to live out here. It's a trip back to look at the place as much as anything . . .'

We were vaguely worried about each other.

She was the sort of woman who, without any obvious show of impatience or ruthlessness, none the less gives an impression of bitter inner speculation: a sense, like the threat of a hidden time bomb, that she'd find out everything in the end so one might as well tell her straight away; it would save trouble.

She would have been just the sort of person to send looking for Henry, I thought. She'd know all the ropes, all the nooks and crannies: a greedy woman, unsatisfied—her feminine intuition not at all domestic but loose and roving: friend or enemy depending on what you fed her, and she obviously regarded my coming to the city as an interesting plate of meat.

'There's another man who often comes out here doing odd articles—do you known him at all—Henry Edwards? He does pieces for the *Spectator* and some of the glossies. Ever come across him?'

I took the question on the run. 'Yes, I've met him once or twice. Haven't seen him recently, though. Has be been out here?'

'I saw him a month ago. I was just wondering, there was a journalist with Mohammed Yunis when he left the airport—you know about Yunis, he's under house arrest now—and I thought

it might have been Edwards. We don't know much about it, the
flight came via Munich, so it could have been a *Stern* man he
was with. We're trying to get something on it. Unless you came
on that flight too—did you?'

She was running it hard. 'No, I didn't, as a matter of fact.
Where did you meet Edwards?'

'Michael knows him really. He comes into our office when
he's here. But how does he make his money at this freelance
business, that's what I'd like to know. He's out here half a
dozen times a year and there can't be that sort of interest in the
UAR—even in the glossies . . .'

Mrs. Moustafa was sprinting now and the trick was to run
with her, past her, pip her at the post.

'Has he money of his own? Or maybe he does rep work for
some firm. Or perhaps he works for British Intelligence. One
never knows, does one?'

'One never does.'

Mrs. Moustafa looked at me, her expression more intrigued
than ever for a second; looking at me, waiting for a sign, a
knowing hint that she and I were in the same line of country. I
didn't hammer it and she lost interest. But I could see she felt
she was on to something, worrying at an idea: 'British agent
arrested in Cairo' and a pat on the back from the Chairman in
London. There was a war brewing up too and perhaps she felt
she might be first in the line this time, to break the story of
another Suez—another 'collusion'.

A small, thin man—narrowed out to the point of emaciation—
weaved his way like a dancer through the tables, tiny feet
skipping across the terrace, out into the last of the sunlight, and
over one corner of the pool, in a frenzied quickstep: a fox face,
a double-breasted linen suit and thin jet-black hair combed
straight back with a central parting completed the picture of a
'thirties dance band leader running from the management with
the evening's takings. He seemed excessively worried as well as
pressed. But closer to, the deeply lined face and springy
movements suggested that his nervous motion was habitual, not
temporary. He waved round the table and there were the barest
introductions before he squeezed himself into a seat next to
Olive. I turned away and engaged Mr. Khoury in concentrated
talk about Egyptian folk drama. I wanted to hear what Michael
Pearson was possibly in more of a hurry than usual about.

'. . . and what about these rural folk-art centres, the one in the Fayoum you mentioned? Are they really inspired by anything local, or just something got up by the government? . . .'

'Certainly they are real, Mr. Marlow: this is the true folk drama, centuries, *millennia* old . . .'

'. . . Hamdy . . . Army Intelligence . . .' I barely caught the words from across the table.

'. . . a drama based on centuries of oppression . . .'

'. . . can't file anything. But we'll see . . .'

'. . . "Words are the only weapons of the poor." You remember your Sean O'Casey . . .' Mr. Khoury boomed, spreading his arms upwards in a half circle. 'A *genuine* peasant drama, Mr. Marlow. These people aren't worrying about your angst like your John Osbornes or your Louis MacNeices—they are *trapped*—', another boom and shake of the arms, '—in a prodigious drama of *real* events, Mr. Marlow. That's what it is, I assure you. And now under the revolution we are uncovering for the first time . . .'

I said, 'Of course if the revolution is making things much better for everyone, if it's lifted the oppression—as it has—the peasants won't have much to dramatize, will they? The *raison d'être* for their fine words will have disappeared rather. When the saviour actually comes he puts an end to the drama, no?'

'Certainly not. You are being subtle, Mr. Marlow. I will take you to the cultural centre at Zagazig and you will see for yourself. Let me get you some more lemonade. I know the drink—at Oxford once, we were visiting with some chaps and we had it there by the river. You call it "Shandy Guff", don't you? "Give me Shandy Guff," I remember the fellows saying.'

Shandy Guff and Colonel Hassan Hamdy . . . a new strip cartoon for *Rose el Yussef* . . . The gaps in the talk between Olive and Pearson had been easy enough to fill: *Colonel* Hamdy and *Egyptian* Army Intelligence. And Mr. Pearson had been in a hurry about him. I noticed now that Whelan had turned round and was talking to them, Cherry having moved back to our side of the table.

Something was afoot about the Colonel, Yunis was under wraps and a journalist had been with him at the time of his arrest. Possibly Edwards, Olive thought. They were building something; the various people were connected in some way—or were they simply being connected by the International Press Agency? Colonel Hamdy and Yunis—I could see a connection there. But Edwards? They weren't going to tell me—unless they came to believe that I held an essential clue to the whole affair.

I turned to Mr. Khoury again and said in a voice slightly sharper than usual: 'Did you ever hear of a good writer, a friend of mine, Henry Edwards? He was fond of the folk drama. Very interested.'

'Edwards? I don't think so. No,' Khoury said reluctantly. 'But we will meet, certainly we will. You will introduce me.'

Pearson had looked up, I saw him out of the corner of my eye, his flat shiny hair reflecting the light for a second—the street lamp affair which had gone on above our table.

He turned away again at once but he'd seen the bait and I knew he'd come for it again. Henry counted for something, I realized now, in the rumours he was collecting—was one of the missing pieces in the puzzle which involved Yunis and Colonel Hamdy. And they weren't looking for this man who'd been with Yunis, this possible Henry, because he was a journalist, but because he was a possible defector. If it had been Henry at the airport with Yunis, then Pearson's interest in him was because he smelt a Blake or a Philby in the whole affair.

Journalists believed that our service, and particularly my own Middle East section, formed an inexhaustible source of sensational copy. They had good reasons for that belief. Like hunters at a rat hole they waited for the next exit—the man who came running from the grimy depths into the light and across the guns for a second, only to disappear down another bolt-hole on the far side of the common. They were rarely caught on this blind run through the dazzle, but they were seen, or thought to be seen, and the presses rolled with half-facts and rumour. And Pearson was a real 'no smoke without fire' man. On some sort of tip-off he was getting his team together outside the warren, organizing the long vigil, and no doubt Whelan would have the exclusive North American rights. Was the rumour genuine, then, that Edwards was on the run, defecting? I'd not believed anything of the sort in London. But it struck me that Pearson wouldn't have been so excited over anything less.

Cherry was squabbling again—with Mr. Khoury this time, wagging his finger at him about an article on Palestine in the last edition of *Arab Focus*. I took another dash of beer. The

Palestine Problem: I'd gone through the Arab press about that for ten years in London—how did Cherry have the enthusiasm for it? It was his expatriate version of the Irish Question, I suppose.

In all this talk what I wanted was a hard fact or two: was Henry in Cairo—and if so, why? Had he defected, or just been caught by the Egyptians? That was the equation.

I got up to go to the pissoir next to the showers on the other side of the pool. There was a row of small frosted glass windows, half open, above the immense porcelain urinals, and I could see part of the driveway that ran round the front of the Club, down past the cricket pitch and out of the back entrance into Zamalek.

A woman had walked past, in the crowd of strollers, with her back to me now, carrying a string shopping bag: tall, in a light cardigan and headscarf, a thin body, coming out suddenly at the hips and in again, down to long narrowing legs; not typical of Cairo at all. Looking at her moving away from the Club I tried to put a face to the body. I imagined myself on the far side, up the drive, walking towards her. That way of walking, the confident brisk step, the flat backside: what would I see if I were looking at that figure the other way about?

And the face I saw when I reversed the image was Bridget's.

By the time I'd run round back on to the terrace, out through the main entrance and on to the driveway she had disappeared. I raced along the grass verge but the road was crowded with people, cars pushing through them, their lights blinding me as I dodged in and out of the traffic. I tried to get ahead of the strollers so that I could look back along the headlights at their faces. But when I did there was no one I recognized in the long pencils of light. Nothing. If not her, I thought, then who?

When I came back up the Club steps again Olive Moustafa was in the hallway. She seemed to have just come out of the ladies' room, but I had the impression she'd been looking for me.

'*There* you are. We thought you'd gone. We're going to play some croquet. Do you play? Morsy has the court for seven o'clock and he's suggested dinner with him afterwards.'

Snapping at the bait again, I thought. I wondered how they would handle it.

Cherry, Whelan and Mr. Khoury came down the drive with us and sat on the balcony of one of the little wooden pavilions which ran along one side of the four floodlit courts. A *suffragi* flustered round them and they ordered coffee; drinks weren't allowed near the field of play. Many Egyptians took this game very seriously, as something mystical, second in importance only to the Koran, and I'd picked up some slight skill in it myself when I'd lived here. They'd never taken to cricket, as had other former British 'Dominions', seeing it as a pointless, long drawn out nonsense which denied any really individual nastiness. But croquet, perhaps because it specifically allowed for this, had some great magic for these upper-class Cairenes and they played it with a passion they gave to few other things in their life.

Mrs. Moustafa partnered Morsy and I played with Pearson.

We knocked the four coloured balls round the first three hoops with the mildest of chatter. Pearson wasn't all that good at the game, I was worse, and the others were several hoops ahead of us as we turned up the back straight.

'You're not *looking* for Edwards yourself, are you?' Pearson said, studiously and suddenly, lining up a shot for the fourth hoop.

'No. Why should I be?'

He smacked the ball up court, passing the wire and going off the edge at the far end, leaving me an impossible angle to get back on.

'Just a little worried about him, that's all. Someone was seen at the airport with Yunis three days ago, just before he was arrested. A journalist, my contact at the airport said. Someone he'd seen out here quite often before. But he couldn't describe him exactly—except for the hair. He said the man had a lot of hair. Henry usually drops in to see me when he's here. That's what made me wonder.'

I tapped my shot back to the far side of the wire, giving Pearson a straight through on his next turn.

'You think there's a story in it?'

'Whoever was with Yunis at the time has a story. No one has any firm details on his arrest or what it's all about. We're scratching around trying to fill them in.'

'You mean if it was this man Edwards—he'd tell you what happened?'

'He used to let me know odd things when I saw him out here. Straight news, agency stuff, things he didn't use himself. If it *was* Edwards, that is . . .'

We'd nearly caught up with the others. Mrs. Moustafa had failed at a hoop and, if played right—it wasn't difficult— Pearson's next shot should croquet her. He'd then have an easy passage through the iron and, once through, could take her on down with him to the pole at the end. He missed. On purpose I'd have said. The others went ahead of us.

I said, 'Who else could it have been then, with Yunis?'

'It wasn't any of the regular correspondents—something would have broken on the story by now.'

'Why a journalist in any case?'

'Passport control. We have a little money on the right horse there. The man who came through with Yunis had a British passport—profession was marked as "Journalist". That narrows it down fairly.'

The others were two hoops and a pole ahead of us. I tried to pull back a few shots but without success. Olive was playing like a demon and Pearson was fudging everything. He put his foot on his mallet like a big game hunter on a lion while the others streamed ahead up the home straight.

'We'll make it worth your while. Very much so. Unless of course you're contracted already. Anything you know about the Yunis business.'

'I'm not doing that sort of work out here, Mr. Pearson. I was telling Mrs. Moustafa—just background stuff.'

'That's what I thought—'

'I haven't got any hard news and I didn't come on that flight. I came in last night.'

Pearson nodded, impatiently. These were preliminaries for him. I could see he believed me—as I didn't believe him. What he wanted was to talk to me, to pretend I was a serious journalist, while searching out my real business in Cairo. And he had to have a good reason for broaching the subject of Edwards with me at all, one that would give the impression that he was interested in Edwards and myself purely from the professional point of view—as journalists who might be on to a good story: he had to cover what I was sure now was his real interest in the whole matter—that he believed Henry was running in the Philby stakes, that he'd used Yunis in some way to get into Egypt, and that I'd been sent out from London to stop him before he went over to Moscow. He'd never really bought the idea that Henry was a Fleet Street man, or that I was even a serious freelance. Pearson had made a reasonable job of the bluff, but he'd left a loophole, intentionally no doubt, knowing I'd go for it, which I shouldn't have done; it was just his cockiness.

'You must have known who was on that flight with Yunis then. If you had his profession and nationality—your contact could hardly have overlooked the name.'

Pearson belted his shot wildly to the pavilion, smiling. The game was over, the others had tipped the post. We walked back after them slowly.

'Now I'm telling *you* something,' he said.

'Why not? What's the mystery?'

'You don't know yourself?'

'Of course not. Was it Edwards?'

'Yes. It was. That was the name on the passport.'

'Why the elaborate front then?'

'I couldn't put it directly, you'd have shied away. I had to get you to ask the questions. You're looking for Edwards too, aren't you? We could probably help each other.'

'We probably couldn't, Mr. Pearson. I doubt that very much.' And I left it at that.

Pearson had got his sights on Edwards all right: Edwards, out of the hole and on the run, in the light for a moment before disappearing again. They'd missed it all with Philby in Beirut and they weren't going to miss it with Edwards in Cairo. It was the same thing all over again. But was it? It was just as possible that Henry had become involved with Yunis somehow, on a job which had gone wrong, and had been picked up with him by Egyptian Intelligence—by Colonel Hamdy, the other man in Pearson's crossword.

Either way he was somewhere in the city. I knew that now and I'd no doubt that Pearson would try and make me pay for the information. He wouldn't have given it to me unless he had been confident I had got something for him in return.

Pearson had a hunch, his network about the city had given him a lucky break, and he was going to play it for all it was worth. At this distance I couldn't read him the Official Secrets Act or slap a D notice on him. There wasn't enough to go on. It was a question now of who would find Edwards first; probably

Pearson would. It seemed he was several steps ahead in the
chase and he was also in the best sort of position to use me. All
he had to do was have one of his Egyptian contacts keep an eye
on me—not a difficult exercise in Cairo where every shoeshine
boy, kiosk vendor and porter were keeping their eyes on
somebody—for somebody else's money.

After the croquet we all walked down the back drive, round
past the Omar Khayyam Hotel and along the corniche to
Morsy's apartment. It was in an old turn of the century building
on the third storey. At the back there was a balcony that
looked on to the Club's cricket pitch while the main entrance
on Gezira Street faced out over the river: a long narrow
apartment with the usual pseudo second Empire furniture caked
in gilt, cracked family portraits, heavy carpets and very few
windows. It must have been awfully dark in the daytime.
    There was plenty to drink and a buffet of Port Said prawns
and rice, grilled delta pigeon, stuffed courgettes and so on.
Pearson didn't bother me. I talked with Morsy's wife, Leila, an
attractive woman, just fractionally plump, in her late thirties,
but with the weary isolated air of so many educated Cairo
wives: a woman who had wanted, and been capable of, much
more than she had ever got, either from her husband or from
life in Egypt. She made suitable sounds about the President and
the sort of society he had created in Egypt, but one felt it
didn't really touch her, not because she was frivolous or stupid,
but because she came from the city's professional upper
class—from a family of bankers or lawyers or whatever—from a
metropolitan society which had been liberated for generations.
She would like to have exercised herself in a larger world, or at
least felt a part of it—of Paris, and London and Günter Grass.
    She was interested in things beyond the narrow confines of
Arab nationalism and such idle preoccupations were no longer
on offer in Cairo. The city was bereft of ideas. There was only
one idea, the war against Israel. It made the fearful middle class
nervous and short-tempered, full of upsets and hangovers, gave
them thoughts of a boat to Canada.
    But Leila Tewfik was committed to something she couldn't
give anything to, stuck where she was, with the latest foreign
papers and magazines stacked neatly about the living room, all
the news of the world her husband got before he censored it.
She—and Morsy too—were part of the 'new class' spawned by

every revolution; except that in Egypt that class was often composed of the children of the old, inheritors of necessary intellect—and unnecessary, unsatisfied longings.

I was exhausted and left early, dropping Cherry off in a cab by the hospital. 'We'll have a drink another night. Seriously,' he said in a slow voice. 'And Edwards is in town,' he added, commenting on my talk with Pearson which I'd told him about. 'That should please you.'

'Vaguely. I could do without Pearson. And I hardly know where to begin.'

'Why don't you climb that tower? You'll probably spot him from there.'

Cherry smiled and disappeared up the avenue of palm trees to the woman who lay like a pencil, stiff and straight, lightly wrapped in a sheet. And I thought of the other woman with the flat backside and narrowing legs who'd walked away from me towards Zamalek. And again, so easily, I saw myself walking towards her, seeing her face.

6

THE Cairo Tower was in the middle of the old Botanical Gardens, on Gezira Island, just across from the hospital, and I went there first thing next morning: a huge 700-foot phallus in latticed concrete wrapped round the central elevator core. It had been built, so we had been reliably informed in our Holborn section, with three million dollars in notes which the CIA had attempted to bribe Nasser with ten years before. It was a pure undisguised folly, with no function whatsoever other than that of being an affront to the 'forces of neo-Imperialism'—and it succeeded well enough in that, facing as it did the expensive bedrooms of the Hilton on the opposite bank of the river—the terraces from which latter-day CIA men had to view it every morning when they woke up, sniffing the airs of the city in their towel-robes and wristlet name-plates.

A drowsy clerk, sipping a glass of milky tea and burning ruts in the pay desk with his cigarette, took my ten piastres and the lift crawled and squeaked for minutes on my way up. There was a minute café at the top, surrounded by glass, with a terrace beyond that and a coin-operated telescope fixed on to the concrete balustrade, leaning drunkenly down over the river.

Apart from an even more sleepy waiter who made me a coffee there was no one else about and the whole pinnacle, though it hadn't been up for more than a few years, had a dilapidated, run-down air about it. The concrete window casements were beginning to flake away at the edges, eroding in the dry windy weather up here, a pane of glass eight feet square was cracked from side to side, and the wooden chairs and tables must have been taken from some back-street café or a mission school that had closed.

The Tower wasn't a popular attraction apparently; perhaps there had been a scare about its safety once. It was a mysterious toy, a Trojan horse which the local people mistrusted, I imagined. Egyptians have little head for heights, theirs is a flat country, and I suppose many of them, particularly those on the bread line and beneath, must naturally have questioned the safety of such a patently useless, expensive ornament.

I went out on to the balcony, forcing the iron door open. Although the vantage point was tremendous the view was unsatisfying somehow. The desert sands, brought by the Khamseen, hadn't yet subsided in the air so that the city was covered in a film of sepia and ochre, and the buildings seemed to flap about in the haze like dirty brown and yellow sacks. There was a monotonous sameness in the view from this height. Nothing, none of the mosques, the minarets or cupolas, stood out. Everything looked as haphazard and dirty as a collection of nomad tents thrown up about the place, which, of course, was how the mediaeval city had begun—'El Fustat', the tent—so I suppose the view was appropriate enough. With eyes half closed against the glare one saw the unchanged continuity of a thousand years—an encampment of ragged cloth by a huge brown river. The modern city disappeared; a ribbon of dun colours took its place beneath a tired lead-blue sky.

I yanked the telescope up on its pivot and put a coin in on the half-chance that it still worked. The machine clicked, the shutter opened suddenly and I found myself looking, with startling clearness, at a plump Levantine gentleman in bathing trunks having coffee on his bedroom terrace of the Hilton. He lit a cigarette and I could see the red and white colour of the pack—'Marlboro'—though I couldn't actually read the lettering. He screwed a finger in one ear, examined the result on the end of his nail, got up and went into the bedroom. He moved around inside, sliding out of his trunks, a brown shadow against the white counterpane of the bed.

I swung the machine round to the left, over the river, the crescent sails of a felucca jumping up suddenly in the foreshortened distance, billowing into the lens, filling the whole view, like the underbelly of some river monster. Further round the battered cricket score-board by the Zamalek entrance to the Club came into view. The last batsman had apparently made 990 runs, until I saw that the 'Batsman' sign had fallen down over the 'Total Runs' sign. And I remembered I'd seen the same incongruity from the balcony of the Tewfiks' apartment the previous evening. Their place would be somewhere above and to the right of the score-board. I swung the telescope up and back along the line of buildings that faced out over the pitch.

The Tewfiks' terrace had two basketwork chairs and a glass-topped bamboo table. I moved the glass to and fro along the buildings. They'd been on the third floor. I counted them up from the ground—there it was, the chairs and the little table and the French windows open behind, and a woman in a black cotton smock dusting the living-room. She came out and shook the cloth over the rail. Would Leila appear, I wondered? Perhaps she'd come out on to the terrace with an open house-coat and without her glasses . . . But she didn't. I was tiring with the strain of keeping one eye screwed up, but the machine was running out with a furious ticking and I panned it once more to the balcony of the next building, upwards to the top floor, where I'd seen something move.

Another woman had come out on to the terrace in sun glasses and a short house-coat and was setting up a deck chair in the corner out of the sun. I tried to focus the lens to get a clearer view. But the shutter clicked and fell. I stood up and stretched. A last shot? I wondered. Yes. Why not? There was Bridget's apartment, round the other way to my right, on top of the block in Garden City. I might as well see if I could get it on the machine. I put in ten piastres and was just on the point of swinging round when I saw the woman in the short house-coat again. She had stood up and was in the light now, talking, arguing, it seemed, to a man who had joined her.

I recognized him first, the fluffy strands of unruly hair through which he was running his fingers, the ancient saucer spectacles, the full, rather debauched, boyish face. It was Henry, so that for quite a while, in my surprise, I didn't bother identifying the woman. Just a girl he was with, I thought, someone he'd picked up in his voracious way—until he moved towards her and they kissed. I felt there was something incredibly awkward in this event—which wasn't in their movements which were perfectly natural—and I couldn't at first understand why I was so struck by the embrace in this way, as a catastrophe, an outrage, coming over the lens to me as a blow in the stomach.

And then I looked carefully again at the woman's profile. The message had simply been delayed a few seconds. I'd known I was looking at Bridget before I could believe it, put it into words, before I could give a name to the woman whose fingers were linked round the back of Henry's neck now, the house-coat flapping open about her in the windy baking haze.

I didn't say anything to Cherry when I met him half an hour later. I'd taken a third ten piastres' worth on the telescope, swinging it round and peering at other parts of the city, so that the waiter behind me would have no exact idea of what or where I'd been looking at if he were asked. And I knew he'd been looking at me—a natural for one of Pearson's Egyptian pound notes.

Henry and Bridget had gone inside. They were in the apartment above and to the left of the Tewfiks'; I didn't know if they shared the same stairway. But I knew enough. It was the same building. I had simply to decide what to do about it. Though even at that point I can remember thinking that just going up to the apartment and knocking on the door was the last thing I'd do.

Cherry had been up to his office and had brought a message back from Mr. Khoury, a schedule in fact, of trips about the city. A visit to the High Court, to the Egyptian Family Planning Association and the steel works at Helwan.

'Where are you going to find Edwards in all that?' he remarked over coffee on the hospital terrace. His wife was in better form that morning and Cherry was in a pushy mood without a drink taken. I told him that one place was as good as another, that I'd pick up something.

'I doubt you will. You'd do better to stick around Pearson.'

'I'll find Henry before he does.'

'What about Usher? Do you want me to make any plan there? You should see him. Perhaps Henry called there.'

'In time, not now. Intelligence here knows all about Usher. His phone would be tapped or they'd nail me if I went up there to see him on my own. If there was some reason, a party or something, then I could call.'

There was only one thing to do now, stall on these various plans and proposals, and find out what was going on in the apartment on the Gezira corniche. How? Wait for them to come out? And then follow them? And then what? Nothing much, unless I could actually hear what was going on in the apartment. And that seemed impossible. There were technical tricks, of course, planting microphones on walls or through telephones, shooting mini-transmitters from an air rifle at the end of a suction pellet, but I barely knew the beginnings of them. There would have to be something else, something entirely in the realm of the ordinary.

We went on to the Club for a beer and a sandwich by the empty pool and I wondered what it could be—how to be *in*, but not *of*, the apartment which I could just make out from where we were sitting, a smudge of white concrete burning in the sun high over the cricket score-board.

Yet it shouldn't have been impossible, I thought. I'd had some desultory training when I'd first come back to London from Egypt ten years before, a few dry lectures in shadowing and concealment, dropping a tail, and so on, before I'd subsided into the Information and Library in Holborn. And in essence was there any real difference in this case? I'd dropped from the sky on a mission and except for the fact that a woman, not a country, had become the dangerous foreign territory, it was much like any other undercover job; the same principals should apply: keep your head, wait, think—*do*; that was the order. I'd found out about Henry, as much as was necessary for the moment. Now I wanted to find out about the woman who had been my wife.

Leila Tewfik stood on the terrace steps, twirling her spectacles round in one hand, shading her eyes with the other, surveying the few people about the place as if they were a multitude. I thought she must have seen us, we weren't more than fifteen

yards away, but she stayed where she was, dilatory and
composed in a sleeveless Greek embroidered tunic with a
dressing gown belt tied loosely round her waist. The dress
disguised her slight plumpness and the rough oatmeal material
accentuated her fluffy dark hair which she must have washed
overnight, for it stood up alarmingly over her ears. Her arms and
face were an extraordinary honey-coloured bronze; it was
probably her best feature. She had some foreign paper under
her arm and it seemed unlikely, I thought with regret, that she'd
come to the Club for a swim. She put her glasses back on, saw
us now, and ambled over.

'God,' she said, 'I feel none too fine.'

She lay back, tilting the chair over, stretching her arms wide
apart. There was a large emerald-coloured ring on one finger, no
wedding ring. She shaved regularly under the arms. A neat, well
tended, unattended woman.

'Morsy was up to all hours—going on with Pearson and
Whelan and Khoury. Drinking, drinking. I wish Mohammed
Yunis had stayed in Moscow—and his journalist friend, whoever
he was. And Colonel Hamdy. Morsy doesn't know anything
about them really. He pretends. With a few drinks he becomes
the President's special confidant. As if there wasn't one
already.'

Leila Tewfik wasn't at all as serious as I'd remembered her.
She had thawed dramatically in the hangover.

'Underberg. You need an Underberg,' Cherry said.

'Ugh!' she said, enunciating the expression exactly, like an
exclamation in a comic strip. 'I hope not.'

'You need something fizzy to get the gas up,' I said. 'A bottle
of light ale, I'm told that's a palliative, administers a sound and
beneficial shock to the whole system.'

'I shouldn't. But I will.'

She slumped forward on her chair, put her elbows on the
table and cradled her chin morosely. Cherry clapped his hands
for a waiter in his irritating way and she looked at me with that
unwavering, warmly intense look that comes with a hangover
for someone you like, when you're no longer afraid of letting
them know it.

'You know all about hangovers, don't you? The Irish are
supposed to drink a lot and we're not supposed to at all.'

'What do you normally do?'

'When?'

'When you've had too much to drink.'

'I never do anything—unless I meet someone like Cherry, or you, the day after. Bed and aspirin, that's what I usually do. But what do *you* do, tell me, what are you really going to write about here? Cairo life? There's not a lot of it, is there: croquet and the fellaheen? Or are you secretly after the Yunis business, trying to scoop Pearson and the others? Whelan annoys me sometimes. He's no eye for details, he gets it all wrong. Egyptians tend to be very formal nowadays, because they're isolated, unsure of themselves. And the *New York News* is even worse. Backs up the dullness all the time. Weevils in the cotton and MiGs in the Fayoum—that's all that seems to interest them. They've forgotten, we've forgotten, there's anything else— forgotten how to live.'

Cherry said, 'That's true of the Americans and the Israelis as well. True of anybody at war. Wars are only fought out of a sense of uncontrollable power. And powerful people become formal bores.'

Leila looked up at the flat sky. Silence. We all looked up.

' "Tell me where all past days are, or who cleft the Devil's foot . . ." ' Cherry broke in mock-mournfully. The waiter brought some more Stella.

' "Waiting for a War"—that might be a title for you,' Leila said to me.

'Oh, I'll find something less grave, I'm sure. I'm not a war correspondent. The lighter side is my speciality.'

'You won't find much of that here,' Leila said. 'Unless—do you play badminton? Morsy's got a net up on the roof at home. He's gone mad on it. That's a lighter side.'

She looked at me carefully again, blinking through her spectacles, either coquettishly or because her eyes were hurting, I couldn't really tell. Cherry lay back and looked upwards again, eyes agape. He sighed and then he moaned—a rising whine which he caught at the top of his nose and which was one of his many preludes to derisory comment.

'Ah-h-h-h no! Not that. Not badminton. You must be out of your mind, Leila.'

'Just because you're past it, you large fellow.'

Badminton, I thought, on the roof of her apartment. Croquet and now badminton. Perhaps I'd get a game of cricket before this was out. The spy as sportsman. I smiled at Leila.

'You can play, can't you?' she said. 'It's just like tennis. Only you don't let the ball bounce. And it isn't a ball.'

We arranged to meet at five o'clock that evening.

7

THERE was a separate entrance to the apartment where Henry and Bridget had been, I saw, when I got to Leila's place that evening. But the two sections of the block shared the same long roof, with a lift shaft and laundry buildings rising up at either end, forming a barrier which prevented the shuttlecock from disappearing too frequently, though under Morsy's indignant, untutored hammerings it sailed over the sides of the roof often enough. He had one of his *suffragis* down below, stationed head-in-air, scuttling round the block to retrieve them.

Cherry arrived towards six o'clock and we had some lemon juice and mopped our faces. I hadn't really found my form, had lost every game but one, and I wandered away from them, walking with a slight limp, trying to ease the cramp which had come up in one thigh.

I looked over the edge of the roof just above the balcony where Bridget had been. It was impossible to see anything on the terrace below. The lift shaft door at the far end was open and I looked in. There was a huge spindly wheel encrusted with grease and a smell of warm oil. The laundry next to it was empty and a door beyond the row of tubs must have led down to the floor below. I couldn't have been more than a few feet above whatever was going on beneath me but I'd learnt more about it from the Tower half a mile away that morning. It probably wouldn't have been too difficult to introduce a microphone into the place, if one knew the tricks, if one had a microphone.

Morsy had followed me, drink in hand, looking very fit and pleased with himself. His shorts were too short and one heel of his plimsolls was working loose.

'It works, doesn't it?'

I looked at him.

'The badminton on the roof, I mean.'

'It's fine. You don't get complaints from the people below, do you? Bouncing up and down?'

'There's no one in the apartment beneath. It's empty. That's the beautiful thing. That's why I got the badminton up here.'

'But aren't there *two* apartments on the floor beneath? There are two lift shafts.'

'There's no one in either of them. All the floors in this block used to be one single apartment. Then they divided them in half, filled in the connecting doorways and put another lift in at that end.'

'*No* one in them? What about the housing shortage?'

'Doesn't apply, not in this part of town, in this sort of place. All these apartments are owned by the original families who bought them and quite a few of them live abroad now, or in Alex. The one underneath us on my side is sequestrated still. It used to belong to an Armenian lawyer who went back home, wherever that is, last year. And the other, underneath us here, was owned by an old lady who's dead now. One of her relations, I think it is, uses the place sometimes. But he's never there. So we can make as much row as we like. That's the beauty of it. We had a party up here a month ago, even some dancing. But don't put that in anything you write, will you? Press censors don't dance, you know. Or give parties. Or play badminton on the roof of their apartment. It wouldn't do at all. Shall we go down? It's too dark for another game, I fear.'

The huge-eyed *suffragi* came up with the last lot of shuttlecocks, clustered gently in his hands like a nest of birds, and presented them to Morsy with all the elaborate courtesies of the messenger with the tennis balls in *Henry V*. Morsy likewise put them away with careful importance in their long cylinder and we trooped back to their apartment. We passed the Armenian's doorway on the third floor and I noticed that it didn't have the usual government sequestration seal across it, the tatty bit of ribbon and wax that I'd remembered on the doorways of British apartments after Suez.

Downstairs in the Tewfiks' drawing room I looked around for the blocked up doorway between the two apartments that Morsy had mentioned. I passed through the sliding doors that led to their cavernous dining room in the centre of the building. Luckily there were a number of appalling family portraits hanging beyond the table in the gloom and Morsy was more than anxious to turn the lights on and explain them to me. A fat Circassian lady, in a frilly bonnet and black widow's weeds, with a remarkable resemblance to Queen Victoria, was the principal oeuvre; and next to it a tiny eaten-up man in a tarbush.

'My grandmother and grandfather. Can you see the order he's wearing? Only just perhaps. The Royal Victorian Order or something. He got it from Lord Cromer and my father had it painted out—when he became secretary of the Wafd executive. And this is my uncle. "Nebuchadnezzar" he was called. I don't know why. You know your Bible. I'm a bit hazy.'

Nebuchadnezzar had a lush beard at the end of a long money-changer's face and an even longer nose. He looked as old as God. His nickname seemed to have the most obvious origins. I didn't comment on them.

Behind the pictures were heavy velvet drapes. I put a finger between them and touched wood.

'Was this where they divided up the apartments?'

'Yes. There are double doors there, several feet between them, bricked up in the middle. They led to a library and study beyond in the old days. My father held Wafd committee meetings there and kept a secret supply of Scotch behind a row of books. I remember as a child seeing them at it when my mother had gone to bed. Just like one of your London clubs. But all that had to be kept very quiet. We were fighting for our independence then.'

Morsy laughed pleasantly.

'I thought the Wafd was committed to parliamentary processes, getting the British out peacefully. You mean they were in there plotting armed rebellion?'

'No—they were drinking the Scotch. Guzzling it. Tippling very heavily. They couldn't do that outside.'

'You used to watch them at it?'

'I used to *spy* on them, I suppose you'd say,' he said deprecatingly. 'I was fascinated.'

'Through the keyhole?'

'Oh, no. I had a much better way. In the old days all these apartments had a row of ventilation strips in each room, at the top of the wall, so that the air from the ceiling fans could circulate all over the apartment, a sort of primitive air conditioning. Well, I worked one of the strips loose and could see most of what was going on next door. And hear everything, the voices echoed up through the room like a loudspeaker. You see this here?' Morsy went over to a huge sideboard in the corner of the room, four feet off the ground, with a tasselled velvet cloth over it.

'I stood up here,' he said with a ringing, sudden enthusiasm. 'Look here—on that very cloth, so it made no noise. And you see the drapes on the wall? They're the original ones too. I got some of the same material and wrapped it round me. And you know, if you stand absolutely still in the identical colour—I was perfectly camouflaged. My father walked past me once, not ten feet away, and never saw a thing.'

I looked at Morsy in genuine astonishment and then up at the ceiling.

'They've blocked them in now, of course. And painted them over. That was a long while ago. What a child—up to every sort of mischief I suppose . . .'

'Indeed.'

'One must "put away childish things" . . .'

'Depends on what you put them away for.'

'Badminton and croquet. And cutting pages out of your *Daily Telegraph*. We're a *young* nation as the President keeps on reminding us. A childish nation, would you say?'

We chattered away late into the night and when I left it was no effort to tell them both that I was looking forward to another game of badminton.

'Come any time,' Morsy said. 'Use the place if you need somewhere quiet to work. I'm at the office in the mornings— there's a study, typewriter, all the papers you need. If Leila isn't here the *suffragi* will let you in. I'll tell him. Or go up on the roof, there are chairs and a sunshade. Feel quite free to come and go as you please.'

I took Morsy up on the offer at once and asked if I could come round the following morning, that I'd some notes to put in order.

Morsy had had set up another table for me in his study looking out over the cricket pitch and Leila showed me the key to the roof and the other two keys that would let me back into their apartment again. Then she went out. The kitchen woman and Ahmed, the other *suffragi*, were padding round the rooms behind me and I pretended to work for half an hour before I picked up a book, my notes and a plastic ruler which I'd bought that morning. Ahmed wanted to come with me, to show me the way, to help 'arrange' things, and I had some difficulty in putting him off. Even so he came half way up the third flight of stairs with me, past the Armenian's door, so that I had to go out on the roof first, settle down under the sun shade, and then creep back downstairs again.

As I'd thought, one of the keys to the Tewfiks' apartment, an old-fashioned mortice type, just about fitted the first Armenian lock; the other, a Yale-type key and lock, didn't. The ruler cracked when I first pushed it in between the jamb and the door, trying to slide open the tongue. I pulled out the bit that was left, a narrow strip now, and suppled it vigorously with my fingers: a shoddy Russian import, I noticed, but it worked eventually.

The door opened quite suddenly, with a resounding click, so that I almost fell into the hallway and I realised that I'd been leaning on it with one shoulder which was what had been keeping the tongue in place. I was as ham-fisted at this sort of work as a bank manager.

The hallway and apartment beyond were in almost complete darkness when I closed the door behind me. But the disposition of the rooms must have been the same as downstairs, I thought, as I touched my way along the corridor, and into the drawing room at the back. A crack of light came through the heavy curtains, great shapes loomed up all around me, furniture under dust covers, and there was a sharp smell of paper, a bookish smell, when books have been stored and dried out for a long time. I pulled the inner curtain back, draped the tail of it over one of the mounds of furniture and looked round me. The books were everywhere; a whole library had been taken off the shelves about the room and dumped in piles on the floor. And on top of them were the other domestic possessions of the family—dresses, carpets, pictures and kitchen equipment. The room next door—the dining room—was empty. Not a stick of furniture, nothing. I had to open the curtains inch by inch as they squeaked on their runners about the empty bell of the room.

I looked up to where the ceiling joined the wall, five or six feet above my head. The plaster was the same colour all the way up. How many books would I need?

It took me another twenty minutes before I'd carried enough

of them from the other room to make a platform to stand on. I started with a large base made up from the heavy paper edition in seventy volumes of the *Hearings of the Mixed Courts in Egypt* 1888-1913, stacked the middle with *English Common Law* followed by the *Code Napoléon*, and ended with a number of bulky modern treatises on Company Finance. The Armenian lawyer must have had an old and comprehensive practice and in the end I had a rock-steady lookout with steps up to the top in both real and false morocco.

I prodded the tip of my ballpoint pen about the plaster just under the ceiling and soon I'd displayed a honeycomb of small holes in what had been a long rectangular metal ventilation grille, about twelve inches high. I wasn't able to pull the whole thing out and in the end I had to chip away at the plaster which held it at the top. Then I managed to bend the whole grille out and down—a section about three feet long. There were no bricks inside, that would have been the only catch, just an empty space two feet wide and with the same sort of grille the other side, with curls of old plaster sticking through the holes, like larvae, from the wall of the apartment next door.

The light was hopeless but I started to work on one of the plaster curls on the far side as gently as possible, using the little trowel-like pen clip to chisel away at it until there was just a flat membrane of paint covering the wall on the outside.

There was a risk, but there wasn't a way round it—I couldn't pull the circle of paint towards me. I listened, heard nothing and pushed. A tiny iris of grey light appeared. I turned my head sideways and pushed it through into the shaft. I couldn't see anything and there was no sound from beyond, only a smell I noticed, a new smell which obliterated the chalky lime dust of the disturbed plaster: like a blocked drain, faint but distinct. But it was fresher than drains, I decided: a recent eruption of the body, diarrhoea or vomit. I chipped away two more holes in a line downwards and by straining my head impossibly for a few seconds I could see across to the far side of the room, from the ceiling down to about the half-way stage of the wall.

Henry's ruffled hairline bobbed into view before I had to get my neck out again, or risk dislocating it, and then they started to talk, their voices coming up to me with astonishing clarity, reflecting off the walls and ceiling, like a drum, just as Morsy had said.

'. . . How long do *you* think then?' Henry said irritably.

'Well, it's not Gyppy tummy is it?' Bridget replied in the same shrill vein. 'It's food poisoning. We've all got it. The place stinks. You put the beer in the fridge and left the rest of the stuff out. Just like you.'

'For God's sake—you've been getting the food fresh every day. It shouldn't be bad.'

'Well, Hamdy's not going to go anywhere. He looks pretty ill to me. There's no point—listening to him. He'll have to have attention.'

'How—who?'

'I'll find someone. Money. We still have that. I'll go to Usher. He'll know someone.'

'Don't be mad. They'll have his place surrounded.'

'Look—if we don't try and contact Usher—there's nowhere to go: the Embassy's closed and the Consulate people aren't likely to know anything about getting us out of here. We can't just stay on here indefinitely.'

'You want to leave him then?'

'Of course not. But we have to *do* something. We *know* they're not on to this building. I've been out every evening for the last three days. And Security here can only have a very hazy idea of what you look like. You've got it into your mind that you're a marked man. If we stay cooped up here much longer you will be.'

'You know what it's like in Cairo—every shoeshine boy is in someone's pay. They'd be on to me pretty quick. And they must be looking for you—they went straight to your house after all. I thought we'd been over all this.'

'What, then? Is there no one else here we can contact? Get a message to London? I mean, there are three of us. I'm not important, but you are and Hamdy must be. Don't you think London has any interest in getting us back?'

'Certainly—but the three of us *aren't* going to get out together, that's the point. However much London wants it they're not going to be able to arrange for all of us to get to the airport and step on to a BOAC flight. That was always the problem here. If you got caught you were stuck. The only chance is to divide up, take it on our own. When Hamdy is better. God, I feel sick.'

I heard the thump of Henry collapsing on a chair.

Bridget said, 'Well, that's the first thing then. There's another doctor I've thought of, he's at the Anglo-American.'

'How well do you know him?' Henry asked with just a trace of tired sarcasm.

'You know him too, you ass. He did first year English with you at Dokki. Gamal Cherif.'

'He won't want to get involved.'

'He won't know. I'll ask him to prescribe for me. We've all got the same bug. We can share whatever he gives.'

I tried to turn my head again in the ventilator, from a listening to a looking position, round to where I could get a glimpse of Henry, but he was out of sight somewhere in the corner of the room. Bridget passed my awkward eye line for a moment—was she taller than Henry? I'd forgotten. Her hair had turned a slight rust colour, it seemed, a mixture now of her parents' colouring, where before it had been very nearly sheer black. And it seemed to have receded too, half an inch or more over her forehead, giving her profile a smoother shape than I'd remembered.

I just had time to see her nose before she passed out of sight, slightly turned up, the same as ever—that feature which had given her a permanent air of cheeky interest and unrest and had made her face so different from the languid boneless expressions of the other women of the city. If Egyptian Security were on the lookout, I feared for her: she had the kind of features you'd pick out in any Cairo crowd, particularly in that nervous time: confident, assured, gentle. I knew them well enough.

Indeed, I knew in the few short moments as she passed across the ventilator that I would try and follow her now myself, wherever she went, and get her back. Something had gone wrong ten years before, the time had come when the fault could be corrected. There had been some simple error in our marriage, a miscalculation, and the answer to it was in front of me now, beyond the wall. It was something which I'd simply had to wait for, which had to mature for all those years, until I'd seen her passing by for a second, a bright face glimpsed through the darkness of a ventilator.

I felt a proper sense of direction again, knowledge of a job to do—a task properly outlined at last, something which could be pursued to an end. I had something to go on, the numbing professional mysteries of the years in Holborn and the nonsense of this present mission were dissolving, clearing into another perfectly grasped pattern: a personal enquiry.

I left the bottom mortice lock open and pulled the door to. I could get back into the Armenian's apartment with the plastic ruler alone now, and I left the keys with the *suffragi* in the Tewfiks' place downstairs.

There was a desolate riverside night club and café about five hundred yards down the Gezira corniche, a few broken chairs outside by the river wall, and a kind of dark-room shack in the middle where they served coffee and Cokes during the day; a place that years before, in the evenings, had catered for the envious fantasies of the poorer middle class. I waited for Bridget here. She would have to pass down on the far side of the corniche, going towards the Kasr el Nil bridge, if she were making for the Anglo-American Hospital.

I didn't know exactly what I had in mind—not to follow her, there was no need for that, just to look at her perhaps, as a free person walking along a street, to see her in a complete perspective which the ventilator had not allowed—someone without the trappings of a woman on the run, or of my following her; free of all that—in a situation where I might have come out of the café and bumped into her by chance: I wanted the temptation of a casual encounter.

When she passed I did nothing. I watched her disappearing down the far side of the road, standing by the curtained window in the smelly, tobacco-stale gloom sipping a gritty, sour coffee.

One's gaze was so drawn to her among the other passers-by that I wondered how she could walk a pace without being noticed. But perhaps that was the trick which had preserved her from Egyptian Security—she was so obvious, open. They were looking in the dark corners.

I thought: I've only got to go to the Council Library at the back of the Embassy, make a report out to Williams, put it in the map flap of the book I'd brought with me for the purpose—a *Shell Guide to the West Country*—and give it to the little lady by the desk. They'd have the message in London by evening and it would be Williams's responsibility from then on; he would have to take the decisions and make the arrangements. I would have done my job, could pass out of the picture, back to my desk, last week's *Al Ahram* and a half view of St. Paul's.

It would have been the sort of thing one did for one's friends, after all, apart from any professional consideration. And even Colonel Hamdy was a friend of sorts, with his quiet blackmail in the Semiramis after Suez: Hamdy who had somehow got caught up with the two of them, either trying to defect or as one of our Mid-East men all along. Perhaps that was why Henry had come out to Cairo in the first place—to make contact with him and get him out of the country. Something had gone wrong and I could put it right, play my part in rescuing them, and we should have civilised amused talk about the whole affair among ourselves for years afterwards in various separate, well appointed apartments in north London—a sweet memory of derring-do. Would Henry have married Bridget by then?—was that how it would all work out, as just a little arrangement among friends? And perhaps, for my part, I'd get some sort of promotion out of Library & Information.

And I think I would have left it at that, given in to some sort of 'better judgment' in the matter, gone over the river with my *Shell Guide*, and dropped the personal pursuits I had in mind as regards Bridget—if Henry hadn't come out of the apartment block a moment before I moved towards the doorway of the café. He walked fairly slowly up the corniche in the opposite direction, his usually neat footsteps shaky now, the way he used to move when he'd had too much. None the less I would have lost him, I think, if, just before he disappeared from sight, he hadn't turned into the drive of the Omar Khayyam Hotel next to 26 July Bridge at the end of the Gezira corniche.

This splendid palace had been built as a rest-house for the Empress Eugénie on her visit to Cairo in 1869 to open the Suez Canal; now it was a stopping place for a package tour holiday organization. A coach-load of tourists were getting down outside the doorway and another group was milling about inside the hall. There seemed little risk that anyone would spot him there; Henry had chosen the place well. He'd almost certainly gone there to use the phone, I thought, but I wanted to see if I could confirm it.

The booths were out of sight behind the reception desk and I stationed myself on the far side of a group of elderly Germans in sandals and plastic straw hats who were counting their suitcases earnestly in the middle of the lobby. A bag was missing.

'A scandal!' one of the ancient Brünnhildes was shouting, and

she was soon joined by a chorus: a stream of vicious gutturals
falling over several beady-eyed, sweating bearers and an assistant
manager.

In a minute or so Henry appeared from behind the reception
desk and walked straight to the door without looking left or
right. It was worth trying. I went round to the booths—there
were only two of them—and picked up the receiver.

'That last call I made—I was cut off—can I have it again?' I
said to the hotel operator, even capturing something of Henry's
sardonic, busy colonial voice.

'The Kasr el Aini Hospital?' the operator asked me.

'Yes, please.'

I let the phone ring and put the receiver down when the call
came through.

The Kasr el Aini? Something for their Gyppy stomachs?
Where was Bridget off to then? Or had Henry some other
contact to make there? Or had I simply not heard some
amendment to their plans after I'd left the ventilator?

8

THERE was a note from Pearson waiting for me when I got
back to the Semiramis towards lunchtime and I took it to the
bar with me just off the main hall, the ancient air conditioning
throbbing and shaking the floorboards as it had done ever since
I'd first come here and had gin and tonics with Bridget and
Henry ten years before. And there was another moment's doubt
then: I should have been drinking here with them now—and the
hell with Williams, the Egyptians and all their various cloaks and
daggers. Henry had wanted an end to all that and I had agreed
with him. I had come out to tell him so. And now, less than a
week later, I was snooping on him and Bridget with all the
gracelessness which characterises the best traditions of our
trade.

Pearson was at the bar, his back to me, leaning over a chalky
drink. I hadn't noticed him.

'Ah! Good to see you, I didn't expect—'

'Just got your message.'

'What will you have? I'm afraid I'm on the wagon. Upset
stomach. I'm prone to it.'

'You should have it looked at.'

'Yes, as a matter of fact I am. A specialist in gastric medicine. Dr. Novak, a Russian chap at the Kasr el Aini. Their fellows pick up a lot of that sort of thing out here.'

'They all go there?'

'Who?'

'The Russians.'

'Yes—why? The hospital's full of them. Those that aren't shipped back home at least.'

'It's an easy way out for them, I suppose—if they were ill. The engineers at Aswan and the military people, the Russian 'advisers' here. They wouldn't go on a normal flight if they were invalided out through the hospital—would they?'

As I talked I was learning—picturing a move, Henry's move. It had never crossed my mind before. Henry the Russian defector, phoning a contact at the Kasr el Aini Hospital, Henry on his way over, without anyone knowing, not even Bridget.

'What are you getting at?' Pearson asked, curious at the direction I was taking.

'Background. Russian influence in Egypt. People want to know.'

'Yes, the Russians come in and out of here as they want. At Cairo West, at Jiyankis and Al Mansura in the north among other places. What are you doing—a piece on how to get from London to Moscow—via Cairo?'

I let that go. Pearson could think what he liked about my being in Cairo. He sipped the chalky mixture, the oiled Dixie Dean scalp and thin nose pecking in and out of the tumbler like a toy barometric duck. He looked up, smiled and spluttered, making an attempt at genuine good will.

'But you've not had one yourself.'

He called for Mohammed. The air conditioning plant drummed under our feet, stirring the whole floor beneath us in odd recurrent waves. It was like being on a ship in the Semiramis bar when the air conditioning worked.

Pearson said, 'Look, I don't want you to get me wrong—about all this. Let me explain: for whatever reason—let's leave that out—I have the impression you're looking for Henry Edwards. And why not? He's a friend of yours—he's a friend of mine too. And he's missing. He came through Cairo airport last Tuesday with Yunis and he hasn't been seen since. And Yunis,

we know, is under house arrest—at the very least. That all adds
up. We should be worrying about him. But now listen to
this'—Pearson looked at me with pretended innocence and
concern—'Someone arrived from London late yesterday, our
contact at the airport picked him up for us, British passport, a
businessman, name of Donald MacMillan. He's staying at the
Hilton. We check them all. Businessman—what business? I said
to myself. So I made a few enquiries with the hotel. Scotch
whisky he was in. They didn't know anything else. Well, I
thought that was interesting enough, something I'd missed, and
there might be something to file, for the Scottish papers at
least, and I called down at the Hilton this morning, gave my
name and asked to see him. But he wouldn't play, wouldn't
even see me. Well, I was curious because although there's a big
market here for Scotch it's all controlled by a single government
import firm. I checked with them and they knew nothing about
any Scots chap coming out.

'So I waited around the Hilton and eventually, about nine, he
came down to the grill restaurant for breakfast. I had eggs and
coffee at a table nearby—that's why I'm on the chalk. Well, of
course, I knew at once who it was. It was that lawyer David
Marcus, the one who used to be at the Scottish office and
moved to the Highland Development Authority.'

Pearson obviously felt he'd come to a dramatic pause in his
tale. But I had to be sure.

'So? He's trying to do some new deal with the whisky people
here. Sounds perfectly straightforward. Why tell me?'

'Because Marcus left the Development Authority six months
ago. Came to Whitehall. One of the P.M.'s special advisers on
security. After Blake. Interrogator chap. That's why I thought
you'd like to know.'

'If you break that sort of thing you'll be in trouble
straightaway. So I can't see why you're telling me about it.
You're just marking yourself and your agency before you've
done anything. And what *can* you do? What's the story?—no
evidence. What have you got when you look at it? Some
assorted people from British Intelligence in Cairo? All right, but
that's not going to make any headlines. You'll just get a D
notice slapped on you if the stuff gets back home. After all
none of these people are smashing up lavatories or having
drunken boating parties on the Nile. There's absolutely nothing
in the open on it.'

'Not now, no. It's what might happen that interests me. I'm prepared to play this perfectly straight. There's something on and I can make a very good guess as to what it is. Something is going to break—at the Number One court at the Old Bailey, in an apartment in Moscow, or more likely just down some dirty back street in Cairo.'

'And you'd like this lawyer to keep you in touch with developments, no doubt?'

Pearson smiled, giving me the straight look. 'It's a good story, you know.'

'I thought journalists had given up suggesting that sort of deal long ago.'

'I don't know, Mr. Marlow. Perhaps you freelance people are a little out of touch. There's a lot of money in a story like this.'

'Well then, you go and ask this man Marcus about it all yourself. Put your foot in the door. You professional pen men are supposed to be good at that sort of thing.'

I lowered half the shandy he'd bought me and got up.

'I will. I will ask him. Usher—you know Robin Usher, don't you?—he's having some people along this evening for drinks. He's asked Marcus. No ambassador here now, so Usher acts as a kind of unofficial host when business people come out from London. Perhaps you'll be there yourself?'

'I've not been asked.'

'You're sure to get a message then.'

'You told him I was in Cairo?'

'Of course. The British are a pretty small community now. We don't get many visitors from home. Everybody knows everyone else. There aren't many secrets between us all out here, you'll find.'

Pearson was a limpet, a little drummer who'd never let up. And why not? He had the makings of a story all right. As far as he was concerned British Intelligence was playing some sort of extraordinary leap-frog in Cairo. He must have known that Usher had some connection with the service, and Henry too with his frequent visits to the Middle East, and he'd guessed that I was in the same line of country. And now Marcus. He had more of a picture of what was going on than I had myself.

But what sort of leap-frog? What was the large view? What had Marcus come for? Enough was happening in the area politically at the moment to justify a visit by one of our senior staff. But Marcus didn't fit that bill—knowing little of Arab affairs, he'd come to our section with a security brief, primarily as an interrogator, a ferret to smell out the vermin, the double dealers and defectors. He was practised in that and it must have been his role now. Presumably he was after Henry—they'd had some definite news of him since I'd left. Or had he come after both of us now?—with the idea that I was on my way over to the other side as well? Marcus was the sort of person who, if he couldn't find a plot, would invent one. And so, I thought, was Williams. In the business of espionage they were always seeing double.

I called at reception for my key. There was another message for me—a phone call from Usher giving me his address up behind Abdin Palace beneath the Citadel and an invitation for that evening. My passport was there as well, back from its police check. I'd forgotten about it. The clerk handed it over with a little less than his usual obsequious bonhomie. He glanced over my shoulder and I knew at once what was up. Someone from the 'authorities' was standing behind me, waiting for me.

In fact there were two of them, over by the huge copper globe labelled COMPLAINTS at the end of the reception desk, dressed in the usual shimmering Dacron suits and Italian winkle-pickers which Egyptian plainclothesmen had made their uniform. With their tooth-brush moustaches, well kept weasel faces and dark glasses they looked like night club owners nervously and unaccountably involved in some dangerous daytime venture. For Egyptians there was something unusually aggressive about them too, a threatening, hair-trigger efficiency.

The taller one approached while the other stood back blocking the corridor which led to the rear entrance of the hotel. I might just have made it down the regal brass-railed shallow steps which faced the corniche but I honestly didn't feel like running.

'Mr. Marcus?' it sounded like, but I must have misheard in the confusion.

'Yes?'

'You would come with us please. Thank you very much.'

'Why—what's up?'

'Something is irregular in your passport. If you would not mind. For a few moments.'

'What's wrong with my passport? I had the visa through your

London Embassy. The press section there . . .'

I opened the passport—and closed it again quickly. The photograph on the first page was familiar enough, a fellow with a receding hairline, balding slightly, not unlike my own. But the chin definitely wasn't me, jutting out aggressively like an icebreaker, or the narrow formless lips and bitten-in mouth: the general air of disquiet and deviousness belonged unmistakably to David Marcus.

The tougher, taller man took the passport from me and his friend closed in on one side. I was certainly coming quietly. I'd got the wrong passport and they'd got the wrong man—a typical Egyptian police muddle—and I'd probably only got an hour or two before they found out their mistake: just time, if I was lucky, to find out what they were on to Marcus for.

'Very well. May we go?'

Pearson had come out of the bar to our left and I think he had it in mind to try and stop us as we moved across the lobby and out of the main entrance. But he thought better of it, his mouth twitching in agitation and surprise. Instead he followed us down the steps.

'Where are you taking him?' he shouted in Arabic, flourishing his press card, as the two men opened the door of a small Mercedes at the kerb. 'He's a journalist. What have they got you for?' He made an anguished appeal to me, a hair or two out of place in his immaculate black shine so that he looked almost unkempt. I shrugged and got into the back seat. I didn't feel like helping him. His interest was so transparent. He wasn't worried about me, whether I was thumbscrewed, beaten about the soles or had my balls plugged into the Direct Current; Pearson was worrying about his story: the plot was thickening about him while he watched, and he was losing his way. I couldn't blame him. He was by temperament a journalist of the old blood-and-smut school—a fiver in a saloon bar in Earl's Court, the dead call girl in the basement opposite—and these present developments were clearly putting a strain on his self-control.

We went across El Trahir, up to Ramses Square, past the station and then along beside the metro towards Heliopolis before pulling off through the main sand-bagged entrance to the military barracks there, the armour depot and G.H.Q. for the

Cairo area forces. This was where Egyptian Military Intelligence
operated from, I knew, and the man I met in the weather-blown
Nissen hut, still doing duty from British days, was no passport
control officer: a Major with an over-keen face and unusually
slim-fitting uniform for a senior Egyptian Army man. When you
got anywhere in his job it was back to the tailor's every year to
let the seams out. They gave him Marcus's passport and he put
it down on the desk in front of him, fiddling with it, but he
didn't open it. And I didn't expect to learn much from him
either, for the moment he did look at it—and me—carefully, it
would all be over. But I was lucky. He started straight away,
confident, going in at the deep end.

'Why have you been bringing messages in your passport, Mr.
Marcus?'

'Messages?' I put in quickly, covering the name.

'Microfilm.' He held up an envelope, opened it, and took out
a card with a speck of dark negative attached to it. I laughed.
How far could I get with him? I wondered.

'What does it say?'

'That is no matter.' The Major looked puzzled.

'I've not been bringing in any microfilm. I don't know what
you're talking about.'

'It was under your—' he took up the passport, opening it at
the end, and read out from the back page '—your Foreign
Exchange Allowance. Why do you deny it? This sheet here—I
see you brought in £200 with you as well.' He spelled the
figures out slowly. He seemed to have all the time in the world,
an extraordinary confidence in the circumstances.

'You were thinking of staying here for some time? What have
they sent you out here to do, Mr. Marcus? Who was this
message for?'

'I told you. I didn't bring any message. And my name is not
Marcus, by the way, it's Marlow. I don't know anyone called
Marcus.'

I'd like to have let him talk on. He was the cocky type and
I'd probably have picked up a lot more. But 1 couldn't afford
to; if I learnt any more they couldn't afford to let me go.

'Are you *sure* you've got the right person? I didn't have time
to see that passport properly before your men took me away.'

The Major opened the passport again, this time at the front.
He looked at the photograph, then at me. I showed him my air
ticket by way of additional confirmation.

He was furious and apologetic by turns. He tried to order me some coffee and spent some time explaining how 'these things happen'. But neither his English nor his temper was quite up to it and he was effusively relieved to drop the whole matter and see me back out into the Mercedes. The two men who had brought me were nowhere to be seen. They had disappeared— probably for a long time.

My own passport had been returned when I got back to the Semiramis. There was nothing I could do about Marcus, they'd have corrected their mistake over him during my drive back. I wondered how he'd make out with the Major. Probably not at all; effusive Security men are as dangerous as wounded animals.

Someone had framed Marcus. I took my wringing wet linen suit off, rang for some ice and soda to go with my bottle of whisky, and went into the shower. Someone had put him into it up to his neck. Or had he just been careless?—had he a message for someone in Cairo and they'd found it? It seemed unlikely. The Egyptians would hardly have checked every passport on the off chance. They must have been warned that he was coming, been tipped off by someone in London. The Spycatcher caught: who could have wanted that? Someone he was on to. That made sense. But that 'someone' would have to have had the opportunity to plant the microfilm. Passports needing visas went through the Staff Organizer's department, a Miss Charlbury ran it on the floor beneath Williams's office, and from there out to Cook's, as if from a private person. There was room for planting something in that chain. Or had it been someone in the Egyptian Consulate, when they stamped their visa?—some devious plot-counter-plot? A possibility. But I preferred the idea of someone within our section tampering with it—someone who had sent Marcus out to get Henry, or me, or Colonel Hamdy, but who had really wanted to be rid of Marcus. Marcus wasn't a courier, that was certain. The microfilm, that dangerous form of communication, was, with equal certainty, a plant.

I looked at the back of my own passport out of interest when I got out of the shower, pulling the gummed flap of the Exchange Allowance form away from the back page. It would have been quite simple, a matter of moments, to slip a piece of film under the gummed part and then stick it down again. Anything up to half a fingernail of negative would sit there very nicely and no one would ever spot it unless they'd been looking for it, unless they'd been told. I pushed the flap down again and started to close the passport.

A little fingernail of negative slipped across the page and into my lap.

Someone hammered on the door and I thought briskly of swallowing the thing until I remembered the ice and soda. The floor waiter came in.

Afterwards I stopped the automatic swivel on the fan, put it on top of the air-conditioning box pointing straight at the bed and lay down, stretched out in my pants and a snowstorm of talcum. It was getting far too hot. I drank a glass of soda and ice straight off before adding a finger of Scotch. 'You should always start by drinking *warm* drinks when you first get to Egypt, tea and things.' I remembered Crowther's advice in the Embassy the first time we met. The little foxy bastard, I thought. And all of them.

It had been me or Marcus but they'd gone for him, as the more necessary man to be rid of. Marcus had been the more pressing concern for someone, but they would have dumped me just as well and that must have been their first intention. Why hadn't they? There could only be one reason. The two micro messages, whatever they were, must have been identical and wouldn't have been believed if they'd turned up on two different Mid-East section men. Whoever it was that had planted them hadn't had the time to take mine out and could never have thought I'd find it.

And that was why I'd been sent to Cairo, not to chase Henry—that had been the excuse—but to be caught with the goods, to be sent down the hatch for some reason. But then Marcus had come into the firing line, had become the target—and then the carrier; the message had been duplicated in his passport and he'd been packed off. And the only man who'd been in a position to do all this posting, this cunning shuffling of the pack, was Williams. Of course. Thames Valley Williams with his violet shirts and polka-dot bow ties, bending down to his drinks cabinet, proffering me his thin pin-striped ass and a warm gin and tonic. 'Drop into Groppi's, I should. That's where the gossip is . . .'

Drop into Siwa Oasis for ten years on beans and water more likely—the prison where Marcus was probably headed after a suitable show trial.

I looked at the colourless negative with the dark full stop in the centre. The print would probably be in white. I wasn't very clear about microfilm but I thought I needed a projector.

As I turned to get up, my heel bit into something hard and sharp on the end of the bed. A long sliver of glass from the top of a soda bottle was sticking out from the back of my foot like a spear. The bloody floor waiter. I wondered if I'd swallowed any.

I pulled the glass out, a neat nasty hole, blood dripping in a trail all the way to the bathroom. I doused it under the bath tap. Every time the water cleared the blood away I could see a piece of glass still caught deep in the flesh. I needed a doctor too. Pearson's Russian friend, Dr. Novak at the Kasr el Aini, might do very well. Two birds with one stone. Three perhaps—he might even have a projector I could borrow.

The Kasr el Aini Hospital lay on the north spur of Roda Island, up-river along the eastern corniche past Garden City—a complex of dun-coloured, featureless Victorian buildings with open terraces and one or two half completed new wings. Like most Egyptian hospitals it had the permanent air of a casualty station in bad times: bandaged figures moved around the main hall, groups of numbed country people had made temporary camp about the passages, seemingly paying court to their confined relatives; stretchers and trolleys were in constant traffic up and down, many of their occupants permanently stalled outside surgeries, operating theatres and dispensaries. There was a feeling of 'maleesh', an overpowering sense that the will of God was having it over the ways of man: a smell of leaking sores and the strongest sort of disinfectant.

I hobbled up to the reception desk, peering over a dozen chattering, frenzied heads all intent on extracting some vital information or permission from a single porter equally intent on withholding it. But the mention of Dr. Novak's name had a steadying effect on him. He gave me a form to fill in where I had to give my own name: Henry Edwards I put. In a moment I had a response. Dr. Novak would see me at once.

He had his surgery in another, more modern wing some distance away at the back of the main building, and the single ward which we passed on the way was full of sturdy Russian gentlemen. Most of them were moving about the beds in baggy underpants listening to Borodin on a radio and reading luridly coloured Soviet engineering journals. It was ferociously hot and unpleasant in the corridor, with wafts of illness coming from somewhere, and I had qualms. If Henry really was running over to the other side it was his business, his affair if he wanted to exchange one toy-town for another, not mine. If there was any mistake and Novak happened to know what Henry looked like, then he would never get out. And neither might I. But I went on.

Dr. Novak had a round bouncy face, hair cut *en brosse*, a curling moustache and a good-natured expression which rather surprised me. He looked like a provincial baker from some French film of the 'thirties. He gestured to a chair in his tiny office, looking at me with an uncertain interest.

'I didn't expect you so soon,' he said.

'I had the opportunity. I've cut myself—so I thought I'd come straight away.' I started to take off my shoe and sock. 'A piece of glass. I wonder if you could take a look at it.'

There was a perfectly appropriate casual doctor-patient relationship between us. But Dr. Novak remained puzzled.

'Can you get up here?' He pointed to a raised couch in one corner and I clambered up on it.

'Yes, I can see it.' He swabbed the wound and went away to get some probes. 'Would you like a local?' He seemed to have a remarkable grasp of English.

'I'll try without.'

'How did it happen? Can you turn round and lie down flat on your stomach?' I twisted away from him so I couldn't see anything of his face.

'A splinter from the top of a soda bottle.'

'You shouldn't have come round here just now, you know.' He lowered his voice. I felt some steel implement clip the top of the wedge of glass, nudging it a fraction further into the flesh so that I jumped forward in pain, the sweat coming out in rivers all over me. 'Jesus!'

'Sorry.' He took the probe or whatever it was out, it clattered in a dish and he went away for something else. 'Have you been able to make some arrangements? Have you changed your mind?' It was just as well he couldn't see my face. I was puzzled now.

'No—not yet. I was—hoping you could help me . . .'

'How?' he said urgently. 'You mean I should come round to

your Embassy? Tell me. Every moment is urgent. I cannot be
sure of things here much longer. You said before on the phone
could I help you?—I don't understand what you mean. I have
already contacted your people here, at the Consulate. I was
expecting you—someone from London, they said—to make the
final arrangements.'

'You will have to wait. A little longer. I came to tell you. A
day or two.'

'When do you think you can get me out?'

Dr. Novak had a pained insistence in his voice now.

'It's difficult, we haven't an Embassy here now. We have to
make different arrangements—Oooch! Christ Almighty!'

A knife, it must have been this time, cut into the skin again,
through inches of it.

'You should have had a local. Keep still now for one
moment. I'm getting it out.' The knife came again. I shuddered.

'Have confidence, Dr. Novak. Do nothing for the moment.'

'But I *must* get out of here, Mr. Edwards. I must have some
firm arrangements from you. It was promised me. You are from
London. We must talk. I have committed myself.' I felt
something grate inside my heel, as if he'd reached the bone.

'I know,' I said miserably. 'But we've had some difficulties on
our side too.'

'I'm not interested in the Americans. Or the French. I
explained that. I want to go to England. That is what I have
prepared. I have prepared my de-briefing.'

'I *know* you have. But it's just not as easy as that to get out
of Cairo at the moment. You'll have to take my word for it. Be
patient.'

He seemed to have started to scoop the flesh out now with
some kind of apple corer.

'For how long must I wait then?' S-c-o-o-p. 'What will be the
arrangements?' Grind. 'When will be the de-briefing?' I thought
I was going to faint.

'I think I'd better have that local. Dr. Novak, you have me at
your disposal. If I—if we—were double crossing you I'd hardly
have come here and let you go through all this with me.'

'I'm sorry. It's finished. I was just tidying it up. You can get
down now.' I hobbled back to my chair.

What, indeed, would the 'arrangements' be? Who was going
to run Dr. Novak out of Cairo—who was going to de-brief him?

There was no counter-intelligence interrogator in Egypt. And then it was clear. The man Novak had been expecting, waiting for, was Marcus. No wonder Henry looked ill at the Omar Khayyam Hotel. His contact man was a defector himself. They had both been looking for the same sort of help. Of course, it was farcical.

The little bouncy face was crestfallen. I could see the horror this whole business had for him—looking for a bolt-hole, never knowing where trust lay.

'Well, what shall we do?'

He was fiddling with his probes and forceps. I wondered if he was more doctor than KGB man, or the other way round. What would he do in England? Where was his family? What made a man like him drop everything and run like this—and why to England? An overwhelming belief in fish and chips and a few broken down carriers east of Suez? It didn't make much sense. Perhaps he had distant relatives in Highgate. I almost asked him, and thought of telling him the truth about what had happened to Marcus.

'Do nothing. One of us will contact you again in a few days. It might be longer. In the meantime, do nothing.'

It wasn't until after I'd left that I realized why I hadn't been forthcoming with him—an unconscious reticence from my years in Holborn: I couldn't trust him; Dr. Novak might simply have been an infiltrator, a Trojan horse. That's why we had men like Marcus in our section, to check such people out before they got into the citadel.

One checked everything and trusted nobody. It was a dull, grubby business. Going over to the 'other side' was worse than staying put, not because you'd broken trust with a country or an organization but because you'd really betrayed all human contact. No one would ever be sure of Dr. Novak again, whether he was playing a double game or not. The guilty can look just as crestfallen as the innocent.

The microfilm was a more difficult matter to unravel. I needed special equipment, a projector not easily come by outside a security organization. But there might be another way of deciphering it, I thought—with a good microscope and a strong light beam under the slide: a science lab would have done, the American University off El Trahir Square for example. But I needed an excuse. Microscopes . . . Wednesday afternoons at school. Botany, stamens and petals . . . Yes, the identification of rare wild flowers. Egypt had been famous for that in previous days—the fabulous carpet of spring flowers on the limestone spur beyond Lake Mariout at Alexandria. That would serve as my background and such flowers as I needed I might pick up from the dazed herbaceous border by the fountain in the Hilton forecourt.

I went round to the University at five o'clock having slept fitfully through the afternoon and picked up some dusty weeds at the Hilton. The University was an impossible building to find anyone in and the porter completely misunderstood my interest so that I found myself, in following his directions to the Science department, at the back of the University theatre. A rehearsal was just getting under way managed by a middle-aged American, shouting quickly at a lot of students standing open-mouthed on the stage. They were doing *Charley's Aunt*. I'd seen the poster in the hall.

'Now, Lord Fancourt—over there in the easy chair. And remember, this is Oxford in the 'twenties: very blue porcelain, very la-di-dah. Jack Chesney? Where is Fawzi, for God's sake?'

Fawzi peered round a door on the set, a thickset Egyptian with Presley locks and campus sweater, smoking one of the new hundred-millimeter cigarettes.

'Fawzi,' the American yelled, 'make that entrance much sharper. And remember you light the cigarette *after* you get in. His Lordship gives it to you. So put that one out and start again.'

The Lord Fancourt in the proceedings, in plimsolls and T shirt, remonstrated at this stage direction.

'Mr. Pershore, it's just an excuse. Fawzi's just smoking all my cigarettes. That's the third one I've given him.'

I crept up behind Mr. Pershore. 'I'm sorry to bother you. I was looking for the Science lab.'

He turned and I explained my purpose, brandishing my nature study which I'd stuck neatly in the pages of a book I'd brought with me.

'It's closed, I guess. But Magda might be able to help. She's majoring in Science—over there. Don't keep her too long. She's Donna Lucia quite soon, goddammit.'

Magda, a tall girl with good legs, was more than willing and only her dramatic commitments prevented her from leaning over the microscope with me throughout. Luckily botany wasn't her speciality. None the less she gave me some uneasy moments.

'That looks like a weed to me.'

'Yes, it is. Quite right. It's the earth attached to the roots that I'm interested in. The properties of the soil—it's quite different in Egypt. The Nile mud, you know. I want to see what bearing it has on the seeding. I suspect pollination here is induced by quite a different trigger mechanism than is usual. And of course this would have an important bearing on the growth and spread of wild flowers generally in Egypt.'

'Of course.'

Magda left me to it. I cleaned the earth from the two glass plates, slipped the microfilm in between them and pushed the tray back under the lens. The magnification was far too high, giving me a bad photograph of light and shadow on the moon. I swivelled to the next smaller lens, and then to the one below that. Now I could make it out, at least the heading and part of the first paragraph.

It was an Israeli Ministry of Defence memorandum from the Chief of Staff, General Yitzhak Rabin, to the Commander Northern Front, General David Elazar, dated a few days previously, May 7, 1967. It outlined a series of recent El Fatah raids made from Syria and the Lebanon on Israel's northern borders: a water pipe line at the kibbutz Hagoshrun damaged on April 29, an irrigation pump destroyed near Kfar Nahun on May 5 and an Army truck mined on the Tiberias-Rosh Pina highway on the same day the memo was written. I moved the slide up a fraction. The note went on to say that in view of this dangerous escalation of guerilla activity General Rabin was authorizing a large military deployment near the Syrian border—six armoured brigades, an engineering corps, commando units and artillery, supported by various detachments of the local National Guard, a supply and pay corps, field hospitals, etc. The memo then outlined primary targets in Syria—the fortified village of Kallah, the hills of Tel Faq'r and Azaziat—and discussed the necessary first-strike immobilization of the Syrian 130 mm and 122 mm artillery emplacements in these areas. The note ended with a provisional strike date: May 17 at 0300 hours, a week hence.

Israel was going to knock the Syrians out of the ring in a pre-emptive strike. Nasser, with all his bellicose trumpetings of the past month, could hardly stand by and watch: with this sort of information in his hands he would be forced to mobilize his own troops on Israel's southern flank in Sinai as a diversionary tactic. If he heeded this memorandum, as he must, he was going to be dragged into a war he couldn't win.

The message, if Egyptian Military Intelligence believed it, was more or less the President's death warrant. And they would believe it, wouldn't they?—having found it on Marcus, or myself, genuine Mid-East section men. Which of course didn't mean that the memo hadn't been forged. But true or false its results would be the same. Who could have wished such ill will on the two of us? And on President Nasser. Williams again. We were one of his 'ploys' in action, implementing his or the U.S. State Department's view that Nasser was another Hitler and must be deposed at all costs. Marcus and I had been sent out to start a war, planted, and with Marcus the roots had taken well, I had no doubt. But why Marcus? What had he done to incur Williams's disfavour? Just then, I couldn't imagine.

I walked back to the Semiramis and called Cherry at the Anglo-American from my room. It was just after six and I could see across the river from my window the usual chocolate box sunset over Gezira; an orange sinking out of a violet and gold sky into the palms of the exhibition ground. And there were all the other sounds and senses of the city waking again, grinding into life, after the hours of silence. It was just the sort of evening, among so many in the past, when one felt like doing something, starting afresh. Going to a party.

'Herbert?—what are you doing? Usher's party—are you coming to it?'

It turned out he'd had a call from Usher that morning and had been trying to contact me. I met him downstairs in the bar half an hour later.

'Well?' he said.

'Well nothing. I've been looking round, that's all.'

'Not with Mr. Khoury, though. He's been on to me all day. You were due with him out at Helwan this afternoon. And he's got a trip arranged for Sakkara tomorrow.'

'One can't do everything. How's Madame?'

'The same. But listen—' Cherry assumed one of his serious expressions, screwing his face up, tightening his skin, like air being sucked out of a bladder '—if you don't make an effort to play the part, aren't they going to wonder?'

'Who?'

'Khoury has friends. In Security. They all have. They talk.'

'Have you heard something?'

'The jump is on about something. They picked up someone else today. From London.'

'You're thinking about me, Herbert. I was. They got the wrong passport. A mistake.' And I told him of my visit to Heliopolis. He would learn of that from Pearson in any case, it would be all round the place within hours. We ordered drinks and I started to try and add up what Marcus's capture might lead to. It was possible, of course, that my *laissez-passer* about the city might run out if they put any pressure on him. Marcus had never had the training to withstand the water drop—or whatever the favoured technique of the moment was with Egyptian intelligence; unless one could expect his native intransigence to stand foil against any torture. It was possible.

He knew about my being in Cairo—and Herbert and Usher for that matter. Perhaps this really was the end of the Cairo-Albert circle—the end of so many good days, on so little money, for even less information.

I tried to think of Marcus under pressure, strapped to a chair or something, a moist and swarthy gentleman moving towards him with a carpet beater. Was that how they did it? But whatever they did to Marcus he wouldn't see Holborn again in a long while. And the rest of the picture suddenly came into focus: I saw why Williams had switched to Marcus, made him take the fall instead of me: Marcus, the spycatcher, had been on to him. Williams didn't work for Holborn or the CIA. He could only have been from the other side, from Moscow. And I saw, too, how the Israeli memo would serve Russian purposes even better than our own: a war with Israel, which Egypt would lose, and Nasser's subsequent fall which would allow Moscow really to take over in Egypt; to make good their battle losses and install a properly Marxist government with someone like Yunis at the head of it. Nothing would suit Moscow better than that Egypt should suffer a quick knock-out blow from Israel, a blitzkrieg war over the cities and across Sinai; such an outcome would ensure the Soviet position in Egypt for years to come.

Williams must have been the fourth man who had come into British Intelligence before Philby and the others, who had outlasted them all, and who now worked alone at the heart of it. Marcus had somehow stumbled on this. And Williams had somehow got him out to Cairo—to interrogate Dr. Novak, but to be picked up before he got near him. It didn't matter that the circle out here would be broken up as a consequence of this highpowered tit for tat; it mattered not at all. All that was necessary was thatWilliams should survive. And he would, with increased credit in Holborn, as the 'war maker', the man who did for Nasser at last—until the Russians made the real capital out of that disaster. For the West certainly never would; we'd be selling arms to South Africa by then. And to Rhodesia.

The Egyptians would be the only ones really to suffer in it all; they, and people like Herbert and Usher who would get ten years apiece in Siwa. They would have to be warned. God knows how many contacts Usher had about the city—innocuous old clerks and waiters who remembered the British affection-ately—or how quickly he would turn them over to ease whatever pains Egyptian Intelligence might have in store for him.

'What will you do, Herbert, when—things come to an end here? Go back to Greystones?'

I was wondering how Cherry might do in Information and Library: a quiet job on £2,380 plus the London weighting. Ten to five, leaving just enough time for an easy stroll down to the wine bar in the Strand before it opened. They were going to need one or two replacements in Holborn.

'Why? Why should things be coming to an end?'

'They are, I'm pretty sure. Though there's no point in giving you details. But if I told you to get out—*now*, this moment, go and buy tickets tomorrow—would you do it? Would you believe me?'

'She can't move.'

'Yes. I see that.' Of course, it was hopeless.

'That's all there is then, isn't it? No point in telling me anything. Talk to Usher. Perhaps he'll have some ideas. He's been getting out of things successfully all his life.'

I'd never seen Usher's genuine Mameluke house beneath the Citadel. I'd not fancied his collection of desert bric-à-brac, or

the boys of the same sort that I'd been told went with it. And
I'd thought of Usher himself as a punishing old rogue the few
times I'd met him: an agreeable monster by the Embassy pool
dabbling in champagne and running a circle with almost
criminal insouciance. Now I could almost look on him with
affection.

By comparison with Williams, Henry, Colonel Hamdy and
perhaps Bridget, Usher had the outlines of a straightforward
man—of someone whose intense sexual preoccupations over the
years, his indulgence and irresponsibility, suggested a kind of
loyalty: he was true to his proclivities, and indeed, from what
one knew, to his country. He was a patriot—but a scoundrel in
the last resort. That was his honesty. And at that moment I was
prepared to admire something certain and unchanging in a man,
even if they were characteristics based on the slimmest sort of
belief, sustained by the grossest appetites.

9

THE house lay in a narrow, steeply sloping alleyway right under
the wall of the Citadel—between the fortress and the towering
wall of the El Rifai mosque which was perched further down
the hill on a large plaza where half a dozen other streets merged
into it. Few people lived up here, in this high corner of the
mediaeval city. The streets were deserted and lit only by one
huge art nouveau lamp-standard with a clover of frosted globes
on top. Herbert knew the way, otherwise one would never have
found the place in the confusing shadows and different levels of
the terrain: an arched doorway in almost total blackness except
for the flicker of firelight coming from somewhere behind it.

Inside was a rough ante-chamber like a cow byre, with soil
underfoot and smoky beams high overhead. A woman was
squatting over a fire of tinder and desert brush, Gagool-like, in
rags, warming herself in the acrid smelling mist. She seemed to
have sunk to her knees a long time ago and never bothered to
get up; deformed by her own ill will rather than by any natural
or unnatural process. She held out her hand. I had stepped past,
thinking we had not yet come to the proper entrance to the
house, but Herbert gave her some coins.

'She looks after the place. Storyteller, sorcerer, witch, fortune teller, jester—the whole pack rolled into one; you mustn't pass without some financial attention. Otherwise the place falls down. Or you do. She has friends in all the shadows.'

I gave her a coin myself.

We stumbled up some steps and along a passageway towards a jaundiced light. At the end was a stained-glass door, in brown and yellow, like the window in a Victorian lavatory. From beyond came a smell of sizzling onions and mince, and from somewhere else, it seemed in the far distance, the subdued roar of party chatter.

'We're on the high level here, next to the kitchens and the old harem. Usher had it converted. Normally one would have come into the building from the other side, where it faces the mosque. But he's turned the proper hall on that side into a garage. You'll see, we'll look *down* on the multitude, like the girls did.'

Cherry opened the glass door and we stepped on to one side of a gallery which ran right round the building, with shadowed haphazard passages leading off it, and a marvellously delicate wooden filigree harem screen built up from the outside ledge. Twenty feet below us was the reception room, the formal Mameluke Salamlek, the size of half a tennis court, paved in blue mosaic, a fountain in the middle, and set about with a quantity of divans, silk bolsters, cushions and half a dozen small pearl-inlaid coffee tables, each with its elaborate silver hookah beside it. Everything was as it might have been in Saladin's Cairo seven hundred years before—except for the people, who, from their uncomfortable dress and apologetic demeanour, were clearly the remains of another and different dynasty, the descended remnants of those northern Caliphs, the last of their kind, who had once usurped and ruled the city.

Usher I could see at one end, dressed in fine cottons and a scarlet cummerbund, draped over the only proper seat in the room, a high-backed mock-Jacobean affair in velvet with tasselled heads, one of his billowy sleeves extending far out over the arm, balancing a crystal goblet between the clutch of fingers. Scattered about him—and having to stand so that they inevitably seemed to be paying court to him—were his friends. In deference, no doubt, to the semi-official nature of the occasion few of these appeared blatantly to suffer, or enjoy, any sexual inversion. Apart from several young *suffragis* in richly embroidered *galibeahs* and dazzling emerald cummerbunds serving drinks, there couldn't have been more than half a dozen Egyptians present—among them Leila and Morsy Tewfik. The other guests were clearly English: just as their faces exhibited a distinct lack of thought, so one could identify their provenance without thinking: several military men, thin and old, with tobacco-stained faces, arrayed in wide pin-stripe suits, double-breasted in the pre-war fashion; several substantial ladies in polka-dot navy blue dresses and cumbersome, sensible shoes; and several thin ladies, dressed like black pencils, in Empire-line silk and gilded slippers; a clergyman in a smart grey lightweight worsted, and a red-haired priest in a soutane who moved one hand about constantly beneath its drapes, as though tightening, or loosening, something of vital importance beneath; some serious, awkward, hunted-looking men and their wives, obviously the skeleton staff from the Consulate; two long-locked youths and a scrubbed girl in a pony tail, a trio probably doing a little voluntary work overseas, made up the more noticeable guests. Mr. Pearson was there too, but David Marcus had obviously been delayed.

We came down the narrow winding stairway on the far side of the harem and I made my way over towards Usher. But Pearson was right in with his feet before I got half-way across the crowded mosaic, gibbering in a state of some energy and excitement.

'Well, my God, man, what happened?' He was obviously holding the front page.

'Nothing. A police muddle. The usual thing. I was given someone else's passport. They hadn't got a proper visa.'

'And Marcus?—our friend Marcus?' Pearson fidgeted nearer, taking a pushy stance. 'Where's he got to?'

'*Your* friend, Mr. Pearson. And where should he have got to? Here, I thought you said. Isn't he?' I looked around.

'He was picked up at the Hilton about an hour after you were.'

'Probably had business with his whisky people then.'

'Like hell. These were jokers from the same pack as you had.'

'How unfortunate. I expect he'll be along any minute. Probably had something wrong with his passport too. They're very careful about that sort of thing out here now, aren't they?' I moved on.

'Mr. Marlow! How long it's been. What a very long time.'
Usher actually stood up. His voice was full of mild generosity. 'I
was so hoping you could come. Feel responsible for you in a
way,' he went on in a lower voice, leading me by the arm up
some steps behind his throne and into a minute whitewashed
cell-like ante-room.

'Have a drink. Some champagne, I remember it was, last time.
How have you been? No hard feelings, I hope; that business
over your wife. I hear it ended badly. She was due along here
tonight but I couldn't get any answer from her number.
Probably just as well. Let old acquaintance be forgot, in the
circumstances, I imagine.'

There was a huge double bed, with a Moroccan weave
counterpane, filling half the space; a camel-saddle stool and a
lot of champagne on ice in several buckets: an austere room,
but not entirely unrelieved.

'Quieter here. And we should talk. Henry Edwards?'

'Yes.'

'Mr. David Marcus, late of the Scottish Office?'

'Yes.'

'Mr. Pearson, the news hound?'

I nodded. 'You know all about it then.'

'I thought so. An awkward business, especially with Monty
here. Truth to tell there'd have been a hell of a row by now, but
for that. They're playing it down. Don't want to spoil their
military reunion. Monty's showing them how to drive a tank.
Otherwise we'd all be in Heliopolis barracks by now.'

'I expect so.'

Usher smacked his lips and, bending down, he nursed a bottle
out of the ice and cracked it with a resounding pop. He relished
the proprieties, holding the foaming mouth high in the air for a
second before quickly dousing it in two gold-stemmed Arab
goblets. The crystal winked in the soft light and the bubbles
sparkled and I thought, 'He has the conviction of his clichés;
you live for ever like that. You become myth.'

How old was he, in fact?—ten years on from whatever he'd
been when I last saw him—had he been sixty-odd then? At least.
But he didn't look seventy now. He had lost weight since, the
eyes were more a pearly watery blue than ever, islands of
mischief and abandon in the parchment map of his face. The
skin here was tired and blotchy if one looked closely, but the
lips were as full and purple as ever, the hair as white and

blossomy. He had obviously put up so little resistance to the attack of age, cared so little how time might damage him, that he had escaped into the last lap of life practically untouched. Contrary to expectation, and all the other grim cold Saxon warnings long ago, fidelity to pleasure had preserved him, even made him younger—that fidelity which, in betraying it, other people grow genuinely old. Usher was a living affront to all his dead nurses and mentors.

He held up his glass, spun the stem a fraction in his fingers, his eyes clear blue orbs surveying the sparkle. There was nothing of the antiquary in the gesture, or the wine snob; it was an expression of genuine, deeply-felt greed.

'Pearson particularly,' I said. 'He's been on at me about Edwards and Marcus ever since I got here. I suppose he can't be prevented from filing something now that they've taken Marcus. He's probably been on the blower already.'

'No, he hasn't. I said I had something for him on all that—later this evening. And I have. It would be *quite* the wrong moment for anything to appear on Marcus in the U.K. While Monty's here. And more importantly, while *we're* here. The Egyptians will keep the whole thing under a lid—as long as we do. If we break anything, they'll be bound to as well. And rope us all in. Our friend Williams has made a cock-up: first Edwards comes out here running, then you, then Marcus. And you're the only one left. Williams has effectively smashed the entire circle. Any idea what's behind it?'

'No. I was sent out simply to look for Edwards.'

'A likely tale. And Marcus to check out a Soviet defector, a Russian doctor at the Kasr el Aini. And the result: at least two of our men in jug—and probably your wife as well. And the rest of us hanging on by the skin of. The whole circle smashed— don't know why they haven't picked you up before now; don't follow it at all. But the message I get from the Egyptian side is clear enough: as long as we make arrangements to break up and clear ourselves out of here in the next few days, or at least before Monty leaves, we won't get the hammer. The others will, no doubt: a trial and what have you—and a spell in Siwa. But there's nothing to be done. Mr. Williams has a lot to answer for. I had three of my Saudis off today to Bahrein; nice boys. I've got an English teacher from some mission school downstairs running round in circles, a ticket man and an airport officer wondering about their pensions, plus Cherry and myself—all to be sent packing in the next forty-eight hours. What sort of arrangements have you made?'

'I have a return ticket.' It was like saying I had wings.

'Well, keep out of the way after this and get straight to the airport tomorrow. You seem to be in the clear, probably the only one of us. And remember, if we don't get back—remember what I've said: find out what the hell Williams has been up to; take it to the highest level if necessary.'

'What happens if they decide to hold you people?'

'I should have a warning, if they're coming for us. I still have contacts.'

'But if you do have to go under—how would you get out of the country? What arrangements are there?'

'You mean you weren't told?' Usher looked at me in some astonishment. 'Williams must really have it in for you. There *isn't* a "way out"—for us, not since Suez. No escape plans, couriers, code messages or false moustaches. If you go under here—you *stay* under as far as Holborn is concerned. Now, you go out and circulate a bit and I'll deal with Mr. Pearson. We shall be all right for an orderly retreat unless he breaks some coat-trailing story about "missing diplomats" in Cairo.'

Usher was approaching this climacteric in his life with too great a show of efficiency and unconcern, I thought. I wondered if he really intended moving out from fifty years in Egypt with just a toothbrush, taking a taxi to the airport. But perhaps the flabby lips deceived the eye; he had been with Lawrence in the Hejaz after all, survived the self-destructive ambitions so favoured by that tortured martinet; there must have been a fiery streak in him somewhere, which this lifetime's interlude of pleasure had damped but not extinguished. I thought how quickly he would age in St. John's Wood.

I found myself talking to the smart-suited clergyman when I came out again into the Salamlek. He was among a group of people, which included the red-headed American priest, being lectured to by Herbert in his best hectoring, low-church manner: he had chosen the Problems and Principles of Ecumenicism as his theme. His argument seemed to be that *his* church, the Church of Ireland, that is—and I remembered the arrogant granite parish building in Greystones—should be the ideal to aim for in the present attempts at a united Christian congregation, that its lack of mystery, its plain speaking, its dowdiness even, represented the proper Christian ambition in these confused times. Cherry had his tongue in his cheek, but they weren't the sort of people to notice that. Just the opposite: the two divines were part of an ecumenical study group visiting Egypt and the Middle East, set up by some excessively wealthy American foundation to consider just such fool-headed opinions as Herbert's. Thus they paid him careful and completely unmerited attention.

'I wasn't aware there were so many differences between the Anglican and Irish communions,' Mr. Rostock said to me, smiling. He was the incumbent of a new town near Aylesbury.

'I think you'd be surprised. We manage to make our version of the faith very dull in Ireland—practically invisible. You're not hoping to rope the prophet Mohammed into your united congregation, are you?'

'No, indeed. Not in any strict sense of a shared communion. Though we naturally hope for greater bonds between *all* faiths—as a result of our deliberations. Our visit here is part of a general look at the Anglican communion in the Middle East. The diocese here, of course, is administered by the Archbishop in Jerusalem.'

'Of course, though you've not actually *come* from there, have you?'

'Well, no, as a matter of fact. There are one or two temporary difficulties in the way of direct travel about the diocese at the moment. We came via Cyprus actually. I'm staying with the Provost's deputy at All Saints' here. Mr. Hawthorn. Do you happen to know him?'

'Not the present occupant, I think. I knew his predecessor. He gave the prizes away one year at a school I was at in Cairo. He had a loud voice—most of them do, I suppose?'

'You ought to look him up then, the Cathedral on the corniche. He'd be pleased to see you. They're doing a lot of interesting work; here in the UAR, in Libya and the Sudan. In fact Hawthorn's making a trip this week to Alexandria and then on to the sub-diocese in Benghazi and the one in Tobruk. They're extending the parsonage there. A tour of the parish, you might say. It could make quite a nice story for your paper.'

'How does Mr. Hawthorn travel on these pastoral missions?'

'Oh, my goodness me, I know all about that. I've been

hearing about it non-stop for days: the *immense* efforts over the past five years with the parishioners here. Raffles, bingo, jumble sales, amateur dramatics—even the lenten collections: they've got themselves a *long wheel-based Land Rover.* Can you imagine? Punitive import taxes, but they managed it in the end. A real go-getter, that's all I can say, Mr. Hawthorn. A very smart affair. He's anxious for a long spin in it.'

'Well, I must look him up, if I have the time. He certainly sounds a forward looking man.'

' "Six forward and two reverse"—as he says of his progress in the parish here. Talking about the gears of course.'

The Rev. Mr. Rostock chuckled, but not convincingly, vaguely aware of the banality of the joke. He was young really, hardly out of his thirties. Only a comprehensive and premature baldness gave him an irredeemably older, care-worn look, as if his hair alone had succumbed to the unhopeful routines of a home counties presbytery—visiting the antiseptic, Scandinavian bungalows on the new estates and counting ten times the plate money at Christmas and Easter—while the rest of his body yearned for gospel safaris in the Libyan desert.

The idea struck me then and there, of course. There was a British air base at Tobruk, a direct RAF Transport Command flight back to Brize Norton. But Usher had said to keep my ticket and go to the airport. That would be tomorrow.

I saw Usher put his arm round Pearson and manoeuvre him towards the little cell at the end of the room, and then Leila Tewfik bumped into me.

Tomorrow, I thought, and that will be the last of it; not any more of it—ever. Not here. For she looked at me with a quite unexpected warmth. There would be an end of that, the chances of women in foreign places, and it might be no bad thing: I had gone through that routine once before in these parts. Yet how easily I could have taken up with Leila at that moment, not for any sort of consolation, just the opposite: we would fall to it with all the skill of trained adventurers, believing that having emerged from the vengeance and disappointment of one affair we were now qualified to avoid those pitfalls in a second. Leila put one in mind of a really professional, joyous few weeks. I don't suppose it was a realistic notion; such thoughts at Cairo parties rarely are—and it was this potential of the city that I was going to miss: its electric vacancy which begins by making every plan possible and ends by making them all unnecessary; the airs of a place whose citizens have long ago come to genuine terms with their ambitions.

'Well,' she said, 'did you get plenty of work done this morning?'

'Thank you. I'd meant to say so before but I've not stopped running. I gave the keys back to Ahmed.'

'How long are you staying here?' She crooked her glass in an elbow, took off her glasses and wiped them.

'What are you thinking? A trip to Helwan on a boat together? I've never done that.'

She put her glasses back on and blinked at me for a moment, focusing, her eyes narrowing a fraction into the smallest of smiles, nose dipping in an even smaller nod.

'Trouble is I'm supposed to be going back tomorrow. If all goes well.'

'And if it doesn't?'

'I'll come and do some more work on the roof if I may. Where do the boats go from these days?'

'Below Shepheard's, by Garden City. Why don't you come? Tomorrow morning. Morsy might come. And he might not. I could find out.'

The little conspiracy was perfectly presented.

'Can I let you know?' A *suffragi* had tapped my arm; Usher wanted me to come to his cell.

'Please. Will you let me know?'

'I'll be back.'

Yes, we could have begun there and then; trips to Helwan and the Viceregal kiosk by the pyramids, cocktails on the Semiramis terrace, and cold hangover beers in the stuffy back bar of the Cosmopolitan: we could have pushed off straight away into the infinitely shoddy glamour of the city which would so soon become precious for us. But again, I was bitten by tomorrow: a half view of St. Paul's lurking behind the vile new concrete, from a matchbox office where one would hardly remember the crumbling architecture of this changeless valley.

I saw that Cherry had been given the same message from Usher and was following me through the crush of people. The festivities were at their height.

Usher was standing at the door and when we were both inside the small room, he closed it carefully and locked it. Pearson was lying stretched out full length on the Moroccan counterpane, legs apart, arms wide in a position of suggestive abandon. His shoes were on the floor and his tie loose. For a moment I thought he was awake and waiting for something untoward, and that Cherry and I had been invited to participate or witness it. And then I remembered Usher's phrase, that he 'had something' for Pearson. He had obviously received it.

Usher was moving round the bed with fussy efficiency. The shoes were back on now, the tie fixed. Finally Usher carefully replaced a number of papers from Pearson's inside pocket.

'Poor chap. I'd forgotten his ulcer. Stomach wall must have very low tolerance for that kind of medicine. Went out so fast I barely caught him. Now I need your help. These knock-out drops will keep his curiosity at bay for forty-eight hours. I want to get him home to his wife in Zamalek. She doesn't care for me; I think she may well come to hate me after tonight. But that's no matter—the point is he'll be too ill to file anything until we're all out of here. And he certainly won't get his ten o'clock news circuit to London this evening.'

Usher bent over him, lifted an eyelid, checked his breathing. He stood up like a policeman.

'Funny things, these new cough drops. You know what they do?—they give you an almighty go of Gyppy tummy. Appropriate, what? Just the same symptoms; clever fellows, those boffins. Like to get him home before that starts. Of course he was filing on Marcus. It was in his pocket—"Informed sources here suggest" sort of thing; he's going to inconveniently mislay the cable; hope he loses his mind as well. Now, if you two could help me downstairs with him. I'm rather too old for much potato work.'

Cherry looked on hopelessly and I tried to find a cigarette.

'Downstairs how? Where? There're no windows or doors. You're not thinking of taking him back through the party?'

'Well, *up*stairs, really. Then downstairs. That's why I needed you.'

Usher stood up on the bed, between Pearson's feet, and pulled at a red silk canopy which covered the ceiling in folds. 'Had no roof in the old days, this room. So I put in a false one when I converted the place. Now you get up there, Marlow— that's right, you'll have to use your arms.'

I had joined Usher on the bed and had started to pull myself up between the frame of an open trap-door immediately above us. When I was up and had turned round, bracing myself against the rafters, Cherry and Usher grasped Pearson by either arm, and the three of them commenced a brisk dance about the bed springs for some moments, trying to steady themselves, in a fearful drunken fandango, Pearson's head lolling about between them, his dancing pumps dragging about the counterpane, marionette-fashion.

It struck me that Usher was doing something seriously stupid, that he'd kill the man, snap his neck or asphyxiate him with his antics. Then Cherry tried to steady himself by grasping the edge of the trap-door but instead managed to drag the entire canopy down over himself and Pearson.

'For God's sake man,' Usher murmured. 'Pull yourself together. Don't tear the material.'

I lay down along the rafters burying my arms in the bouncing red shape, crooking my arms beneath two armpits. Then I pulled hard.

'Wrong one, old fellow,' Usher said after a moment. 'Pull the other one.'

We got Pearson up, Cherry followed, and together we hauled Usher after us. We even managed to replace most of the canopy.

'A ladder would have been useful,' Cherry suggested, as we carried Pearson across the beams to some other part of the Mameluke warren.

'No doubt,' Usher puffed. 'Never got round to it. I don't normally use this exit myself. It's really a direct entrance from the garage to my bedroom for some of my more limber acquaintances.'

We came to the end of the attic, moved through some angled joists, through a plywood door, and nearly fell headlong into a garage twenty feet below us. Here there was a ladder, and we moved more quickly now, with Pearson in a fireman's hold over my shoulder.

Usher opened the back door of an immense old navy blue Rolls and I toppled Pearson straight in.

'This used to be the main entrance,' Usher said. 'It gives straight out on to the street behind the mosque. Open the doors and I can run down-hill as far as Abdin Palace without starting the engine. Very convenient.'

'This car is a bit much, though, isn't it, Robin? Bit

conspicuous for a job like this. I didn't think you still used it.'
Cherry was excusably nervous and was trying to work off his
forebodings on Usher. 'Doesn't it rather irritate people out
here?'

And it could well have done with its shapely arrogance, its
immense spokeless wheels and tall coach-like box for the
passengers behind. The radiator might have caused particular
offence for instead of the usual winged angel there was some
antique automobile club emblem--a wheel in the shape of a
large Union Jack.

'It belonged to the editor of the *Egyptian Mail* in Alexandria.
He had it specially made for him in the 'twenties. Why should it
irritate anyone, Herbert? Envy, perhaps. But not irritation.'

'I didn't think we wanted to draw attention to ourselves,
that's all.'

'One of the secrets of secret work is to *be* conspicuous; I've
often told you. The more obvious you appear, the less suspicion
is aroused. To slink round town in a Morris 8, in my position,
would be to invite both mistrust and cramp. Come now, let's
not argue methods of approach at this juncture: I'll prime the
motor, open the doors, and I'll drop our friend back home. You
two go back to the party. If anyone asks you can tell them I've
been helping the press in their inquiries. And I think one could
hardly deny it. Drunken sods . . .'

Usher climbed aboard and began tinkering with various levers
attached to the central rung of the steering wheel. Things
whirred and clicked and groaned beneath the long bonnet.
Cherry and I opened the two doors. The garage gave on to a
narrow unlit side street, which ran across the hill, away from
the El Rifai and Hassan Plaza on our left down towards the El
Azhar mosque and the Mousky bazaar northwards to our right.

There was no one about, a moonless, close evening with the
ticklish smell of pepper in the air, and no sound apart from the
distant crash of traffic down in the city. Cherry saw them first,
he was on that side of the door looking along to the Rifai Plaza
a hundred yards away, though we had heard the sounds half a
minute before, standing rooted to the spot: the groan of heavy
diesel engines changing down through the gears as they came up
the hill; a line of military vehicles circling now round the plaza
and going on up to the higher road which led to the new
entrance to Usher's house; a small convoy of jeeps, followed by

several police Fiats, and two Military Police lorries with bren-guns mounted on the cab roof.

Another historic ambush which would end a dynasty was under way: it was Mohammed Ali's massacre of the Princes at the Citadel all over again; the remnants of the Saxon Raj as victims this time, rather than the last of the Mamelukes. Amongst the startled multitude damask and richest silk would have given way to cotton polka-dot print, chain mail to faded pin-stripe, and there would be no caparisoned chargers at the door, just a few ruined Hillmans; but the result would be the same: trapped in a narrow defile beneath the fortress walls there would be no escape for the lumbering Lords and Ladies as they sought vainly for release in stout Northampton boots.

Usher got down from his bridge on the Rolls and looked out with us.

'Pearson must have got something through after all,' I said.

'Or they may have just changed their minds about us. They're like that.' Usher seemed unaffected by their arrival. Was there a hint of relief even in his voice, now that he realised he might not be seeing St. John's Wood for some time?

'Never mind. I've burnt all the papers. Never kept many papers anyway. We might as well all go together then. Rather fortuitous even.'

'Go *where*?' Herbert asked bluntly, shades of anger and despair gathering in his voice. The M.P.s had left their lorries and were ringing the plaza, blocking off the south end of the lane, their backs towards us. 'I'll really have to be getting back to my wife,' Herbert continued. 'I've been out long enough already.'

Cherry and Usher had commitments in Egypt, I realised again, ties of pleasure and misfortune, and I suppose it must simply have been Usher's dedication to form which made him run that night: a sense of keeping his end up. Or he may just have felt it was too good a chance to miss, a last excessive raspberry in the face of authority.

'Come on then, Herbert. I'll drop you home.'

The chatter above us had suddenly died. There was a sound of glass breaking.

'I wonder who that was,' Usher said with real indignation. 'That's the second tonight of those goblets. Shan't bring them out again.' He got back behind the wheel. 'Give us a push.'

The huge car glided out of the garage like a boat, a noiseless blue craft indistinguishable as velvet in the darkness, the Union Jack moving in a steady circling arc at the distant end of the bonnet like a gunsight on the bows. Usher locked the wheel to the right with vigorous pumping movements, one hand flashing over the other, thwacking on the wood as it spun, his jowls shuddering, white hair bouncing in strands over one ear. With a yachting cap he would have been Sir Thomas Lipton caught in a squall.

Cherry and I crouched in the leather cathedral of the huge interior, Pearson propped up in the seat behind us. But as we moved away down the lane with nothing following us we got up off the floor, pulled the jump seats out, and sat down.

Usher still hadn't fired the engine and I couldn't make out whether he was trying to or not. We had long since left the lane, turned into Bab el Wazir and from there into the narrow streets which skirted the Mousky bazaar, going downhill, heading northeast, roughly in the direction of Opera Square. Market stalls lay within a foot of either side of us now, pressure lamps flaring above each of them in a snake-like dazzle that went all down the street, and a huge crush of people moving in between them, buying their evening meal. We had arrived in the middle of that interminable Egyptian supper time, in which whole streets of the city become dining rooms, and the going was difficult.

Usher fired the engine now, a delicious warbling, throaty roar, which was drowned only by the klaxon on the vehicle which he started to exercise violently. Whole families sprang from their food, running for the gutter in a clatter of tin dishes, *galibeahs* pulled about them, jumping for their lives. Our progress could not have been more noticeable or better judged to support Usher's theories on the art of inconspicuousness.

And strangely enough few people seemed to pay us any real attention; no one shook fists after us in the rear mirror or threw marbles under the wheels. True, we were passing down one of the oldest parts of the mediaeval city, between the Blue Mosque and the Bazaar, whose populace, since the days of the Fatamids, had long been inured to foreign arrogance in a variety of the most eccentric forms. Not half a mile away the insomniac Caliph Khumaraweh had had himself rocked to sleep on an air mattress in a lake of mercury, a sybaritic transport not far removed from our own extravagant progress in the Rolls. For some of the older bystanders our headlong career may have seemed no more than happy evidence that the British had at last returned to Egypt and they could look forward to sharpening their wits and financial idioms again.

And we would have made any destination we chose in the city that night, I think, if an elderly, courteous policeman at the entrance to Opera Square had not spotted the car and its proud enamel colours on the radiator, and thought almost exactly this: not that the British had returned in any permanent form, but that they had come back temporarily and were on their way to a little reunion downtown, which he, among many of his colleagues, was helping to effect smoothly.

The man stepped gallantly up on the wide running board while we were at the lights at the top of Adly Street, saluted Usher with one white-gloved hand, while holding on to the side of the car with the other. The white gloves gave me the clue. Cairo police wore them on only the most auspicious occasions. But I couldn't get any further. It seemed simply that we were being arrested with more than the usual Egyptian courtesy.

Then the blossomy round old face shouted at Usher above the din of traffic, 'Montgunnery, sir! You wanting Montgunnery party. Follow me!' The man tightened his grip on the car, urged Usher forward, while at the same time lashing out at some luckless pedestrians with one foot. I would have run for it there and then if Usher hadn't driven off smartly, breaking the lights, while thanking the old fellow effusively in Arabic.

Other traffic police waved the car on now in a gale of whistles, and we were passed through a barrier at the end of Adly Street and into Soliman Pasha which had been cleared of all traffic. The crowds were fairly thick on either pavement, held back by police every few yards, and further down by Lappa's and Groppi's they were six-deep, quiet, full of interest, devouring ice cornets.

Cherry and I sat rigid in the jump seats; prominent, upright men—detectives I supposed they'd think us—accompanying some Ambassador who had unaccountably dozed off in the back of the car. I straightened my tie and wondered if we should wave to the crowds in lieu of our master. Cherry drummed his fingers on the upholstered floor, his arms hanging down across his body in the minute seats, like an ape about to spring.

'What *does* Usher think he's up to? We'll never make it. Not a hope.'

'I should think that was exactly what we were going to do,' I replied.

The moon face was wild and sweating now, as he shook his head from side to side in desperation. He had at least managed a suit in place of his usual crumpled flannels and stained linen coat. Usher, of course, was resplendent, while my linen tropicals were still in fair order. From the sartorial point of view it struck me we would make it all too well. Conversation, on the other hand, might be more difficult.

'What was your war like, Herbert? A good armoured regiment, I hope. Monty has a horror of backsliders. And he's northern Irish, isn't he? Not southern.'

And there was Mr. Pearson of the International Press Agency dreaming of a Stop Press behind us. I wondered what Monty would make of him? He might take it that, on this occasion, the press had gone a little too far.

We swung round Soliman Pasha quickly and on down towards the river. There was a queue of limousines in front of us, turning off to the right at Bustani Street, light blazing from the covered terraces of the Mohammed Ali Club on the corner. Usher had stumbled on a suitable place for our Valhalla; the Club had been previously only less select that the Khedival Club; now it was where the Egyptian Foreign Ministry held their most dignified receptions.

We turned—there was no alternative now, the rest of Soliman Pasha was barred against us—and drew up outside the huge doorway with its two glittering brass street lanterns illuminating the red-carpeted space between us and the marble steps. A young army officer in full dress uniform approached and opened the back door. There was absolutely nothing for us to do but get out, leaving Pearson where he was, propped up in the corner of the seat, eyes closed, the foxy nervous face perfectly at peace, the not-too-popular 'thirties bandleader coming into a show stopper now, a sweet melody that would fell them all at the Metro Ballroom, Huddersfield, next week.

And then—I can't think how or why, his unfailing nose for a good story prodding him, perhaps, even in this deepest unconsciousness—Pearson stirred. His eyes fluttered and opened and he licked his lips, before he began to push himself forward, slowly, a ghostly man, from his upholstered tomb. The officer,

still holding the door open, turned and the three of us helped
him out of the car.

It looked all right in the event, Pearson seeming to be
afflicted with no more than a bad leg, earned gallantly at
Alamein in the circumstances, stumbling with game dignity
across the red carpet and up the steps in our arms. In fact he
was in a speechless dream, his mind had not yet begun to catch
up with events.

The young officer showed us all into a small drawing-room
off the hall and we got Pearson down on to a sofa. Usher came
in shortly afterwards, having parked the car, all bustle and
British, going straight over to tend Pearson.

'I'm sorry about this, Captain. He so much wanted to come.
An old wound. We did our best to warn him. A glass of water
perhaps?'

'Certainly.' The Captain, extremely solicitous, went away to
fetch the refreshment.

'That's one of their Military Intelligence people,' Usher said.
'Foreign Ministry is giving the do for Monty.'

Pearson had begun to doze again.

'I don't suppose they're likely to look for us here then,'
Cherry offered, though his face suggested no sort of belief in
the statement.

'Where can we go?' I asked. 'What's the point?'

'We shall go where we set out to go,' Usher retorted heavily.
'We are not going to have orange juice with Monty, I can assure
you. I'll try and get Pearson back home, you no doubt to your
hotel, Cherry to his wife. We must do as we set out to do.'

Usher immediately seemed to contradict his plan of campaign
by sitting down suddenly on a tiny gilt chair, his bulk enclosing
it completely, like a hen settling on a nest. He looked beaten. A
pair of French windows behind the sofa led out to a closed
terrace which ran all the way round the ground floor of the
building. I couldn't see any of the blazing lights coming in from
the street so I assumed the room beyond must face away from
Bustani Street and on to a side street.

'Perhaps there's something out that way. Might be able to get
over the balcony.' The others looked at me dully and I saw
Pearson swivel with me as I moved towards the window, a look
of hate creeping into the doped lines of his face.

I pushed through the half-opened curtains and went into an

empty unlit terrace beyond. There was a balustrade on the outside and a drop of about ten feet down on to a side road crammed tight with cars, their drivers chattering in groups here and there up its length. I could make it, I thought. But the others? We might possibly have to run from the chauffeurs as well. And run *where*? I turned back. A door opened. Several people had come into the little room. One of them had started to talk. I recognized the stumbling accents at once, the extraordinary arabesques decorating the English vowels: it was the Major I had seen earlier that day in Heliopolis welcoming his unexpected guests.

'A pleasure, Mr. Usher,' he said, a caricature opening in the circumstances. He'd seen too many films. All Egyptians have. 'We were just looking for you on a call to your house up-town. You were giving a reception there yourself—no? We did not expect you here. But you are—not very well—yes? But very welcome . . .'

I heard the tinkle of a tray and saw Usher's arm stretch across the window. He took the glass of iced water, then his head bent into view, the long nose dipped and he started to gulp it down in one swill. Greedy to the end, I thought. I turned and cocked one leg over the balustrade, suddenly feeling an appalling thirst myself.

The chauffeurs heard me as I hit the ground. There was a group of them fifteen yards away, probably security men as well. I brushed myself down, saluted them formally and walked casually towards the main street. I had ten seconds before they made their minds up about me, then I'd have to run. I turned the corner into Bustani Street. Ten, twenty seconds; nothing happened. I walked past a deserted police barrier towards the bottom of Kasr el Nil, stragglers moving with me now that the gaiety was over. Constables gathered in groups mopping their faces on the other side of the road and a few white-suited officers directed the returning flow of traffic.

Then they came—a whistle and raised voices behind me. I had gone beyond the point of running; they'd seen the direction I'd taken; it could only be a chase which I would be bound to lose: police were in groups every ten yards or so along the road in front of me. I pulled off my coat and tie in almost a single gesture, heeled right round in my tracks, and walked smartly back, slightly crouched, in the same direction as I'd come.

They passed me on the run, pushing the stragglers out of the way, a group of security men and an Army officer, shouting hard. One of them barged me off the pavement into the arms of a startled traffic policeman standing by the kerb. I stopped and looked after them with annoyance, but not for long. 'The foreigner,' they were shouting, 'in the tie and suit. The tall one!' I turned to the bemused policeman, smiled, shrugged my shoulders as he gazed at my open-necked shirt: Marks & Spencer some months back, one of the last they'd made in pure white cotton. The little man saluted me, helped me back on the pavement, and I went on my way, returning the salutation. Egyptians are much given to that form of address.

It was after ten o'clock when I'd crossed the bridge and let myself into the Armenian's apartment on Gezira. The darkness smelt of paper; fine weave and heavy rag, manilla and best hand laid; years of warm paper. I lit the matches, one by one, carefully dousing them on the floor as I made my way across the apartment to the perch; circles of light, flaring up, dying, briefly illuminating the chronicles of the Law. I felt as secure as the passengers in the next cabin, all of us inmates now, the ship stalled and perfectly camouflaged in a Cairo backwater.

I had almost fallen asleep by the ventilator, for although there was a light on in the room next door, there wasn't a sound from the place.

The smell of illness had disappeared almost completely. Had Colonel Hamdy decided to run as well? I had turned away, was resting my head against the ridge of the ventilator, when I heard the telephone start, a faint, insistent buzz from the far side of the sofa. My head was in the grille again, just in time to see Hamdy crossing the room smartly in a bath robe, eager and quick indeed for an ill man.

He answered in Arabic, calling himself Mahmoud, listened for a minute and then seemed to confirm some details about fruit, the importation of so much dried fruit, coming in on a Greek boat the following day at Alexandria. The *Salonika*. He repeated some customs and consignment numbers, thanked his caller in a bored way, and that was it.

A code call. Their way out. Arrangements had been made; the call they'd all been waiting for—if they could make it to Alex and get past the harbour authorities. The Colonel, not Crowther or Usher, must have been the king pin in Cairo, to be protected at all costs, and now he was on the run with the rest of them.

He came into view, slumped on one end of the sofa, lit a cigarette. His head knocked against the wall and a shudder of nausea closed up the lines over his face and neck. He rubbed the back of his skull. Then he seemed to settle, composing himself with a drawn hang-dog look, a man waiting for someone to be sorry for him; pretending.

Some time later I was in the shaft again. A door had opened and now Bridget came into the room with a package. The Colonel looked asleep.

'Hamdy? Hamdy!' She bent over him and wobbled his shoulder gently. 'I've got the stuff at last. You'll need some water with it. Has he come back yet?'

The Colonel opened his eyes but didn't move. He certainly looked ill now. 'No. No, I don't think so.'

'What are you doing here—what did you get out of bed for? Did they call—did the call come?' Bridget ran through the sequence of thought with increasing urgency.

'No. Nothing came. No one. I went to the bathroom, must just have dropped off here.' He looked up at her with genuine exhaustion.

Bridget left the room. I heard a tap go on and tried to think what the Colonel was up to. He wasn't running in their direction at all.

'Take two of these now, and a sleeping pill. It's food poisoning of some sort. Rest, Cherif said, just rest.'

She gave him his medicine, then sat down next to him while he was getting it down.

'Now what?' he enquired when he'd finished. 'He's been gone since midday. Probably the sensible thing. We ought to have split up long ago.'

'Fine, fine—split up and go. But *where*?'

'He's obviously thought of somewhere.'

'He'd have just gone off like that, you think, without letting us know?'

'Why not?'

'He went for a walk. That's all. He went out and got picked up somewhere. How could he think he'd make it out of Cairo on his own?' Bridget turned on the Colonel almost angrily. 'How could he?'

'Well, he's gone. And if he's been picked up he'll probably

start to sing. Unless you want to go phoning the hospitals and
police stations?'

How like Henry, I thought, to fall under a bus at this
moment. But of course he hadn't; he'd sidestepped Dr. Novak
and made his way direct to the Russian Embassy. The Colonel
must have been thinking of some similar asylum—where
though?

'Obviously I'm not going to get out of here,' Hamdy
continued. 'Even if London is able to make some arrangement.
I'm not fit to walk, let alone jump a ship. Why don't you go to
the Consulate? Just give yourself over. They'll manage something for you.'

'Mad. Just madness. Why do you think that?—that I'd leave
you here?'

Tenderness for the Colonel—I shouldn't have been surprised
by it. She had always had those sudden gusts of unthinking
tenderness for everyone—even for someone who in this case was
going to bolt and leave her. I'd seen the Colonel move across the
room like a long jumper starting his run, frisky as a fox.

'Go back to bed, Hamdy. Wait. We'll just wait longer. That's
all. When you're better, there'll be something then. I promise
you.'

She helped him up and the two of them went through the
charade of his being lumbered back to bed. They passed out of
my eye-line, father and daughter, linked bravely together,
refugees starting out together on the long journey away from
the holocaust.

Hamdy was working for someone else. There was no end to
it. The Americans? The French? The Israelis? For someone, or
some country, so violently antagonistic towards Egypt, that he
couldn't trust Bridget with the information. But perhaps I was
being hard on him; he was simply protecting her, as Henry had,
from dangerous information. One protected people one loved.

It must be the Israelis, I thought. With any other country
he'd be in their Cairo embassy by now. It was perfectly
possible. There had always been Jews in Egypt, and some of
them had 'gone under', changed their names and covered their
tracks, in response to the difficult circumstances; Turkish and
Armenian Jews—and others from the diaspora—who had long
before intermarried among the upper class of the city, merged
completely with their Moslem neighbours. The Jews had never

been persecuted in Egypt. Certainly if he were with the Israelis they would make very effort to get him back, unencumbered with friends or colleagues or mistresses. And that was his plan. He would bolt when the music stopped, when only Bridget would be left standing.

She came back into the drawing-room, passed out of sight then back again with a whisky in her hand. She sat on the edge of the sofa, legs forked outwards, elbows on her knees. There was nothing vulnerable in her, nothing nervous in her calm expression: a sensible dark skirt and a long-sleeved blouse with a panel of embroidered lace down the front, Bahaddin's gold cross still about her neck.

She had weathered the years, and the men that had gone with them, with the faith of a missionary. She had believed in men; they had been her disciples. Though I had tried, I had never really been able to see her infidelities as a flaw of character, as simple greed or selfishness or stupidity: they were simply a reflection of a great need, an impossibly generous gift in a small and mean world; a gift centred on sex merely as the outward and visible form of all the other passion which for her lay behind that communion. Thus she repeated it, as gesture and symbol, with whoever came to the altar. There was, indeed, nothing possessive about her, nothing exclusive; she quite lacked self-regard—and that was her message to mankind. I had tried to tie her with those self-centred flaws, the perversions of her faith. The others, Henry and the Colonel and who else I didn't know, had learnt to freewheel within the orbit of her love; I had always pedalled hard in the wrong direction. And it wasn't the time to change things, just time to go. The only call I could have upon her now would be as a voice from the clouds.

'Bridget!'

She looked round towards Hamdy's bedroom door, casually.

'No—not there. *Here*—up at the ceiling. The ventilator shaft.'

She turned back, lit a cigarette and took her drink. She had heard some whisper and forgotten it.

'Bridget—*here*! Look *up.*' I repeated the performance. It was an extraordinary sight. From my height above the room she got up and moved about like an animal, testing the bars, looking everywhere, then coming towards me, dipping out of sight into the wall below me.

'Henry?' Her voice rang up to me. 'Henry?'

You silly bitch, I thought. And I had to stop myself from yelling next time.

'Here,' I said. 'Not Henry. Marlow. Peter Marlow.'

She had come out from the wall now and was looking straight up at me. She closed her eyes for a moment and shuddered, all the top half of her body shaking involuntarily, as though facing an icy blast from the ventilator.

'Listen—I'm coming round to your door. Have it open. *Don't* wake the Colonel.'

She looked at me without seeing anything, nodding wildly, her head bouncing up and down, breathless, an expression of insensible abandon on her face.

She closed the hall door noiselessly behind me and we tip-toed along the passage. How quickly she joined herself to the silent conspiracy, assuming all the skills of the dedicated lover: whispers from a window, the illicit meeting at the door, the utmost care in approaching the last hurdle of the creaky stair, before the vehement release in the spare room. She had, of course, just the right qualities for her job.

The remains of their tummy trouble hung in the air, a smell of rancid milk, but it had gone completely by the time we reached her bedroom at the end of the apartment, submerged in a rich blanket of powder and eau de cologne which she had doused the room with. It was stifling by the big bed; air couldn't have reached the place in months. I took my jacket off, while she closed the door behind me, carrying whisky and two glasses.

'Henry said they might send someone after us. But not you. We never thought of you.' She stood in front of me, pouring a drink, watching the golden trail of liquid, then gazing up at me. She looked more her age now, smaller, thinner, the hair seeming to fall back from a higher point on her forehead than I'd remembered. It only made her other features more prominent— the eyes larger and more widely spaced, the nose more abrupt, turning more pointedly at the end, the mouth a fine mobile line right across her jaw: the flesh had receded with time, had left these quirks like emerging islands; startling, unvisited shapes in the drought of the years.

'I'm sorry. Yes—they sent me.' I swallowed some of the neat whisky. 'Do you have any water?'

'I didn't mean *that*. Just—the surprise. It nearly killed me. How long have you been up in the wall?' She turned away.

'Just now, this evening.' I explained, briefly, how I'd got there. But the mechanics didn't interest her.

'Thank God you've come,' she said. That was what interested her. 'They got Hamdy's message in the end. It took them long enough. What—plans have you got? For getting us out of here?' And she rushed on, not wanting to seem pressed by the impersonal—'I never thought I'd be so glad to see anyone—and it's *you*, of all people.'

She looked at me warmly, full of trust, as though I were a sensible friend come to sort things out with a family after a bankruptcy. We might have been in each other's arms after a few more drinks. Not for love, for mere formal relief.

'Your hair's going further back your head; that's all.' She seemed to feel her way round my body with her expression.

'So's yours.'

A smile between us, then—acknowledgment that though passion had waned to nothing, it had existed once, and might again. She was making polite inquiries. So was I.

But suddenly I couldn't see Bridget in those terms any more, couldn't see myself sharing any kind of emotion with her. In a second it was all finished and done with, the years of pain, the suppressed longing which had risen again when I'd seen her from the Tower, and from the café as she walked along the corniche; another man had experienced all that bright resurgence, not me.

I had re-achieved her in those seconds during which we had looked at each other warmly and talked about our faces. We had gone through all the teasing preliminaries, and I felt that I could have tossed her on to the bed beside us without more ado. And since that was possible at last, I couldn't contemplate it seriously.

She was someone to help in a professional way, someone in trouble. It was she who must face the disappointment now.

'Henry's disappeared,' she said lightly, after the silence. Henry in his sailor suit who had run away behind the bandstand—as though she had been given the boring job of keeping an eye on him for the morning and had no other connection with him.

'Oh,' I said. I had nothing to offer her there, not yet.

'But what shall we do—what plans do they have?' she went on, like a traveller stuck at a midland junction on a winter Sunday morning: upset but still confident.

'There aren't any. I haven't any plans. They sent me out to see if Henry was here. And bring him back if he was, I suppose. But I don't see how any of us are going to get back.'

'Have they got on to you as well?'

'Yes. Cherry and Usher too for some strange reason. The whole circle.' I told her what had happened earlier in the evening.

'But what about the people in London?' she said, inisting now, but still controlled. 'At Holborn?'

I tried to think of Bridget at a meeting with Williams or having a drink in the wine bar in the Strand, just as I'd tried to imagine Cherry and Usher getting the number eleven bus—and it didn't work. Bridget, like them, was a part of Cairo, part of its very core; they were natural seismographs alive to its smallest tremors. They had not always been happy there; so much the more were they bound to it: they had lived a real life in the city, had given nothing false to it, in every minute passed there. Their dreams of elsewhere, of rain, ploughed fields, sloes in the hedgerow or London Transport, were as unreal as mine would have been for sun and coral, and clear blue water. The known years spent in a landscape never tie us to it, the marked calendar from which we can stand back and reflect or think of change; we are bound to a place by the unconscious minutes and seconds lost there, which is not measurable time or experience, and from which there is no release.

'Holborn doesn't know anything about getting out of here. But I'll let them know tomorrow. I have a contact through the library.'

She had begun to look glum and a little hopeless now, sitting on the dressing-table stool, drink in her hand, swaying out in a clumsy arc from the balance she'd made, elbow on her knee.

'But why should you want to leave? You haven't told me.'

'We've been here for days. They picked Henry up at the airport. He got away. They got on to Hamdy. We came here, it's his place, they don't know about it.'

'Hamdy's with us, of course?'

'Yes, of course. Didn't you know?'

'I was never active. You knew that. I'm in Library in

Holborn. I don't get to hear much about people in the field.'

'Yes, Henry told me.'

'You've seen quite a lot of him?'

'Odd times. When he was out here. Didn't he tell you?'

'No.' And I could see she knew he hadn't told me. 'No, he didn't tell me he saw you. Why should he? Why drag it up? I knew nothing about you.'

'Yes—but why? I wish you'd bothered. Sometimes.'

'Come on. It was finished, done with. We had a merry time. Then there was an unfortunate "professional arrangement"; if you remember.'

'Our marrying, you mean?'

'If you can call it that. I meant the other thing—getting married because it suited the professional circle you all had out here.'

'It wasn't *just* that.'

'No. All right, not *just* that, then. There were a lot of other funny things, *before* that. It passed off well enough, really. It could have been much worse. We could have stayed together and clawed each other for years. We were lucky to miss that. But you can see—it's not really the sort of thing one "bothers" about afterwards. One tends to want to forget it.'

My tone was so much the lying pedagogue: I had wanted to 'bother' her about it—for years afterwards—so much. Now it was her turn: she wanted to be bothered and worried about things like that; to feel, even at this late stage, that in distant conversations between Henry and me, she had been included: I worrying, Henry consoling.

Her sense of indispensability, of course, was part of her great attraction—when you were with her, when you thought you were the only person who shared her exclusively: when she was indispensable to you.

She put her drink down behind her and looked at me, hand cupped about her chin—that gesture I knew so well, when she turned from provocation to trust: the tired child, gazing into the fire, waiting for a story. Now for the first time since I'd emerged from Colonel Hamdy's office ten years before, it didn't have to be, couldn't be, a fairy tale.

'Anyway, the talk with Henry is finished. He's gone over to Moscow. He's probably at their embassy here now. That's where he's disappeared to.'

I wondered what her first words would be in reply, thinking that I could measure in them the strength of her affection for him. 'I don't believe you' would have been a natural response, for Henry had hidden his real self just as well from her as he had from the professional spy catchers. But instead she did the most natural thing, saying in a hardly surprised, serious voice: 'How do you know?'

I showed her the plaster round my heel and told her of my visit, under Henry's name, to Dr. Novak at the Kasr el Aini Hospital.

'You mean you suspected he was going over—London thought he was?'

To cut a long story short I said, 'Yes, that was what happened.'

'And what if he were to walk in here— now?' She wanted so much to see me wrong, almost believing about Henry, but not quite, not yet.

'If he were to do this, do that—Bridget, he's *not* going to walk in the door. He's gone out, over. He's with Moscow. It's the one thing he'd *never* have told you; nothing to be upset about.'

'I thought you knew him—as well as I did.'

'Yes, and I'm not surprised. Henry was like that, one knew everything about him except the boring things that mattered.'

'What on earth is he going to do in Moscow?' she went on with mystified concern.

'Write books, perhaps. He was good with words. Books and drink; argue with the housekeeper, read the English papers. A medal later on when they've squeezed him dry and put him out to grass. There are girls in Moscow too.'

I couldn't resist the easy cruelty.

'That's just spite. You might just be inventing the whole thing.'

'You know I'm not. I didn't come all this way just to do you down, I can tell you.'

'Why did they send you then?' she said in a higher, faster voice, heading for a point where she would break. 'You said you only worked in Library.'

'I don't know why they sent me. Because I know the place, the language—and wasn't known here now. That was the official reason.'

'You're just the same sort of vague fellow, aren't you? Bumbling round the place, letting everyone use you. It used to be teaching, now it's spying—but never really knowing what you're doing. Or why.'

'You're overdoing it. You're probably the only person who "used" me, as you put it. But that doesn't matter, as I said. What are *you* going to do? That's the question.'

'There are the other arrangements.' She was almost prim now. 'Hamdy was making them through a contact in Athens. That's through central office, not Holborn. I thought for a moment you were that contact. That's all. We just have to wait till he calls back. Hamdy's ill anyway.'

'He's not. And there won't be any call. Hamdy has nothing to do with our section, or with central office. That's why I wanted him kept out of the way.' I stood up to fill my glass for I honestly thought she might go for me on the bed. And I wanted to stop her too if she decided to make a run for his bedroom. But she did nothing except ease her legs on the stool.

'I suppose you think he's going over to Moscow as well—for a row with the servants.'

'No, I don't. Somewhere else. As far as I can make out he's with the Israelis.'

'Ha, ha,' she said in a dry way. 'Give me some more too, will you?'

I moved across, poured, added some water.

'You've let your imagination get the better of you, you really have.' She looked at me a moment, questioning. Then smiled, suddenly at ease. I was mad. Henry would be back later, a little drunk but safe, and Hamdy was recovering in the other room. They'd be off together as soon as the call came, as it would come. I had given her hope at last because, of course, I was mad.

After the years of bureaucracy in Holborn, doing nothing but thumb through *Al Ahram*, this trip into the field—into the world of guns and golden Dunhills and dark glasses—had driven me off my head: I was a gambler speculating wildly, suggesting complex allegiances, where, in reality, everything was as it seemed. For Bridget, the business of espionage was dull—but true, and it was wearisome enough to have to accept that situation. That it and the people involved were dull but *un*true, as I had suggested, was beyond her comprehension. It was time to humour me. The man who calls 'Wolf' once too often—I was the child now who need never be believed. Relief flooded across her face.

'You really worried me.' She got up, walked over and bent down for a moment, hands on knees. 'Why do you do it? After so long—what was the need to try and hurt again? You really didn't have to. To hurt and possess, always that, never giving up. It's what went wrong before and you're still at it.'

She stood up. The grave, widely-spaced eyes were an admonition linking past with present. It was part of the same expression that had brought things to an end ten years ago—and it was intended to serve the same purpose now: a look of kindness, even worry, above all a deeply mystified, discursive inspection, as a drunk might study someone overboard from a yacht.

'I'd better see how he is. But for God's sake don't be stupid. I won't tell him. Let's just concentrate now on getting out of here without all this drama. *All* of us. That means you too.'

'That's good of you, I'm sure.' She moved away towards the door. I swivelled the drink round in the glass and sighed.

She called me a few moments later. The light was on beside the bed, the table next to it piled high with old French novels, even an early Colette. There was a bottle of chalky medicine and an open box of pills. There were cigarettes and matches and the coverlet was nicely turned down—slippers, pyjamas, dressing gown at the ready. Someone was expected.

'Who sleeps here?' I asked. 'Henry?'

'No, Hamdy.'

'Where is he? The bathroom? Is he ill again?'

'No.' Bridget closed one of the paperbacks lying on the pillow, tucked the sheet in, pushed the slippers under the bed.

'He's gone.' Then she turned the light off. 'Why the *Israelis* of all people?'

'I don't know.'

We went back into the drawing-room.

We talked in more normal voices now; it made the apartment all the more silent.

Bridget went into the bedroom, and brought the drinks back in with her five minutes later. She had tidied her hair, powdered herself or something; there was a physical difference I couldn't quite identify. It wasn't a fall of confidence, much more a careful self-regard. She moved about the drawing-room settling things, rearranging cushions, emptying ash-trays. I had become a visitor who had dropped by at an awkward moment.

'If you work it out—I don't see who else he could be with. Moscow would have got him out of here long ago—'

'—No, you don't have to go on about it. It fits. Everything fits.'

I wondered if she would cry, once. But of course not.

'Before you came back this evening—that call did come, when I was up in the ventilator. He mentioned the name of a Greek boat in Alex. You could get—'

'—Something Tel Aviv must have fixed up for him,' she said brightly.

'Couldn't you have gone with him?'

'No, I couldn't. You don't run risks getting someone like him back home. Nor would Henry. I can see the problem. Now that I can see who they were really working for.'

'You couldn't have guessed.'

'I should have. I've known them long enough. Both of them. Hamdy better than any. You wouldn't know that; Henry didn't.' She started to talk quickly now, to herself at first, then to me, turning, pecking her face in quick starts like a hen querying something. 'Hamdy knew my parents. I'd known he was working for the British almost from the start. I thought it was the only thing he never told me.'

'I told you once in the Semiramis—there've been too many men; still. We've all been playing games. You and I, Henry and the Colonel. Point is, though, they've kept a last trick up their sleeves. We should have had one too.'

She raised her eyebrows, blew some air into her cheeks, trying to give her face the one expression it could never naturally assume—a stupid, deceived cast.

Blinded by these men? Could it ever have been so? Was she really one of those women who are natural camp followers, taken and used everywhere, only to be discarded at the final battle? I didn't think so.

There was a simpler explanation. She had been as close to Henry and the Colonel, as involved, as it's possible to be. She had given them every truth about herself. But she didn't really know them at all. So the passion was maintained—on mystery, on things that could never be counted. In my case, where there had been gross expectations and disappointment, she had come to know everything about me, so that we fell apart.

'If you ever do get out of here what will you do? What do you want—something in Holborn?' It was a rhetorical question; I knew she'd never be sorting cables on the fourth floor. The risk would have been too great with anyone who had been so directly involved with Henry. I supposed, if she did get back, they would give her some money and help her to find a small flat. Already I saw her as a burden, as someone I might have to remember Christmas cards for, wilting away like a poor cousin in Kensington. But perhaps she might decide to go to Israel.

'Or go to Israel?'

'No. Not that and not Holborn. I can get out of the whole thing now. I can do that at last.'

'I'll go to the Consulate library tomorrow morning, get a proper message through to London. Then we can decide.'

'You surely won't get near the Consulate. Or the library. They'll have the place surrounded.'

'We'll see. We'll think of something.' I didn't know what, for she was right.

'Yes,' she said easily, 'let's think about it tomorrow.'

The heat, with the whisky, had made us sweat. I got up and poured some more. There was nothing else to do. The apartment smelt of rotten lilac, powder and tobacco—curtains of different steaming smells as one moved across it. My face was burning, pumping with blood; and my heel had started to throb. I gave Bridget what was left in the bottle.

'You always dress out here like an Arctic explorer, Peter. Why is it?'

I looked at her, wondering if she had introduced this old sartorial theme with the same sexual innuendo behind it that we had understood so readily years before. But her expression was no more than tired inquiry; she seemed to have quite forgotten its earlier implications. I was annoyed at thinking differently. For me she was a woman who had come to mean exactly what she said; there were no overtones with her now. It was all precise words; and the words would support us as long as we used them officially, kept them to the professional matters in hand. They would bear no real weight.

Yet her remarks about my dress reminded me—as something dead but otherwise intensely real in a museum—of the life they once had: a talisman still capable of stirring desire. She had used those same words once, with feeling, and they would do now as encouragement for any woman.

'I'm hot, that's all. I'll take a shower and lie down. I'm exhausted.'

'Don't eat any of the food.' Her voice trailed casually after me as I left the room. 'It's all bad, I'm afraid.'

She had tucked her legs up beneath her on the sofa, shoes spilled on the floor, knees bent double like two delicate ivory ornaments, Buddhist carvings beneath the dark hem of her skirt which had risen up her thighs. She was sitting in a way she never used to—except when we were alone together, high up in Garden City, the windows open, waiting for the evening. An unthinking remnant of our intimacy had survived at least, I thought, but only as a formality, with no more meaning than the chivalry we mimic in shaking hands with a stranger.

I let the shower play over my face and through my mouth, spitting out water and saliva and the taste of whisky every now and then in white-flecked oily globules which ran slowly in the rushing stream along the bottom of the bath, before gathering speed in the current and spinning furiously into the whirlpool of the drain.

I almost fell asleep on my feet looking at the liquid cone of water, and I would certainly have dropped off had I been taking a bath. But I wanted to stay awake.

The drawing-room was empty when I got back, towelling my hair, just wearing my pants, and I went along the corridor to the bedroom we'd been in. The door was half open, light shining through into the darkness beyond. Bridget was in the huge bed, beneath a single sheet, arched on her side, facing me. She opened her eyes.

'I'm sorry.' I let the towel fall around my shoulders. After the long rush of cold water I felt a moment's chill run down my back and shuddered. 'I'm going on the sofa. Goodnight.'

I had my hand on the door ready to close it. 'Shall I close the door?' But already, in asking the question, I had opened the door slightly, moved a fraction into the room.

'Come in. Close the door.'

She pulled the sheet back as I walked towards the bed.

Of course, I said to myself, if we hadn't drunk so much, been so tired, it would never have happened. It was a combination of despair, drink and exhaustion which had made our bed for us that night, I thought. But I thought wrong.

She wanted me as much as I did her: we were equally dedicated to the idea. Now that there were no overtones, no emotion, no backlog of frustration and no future to the business, we could give ourselves to each other with the same uncluttered vehemence as we'd done on the first occasion we'd met. There was nothing perverse in it; it was purely self-seeking. We took to each other with the sharpest sort of appetite—that of perfect strangers.

No sixth sense warned us that the future might be sour, the next morning or a month hence. We didn't have that sort of future and we knew it. No debts would have to be paid, nothing lay in wait for us; no days over the smelly summer river, arguments over coffee at the Semiramis, or lies with dinner at the Estoril; no plots, misunderstandings; no tears or departure; no Usher and no Henry—no one to manipulate the slight events we might try and shape our lives with. There was no more of that life to shape. The professional, the personal, exploitation was at an end.

I had arrived in a country years before where nothing was as it seemed, a territory defended everywhere against trust, and I had come now to a broken barrier at the end of a smashed and empty landscape, a deserted customs post—to a point where no one stopped or chased you; where you simply stepped over the border and walked away.

She must have gone very early. I had woken once in the night and had seen her leave the room, the long naked back and widely-spaced legs moving in clear silhouette towards the shaft of light in the corridor, sharply isolating the narrow rectangle between her thighs.

And then I had woken a second time, abruptly with a headache in the darkness, the place beside me empty, and I had stayed where I was, waiting for her to come back as before, eager for her again. But I knew within moments that this time she had really left.

I moved fretfully around the apartment, wondering what she had taken with her, looking for some evidence that would tell me she had gone, and where, perhaps, and why. But there was nothing; a few of her clothes in the wardrobe, a sleeveless white dress I'd remembered her in, some soiled cosmetics on the dressing table, a small pile of underwear on the bathroom floor.

Not London, she had said. And not Israel. She was simply
getting out of it all. But where? I almost began to miss her—that
infection of sex, as if she and I had, after all, a future. There
was a surge of bitterness, a moment's fierce resentment that I
had lost her once more and would now have to start the search
for her all over again.

I went to the window in the drawing-room, eased the heavy
curtain back a fraction, and looked out on the brown grass of
the cricket pitch at the Club. The early sun slanted over it in a
bright golden wave. A man with a hose paddled about the edge
swamping the boundary in pools of grey-blue water. Kites fell
about the sky like footballs and the flame trees by the back
entrance were just beginning to explode into rusty crimson
light.

The minute Egyptian spring was finished, the Khamseen had
whirled itself out over the dunes to the south; the dog days had
arrived on the dot, when the heat would lie over the city for six
months like a plate. From now on one would need the Stella
really cold.

I wanted to be out of this too known country, where the
seasons were invariable, where duty and pleasure and sleep rang
out as clearly as a monastery bell, but where I could never again
be an indistinguishable part of the foliage. I was no longer part
of the timetable, had lost all the habits. I wanted to leave it
quickly and violently as I could, and I thought for a moment of
just going out to the airport and chancing it. But the chance
didn't really exist. And then I remembered the Provost's deputy
at the Cathedral: Mr. Hawthorn was going on a tour of his
Christian dominions in a long wheel-based Land Rover. Anything—anything would do.

I left the apartment, making as quick a passage as I could
from the darkness to the light.

11

THE Cathedral of All Saints' stood up on the left as I walked
over Kasr el Nil bridge, dun-coloured, with its bulbous central
tower like some atrocious chocolate shape; a boast of some
Scottish bishop fifty years before, an empty fortress now,
relegated to an imaginary holding operation against the alien

faith. For many years the City Corporation had planned to build a bridge over the river at the point where the Cathedral fronted on to the corniche, but the cost of demolishing the gigantic pile had disheartened them. It was now the fourth pyramid within the city's boundaries, only thirty years old, but already eroding, chipping away at the edges, taking on the mysterious patina of the other three: an abode of men who had been gods, who like their Pharaonic predecessors had disappeared without trace.

Mr. Hawthorn was at a meeting, I was told by his secretary, a defiant middle-aged English lady, when I called at his office on one side of the Cathedral forecourt. 'An Ecumenical Committee.' Perhaps I'd care to call back? The lady moved from one outer room to the other, very fast, carrying envelopes and brochures to and fro with terrible concern. I was barely able to keep up with her.

'I'll call back,' I shouted, as she settled in one room and began cranking an old duplicating machine.

'Do. In half an hour Mr. Hawthorn should be free. Before he goes to the Jumble Sale at twelve.' She stopped cranking. She looked at me, pondering my credit worthiness.

'Oh, there's a sale, is there?'

'Yes. In the hall opposite. You may like to buy something while you're here in Cairo. It's in aid of the new extension at Tobruk.'

'I'll take a look in, certainly.'

The lady warmed. 'Here!' She drew off an early sheet from the machine and handed it to me. 'It's our Libyan plan. It may be of interest.'

'Indeed—it was just what I wanted to talk to Mr. Hawthorn about.' I looked at the page of rough yellow foolscap:

> *The Churchwardens again take this opportunity of announcing the opening of a fund to provide an extension to the present severely limited office and domestic accommodation at the parsonage in Tobruk . . . .'*

The gods were not quite dead yet; the remnants of the last dynasty were counter-attacking; a message was on the way, an outpost would be relieved; once more the infidel would be repelled. There was even talk at this very moment of a united army gathering in the north, implacable legions blessed by nearly all the disparate Princes. God had been mocked and had retreated; but now there were plans at last: this was the second front.

The lady in the long cardigan cranked the machine again, the inky paper peeling off ominously, orders for the day; a General Mobilisation: 'The dogs of war . . . The Cannon's Mouth . . . Citoyens, aux Armes . . .'

I went into the Cathedral to pass the time, through the minute side door into the dusty golden-moted cavern beyond. One's eyes were lost at once following the Odeon curves and pillars into the shadows above; mid-'thirties, high renaissance ferroconcrete. A silver grille in front of the Lady Chapel at the top of the Cathedral, a distance that seemed hundreds of yards away over an empty no man's land of wooden trenches, the chairs running from north to south in yellow, untrammelled pine, disused communication lines between the opaque glass of the high windows on either side, last occupied by the Eighth Army.

On the walls, at distant intervals, like brief footnotes to a lost history book, were plaques and memorials from other long since ruined churches within the diocese; headstones and memento moris rescued from Port Said, Suez, Zagazig and even further afield.

In Memoriam
Colonel Campbell Scott Moncrieff
killed in an attempt to
prevent a dervish rising
Tigr Blue Nile Province
April 29 1908

Major Esme Stuart Erskine Harrison DSO
11th Hussars
who died on the polo ground
Gezira Nov. 1 1902
'In the midst of life we are in death.'

'Lt. Col. R. W. T. Gordon, 93rd Sutherland Highlanders. Died at Port Said from a fever contracted during the Suakin expedition . . .' 'Robert Septimus Grenfell, Lt., 12th Lancers. Killed in charge of the 21st Lancers at Omdurman, aged 23 . . .'

'Lt. Col. Baker, who died in Egypt, November 17, 1887. He highly distinguished himself at the battle of Tachkessen while in command of a small Turkish force . . . a service which was brilliantly and successfully carried out . . . sincere friends and admirers—a token of their respect . . . qualities of the highest order which he possessed as a soldier and commander.'

'Justice is the foundation of Empires.'

In the dust-inflamed Cathedral with its soft and pulpy curves, its neutral colouring, the men became a film, a coloured epic; lancers and swordsmen in red or blue tunics. They were the only thing that moved in the yellow spaces, the shafts of empty light. There was nothing of any god here; no mercy, pity or resurrection; nothing remotely Christian. The building was simply a memory of violent life, the plaques an album of adventure turned to stone. Battles and games—sunrise, noon and night; exultation falling, nipped by a mosquito finding the one flaw in the net after an exhausting day's march from the coast towards some empty quarter; fantasy dying, killed by some small, frightened men with greasy hair rising from behind a thorn bush in the Blue Nile Province while your back was turned; a dismal winter rectory in Worcestershire thrown into real mourning, nanny weeping on the servants' stairs, through just a piece of bad luck as the pony swerved in the last chukka at the end of a warm afternoon at Gezira: it was the rumour at nightfall, the sound of drums, the parley on the hill top, the pipe of a false peace and a lot of liberal politicians at home, umpires blowing shrill and distant whistles, calling foul.

It was just a lot of bad luck really; they always sold you short—just as you'd got the boot in and had cracked a first skull. When the maxim platoon had a proper alignment and trajectory, and it was going nicely, the black gentlemen scurrying over the hill, you had a telegram from some competition wallah in Whitehall and picked up a dose of blackwater fever on your way back to H.Q. You never made that first class cabin on the Port Said boat; another telegram to the War Office took your place instead, while you lay up in the little cemetery beyond the French Club, looking over the canal, watching the boats go home forever. Justice is the foundation of Empires.

It wasn't so very different these days, I thought. The fevers and the maxim guns had gone, and nanny had died weeping for the brave and foolish. But the umpires were still around in Whitehall, men like Williams, and far from liberal. And in Washington. And Moscow. There wasn't the sound of any whistles now. They knocked on the door late at night; and there was still no boat home.

The Blue Nile Province had become an acrid-smelling barracks, or a nissen hut in Heliopolis—or in Athens or in Saigon. But the men died just the same, on the direct current, with ruptured kidneys or gangrened shins. The brave and foolish went to the wall, just as they had always done, but at midnight now, not high noon; in a cellar, not an empty quarter. And there wouldn't be any memorial; no one would weep, for no one would ever know. It was a foolish story about history.

Something scraped over the glass in a corner window, high up; a shadow flicked across a row of yellow pews like a bird flying quickly over furrowed stubble. I turned and saw a lizard, six inches of still, mottled-green flesh, splayed out on the Gordon memorial window, a tiny cross of Lorraine stamped in the sun above the legend 'I have done my duty for our country'. I moved down a row of benches to take a closer look at it.

Charles General Gordon, C.B.,
1833-1885

I thought the lizard had moved a second time when I heard the scraping sound again. But it was in just the same position when I looked up—a misplaced heraldic device, an idea the artist had forgotten to rub out in the cartoon of the window. I looked to my right.

Henry was standing beside a pillar at the top of the wall aisle, just beneath psalm numbers for the previous Sunday. For an instant I thought he might have been one of the Church-wardens. He was wearing a navy blazer I'd not remembered him in, and his hair toppled about in wild growths, grey matted strands, some upright, some flattened like an unsettled harvest. His eyes sloped down on either side of his face, with tiredness or drink, as if someone had tried to make him up as an oriental and got it wrong from the start. There was nothing sinister or hunted about him; there never had been. When Henry was worried he simply looked in need of a bath. A shave and a haircut wouldn't have been wasted either. He seemed to me defiantly conspicuous.

'Sorry,' I said. 'I thought you were one of the sidesmen or something.'

He came towards me, those busy small steps neatly and exactly marking out the space between us as though he were measuring a pitch.

'Didn't mean to give you a fright.' I put out a hand in astonishment, but he didn't see it. 'I saw you walking along the corniche, couldn't think what you were coming in here for.'

'I came to see the Provost.'

'Didn't know you'd taken to good works.'

'I may be able to get a lift out of here with him. He's going to Libya. By car.'

Henry considered the idea and I looked at him, waiting. I wanted to see what he had in mind. But he said nothing.

'It seems there's only you and I left.'

'You think there'd be room?' He smiled briefly, an expression half meant, half not; waiting to see how the land lay as well.

'I didn't know you wanted to go back. In that direction.'

'Where are the others then?'

'The Colonel disappeared last night, Bridget this morning. I don't know where they went. I thought she might be with you. The others—Usher, Cherry, Marcus—they were picked up earlier still. Probably in Heliopolis now.'

'In the Army hospital at Maadi. But that's another story.'

He brushed his hair back, put a finger in one eye, wiping sleep away. His glasses had broken, I noticed, and he'd mended the hinge with tape. We started to walk down towards the font at the west end of the Cathedral.

'Why didn't you go straight to the Russian Embassy—when you got the wrong end of the stick from Dr. Novak?'

Henry stopped and began fiddling with the metal ring on top of the covered bowl.

'You've really been working.'

'I haven't done a stroke. You'll have to go somewhere. Won't you?'

'I don't have to go anywhere. That's the nice thing. I don't have to spin off anywhere and get broken up. I just have to stay put. Wait till they've forgotten about me. Then I can move off. Not somewhere Williams knows of, or Moscow. Or you. Leave the busybodies out.'

'The toytown, you told me—last week.'

'And you came running with a miniature baton and a set of traffic lights. That was a trick to buy from Williams—invoking the old pals act.'

'I've been just as cunning as you.'

'Why haven't you "turned me over" then?'

'If you thought that, you'd hardly have followed me.'

'I didn't think it. I was curious. Can't seem to drop the habit. What was Williams up to? Why did he send you?'

I told him nothing of the microfilm. I supposed, even then, that Henry might make it back to Moscow and would warn them that I had my theories about Williams—and I wanted to be left to deal with Williams entirely on my own.

'He thought you might have had an accident, that you'd just disappeared, been abducted or something. I thought you might have come here—so he sent me after you, said I had good "connections" in the place. What did you come here for?'

'Some cockeyed idea Williams had about subverting the ASU. I knew he was on to me the moment he suggested it.'

'On to your being with Moscow? Listen, if you've spent twenty years doubling for the KGB you might as well get out of it in one piece. Take the pickings, go home. Go to Moscow, for God's sake. Don't hang around here, you'll get nothing but fifteen years for that, or a bump on the head in some alley. They can get you out of here with no difficulty. Go. Good seats at the Bolshoi, a pass to the dollar shop. Take it. And stop frigging around the Nile in dark glasses. They shoot people out here for that sort of thing, you know.'

'Good news from Her Majesty's Government. I never expected to hear the like. Aiding and abetting treason. You'd get fifteen years yourself.'

'If Williams is on to you—run. You could be on a plane out of here tonight.'

Henry was indignant. 'You met Novak, didn't you? He's the Moscow Resident here. One made for the hospital, not the Embassy; that was the way out for people like us. And when I used it, I found him coming the other way. If a Resident wants to come over, finds things that bad—you think I want to swap places?'

The Cathedral door creaked—a whine of pity that seemed to last forever.

An old *suffragi* in a skull cap and patched *galibeah* crept into the arena and made his way gradually towards us, pretending carefully to dust the immense spaces which separated us. While he was still some distance away I turned and scowled at him, but he took this as his welcoming cue; yellow-faced and obsequious, he saluted smartly, and padded forward in the busy, unstoppable way these men have; a manner which fawns and insists in exactly equal measure.

'Good morning, sah! I will show you Gordon's Window, King Farouk's Golden Gates and very interesting things. Come with me.'

'No. No, thank you. We're just looking round on our own.' I tried to tip him off but he brushed past us, wiping his nose with a sleeve, the bright dark eyes close together, glittering like a conqueror passing over the border who knows the few essential phrases of command but nothing else of the language of the people he has set upon.

'Come this way, *please.*'

We wandered after him. He might have started to make a fuss. He was determined to do his duty, echoing the General's sentiments, as he stopped in front of his window.

'Great General Gordon, sirs. His head was taken off by the Mahdi and sent down here. This is his window. Very fine glass made in England by Pimplingtons, the extraordinary manufacturers. You are English—yes?' We weren't paying attention. He looked at us doubtfully, two laggards who might be American and upon whom he would thus be wasting his eccentric knowledge of Sudanese and British industrial history. But he chattered on comfortably when I nodded.

'Novak wouldn't have stopped you, Henry,' I said quietly. 'Don't be stupid. You're twice the size. After twenty years with us they'd do anything to get you back.'

'. . . . "done my duty for my country." This notice was put here by Bishop Gwynne . . .'

'You don't want to go back, that's all. What have you been doing for Moscow all these years anyway?—Snooping round Farnborough on press day?'

'. . . . the Cathedral was consecrated by the Rev. Dr. Temple on St. Mark's Day, April 25, 1938, who later became your Archbishop of Canterbury . . .'

'I believed in it all,' Henry said. 'That may surprise you.

That's why I don't want to go back.'

'The Moscow trials, Stalin, Hungary?'

'I believed in the belief, not the facts. I've never been to Russia.'

'. . . and the foundation stone was laid by Bishop Gwynne on November 20, 1936 and can be seen on the outer wall of the east end of Lady Chapel . . .'

'That was rather careless of you, wasn't it?'

'No one believes in the loaves and fishes. He was a fraudulent caterer and quack doctor. But that doesn't seem to have mattered.'

'. . . the architect was Adrian Gilbert Scott . . .'

'The English martyrs, the Thirty Years' War, the Huguenots—Christ!—the facts. I'm not talking about them. They never interested me. I was interested—I had to be, I was on the outside—in the selfishness of the creed. It had no message for anyone but me. It was mine. And the more the others said it was a fraud and a lie, the better I liked it. The more Hungarys there were, the more I said, "Screw you with your liberal notions—what have you been doing all these years? Reading *Encounter* by courtesy of the CIA?" Though they don't know it yet. Moscow seemed a better pitch than weeping tears on the box and paying super tax. I wasn't interested in being a professional left winger writing for the *Telegraph* colour mag.'

'. . . and the general contractors for the Cathedral were Messrs. Hettena Brothers, of Shrubra, Cairo . . .'

'If I had to argue that's how I did it. But it was never an argument for me. It was a *suffragi* who broke a decanter in Shepheard's Hotel.'

'What happened?'

It was the story of a genuine cradle socialist, of an old Nubian waiter wounded by his father in Shepheard's thirty years before— a cut-glass decanter more valuable than the man's annual wages; the story of a child who smells justice down the servants' stairs and learns to hate his father over the stench of boiled cabbage. Though of course the child wouldn't know—and I wondered if Henry did—that it was the other way round: it was the denial by his father which had driven him underground in anger, into the warrens of duplicity and subterfuge, and bruised love, where he had remained all his life. Children are the most undetectable double agents; Henry had become a professional child. Belief lay behind the tins of raisins and the candied peel. He had found Marx in the larder, the road to Moscow through the cellar door.

Hungary, five million peasants—the greatest repression—can mean nothing to such people whose political faith is formed in childhood, a creed inextricably related to the pain and happiness of a seven-year-old. A man, once set to the task, will seek to restore imagined innocence ruthlessly and without question. Henry would justify every sort of betrayal and repression because his own identity had been formed by just the same things. He would accept every sort of collective pain because he would be denying that identity, his childhood and an old Nubian, if he didn't.

'Gentlemen! This way please.'

The old fellow shouted for our attention. He had tired of his descriptions and had led us now quickly up towards the Lady Chapel.

'King Farouk's Gates, the "Gates of Heaven",' he said peremptorily, pointing to a sort of boudoir grille that divided the Lady Chapel from the Cathedral proper.

'I thought that was a brothel in Port Said,' Henry said. And then the man was looking for his tip in a business-like way. And afterwards he produced some half-crowns and one-franc pieces, asking Henry for Egyptian change.

'No,' Henry said shortly. 'No, you've had your money. That money is no use to me.'

I gave the man some change instead and he disappeared without another word.

'So you're going to Moscow then?'

'They expect everything these days. Expect it,' Henry said, looking after the swinging *galibeah* rounding a pillar. 'They crawl, they force themselves on you, then they insist, then they want paying twice over. Then they just fuck off.'

'That sounds like the Reform Club, not the Central Committee.'

'I know. I thought last week it was a village in Galway I wanted. Now it's just a castle with a moat. The other view—the East: you know, the desperation, the shoddiness, the eternal damp of six months' snow, fashions five years late and lashings

of raw alcohol on rough counters—all the things you saw as
necessary, which you looked on with nostalgia, when you
thought the Wall and the barbed wire was *your* prison—all that
seems now just like a bad copy of the professionals, a cheaper
show, a swindle bigger than the swindle of the West. But I used
to think of what happened over there as a genuinely amateur
performance.'

We had walked down to the end of the Cathedral, next to the
mission boxes by the door, the lepers and all the penny charity
of darkest Africa.

'The cold must have had something to do with it. In my
mind. It was so cold there, so much snow; there was some
marvellous quality there which we didn't have in Africa.
Wordsworth's daffodils for someone in Capetown who'd never
seen more than a flame tree or a thorn bush or a prickly pear. I
fancied myself, I suppose. In Astrakhan.'

'It's just as cold in North America surely?' I said. But I didn't
press it.

Henry confessing; supplication in a place cracked with the
sun, rotten with heat, summoning a frozen creed. It was an odd
sensation, hearing this memoir of belief from someone you
thought only really cared that the champagne was cold enough;
like seeing a man circled by birds, the true words homing at last,
falling suddenly from nowhere, completely engulfing the
isolated figure, so that one couldn't tell whether he was being
savaged or saved. And could do nothing anyway. One doesn't
'lose' faith; that would be a charity. It simply grows cold in you
and stays there, a dead limb that you can never throw away,
never replace. There was no use my offering anything.

'What will you do then?' I asked. 'A farm in Kenya or
something? Algeria?—they're taking on every sort there these
days, I hear.'

'Do you expect to have to tell them—that you've met me?'

'I won't tell them anything. Except that they sent me out
here on just as much of a goose chase as you.'

'And Marcus? Was he sent out here to fetch us both back?'
Henry smiled briefly. '*Who will they send to fetch him away,
fetch him away, fetch him away? Who will they send to fetch
him away* . . .' He sang the little rhyme joyfully, not a trace of
the cynic. But he slowed on the last line, a little bitterly, as if he

really wasn't expecting it: '. . . *on a cold and frosty morning.*'

'There wasn't going to have been anything of me left to take back. Too long to go into.'

'Same sort of boat then, aren't we? They won't care to see you back home. If you ever make it home.'

'That's why I'm going. Or trying to.'

'If they tried to dump you, as they did me, they won't believe you, you know. They'll just lock you up.'

'Go to Moscow, Henry. Worry about yourself. Even if you don't believe in it any more—what does it matter? None of them do, you know; Blake and the others, that's why they had to run there: they weren't safe in the West any longer, their ideological cover was broken.'

'A plausible line. You'd go down well in Dzerzinsky Square yourself.'

'You'll just have some stupid accident otherwise. Walk over the bridge, take the pyramid road past the zoo, you can't miss it. They'll probably give you a vodka and Coke if you ask nicely. It's the new drink, hands across the ocean. A great cure. Gets the gases up.'

'We should have it together.'

'Don't forget to send me a copy of your book,' I called after him.

He walked out across the forecourt, busy as ever and less shaky, hands stuffed in either pocket of his blazer, pot-bellied, head down, breasting the waves of brilliant light, anxious to make it by opening time. In reality, he might have been . . . I couldn't say. You could never really tell with Henry what he intended; fair enough, I suppose, for a man whose job it was to conceal things. We were friends in other ways.

I gave the half-crowns and francs to the lepers and before I went back to the Provost's office I stood on the corniche for a moment, watching Henry pass the Trafalgar lions and turn on to the bridge.

12

HE came from Gloucestershire, or perhaps Somerset.

'You're keen on ecumenicism then?'

'Very.'

'I can't say it's making huge progress in these parts. Don't quote me, mind you. With the Coptic Church we already have several amicable arrangements. On the other hand they and the Romans are rather wary.'

'I'm sorry to hear it.'

'Only the other day they'd achieved what I felt was a commendable *rapport*. The Sisters of Charity here started a Sunday School on the roof of a Coptic recreation hall at St. George's. But it was stopped. The Mother Superior suggested the rafters weren't all they might have been. Of course the building there is Old Testament, so she may have had a point. Don't quote me, though.'

'I suppose it's a question of two steps forward and one back in these matters.'

'I sometimes think it's exactly the reverse. Still, this needn't concern you. It was the Anglican community in the diocese here which you said interested you.'

'Very much so, yes. Especially your plans in Libya. I hear you've just acquired a long wheeled Land Rover.'

'Long wheel-*based*; yes, indeed. It will ease the visiting considerably. In fact I'm off on an expedition to Alex and then on to Libya in a day or so. You're welcome to come along if you can spare the time, though I expect you're pretty busy with the Field-Marshal's visit. Yes, we're extending our premises in Tobruk, a very useful addition. You know, we've really been rather *cramped* in Libya.'

'I'd like to very much if there's room. I—'

'Well, come along then. You can pay for your way, as it were, at the Jumble Sale now. Add your brick to the extension—what?'

Mr. Hawthorn laughed deeply and stood up, and then seemed to go on standing up. He was a tall man in any case, but his face was long too, and perhaps his heels were more than usually thick, and with his full crop of silvery hair he topped out at well over six foot six. I could hear the voice long ago in some West Country choir, sharp and true, rising clear above the other surplices, just as the boy himself had done the previous afternoon in the rugby line out.

'What B.B.C. programme did you say you worked for?' he asked as we walked across to the sale.

'I'm afraid it doesn't go out on the Overseas Service. Just the domestic. I'll try and see if they can send you a transcript.'

'I'd be most grateful. And if I may I'll give you the names of one or two people at home; if you could let them know when it's going out. And there's the Church Press Office in Lambeth, you might just let them know about it too.'

'Of course,' I nodded, trapped in the hopeless lie. Though perhaps, if he'd known, he would have excused it as rendering unto Caesar. I wouldn't, but Hawthorn was an honourable man.

I said goodbye to him before lunch.

'Be here Monday morning, then, say ten o'clock. We'll go straight to Alex. And you'll need a Libyan visa. They'll give you one at their consulate in Zamalek.'

I crossed on to Gezira over 26 July Bridge and got to the Consulate just before it closed. They tried to get me to call back on Monday but I pleaded urgency: a Church mission, a parsonage in Tripoli . . . I was hoping to leave straight away.

In fact, I had an awkward two days to fill. The Armenian's apartment was no use. Bridget might have been picked up by now, or Colonel Hamdy. They'd ransack his place next door, find the ventilator perhaps. My luggage was still at the Semiramis, but in any case I couldn't risk an hotel. Necessary risks, yes, but nothing else. But I had money, most of £200, and nearly £50 in piastre notes.

I walked back down 26 July Street and on to the bridge again. It was early afternoon. All work would cease in the city within half an hour, people would have vanished from the streets, and I'd stick out like a madman. It had to be something soon.

I watched the feluccas with cargoes of terracotta pots from Luxor easing themselves down the Gezira bank, their huge thin moon masts creaking down as they came towards the bridge. It was the one thing I'd never done in Egypt, a proper trip on the river. It was a comfortable two-day journey to Helwan, fifteen miles south, there and back in one of the small cushioned feluccas that one hired below Shepheard's—cushioned and hidden from the glare in a brown tent that covered the stern in a round awning like a nissen hut.

For a a few extra pounds one could stay on the boat overnight. And for a few more one could ensure that there were no questions. Informers in Egypt were a business-like lot; it was simply a matter of paying them something more than the last

policeman had. I would go to Helwan for the week-end: a
perfectly appropriate voyage for an inquiring Englishman. The
man might question my lack of company; I questioned it
myself. In better circumstances I might well have made the
journey with Leila Tewfik. Cairo used to be famous for this sort
of leisurely waterborne *affaire*; one took hampers and small
lanterns for the night. But that was before my time.

I took a taxi down to Garden City and did a deal with one of
the boatmen. Not too much money. And not too little. £15 for
the two days, with a promise of a further £5 on safe return.

The man seemed not in the least surprised; I played my
slightly eccentric role to perfection. Williams, I remembered,
had recommended just such a front less than a week before—the
only piece of advice that I took from him that wouldn't have
landed me in jail. Williams by now would have heard about
Marcus and the others and been well pleased. He must have
thought that every one of us was on beans and water already.
But he could wait; every dog has his day. With luck, one man
was sailing gently back to him now—dog-in-the-manger, skeleton
in the cupboard, to take his bone away.

I lay back inside the awning, stretched my feet out over the
scrubbed white floor boards . . . the man cast off and poled the
boat out into the stream.

He was old and immensely practised; a small, tight, ebony
face with a white half-moon of stubble, eyes that understood
everything in a glance spared from the business in hand. He
flapped about the wide edges of the boat in his bare feet,
stabbing the water judiciously with his pole, like a bored
snooker master, chipping into the triangle and putting away the
colours in a mammoth break.

We punted along the shoreline, very gradually pushing out
towards the small wind which we would catch near midstream
once we had passed the tip of Roda Island jutting out into the
river in front of us. The water began to flip and scurry along the
bottom of the boat, singing between the runnels of the old
wood—the slow current which would take us back to Cairo, just
as surely as the breeze from the sea would carry us gently
upstream.

The boatman stood up for a moment in the prow, resting his
pole in the current. A minute squall of wind flapped his long

sleeves, a series of small pistols going off in an ocean. Then it
was quiet again. The reedy whisper of water beneath us slowed,
almost died. The man turned against the flat blaze of light in
front of us and looked back at the city. It had come into its
proper context now that one couldn't see it clearly any more,
the ochre ribbon of buildings disappearing in the haze. One
forgot completely the cracked and broken glitter of the streets,
the slops by the doorways, the years of rubbish congealed in
hillocks of tar by the pavements. The detritus of all its history,
from Pharaonic shards to Coca-Cola bottles, belonged to a
country one had heard much of but never visited, passing slowly
half a mile off the coast, looking to the land as though it were a
territory in permanent quarantine.

People suffered there, mysterious plagues beyond the medicine books; the sky burnt them mercilessly, fevers never
dropped; flies pursued them, a hybrid super-species; they were
watched from doorways, sent on endless last journeys; no ease
and little joy—characters bound up in a long book of pain,
exiled in this desert for no other reason than the water which
had brought them here, and was now their only relief. And to
be far out on that huge brown stream was never to know the
illness, only the cure.

We journeyed to Helwan, stayed there overnight on the shore
beyond the town, and came downstream the next day. A day
and a night and another day. We travelled like a nineteenth-
century Arabist and his dragoman, self-sufficient, but always
concerned; a page from Lucie Duff Gordon's memoirs, a
dazzling white-sailed caique moving slowly through the curves
of the river by day, suspended at noon under a clump of palm
by the water's edge, making good passage in the wind that came
with the last hour of light, finding refuge in the darkness, when
the sky lit up the river with tinsel and a shaft of undulating
white marble from a large moon.

The man cooked beans on a paraffin burner he had with him,
stuffed them into bladders of dark bread, and we brewed a
milky tea, spitting the leaves overboard.

I asked him about his life on the river and he talked about it
slowly in a whisper-harsh voice, ragged and disrupted from years
of calling across water.

As with his ancestors he didn't speculate about the river; his involvement was uniquely practical. He had no other curiosity about it. It sprang from mud, meant toil, gave life. It flowed northwards, like every river. And when I told him that there were other streams which ran south, in just the opposite direction, he looked at me as if I were professing a new and dangerous faith.

'How could a river flow uphill, against itself?' he said. 'What would it do to the crops—if a river worked like that? And where would you put the High Dam then?—in Alexandria? And how would a boat get back from Luxor to Cairo?—for the current would be running in the wrong direction. A river can't flow backwards.'

Don't worry, I thought, we're working hard on it; all the rivers will flow the wrong way soon. We'll do everything before we're finished.

We arrived back near Cairo the following evening, cool and silent, the water like a lake, cargo feluccas drifting with us, their crews asleep or crouching round small fires in the stern—a smell of river clay and burning tinder and grilled fish coming over the water which had gone bronze and violet with a burning orange dipping over the western shore.

It had been dark for several hours when we reached the first of the bridges at Giza so that we saw the finger of light from the police launch, prodding the velvet between the piers of the bridge, from some distance away.

I was about to tell the boatman to pull in when he said in the simple easy phrases of a professional describing something seen many times: 'They are looking for someone. He has drowned.'

'Couldn't they be trying to rescue him?'

'No. No, it couldn't be that. They have a grapple with that boat. They only take it out to look for the ones who are dead.'

It was well after midnight when we finally tied up. I paid him the additional money and said I would stay on board till morning.

Mr. Hawthorn had a funeral on his hands when I got to the Cathedral in the morning. Two funerals, in fact.

'I don't know if you've heard about it, there's been some trouble,' he said. 'An old lady at the Anglo-American—her husband is in police custody. And another man from London—

apparently he had some sort of boating accident over the weekend. They found his body above Kasr el Nil last night. I'm sorry, it will mean twenty-four hours' delay on our trip. I've been on to the Consulate. Neither of the people had dependents in the U.K. They're to be buried at the British cemetery tomorrow.'

'I'm sorry to hear it. I've been up at Helwan over the weekend.'

Madame. And Henry. I couldn't think of anyone else falling out of a boat at that moment.

'How did it happen?—the accident, I mean. On one of those small boats?'

'Yes, the man hired the boat apparently, after dark. Either from the Garden City pier or from the island. No one seems to know. The thing overturned—they do if you stand up in them or do anything awkward. The boatman managed to swim back. The other person, a Mr. Edwards, didn't.'

'Oh dear me.'

Henry had been wild drunk. He must have been. I thought how easily it could have been me.

'But why had he taken the boat in the first place?'

'They'd closed all the bridges to Gezira yesterday.' Hawthorn paused and looked at me briefly. 'They were looking for someone. Someone on the island. I understand a woman was abducted, kidnapped or something. The Russians are supposed to have had something to do with it. Probably a wild rumour, you know what the place is like.'

'Yes.' Was he just trying to get off the island, back to town? Or had he been making in the other direction, for the Russian Embassy on the Giza Bank? One would never know. It was just the sort of ambiguous exit Henry would contrive for himself. And the woman? I felt equally sure that it must have been Bridget. She had never made a mistake; the first one would be decisive.

'Did they find this person—the one they were looking for? Or was that the woman?'

'They've been asking me that. Your colleagues. As if I knew. You're the ones to know all about that.'

'Oh, I don't handle news. Just background. The price of rice, how the people live—your new extension in Tobruk for example; that sort of thing.'

'Of course. "Colour" material, isn't it called? Anyway there

seems to have been some considerable unpleasantness. I'm glad
that still doesn't count with the B.B.C. . .'

Hawthorn got up and moved a pile of circulars from his desk
to a table beneath the window of his office, thumping them
down. Dust blew up into the light, like a small explosion,
bringing with it the utterly dessicated odour of lime dust,
peeling wood, baking concrete. The office was surrounded with
diocesan photographs, groups of clerics in strange places
including some recent ecumenical ones: a Nubian priest in full
regalia stood on a muddy river bank blessing naked figures in
the shallows of the stream; a craggy, Anglican bishop glared
angrily across the mock-Jacobean refectory table with a plastic
fan in front of him.

'The woman's husband is coming to the interment tomorrow.
A Mr. Cherry. He was a schoolteacher here. Tragic really.'
Hawthorn gazed out of the window on the small border of
shrubs and bushes, tar-spattered, sand-blasted, oiled from the
years of traffic that came roaring down from the station to the
corniche. 'The police telephoned me this morning. They're going
to come with him.' He turned. 'One didn't expect that, you
know. One really didn't. One doesn't usually get that sort of
co-operation out here you know. Don't quote me on it.'

'They respect the dead in Egypt though, don't they? More
than the living.'

'Ah, that's much too big a question, Mr. Marlow. We haven't
begun to answer that one. But it's true, the Egyptians have a
tradition in that matter.' He came with me to the door. 'These
days, of course, we fly our nationals home. We haven't buried
anyone in the British cemetery here for, oh, goodness me—it
must be more than five years.'

'Now there are two.'

Hawthorn looked at me critically, as if I intended continuing
with some aphorism or nursery rhyme, a query in his long face:
I had stopped half-way through a message which would explain,
alleviate. But I'd nothing to say.

'Yes, tragic really. They don't seem to have had anybody at
home. But—there you are.' He put his hands in his side pockets,
thumbs sticking out, an umpire considering a critical decision.
'Come round tomorrow then. Say around eleven-thirty. We'll
try and get away as soon as possible after the funeral.'

I went out into the scorching light, numb in the heat that

danced off the water, conscious only of the steel that brayed
down the corniche like bullets; the passions that led people
somewhere in such a hurry: to drinks in a shadowed bar, lunch
back home, to see a girl. Such appointments seemed all the
more necessary now, vital.

I'd never really thought of Henry dying; it hadn't seriously
crossed my mind. Something stupid at worst—but then over to
the other side: a dacha, snowshoes and hot toddy in the
Moscow woods. I was sure that in the end he would be faithful
to the fun of it all, if to nothing else. I thought he would
sacrifice his soured belief for the life principle which he held so
strongly. I saw now that the belief and the principle had been
identical in him. Champagne for Henry was a manifesto, not an
indulgence.

But still, there was something so corny about his dying which
I couldn't follow, and couldn't see him following: such an
unnecessary bore, as he would so surely have said of it himself.
He'd done it without really meaning to, like an insult late at
night in the saloon bar. It was a mistake he would regret briefly
when he was half-sober next morning, with a roaring headache,
on the way to another pub; just a foolishness among so many in
the midst of a tattered vibrant life; something he would redeem
later in the continual apology Henry made with his good
fellowship.

I really couldn't see him in the river, the skin going blue,
orifices suppurating, the slobber of that kind of death. He'd
have lost his glasses, I suppose that's why I couldn't see it;
Henry would have been unrecognizable without them. Waters
from Home Security could clear his fridge out now, the solid
horseradish and the bag of olives. And cancel the *Bookseller*.
That was all I could really see.

I spent the afternoon—and later the night—lying in the shade of
some flame trees on the far side of Gezira Club, reading *Al
Ahram* which I'd picked up at a kiosk on the way. The
President was pushing it—or being pushed, of course; war
seemed inevitable now. If the Army needed any more confirmation to send them over the brink, the microfilm would have
done it: Marcus's little message from the Israeli Chief of Staff.
Nasser could no longer restrain his generals; like Farouk, he had
signed the instrument of his demise before anybody had asked

him, for, of course, the more the Arabs clamoured for war, the more unready one knew they were. They were like schoolboys, taking Dutch courage with shouts and teases, for a fight against a bully. But the bully would smash them quietly behind the bicycle shed before tea. The Charge of the Light Brigade; they would need a Tennyson to salvage anything from this blitzkrieg.

I'd always suspected that the dry men in our department, and in Whitehall and Washington, would try sometime or other to get Nasser off his perch, go for him with some new trickery, another little bit of collusion—this time undetectable, except for the microfilm I still had. The headlines in *Al Ahram* told the whole story: six Israeli armoured divisions massing on the Syrian frontier: Marcus and I had been given the same message all right.

And Williams was the driest man of them all; Moscow's man. A war for them would have even more favourable conclusions than it would for the West. Russia was an ally in these parts after all, a friend with a foot in the door. After this they would be running the household, sacking the servants, commandeering all the stores.

That was the only thing I had not foreseen: that the powers had identical interests in this airing cupboard, in seeing matron topple. That was the new collusion. Perhaps, Yalta-like, they had already agreed among themselves that the Middle East should be a Soviet sphere of influence: as long as we could still have the oil. And keep the Jewish vote in New York.

It was like an exotic English garden to a great house, with flame trees round the side, bougainvillea clambering wildly over the yellow sun-burnt walls, clumps of some sort of flowering laurel, paths as neatly run as designs in a blueprint, the grass edged and clipped and watered, untrodden and undisturbed—the one park in the city where no one took his ease in holiday groups; the fruits, the first fruits of them that slept.

The weather wasn't typical National Trust though: the usual lead-blue Cairo dome, the light so harsh and stinging that one didn't dare look up and see where the sun had got to, how far on the day was.

They had dug the graves at the bottom of the cemetery at St. George's: they were just under the high walls, looking back over the Mokattam Hills, in a small patch of empty ground left over from the thousands of other tombstones which raked the area, neat war graves for the most part, plain white stones, like little cupboard doors; name, rank and number: model prisoners, withholding everything to the very last.

The two sandy hollows were at the end of a line, which started with the children drowned in the Comet disaster of the early 'fifties: a watery corner, in a place where everybody seemed to be the victim of some awfully foolish mistake: a piece of shrapnel that had chosen to share the line you lived along, a faulty bolt in the fuselage on the way to see your parents, a bright day on the river that had gone on too long, with too much drink, so that you knocked yourself out on the keel which had risen like an iron reef in the darkness as the boat reversed itself. It was all a dreadful mistake.

Madame Cherry was the only person who seemed to have gone quietly, willingly perhaps. Herbert watched her now as they began the process of lowering her away, his head bowed, the bald pate stooped earnestly, the better to hear some scurrilous Dublin story. A story beyond all telling. His hands were linked together over his belly. 'I'll rest this round, thanks all the same.'

Two plainclothesmen stood behind him. The ropes shrieked quickly against the side of the wood.

Then Henry went, in a larger box, like a lift plunging down a shaft, going under once more. An over-confident conjuring trick, one could see the ambitious pretence immediately.

I was almost ready to believe in the spirit then—complaining, implacable—rising up to indict and slander the barman, resisting the petty regulations of closing time, invoking other more civilized places.

I couldn't hear much from a hundred yards away, pretending to look at another grave by the wall, turning my ear, bending down to look at an inscription, shielded by a flowering bush.

'. . . *it hath pleased almighty God of his great Mercy to take unto himself* . . .'

I lost the rest of it. Herbert had stepped back into the custody of the two men, willingly, as though in all that staring masonry any protection was better than none.

Hawthorn wrapped his surplice around him and moved carefully forward towards the holes, a golfer checking an eagle.

I tried to feel that in other circumstances I would have

comforted Herbert in some way, taken him on to the Estoril for a solid lunch, a long afternoon of drinks, a wake that might have eased things. And the idea came very clearly into my mind, absorbing every other thought: the dazzling linen table-cloths, moist *arak* glasses, the smell of lemon juice and burnt perch; purple bubbles in the Omar Khayyam and the living, stupid chatter around us.

And I saw the two of us, Herbert and me, so precisely, at the cemetery gates, the taxi humming by the kerb, waiting for Henry to join us.

Instead, I met Hawthorn back at the Cathedral and we were half-way down the Agricultural road to Alexandria by lunch time, taking a stomach-turning snack at the rest house in Tanta: raw oiled tomato salad, dry bread sandwich and a warm Coke.

We talked about the challenge of the church today, glancing now and again at the magnificent olive Land Rover parked beyond the fly-smeared windows. A hopeless old man kept on trying to sell us fifty used ball-points; two scabious dogs watched us with equal hungry patience, hunched up, shifting their paws miserably, going 'click-click' like knitting needles on the old linoleum. The waiter made an error in his count, somehow getting an extra figure one in front of the fifty-three piastres total. We pointed this out to him—to his apparent delight—and he took the opportunity of wondering if we could change a few deutschmarks he happened to have on him.

The journey back was uneventful. I was so genuinely tired of it all, so divorced in my mind from the plots and machinations of the past week, that I really didn't believe myself that I had anything to do with British Intelligence. I was what I said I was, a journalist interested in a piece on Ecumenicism and the future of the Anglican community generally in the Middle East; it was, by its very nature, a restful, self-effacing, unsuspicious role and I immersed myself in it completely.

We passed through Egyptian control at Soloum on the Libyan border without their giving me a second glance. It was not a crossing they could have expected me to leave by, nor the impeccable company I kept likely cover for a spy. In fact, of course, the heat must have been off us all by then if, indeed, it had ever reached the slow men at this distant frontier. Egyptian Security must have been suffering an embarrassment of riches;

Alexandria had been alive with the story the previous day: a nest of spies had been uncovered in Cairo and one man had been taken in the western harbour that morning, an Israeli Intelligence officer trying to make it home, head of their entire circle in Egypt, the king pin.

At Tobruk I went to the church hall and talked with Hawthorn at length about the extension; I took measurements, made little drawings and interviewed the foreman in Arabic; I licked my index finger and discussed erosion and the prevailing winds. They were impressed by it all, pleased. It was the saddest afternoon of my life.

'Thank you,' I said to Hawthorn afterwards, 'I've decided I'll have to go straight back from here. Time has rather run out for me and there's a piece I want to do on Libya in any case before I go.'

'But what about your luggage and things in Cairo?'

'You know what it is in this job—here today, gone tomorrow. I'll have the hotel send it back. Don't worry about that. And thank you—very much indeed.'

'It was nothing,' Hawthorn said. 'Nothing at all. Glad you were interested. "Always something new out of Egypt" as they say.'

We laughed and shook hands in the wretched featureless street, Hawthorn in his grey lightweight clericals towering over the rubble of new buildings, the flat land beyond the edge of the road. Sand whipped around our shoes from the desert, piling up against our heels in minute dunes even as we stood.

I took a taxi to the British air base and two days later the VC 10 was falling through heavy cloud above Burford, the jets thrusting once more over dripping parkland, before we scudded down in a cloud of spray at Brize Norton.

13

TWO Special Branch men were on the tarmac to meet me, a senior inspector, a tall pipe-smoking, academic-looking fellow called Kirk, and a burly junior officer, who probably hadn't got more than four 'O' levels but looked as if he could run fast and had done well in Police Federation boxing.

They drove me to London, to Scotland Yard, where I was asked to make a statement.

'I've nothing to say. The only statement I can give is to my own department—you must know that, the Official Secrets Act. What's *your* explanation—wouldn't that be more appropriate?'

Kirk looked unhappy and unsure of himself. He wrote something in the margin of the Crown document in front of him.

'I can understand your position, Mr. Marlow. You are not of course obliged to make any statement. We've been asked to interview you about your recent activities in the UAR—'

'Don't go on. What are the charges and then I'll contact my solicitor.'

Kirk was horrified by my peremptory stance.

'It would come under the Official Secrets Act,' he said at length.

'Well, I didn't suppose it would come under the Foot and Mouth regulations. What is it, for God's sake?'

He sighed and read from the document in front of him, going through the legal preamble before coming to the application proper: ' "... that on dates between the 7th and 10th of May, 1967, and on other dates prior to that period, you did knowingly communicate to foreign agents information which was calculated to be, or might be, or was intended to be useful to the enemy, entrusted to you in your capacity as an officer of the Crown; and that further, you did, between the same dates, knowingly communicate, to the agents of a second power, the names and rank of officers of the Crown resulting in their subsequent apprehension and arrest." One charge to answer, under section—'

'Is someone being funny?''

Kirk looked up, aggrieved.

'You think I'm an Egyptian agent?'

'Not I, Mr. Marlow, I assure you. The charges are being brought by the Crown, on an application made by the Chief of your department to the Director of Public Prosecutions. They've accepted that there is a case to answer.'

'You think I'd come all the way back here in the circumstances—if I were working for the Egyptians?'

'I've no idea. No doubt that's a point your counsel will have every opportunity of presenting on your behalf in due course.'

'I'll call my solicitor then.'

'Certainly. Meanwhile you will be held in custody. Oh, "and I must warn you that anything you say will be taken down . . ." '

He ran on with the legal procedure hurriedly, an old lady scrabbling for something forgotten in her bag, trying to tumble it out as I stood at the door, waiting with a sergeant. When he was finished I was taken downstairs. They made a list of my belongings, including my passport. They didn't, of course, spot the microfilm behind the foreign exchange allowance, and I didn't tell them about it. I thought, somehow, that once that emerged in the right quarters I would be done with the whole business and Williams would start the first of his many turns with the gentle Inspector Kirk.

I was given some warm buttered toast on a large tin plate and a cup of sweet tea. Looking up from my cell through the area window I saw a narrow ribbon of gusty blue and grey spring sky over the embankment and I thought: 'I'll be out in that in a minute, get caught in a nasty squall on my way home if I'm not careful.' I've since learnt that this is a common delusion suffered by prisoners during the initial part of their confinement.

My solicitor came afterwards, when it had got dark and the lights had mysteriously gone on in the tiled cubicle. That was the point when I knew I wasn't going to get home that night—when I realized that they did things here for you literally without asking.

I told the solicitor that I wanted to bring a counter charge against the head of my department, and wished to make a statement about that, and he said, when I'd finished, that he would lay the information with the Special Branch and if they took no action it would undoubtedly form a major part of my defence when I came to trial. He seemed hopeful about this new evidence, said it gave us something positive to work on. I thought so too.

After he had gone I thought about Williams; there was little else I felt like thinking about. He hadn't ditched Usher, Herbert, Marcus and the others—*I* had, and no doubt he would manipulate the evidence to convince any jury. What would my piece of microfilm be worth then? Just something I'd been given by the Egyptians to frame him with. 'A *Russian* agent, my good fellow?—you've got it *all* wrong . . .'

And so it went at my trial twelve weeks later, some of it held *in camera*, at the Number One court in the Old Bailey. They'd had their war by then, of course; the Russians had swamped Egypt in the meantime; Williams's plan had gone off without a hitch—unless one looked on the five thousand Egyptians slaughtered in the Mitla Pass as a hitch, but I'm sure Williams didn't; they were running away after all.

My counter accusation against Williams looked pretty thin when one got down to it: pure supposition with all my possible witnesses in Siwa oasis, for, of course, the Egyptians had dealt with them very summarily before the Six Day War.

The evidence against me on the other hand, though almost entirely circumstantial, sounded pretty convincing: if not I, then who was it who had betrayed a whole circle within the space of four days? It was Blake all over again. I was the only person present at the place and time in question (that was a typical phrase) who had comprehensive knowledge of the people involved; I was the only one subsequently to remain at liberty . . .

What was the motive then? And here a principal point of evidence was brought against me which was quite unexpected and which tore to shreds the remnants of my own case: it was that I and my former wife had been Soviet agents in Cairo for more than ten years. This staggered me until I saw the evidence: a recent photograph from a West German magazine of Bridget walking away hurriedly from a store in a Moscow street, a haggard, frightened, unwilling, unhappy shape in a headscarf, but undeniably her.

The story beneath described her as part of a KGB husband-and-wife team active for many years in Cairo who had infiltrated a British Intelligence circle there during the Suez adventure. Subsequently the husband had arranged to divorce the woman and he had left Egypt to take up an important post with the SIS in London.

The whole thing was a carefully executed plant by Moscow, but other than denying it completely there was no way I could prove that it was untrue. Only Williams, who had arranged it, could have done that.

Of course, I remembered Hawthorn's rumour the day before I left Cairo, the woman that had been kidnapped by the Russians that week-end on Gezira: Williams had thought of everything. My counsel thought it barely worth bringing up, but I insisted. They could check with Hawthorn if needs be.

The Attorney-General, a well meaning, confident fellow who had behaved during the whole trial like a tall man knocking-up at the net, dealt with the matter immediately: 'If I may say so, my Lord, Cairo has been a hotbed for this sort of story since the Holy Family were rumoured in Heliopolis. But let us take it in this instance the rumour was true: I would suggest that it was leaked by the KGB for the obvious purpose of clearing the defendant of any connection with Miss Girgis. If they abducted his wife it was hardly likely to be thought that the defendant was working for them. In reality I would suggest that what happened was that things had got too hot for Miss Girgis, she was being withdrawn from the field, while her previous husband was thus left free to pursue his subversive activities in London. We must thank the German press for some smart detective work and, in this case, we may safely allow our credulity rein in a climate notorious for its deceitful airs: very well, then, Miss Girgis was "kidnapped", I accept that; but *willingly* . . . *knowingly*. She was not deceived, nor should we be.'

We argued that if such were the circumstances I was hardly likely to make such strenuous efforts to get back to England; I would have returned to Moscow myself.

'Experience in these matters clearly shows that this is exactly what the KGB do *not* do,' the Attorney-General put in. 'Once a man has a good placing, impeccable bona fides, as the defendant had, they do their utmost to ensure that he remains at the station he has penetrated.' The man paused, looked around the court, making one of his rare but beautifully timed applications to Actors' Equity; then he continued in an off-hand way: 'My Lord, ladies and gentlemen of the Jury, one has only to consider the case of Harold Philby to appreciate the lengths to which the KGB will go to ensure that their men remain at a penetrated station.' There were suitable mutterings all round.

His final address came shortly after and at the end he returned with relish to the same theme:'. . . It has been the folly of the past to retain such men as the defendant in British Intelligence—even after their disloyalty was strongly suspected, even to the extent of *unofficially* re-employing them, making them privy once more to the most sensitive policy areas, when they had been *officially* sacked. Such was the case with Philby; he was trusted in high places to the bitter end; and that it was such, and worse, I think no one here need contend. Let us not dally with that trust ever again. Let us be firm for once, not fools; let us be forearmed, since certainly we have been forewarned.'

He paused once more, just for a moment, nothing dramatic this time: 'I ask that the defendant suffer the full penalty which the law allows,' he said in a small voice, suddenly bowing his head and starting to put his papers together before he'd begun to sit down.

I did: twenty-eight years. After Blake they were obviously being more cautious with their sentences.

I remember glancing up at Williams in the public gallery as I went down. He had got up and was moving out with McCoy and some of my other colleagues, straightening their coats, blowing their noses, chattering to each other in business-like whispers. I could almost hear the fatuous, facile talk: '. . . a meeting has been arranged . . . we shall need someone . . . a new Cairo circle? . . . well, I hardly think at the moment . . . operate strictly from Beirut from now on. McCoy, make me out a work chart on our Beirut commitments, what we can spare from there . . . had quite a blow you know, losing all those chaps . . . dear me, yes . . .'

They shuffled on out into the bright afternoon, the baking weather which lay all over London that summer. It was just coming on to 5:30 when I got down to the cells, but by then I'd ceased to miss opening time; the piquancy of the hour barely crossed my mind.

I wondered how long Williams would last as we rolled along out of London, in convoy, and up the M1. I caught a glimpse of a fast bowler just starting his run towards the last of the sunlight in a park below the North Circular flyover. Yes, his reputation must have taken a fearful knocking over the whole business and Marcus might not be in Siwa Oasis for ever. On the other hand they were right about the KGB: Williams would stay where he was to the bitter end; and so, in the nature of things, would I.

I was surprised all the same, some time later, when I came to go over the case for my appeal, to hear from my solicitor that my allegations against Williams would now have to be directed to the Deputy Chief of Service of British Intelligence. Williams had left his Holborn office for good.

Of course, he'd been kicked upstairs after the fracas in Cairo;

perhaps the KGB had intended that in their plans from the beginning: a kick it may have been, but the fool now had free run of all the secrets in the attic: a pawn for a queen. It was a good move.

'I don't know how far we'll get with this appeal,' my solicitor said, a touch of weariness in his voice. He had travelled all that day on the way up to the top security jail in Durham and was understandably tired. 'People at that height tend to be pretty sure of their ground—tend to protect themselves thoroughly, you know.'

He looked at me anxiously, seemed to gaze through me, as though searching for something, a spot a long distance away on the horizon.

'I know,' I said. 'I know.'